www.hants.gov.uk/library

Hampshire
County Council

Love
YOUR LIBRARY

Tel: 0300 555 1387

THE
HOUR
OF
SEPARATION

Katharine McMahon studied English and Drama at Bristol University, and has taught and trained extensively both in creative writing and within the criminal justice system. She currently works for the Royal Literary Fund, developing projects that help writers use their unique skills in the community. She is the author of ten novels, including *The Alchemist's Daughter* and *The Crimson Rooms*, that focus on astonishing women and their ability to find a voice, even at times and in societies when they are risking everything. *The Rose of Sebastopol* was a Richard & Judy pick and a *Sunday Times* bestseller.

Also by Katharine McMahon

A Way Through the Woods
Footsteps
Confinement
After Mary
The Alchemist's Daughter
The Rose of Sebastopol
The Crimson Rooms
Season of Light
The Woman in the Picture

THE
HOUR
OF
SEPARATION

KATHARINE MCMAHON

WEIDENFELD & NICOLSON

First published in Great Britain in 2018
by Weidenfeld & Nicolson
an imprint of The Orion Publishing Group Ltd
Carmelite House, 50 Victoria Embankment
London EC4Y ODZ

An Hachette UK Company

1 3 5 7 9 10 8 6 4 2

A CIP catalogue record for this book is
available from the British Library.

ISBN (Hardback) 978 0 297 86606 0
ISBN (Export Trade Paperback) 978 0 297 86607 7
ISBN (eBook) 978 0 297 86608 4

Typeset by Input Data Services Ltd, Somerset

Printed in Great Britain by Clays Ltd, St Ives plc

www.orionbooks.co.uk

For Martin, and my Watford friends

'And ever has it been known that love knows
not its own depth until the hour of separation'

Khalil Gibran

Christa

A memo appeared on my desk at the Board of Trade ordering me to report to Room 115, Northumberland House, at eleven o'clock that morning. The massive building near Trafalgar Square used to be a swanky hotel. In the marbled lobby, a bored ATS corporal ran her pencil down a list and sent me under an arch to a service staircase. A row of hard chairs was lined up along the wall of a poorly lit passageway on the first floor. Uniforms strode by, deep in conversation or clutching buff folders.

'Corporal Geering?'

The room into which I was ushered had retained its floral curtains and carved oak panels. Two men stood to greet me. The first, an elderly colonel with woolly hair and a fierce handshake, introduced himself as Fairbrother. The second, in civilian dress, was all too familiar. Doctor Sinclair had aged considerably since our last encounter.

'Before we begin' – Fairbrother's vowels had been clipped by Sandhurst and generations of overbreeding – 'I trust I need not remind you of your responsibilities under the Official Secrets Act.'

I picked up the document and reread the requisite paragraph of the Act, aware that my hands were icy.

'I'm told that before the war you were a close friend of a woman called Estelle Cornelis-Faider.'

'Oh God.' The room shrank about me. 'Is she dead?'

'As far as we know, she is alive.'

'What's happened to her?'

Sinclair opened a file. 'Corporal, can you confirm that you spent the summer of 1939 with Estelle Cornelis-Faider at her

1

home in Belgium – De Eikenhoeve, which I believe translates as the Oak Farm?'

'You know I did.'

'And whilst at De Eikenhoeve, you became closely acquainted with Estelle and her two brothers.'

'Please tell me what's wrong.'

'Given their mother's history, you will not be surprised to learn that, since the Nazi occupation of Belgium, all three have joined a resistance organisation.'

'Why didn't you—?'

He raised an index finger to silence me while Fairbrother slid a glass of water across the desk. 'We need urgent information from you about De Eikenhoeve. One of our airmen, shot down over Belgium, was rescued by members of what we shall call Unit J. He was hidden in cellars then blindfolded and trans-ferred to a wagon which smelt strongly of cigarettes and animal feed. It was to convey him, as he thought, to the next place of safety. Instead, when the wagon was halted at a roadblock, he was passed directly into Nazi hands.'

Both men watched as, with infinite care, I placed the glass on the desk before me. Perhaps it was obvious that the very name, De Eikenhoeve, had tumbled me into a landscape perfumed with cut hay and strawberries, of young voices in the twilight, of leaves trembling in a dark wood. And of Estelle, bathed in sun-light on the low stone parapet of the bridge, honey hair caressing her face.

'Against all the odds, our airman managed to escape and work his way back to London. We are convinced that he was betrayed. Although he never saw the traitor's face, he does remember his voice: forceful and deep. In the seconds before he was handed over, one sentence was repeated several times, sotto voce. *Lass meine Schwester in Ruhe.* Leave my sister alone.'

'No.'

'Which brother would that be?' Fairbrother said.

Robbe walks up from the river path, jacket slung on his shoul-der, hair tousled, tossing aside his cigarette as Pieter calls his name, breaks into a run and holds out his arms.

Sinclair added, 'You have such ... intimate ... knowledge of the family, you must be best placed to tell us which is the traitor.'

'I can't.'

'At least give the matter some thought,' Fairbrother said.

'These are my *friends*.'

'Oh come,' said Sinclair. 'At least one of them was rather more to you than that.'

'We need your help, after the months you spent with the family in 1939.' Fairbrother forced me to meet his faded blue gaze. 'Several of our people, and some of the unit's key players, have already fallen into Nazi hands . . .'

A tea trolley rattled along the corridor outside.

'I simply don't know. It would be a guess, at best.'

'You need to think it over, of course. Come back tomorrow and tell us your conclusion.'

PART ONE

March 1939

Christa

My father had darkness in his soul. Most of the time he was just my Pa, a port in the storm. If I happened to be in trouble with Ma when he arrived home from the print, I'd climb on his knee, press my face to his waistcoat and smell the metal of his fob watch and the tweed of his jacket while his inky fingers buried themselves in my hair. Pa was a digger of an allotment, a devotee of Watford FC, a family man who unfailingly signed Christmas and birthday cards to his wife: *Your loving and grateful husband, Ted.* But sometimes when I clambered onto his lap he was unyielding, as if he didn't even know I was there. Sometimes he didn't speak for days on end and, instead of leaving for work, would put on his gardening overall and spend all day among his runner beans and potatoes. On such days, his handsome features were forged in iron and no end of tugging at his hand or whispering secrets could bring him round.

Ma had a name for the darkness: The War.

Pa's war had been much more complicated than that of other girls' fathers or uncles. The story went that having been wounded in the head and chest and exposed to more than a whiff of poison gas, Pa had staggered about close to enemy lines until he was eventually captured and hospitalised in Belgium. By some fluke he had escaped into friendly hands and been whisked away to the north via a hay barn, a crevice on the underside of a canal bridge and a hideaway in deep woodland. A truck transporting chickens delivered him eventually to the border with Holland, which was heavily defended by an electrified fence. Fortunately, by the time he reached that final hurdle he was in the charge of a woman known as Françoise. She came armed with two halves of a beer barrel lined with rubber inner-tubing, which she placed across the wires, thus permitting Pa to slip through to freedom.

One day, when I was a child exploring our limited bookshelf, I lifted out a worn family Bible with pages so thin I hesitated to turn them over. When I placed the book on my lap, two frayed markers, one blue, one crimson, fell out, as did a stiff little card bearing the name of a photographic studio in Brussels and a sepia picture of a woman whose name was handwritten in gold ink beneath it: *Fleur Cornelis-Faider. 1912.*

The subject was in three-quarters profile. Her skin was deathly pale, her brows arching steeply then tapering, and she had a perfectly straight nose with a tip that slightly overreached itself, so that together with the high cheekbones she looked a touch haughty. Her mouth, with its unusually full lower lip, was unsmiling, and her glossy hair, arranged in coils and waves above her forehead, was so plentiful that you'd think her slender neck would struggle to support its weight. She wore one of those marvellously complicated Edwardian blouses tucked into the diamond-shaped belt of her skirt.

I brought the card closer to my face so I could peer into her eyes, but the Bible slid to the floor with a crash and Ma came running. Anger in her was so rare that when she so much as raised a finger I trembled. Snatching the picture, she pushed it back between the pages of the book and replaced it on the shelf between *Hymns Ancient and Modern* and *The Wide, Wide World.*

'You shouldn't touch things without asking.' Her voice was strangely low and hard.

'Who is that lady?'

'Nobody you know.'

'Can I look at her again?'

'Another time. And don't let me hear you say anything about this to Pa because it will upset him terribly.'

But Ma was a stickler for the truth and later, as she tucked me into bed, she admitted that Fleur Cornelis-Faider and Françoise, Pa's rescuer, were one and the same and that the photograph had been sent to my grandparents in 1920 after they had written to the Belgian Consul asking if Françoise might be traced so they could express their gratitude. For months they had heard

8

nothing. Then a letter had arrived, written in French, from Françoise's mother in Brussels.

'Where is it?' I asked.

'Oh, upstairs somewhere, I expect, if Pa kept it. They had to have it translated by a French teacher from the church. All it said was that Françoise was the name used by a woman called Fleur Cornelis-Faider, who had been captured shortly after Pa's escape and had died in prison of typhus.'

'What's typhus?'

'A nasty illness you get in dirty places.'

'Why did she have two names?'

'If you were doing dangerous work in the war, you used a false name. And it's no use asking any more questions because that's all I know.'

On weekend mornings thereafter, while my parents slept in, I would creep downstairs, lift the photograph from its place in the Bible, carry it up to bed and stare at Fleur's face. Her expression – searching and fierce – contrasted sharply with the softness of her clothes. How could she have been that brave; to leave her home in order to rescue strangers, to die on a filthy prison bed, her body wasted with disease? I made up adventures for her in which she led lost soldiers to safety, brilliantly dodging the enemy and racing through the night, unseen. Ma was a Methodist, Pa not much of anything, but I worshipped that portrait, all the more because Fleur's name remained largely unspoken.

She became my personal heroine, my Joan of Arc, Florence Nightingale and Edith Cavell all rolled into one. Ma had shown me Nurse Cavell's statue when we went to feed the pigeons in Trafalgar Square and the inscription was a thrilling reminder of my own connection to tragedy and splendour:

BRUSSELS
DAWN
OCTOBER 12TH
1915
PATRIOTISM IS NOT ENOUGH
I MUST HAVE NO HATRED OR
BITTERNESS FOR ANYONE

9

As soon as my schoolgirl French was proficient enough, I pestered Ma to show me the letter from Fleur's mother and at last she produced an envelope, slit open at the top and containing a letter exquisitely foreign, right down to the embossed address at the top:

M. et Mme. Faider,
7, rue d'Orléans
Bruxelles.

The note inside was formal and brief, and contained exactly the information that Ma had described.

'So did anyone write to them again, to thank them for taking the trouble to reply?' I demanded.

'Of course not. We can't speak French and there was nothing else we wanted to say. Besides, the family was in mourning.'

'I know French. I could write now and say thank you. After all, if it wasn't for Fleur, I wouldn't even be here.'

'I don't want you to.' Ma looked terribly distressed. 'Please don't. For Pa's sake. Imagine how he'd feel if he knew you were raking up the past. And think of that poor family in Brussels. It was all so long ago. I'm sure they won't want to be reminded of what happened either. You must promise me, Christine.'

She was so emphatic that of course I promised. But the idea of Fleur continued to haunt me. Largely as a tribute to her I chose to study French as well as English at Queen Mary College in East London. My coming of age, in March 1939, coincided with jackbooted troops thundering into Czechoslovakia. A mere twenty-two years after Fleur's untimely death, a friend collapsed in tears during a tutorial because her uncle, who lived in Prague, had been shot in cold blood – *executed* – for making a speech protesting against the invaders.

With history pounding its drum, my undiminished admiration for Fleur-Françoise now seemed overpoweringly relevant. Unable to resist the impulse to *do* something, to make a connection, I wrote to Fleur's family to express my personal gratitude, as the daughter of a survivor of the last war, for being alive.

10

Estelle

I remember it was the end of March 1939, a lifetime ago, Céleste was serving petit dejeuner in the small salon overlooking the street when Grand-mère produced a letter with an English postmark, from one Christabel Geering.

I conjure up that high-ceilinged room; floor-length lace curtains, chiming clock with gold scrolling and tiny pink and blue flowers, the white tablecloth, the bread still warm in its linen nest and with a gloss on the crust, the blackcurrant jam I'd brought from the farm oozing into the butter.

Céleste was fussing about with the coffee pot and Grand-mère's mild gaze was upon me as she tore a morsel of bread from the crust and dipped it in her coffee. She tried to appear disinterested, but she couldn't fool me – she was watching me like a hawk.

Christabel's letter then. Her careful schoolgirl hand and near-perfect French. A letter too immaculate to be casual, without a single crossing-out.

13 Harewood Road
Watford
Hertfordshire
England
16ᵗʰ March 1939

Dear Famille Faider,
My father is Edward Geering, formerly of the London Regiment, and he is one of the men Fleur helped to escape during the war.
All my life I have been aware of how much I owe Fleur Cornelis-Faider, or Françoise, as my father knew her. Having just celebrated my twenty-first birthday, I wanted to write to you

11

myself to tell you that I will never forget what she did for my father. With every year I become even more conscious of the sacrifice she made for a stranger and at such great cost. I long to know more about her. If there is ever any way I can repay her extraordinary act of courage, I would be very glad.

With my very best wishes to all the family,
Yours sincerely,
Christabel Geering

'What do you think of it?' I asked.

'A bit gushing.'

'Will you reply to her, or would you like me to?'

Grand-mère took back the letter and read it again. 'I thought you'd be intrigued to know that this Edward Geering had a daughter. She doesn't mention other siblings.'

'I should like to meet him. Wouldn't that be something? I was thinking of going to London anyway, for my dissertation.'

Her claw of a hand touched my wrist. 'I'd credited you with more sense.'

'Why do you say that?'

'Because you're bound to be disappointed, one way or another.'

'But I want to find out what this Edward Geering remembers about my mother. Aren't you curious too?'

'I don't need someone else's version of my daughter.'

'Whereas since I have no version of my own, I have to make the best of any scrap that's offered me. I was just a baby when she died, remember.'

Everyone warned me against it. They too said I was doomed to be disappointed, that I'd learn nothing. Marthe was the most insistent. 'You will only give yourself pain. Let sleeping dogs lie.'

I thought: Typical of her to spoil my fun. We all know why she hates the past.

I decided to consult Père Borland. Any excuse, though pointless really because I'd already made up my mind. He was holding a tutorial so I waited outside his room. I felt at home perched on the radiator in that long corridor amidst the smell of warm paint. Young men passed by deep in conversation – some cast sideways glances at me. 'Hey, Estelle.'

Père B. ushered out a couple of students, spotted me and glanced at his watch. 'Ten minutes?'

Ten minutes was all the time Borland ever had to spare. He was always in a hurry, at least when I was around. I dropped into the easy chair while he beat a retreat to the far side of the desk and reached for his pipe.

'And so,' he said in that lilting voice of his, in the purest of French, 'to what do I owe this honour?'

'I'm off to England for a few weeks.'

'Very good. When?'

'On Monday. Papa is paying. I need to research my dissertation.'

'Can *anything* help that dissertation? I have a sense it isn't going anywhere. Am I right?' He was resting the bowl of his pipe on his hip and the tobacco pouch against his chest while he pinched out a few strands. His eyes were humorous. 'The subject, I've always felt, is a little too dry for you.'

'Which is why I intend to expand it to include Rubens and Van Dyck.' Borland's room was one of the few places I ever wanted to be; warm, intricate rug, row upon row of old books, a many-paned window. 'And anyway, Grand-mère was sent this letter.'

He took a very long time to read the short letter from England. Afterwards he spoke lightly. 'So you intend to look up this Christabel and her family.'

'I do. I was wondering if you remember an Edward Geering . . .'

Always the same, when the war came up; a slowing of his speech, as if he were spelling something out to a small child. 'Of course I don't. As I've said many times before, we were never told their real names, and they never knew ours. Even if I had come across him, I doubt I'd recognise him now. Do you really think this is a good idea, Estelle? You're bound to be disappointed.'

'That's what everyone keeps saying.'

'Well then.'

13

'It's worth a try, don't you think? He might remember my mother. I might learn something.'

He had not yet lit his pipe. With his back to the window he looked as thin as a shadow. 'What precisely are you hoping to learn?'

'I just want another angle on her. Surely that's not too much to ask? I intend to get in touch with all four of the families in England who've written to Grand-mère since the war. I thought you, of all people, would be pleased.'

'On the contrary, my advice is that you should let it rest. Despite what this girl Christabel says, nobody will want you to go stirring up old memories, especially with the prospect of another war.'

'That's precisely why I need to visit England now.'

'At some stage you must let your mother go—'

'*Let her go?* Is that what you've done?'

He was spared by a knock – his next student. But as I reached the door he called me back. 'Listen, I have an old friend in England who's a specialist in art history. If you must go, he might be prepared to help with your exiled engravers.'

He wrote a name and an address on a scrap of paper which I crammed into my pocket. I forgot about it until he dropped me a note the next day to say he'd written to this friend, Sinclair, and made a tentative appointment for me.

He was right about the dissertation. I couldn't have cared less.

Christa

On Easter Saturday 1939, with the blossom on the flowering cherry outside our house as madly pink and hopeful and heart-breaking as ever, there was a ring on our doorbell.

I had been lying on my stomach revising Molière's *Les Femmes Savantes* for my final examination whilst Ma was at work in the kitchen with the rolling pin. I yelled: 'I'll go,' and clattered downstairs, expecting Auntie Maisie or a neighbour; instead I found a perfect stranger, hand raised to ring again, head turned to look up the street. The sun blazed down on her red hat, the shoulder of her blue jacket and a bunch of pungent narcissi, pale as paper.

Before she'd announced in confident English with a slight European accent: 'I am Estelle Cornelis-Faider, Fleur's daughter,' I was already ushering her in and absorbing her. We had so few interesting visitors and she had a light of her own, with the fall of her honey-coloured hair across her brow, her height – three or four inches taller than me – and the animation in her grey-blue eyes. Her skin had a peachy bloom that I had never seen on an English girl.

I said something like: 'How wonderful. Please come in. This is so ... unexpected ...' as I showed her into the chilly front room where the fire was never lit until teatime. That space was all wrong for her; even Ma's best ornaments could not fail to look shoddy beside such a creature.

Our house had never seen anything like her. She wore a dress of indigo crêpe – 'Real silk,' said Ma, after she'd gone – and resembled a McCall's model, too willowy and composed to be real. It took me a moment to realise she was studying me with blatant curiosity.

15

'You must be Christabel. You wrote to us.'

'I am. Yes. I can't believe you came. I must tell Ma . . .'

The pair of us burst into the kitchen together and found Ma untying her pinafore, full of consternation, as if she knew even before I'd gabbled an introduction that, Pandora-like, I'd opened the box.

'I don't think I mentioned that I'd written to that family in Brussels. You know, Françoise . . . Fleur, who saved Pa. Isn't it amazing? Her daughter has come all this way to meet us.'

It was the first time I'd actually seen the colour drain from a face, but Ma recovered enough to say, with a stiff smile: 'It's certainly a surprise,' and then she shook Estelle's proffered hand as if it might poison her.

'And Mr Geering?' Estelle asked. 'Is he here? Is he alive even? Your letter didn't make it clear, Christabel.' My name, on her tongue, sounded quite beautiful – Chreestabelle – and I felt a surge of joy that she had transformed it into something exotic.

'Oh yes,' said Ma. 'Very much so. Thanks to your mother.' She nodded several times and clenched her hands together for emphasis. 'But he's at football just now I'm afraid, and won't be back for an hour or two. Wouldn't you rather sit in the front room? As you can see, I've been baking because it's Easter tomorrow.'

Estelle dropped into a chair and looked about as if she were in a museum of curiosities rather than our kitchen with its yellow Formica-topped table cluttered with scales and mixing bowls and a dusting of flour. 'Grand-mère passed your letter to me.' She reached for the scissors and snipped a ruthless couple of inches from the stalks of her flowers.

The severed stems bled sap and Ma hastily provided a vase and a dishcloth while I cleared a space on the windowsill. Arranged by Estelle, the flowers contrived to look both careless and exquisite.

'I can tell that I arrived at exactly the right moment,' she added, having followed Ma's movements as she put the kettle on, whisked scones from the oven and banged the tray onto the top of the stove. 'I was about to leave for London anyway, and thought I must look up this Christabel and her family.'

'Oh I'm so glad you did,' I said. 'So you live in Brussels too.'

16

'I've been studying in Louvain, but my home is a farm called De Eikenhoeve. But why I'm here, what I'm hoping, is that your father will remember his journey through Belgium in the war . . . My mother . . .' The eager anticipation in her eyes was shocking.

'Oh dear, he hasn't spoken about the war for years.' Ma was transferring the scones onto a cooling tray. Not once, since shaking hands, had she so much as glanced in Estelle's direction. 'Would you mind . . . not talking about all this to him straight away? You see, I just don't know . . . I really don't know what he'll say when he sees you, how he'll react. I need to give him a little warning.'

Estelle was regarding her with a fixed expression I came to understand very well – it meant that though she was listening, she was nonetheless completely committed to her own agenda. On that first occasion I mistook it for sympathy. 'Of course,' she said. 'I will be very gentle with him.'

'In any case, he might not be in for some time. He often goes for a pint after the match.' Ma was obviously hoping that Estelle would give up and depart, but our visitor merely crossed her legs at the ankle, tossed her hat onto Pa's empty chair and ran her fingers through her hair as if she was settling in for the duration.

'It's so good of you to come all the way out to Watford. You mentioned you were visiting London anyway,' I said. 'Do you have relatives here? Your English is astonishingly good.'

'I'm glad to hear it, considering it is my third language. In fact, I am writing a dissertation on seventeenth-century engraving. I must take after my mother – she was an artist before the war.' Whenever Fleur was mentioned, Ma's movements slowed and I drew breath. 'So I needed to visit at some stage. For research. A lot of artists from my country became exiles here.'

Estelle spoke distractedly because she appeared to be spell-bound by Ma preparing the tea things. Poor Ma; through our visitor's eyes I saw with ruthless clarity her perpetually worried features, round shoulders and bunioned feet in the faded pink slippers and was sorry she'd not had time to put on a better frock and change her shoes.

'How do you like your tea?' Ma asked. 'Milk? Sugar? I'm afraid I tend to make it rather strong.'

'Weak, with lemon,' said Estelle.

17

More agony for Ma: should she send me dashing down to Frobisher's to see if they had any lemons?

'Ah, no.' Estelle spotted her mistake. 'I'm forgetting where I am. I would like tea the English way. Thank you.'

'So,' I said, 'you were brought up on a farm?'

Estelle buttered the scone Ma had offered her. 'Near the village of Oostervorken, to the north of Brussels.'

'And do you have brothers or sisters?'

'I have two older brothers. Pieter is thirty-one years old and he will inherit the farm from our father. Robbe' – she pronounced this name as Rawbe – 'is three years younger, but has not yet decided what he will be.'

'How lovely. Two brothers,' Ma said, thawing the merest touch, 'just what I would have wanted for Christine. But it's so sad that you all grew up without a mother. Who looked after you? Did your father ever remarry?'

'He did. Yes.' Neither Estelle's posture nor her expression changed and yet it was as if she had turned into some brittle substance. 'I've no doubt you'd like to see some photographs of Maman.' Nudging aside her teacup, she hooked her toe into the strap of a bulging satchel and pulled it closer.

Ma again glanced nervously at the door. 'We already have a photograph of Fleur,' she said. 'Your grandmother very kindly sent it to us.'

'Oh, I know exactly the one. There were hundreds printed after the war, when Maman became famous. It was an engagement photograph, so quite out of date. These are much more like her, or so I'm told. I'm not the best judge, obviously, since I have no actual memory of her. I was just a baby when she died.' She produced a brown envelope containing a few photographs that she slapped down in a row, as if dealing a game of Patience.

At that moment we heard the sound of my father's boots clomping down the alley at the side of the house, his ponderous tread suggesting that Watford had lost.

'Ted,' Ma said, waylaying him at the back door. 'We have a visitor.'

Pa's reactions were always a little slow and at first he merely removed his cap and glanced kindly at Estelle, greeting her as he might any of my friends. But he must have registered something about her poise and foreignness, or maybe he glimpsed one of the photographs on the table, because his head snapped back as if he'd been punched on the chin.

'This is Miss . . . the daughter of Françoise . . . Fleur.'

'My name is Estelle Cornelis-Faider.' Our visitor held out her hand.

He was still a handsome man, my Pa, with the well-defined features that were said to have broken many hearts and made it all the more touching that he had married my mother, plain Joan Myers, ledger clerk at the print. Having stared at Estelle from under lowered eyelids, he lurched towards her, knocking a chair out of the way.

And in a flash, as Estelle placed her hand in my father's and I glanced at Ma's face with its sagging skin and tired eyes, it occurred to me that all this time I'd been missing the blindingly obvious. Beautiful, reckless Fleur. Wounded Ted Geering. Nights spent half-buried in leaf mould deep in some ancient wood or slipping by moonlight from shadow to shadow.

Estelle and Pa, who were the same height, stared at each other, she suddenly tongue-tied but holding his hand tightly while he, most uncharacteristically, carried hers to his lips and kissed it.

'Isn't it kind of her to call in?' Ma said, and I could have wept for her, with her shapeless skirt and her too bright voice. 'Won't you be wanting your tea?'

'Yes, tea,' Pa said. He pressed his fists on the table and hung over the photographs, picking up the first and tilting it towards the light.

'That's our farm,' said Estelle, standing behind him. Close up, I noticed that her own hands were, somewhat surprisingly for so beautiful a young woman, large and workaday. But then she was a farmer's daughter. 'You see it's very old, typical of its kind.'

'Oh it's beautiful . . .' Ma moved closer to Pa, as if to offer him protection. 'Enormous. There must be so many rooms. Look, Christine.'

The farmhouse was a long, low building with a turret at one end and a tunnel or archway leading through it.

'De Eikenhoeve translates as The Oak Farm,' Estelle explained, 'so called because of that enormous oak tree. We think it's older than the house.' She picked up another photograph. 'Here is Maman with the two boys, before I was born.'

Fleur had one little boy on her lap while another, slightly older, leant against her knee. The younger child had huge dark eyes and wilful curls, whilst his brother was rather solemn and stolid. Their mother, though clasping each lightly by the waist, looked uncomfortable, almost as if she longed to get up and dash away. 'Pieter,' said Estelle, pointing to the older. 'Robbe is the dark, pretty one.'

'Oh, I wouldn't say pretty,' said Ma. 'They're both very handsome. I can see your mother in them.'

'And here's Maman again, in my favourite photograph.' Estelle pushed forward the last as if she were playing a trump card: a photograph of a woman seated at a table and holding a paintbrush, her wavy hair twisted over her shoulder so that the tail of it hung to her waist. She was wearing some kind of loose frock with a tabard over the top. Her eyes were momentous – very bright, with a mischievous gleam.

'She is so like you,' I said.

'I really hope so. What do you think, Meester Geering?' She glanced up at Pa, who had hung so long over the photograph that a thread of saliva dangled from his lip.

Ma had bustled away and was rinsing the teapot at the sink, emptying it over and over until the water ran clear. At last, Pa shifted from the table and made for the door. 'No more,' he mumbled. And then he came back, lifted a strand of Estelle's hair and turned it in the light. 'Her hair . . .'

For a moment I wondered if he might kiss it too, then he disappeared into the yard.

'I'm so sorry,' Ma said. 'Such a shame he wasn't able to tell you more. I had a feeling something like this would happen.'

'It doesn't matter.' Estelle's hair fell forward so we couldn't see her face as she thrust the photographs back into her satchel. 'It was just . . . so good to meet you all.'

'Don't rush off,' I pleaded. 'Or if you must, please come back. Next time we'll be ready for you, won't we, Ma? We'll hold a proper feast in your honour.'

'Maybe. We'll see. I'll be in touch.' Estelle walked into the hallway, flung open the front door, waved and strode away.

Ma emerged from the kitchen with a splash of red in her hand. 'She left her hat. Run after her. I don't want it here.'

By the time I caught up, Estelle was already in Whippendell Road. 'You forgot your hat.'

She turned to me, her eyes wet.

'Don't worry about Pa. He's not quite right. You mustn't mind.'

'I had such hopes that he would remember her.'

'And he did. You heard what he said about your hair. He'll soon get used to you. Come to dinner tomorrow, or next Sunday. How long will you be in London?'

She took the hat and clapped it on, then adjusted her satchel so that it sat more comfortably across her body. 'Maybe the following Sunday, I'll visit again.' As she strode off, the tension in her shoulders suggested that she was conscious I was watching.

On the way back to Harewood Road, a fleck of blossom caught in my hair and a bicyclist – a young colleague of Pa's – yelled hello. Our front door was ajar and the familiar gloom of our hall seemed to reach out and pull me in, the slight smell of soot mingling with beeswax. I shut my eyes and relived that astonishing handshake, Fleur Cornelis-Faider's daughter and my father. It was I who had achieved that historic encounter, through my letter, and the responsibility filled me with awe.

When I went into the kitchen, Ma stood with her back to me at the sink. 'I told you not to write to them. You have no idea the effect all this might have on Pa. I'm the one who has to deal with him.'

I dried a cup and fumbled for soothing words. 'Sorry Ma. The point is, Pa survived and he has you and me, whereas Estelle was left with no mother. Don't you think we should help her?'

Perhaps, as she scoured the top of the stove, Ma was thinking of a youthful Ted Geering and Fleur Cornelis-Faider skimming between hedgerows under the light of a treacherous moon. She appeared to relent somewhat, as she wondered what Estelle would think of Yorkshire pudding, and whether or not to invite Auntie Maisie and family to meet her if she visited again.

21

Estelle

Papa's allowance didn't stretch to more than a hostel in Highgate recommended by my friend and erstwhile travelling companion, Edouard — trust him to be an expert on women-only accommodation. Clean and convenient, with rules about noise, curfew, use of the kitchen, everything. The local locksmith did a roaring trade duplicating keys, and the warden, a bit of a harridan over lights left on and food left out, was either too naive or — more likely — turned a blind eye to the fact that we all let ourselves in whenever we chose.

The best thing about the hostel was the nearby park of the type the English do so well: landscaped, on the side of a hill with tennis courts, a pond hidden by trees and, above all, not a straight line anywhere. Even the markings on the court were wonky. I used to play in the early morning with a German girl called Heidi.

She and I avoided the subject of politics; she never said, but I guessed that she had a sneaky admiration for her Führer. Or perhaps I maligned her. Despite her fearsome serve she was a very good sport. I helped her develop a more effective backhand. As I stood behind her shoulder, my hand on hers, and guided her arm to make the full sweep, I used to think I could smell alien sweat.

I loved the thwack of tennis balls, the rattle of rubber against the high wire fence, the spring sunshine. I made a point, that April, of watching the flowers bloom from day to day because I knew that everything was coming to an end. Couldn't ignore it. The English were digging air-raid shelters in the park and in the gardens of private houses.

Meanwhile I mooched around art galleries and wrote to the

address of people who'd been in touch with Grand-mère about Maman. Three were pretty hopeless. The first letter, to Lancaster, led nowhere at all – twice, my envelope came back, return to sender, even though each time it had been opened and resealed. Turned out the second person had died half a decade ago.

The third man asked me to dinner. A disastrous evening in Birmingham. He was accompanied by a beady-eyed wife, Irene, who'd pulled out of a bridge engagement at the last minute so she could join us. She said she was curious to meet the daughter of a war heroine. 'Although I'm quite sure my Harry would have found the Dutch border on his own had he not been picked up by your mother.' Venom.

We ate at one of those vile, expensive restaurants of the type that Papa used to choose in Brussels: red plush, dusty chandeliers, half-cold food. As soon as I'd clapped eyes on Irene I wanted to leave. Harry was cagey about Maman and kept glancing at Irene and cutting me off if he thought I was about to say anything provocative. It was obvious that he'd intended to have a cosy dinner alone with me.

Irene revealed that since the war he'd dined out on a glorified version of his escape in which he was the star. When I showed him a photograph of Maman he said he thought he remembered her but couldn't be sure. After that, Irene's attitude changed from gushing to downright hostile. She was probably shocked to discover how beautiful Maman had been, especially compared to her.

But when I got up to leave, Harry grabbed my hand. 'You know you are so very like her,' he murmured, and I saw the shadow of a much younger, more vulnerable person. His dreamy gaze shifted to my mouth.

'*Harry*,' Irene snapped, and he shuffled off.

After the meal, I stayed the night in a cheap hotel near the station. I'd rarely felt so sorry for myself. Sleepless on a lumpy mattress. Unironed, grubby sheets. Why on earth would Maman risk her life for such a man? Surely she hadn't slept with him? But why else was the wife so hostile, and why had Harry looked at me like that when we said goodbye?

So I pinned all my hopes on Christabel Geering's letter. The train between Birmingham and London stopped at Watford, it was a Saturday and, even though I'd given her no warning, I got off there and wandered around a street market in the town centre for a bit; curtain fabric – white with blue birds, red checks – a stall with oranges in pyramids, gloves displayed on spooky wire hands. Eventually I plucked up the courage and asked someone the way to Harewood Road.

The house itself was very small, red-brick, English. The type you see from the train window when approaching the centre of any town in that country; one of a long row all joined up, but the Geerings' stood out for being the tidiest with a polished step and fresh paint. At the front was a low trimmed hedge behind a brick wall. I walked up and down the street several times before knocking. Cursed myself for not writing in advance. What if they were out? But in the end I did knock and there she was – a sweet, nervous girl with her hair tied up in a ribbon and a yellow cardigan worn like a cape around her shoulders.

Not just sweet though. I soon revised that idea. After all, this was the girl who had written the letter, and from the moment, the *first* moment, that I walked through that door, I felt it: competition. Christabel, star-struck, couldn't stop staring, tried to dig Maman out of me and shine a spotlight.

So, initially it was the mother, Mrs Geering, I liked the best. Different to any other mother I've known – women on the farm, mostly, who nurse behind hedges and whose children swarm in the fields at harvest time and are carried home, clinging like limpets, awarded sticky kisses as they knot their filthy hands in their mother's hair. Mrs Geering was shy but never thrown off balance. She used to be a servant – a housemaid and then a housekeeper and then some kind of clerk. I visited Harewood Road many times and she was never without a task – preparing a meal, clearing up, knitting. Through everything there was this consciousness of me. At first she was shocked and wary, a touch hostile. No wonder. It became clear Christabel hadn't even told her she'd written to us.

A footfall. Dogged. Uneven. All eyes on the door. The father, Ted Geering, had his head down and a rolled cap under his arm. Lots of grey hair. A big man, heavy-shouldered. He looked about him, bewildered, when he first came in, nodded at his wife, followed her gaze to me. And straight away I knew he really had met Maman. I saw just a flash of it, like when the shutter clicks open in a camera.

My whole body juddered when he grasped my hand. Later, he held a lock of my hair to the light and she flickered in his eyes. Had I been quicker, I'd have seen her scorched onto his retina.

It was too much and I ran away. But I wonder, did I leave my hat behind on purpose? Because I hoped Christabel would come after me?

After that, I went back time after time, I couldn't help myself; I stood at the green front door with the polished knocker and the doorbell that rang like an electric shock. Stepped into the little entrance hall and smelt whatever was cooking, maybe those plain English cakes that clog the roof of your mouth. Or a dessert called apple crumble with hot yellow sauce. Sweet buttered scones and jam. Gingerbread, sticky on top, or crumpets where the tip of my tongue fitted into little yeasty holes.

I thought to myself: this is Maman's gift to the world. This family.

The first time I went back was a Sunday – fires lit in every hearth, the scent of roast beef. A waffle mix that puffed up in the oven, sauce called gravy, dark as treacle.

The table had been set in the back room with a checked cloth because it was Sunday, they said. Normally they ate in the kitchen, which I much preferred.

Joan Geering had invited her sister to inspect me. This Maisie – short for Margaret, bizarrely – sat in the front parlour, smoked a cigarette and asked me, when we were alone together, how long I intended to stay. 'Joan has a very hard time with Ted. He suffers from dreadful headaches and nightmares. They've got worse these last two weeks. Just so you know.'

'Are you saying it's my fault?' I said.

'I'm afraid I am. That's why Christine shouldn't have written to you.'

'I'll try not to upset him but there are obviously questions I'd love to ask.'

25

I wasn't sure about Maisie, who was much harder-edged than her sister. She gave Christabel a difficult time at lunch. 'Have you told Estelle the saga of your name?'

'Must I?'

'She might find it amusing.'

Christabel became much more childish, blushing, a shy glance at me. 'When I was thirteen, I came across this poem called *Christabel,* and it's also the name of a famous English suffragist, so I insisted that's what everyone should call me from then on. I even had my name changed on the register at school.'

Mrs Geering said: 'I liked the name Christine when I chose it. I thought it was quite daring, compared to my own. You can't get plainer than Joan. But that's typical of Christine, once she gets a bee in her bonnet . . .' She gave her daughter a look that twisted my heart: I love you despite our differences. Because of them.

'I tell you what. I will call you Christa,' I said. 'Which is in the middle of the two names.'

'*Christa*. I love it.'

'I'm told that Maman was the one who named me.' They all jumped to attention when I mentioned her. Solemn expressions. Except for Ted Geering, who just went on eating. 'It's French and means star, because I was born just before Christmas in 1916.'

'But your brothers don't have French names,' Christa said.

'That's because they were named by my father, who speaks only Flemish. Belgium is a complicated country. My parents were unusual – Flemish- and French-speaking people generally tend to hate each other rather than get married.'

'Didn't your grandparents mind that your mother married a Flemish person?' asked Christa.

'Everybody minded, especially my Flemish – Cornelis – grandparents, who were very severe, and wished that Papa had chosen a woman who knew about farming, instead of a French-speaking artist like Maman.'

'She also spoke a bit of English,' said Ted Geering suddenly. We all went absolutely quiet for a moment.

'Steady now, Ted,' said his wife.

'I understood her perfectly when she talked to me in English.'

'What else do you remember?' I asked.

He shook his head and looked imploringly across the table at his wife while wretched Maisie turned the subject. But just for a moment, as with Harry in Birmingham, I had seen a different person in Ted Geering – younger, like in his wedding photograph on the parlour mantelpiece. Film-star good looks. Half a metre taller than his bride, confident. That was 1916, before the war got him.

Christa and I washed up. I didn't like to admit that I'd hardly ever picked up a tea towel in my life. I took ages over each glass in case I broke it, whereas she was slapdash. Clashed plates in the bowl, tossed the cutlery in heaps for me to dry. Meanwhile she asked lots of questions about the farm and my work. She was studying English and French, partly as a tribute to Maman, and would become a teacher in the autumn.

'They'll be lucky pupils,' I said, and she flashed me a look of sheer pleasure. She'd tied an apron round her waist and it had got wet where her thighs pressed against the sink. 'I hate studying. I'm supposed to be writing a dissertation but I can't be bothered. Even here in England there's research I should be doing.'

'Just say if you want to talk over anything or need help with looking things up in the library, that sort of thing.' She turned to face me, gripping the sink, eager to do anything she could for me. How easily she provided us with the chance to meet again and again . . .

Christa

Estelle blazed through my life like a comet, shining light into all the dull corners, and when we were apart she left me yearning for more. I had never met a woman so lacking in consciousness of her own physical beauty, and I was struck by her resemblance to the photographs of Fleur I had studied constantly since girlhood. Except that Estelle, unlike her tragic mother, was intensely alive, with a shimmer of gold in her hair and a pulse in her strong throat. Her boldness and unorthodoxy were infectious; she was hoping to take a postgraduate job at the University of Louvain in the autumn, her brother Robbe had been fighting in Spain on the Republican side, her Aunt Julia owned a smallholding and was never seen in any outfit other than a raincoat and muddy boots, and one of her closest friends, or her mentor, as she called him, was a Jesuit priest called Père Borland who'd been her mother's fellow Résistant during the war.

Far from finding us dull or disappearing without trace after that first visit, she turned up again and again, usually at mealtimes.

'She's always ravenous, that girl,' said Ma – which was quite sardonic, for her.

Estelle *was* hungry, for anything to do with our family, and for company. After she'd accepted my invitation to Sunday dinner and met Auntie Maisie, I realised that all she really wanted was to belong. And there was a defensiveness about her affection, a determination not to seem dependent that I found endearing. 'If you like, we could meet in London,' she said, 'and you could show me the sights. It doesn't matter in the least if you don't want to, though. I'm going anyway.'

Predictably enough, she knew far more about the places we visited than I did. Our first stop was the Edith Cavell memorial

28

on St Martin's Place, which we viewed from both sides of the road and then close up.

'Don't you think it's very imposing?' I said as we walked around it, craning our necks. Pigeons were perched on stone ledges and one, particularly irreverent, nestled in Cavell's hair.

'I think it's hideous. You should see the one of my mother. Totally different.'

'There's a statue of your mother?'

'Of course. In Brussels. But it's life-size, not a monument like this. Why did they make it so big and stick it on a main road where everyone's too busy to look at it? What is that carving of a mother and child doing on the top? Cavell wasn't a mother.'

'Do you think your mother would have been acquainted with Edith Cavell?'

'She'd definitely have known about her. Cavell made herself famous by being executed. As a matter of fact, I suspect that she was a liability not only to herself but to other escape organisations operating in Brussels. We had so many heroines of our own, you know, besides Maman. Gabrielle Petit, for example. Have you ever heard of her?'

'For Pete's sake,' I said, 'you'd better not criticise Cavell too loudly. In this country we have schools named after her.'

'It's the same in Belgium. It must have been blindingly obvious to the Germans what she was up to, all those English soldiers traipsing in and out of a school for female nurses. Poor thing. I've been to the Tir National, you know, the old shooting range where they killed her.'

We stared up at the hem of Cavell's stony gown. 'Which would you prefer,' said Estelle, 'death by firing squad, or death in a prison cell from some horrible illness like typhus which means your end is prolonged, painful and undignified?'

There was such a contrast between the living Estelle, with her hair blowing in the April breeze, coat undone and her warm arm pressed against mine, and the immoveable image of Cavell. And there was such desolation in her voice that I tucked my hand under her elbow, feeling very young and inadequate as I groped for the right thing to say. 'I wouldn't choose either. I don't know if I could be brave enough even to stand upright if I had to face a firing squad.'

'Imagine leaving your prison cell before dawn and being driven through the city. Thinking to yourself all the time, this can't be happening; nobody kills middle-aged English ladies in cold blood. It was just her and a man who had worked with her, a Belgian father of young children, shot side by side in the cold early morning. When they tied her to a post and bandaged her eyes, she was weeping.'

'*Patriotism is not enough*,' I read. '*I must have no hatred or bitterness for anyone.*'

'Easily said, considering she knew she was going to die anyway.'

As we left Cavell behind, her noble eyes forever fixed on St Martin's Church, I had a thrilling intimation of how Estelle was shifting my perspective and binding me even tighter to the moment of history that she and I shared. For a few moments I was Cavell, braced for the bullet, the weight of my tweed skirt pressed to my knees by a chill wind.

The minute we were inside the National Gallery, Estelle's mood changed again. She marched me through room after room, dismissing any painting of a woman in a long gown, from Pre-Raphaelite to Gainsborough, as a *frock* picture, and heading for her own special subject, the artists of the Netherlands in the seventeenth century.

'Why did you pick that particular period for your dissertation?' I asked.

'Because I had to write about something. Any excuse to stay on a bit longer at university. Unlike Maman, although I'm artistic, I am no good at actual painting, so I am studying the history of it instead.'

She stood with folded arms before Van Dyck's *Portrait of a Woman* and appraised it as fondly as if it were an eccentric family friend. 'You see now I understand Van Dyck better,' she said, 'because he was a visitor to England from the Low Countries, just like me.'

We shared our sandwiches with the pigeons in Trafalgar Square before heading east past St Paul's on the top deck of a bus. Père Borland, Estelle's Jesuit tutor, had provided her with a street map, which she'd marked with crosses to show the sights we mustn't miss. One of them was the London Hospital, where Cavell had trained, and we stood inside the lobby to soak up the atmosphere; the aromas of disinfectant, soot and outdoor clothes, the long corridors leading to the mysterious world of sickness, death or healing, and the staircase up which nurses dashed purposefully.

Lastly, we trekked along the Mile End Road to Queen Mary College, where I was in my final year as a student. The sun slanted through the high windows of the Octagon Library onto the oak tables and endless bookshelves. 'Well, this is lovely,' Estelle said. 'Even I wouldn't mind working here. Will you be sad to leave? Have you made many friends?'

'I will be sad, yes. But it's time.'

'Why did you choose here and not Oxford or Cambridge?'

'It never occurred to me that I might be bright enough.'

She subjected me to one of her ruthlessly appraising stares and I thought I'd be dismissed as timid, but instead she kissed my cheek. 'Anyway, I don't expect you'd have wanted to leave your mother. I wouldn't.'

She paused, suddenly diffident. 'The thing is, Père Borland has given me a letter of introduction to a friend of his, a tutor in Cambridge, who might have some thoughts about my dissertation. I suppose I ought to follow it up, if only for the sake of good manners. Will you come with me?'

Of course I would. An expedition with Estelle was far too intriguing a prospect to miss. Our days together were numbered and she made me feel reckless and eager for more adventure.

31

Estelle

Mrs Geering wasn't that keen on me at first. She was always nervous when I was around. I'd catch her studying my face, and once she dropped a glass bowl when I walked into the kitchen. I discovered that the surest way of buttering her up was to ask about Christa.

Christine's first word, I learnt, had been *button*. Then *garden*.

Christine's hair had always been thick and wavy, even as a baby. Took after her father – his hair had also been that beautiful dark mahogany when he was younger.

Christine, aged eight, had been cast as an angel in the school nativity play. Made the audience laugh by wobbling her front tooth for the baby Jesus.

Christine had been deputy head girl. Would have been head girl, had it not been for the business of changing her name. Just a little too eccentric. 'She can be a bit wilful, but then I think that's a good trait in a girl,' said Mrs Geering, who clearly didn't believe this at all.

If Christa came into a room, her mother's eyes lit up. Mrs Geering, I soon decided, would never, ever, abandon her daughter, not even to save the lives of fifty men.

Really, Maman, I thought, you had three children, *three*, and you risked everything.

As for Mr Geering, for the time being I gave up getting anything else out of him. He was a restless soul, rarely in the house. One Sunday afternoon Christa took me up to visit him at his allotment. He was feeding dead stalks and the prunings from raspberry canes and blackcurrants into a bonfire and smiled at us across the flames. His face quivered in the hot air and I saw the young man again, yearning in his eyes. The moment passed and old Ted was back, a closed door. He allowed me to poke my nose into his shed, though – immaculately tidy, about two metres square – and showed me the seedlings he had planted in his cold frame. He was on nodding terms with his fellow diggers, whom apparently he'd known for decades.

Ted Geering clearly adored his wife. Followed her with his eyes. If he was home, he was always listening to us women, even if he appeared to be reading a newspaper.

While Christa was at college one day, Mrs Geering escorted me to Sun Engraving because I wanted to see where Ted had been working all these years; in other words, to witness the life Maman had given him. I took the Metropolitan Line train to a little station near a park and walked under trees with bright unfurling leaves, past largish houses fronted by privet hedges and rose bushes. Mrs Geering was waiting for me under a clock tower, amidst a crowd of workers rushing home for their lunch. She was wearing a pale-brown coat and a worried expression and she waved when she saw me as if I wouldn't have recognised her otherwise.

The gatekeeper doffed his cap to her. The factory seemed boundless. Half empty because it was lunchtime but still vibrating with machinery. A good place, smelling of ink and chemicals and metal. We passed along deep alleyways between buildings. Mrs Geering pointed to a warehouse which had replaced the office where she used to work as a ledger clerk. 'That's where Ted and I first met, at the start of the war. The door burst open and in came this young man in a great hurry because he was behind with an order. I had to enter the details and he fretted until I'd finished. Later he came back to apologise.'

It turned out they'd been brought up a few roads apart. A couple of days later they'd met again at a Saturday night dance. He'd joined up soon after that. 'We courted on the couple of times he was on leave. Dear Ted, I never could believe my luck.' She smiled like a young girl. Lucky him, you mean, I thought.

We peeped in at the brand-new composing room where Ted Geering was at work in a white overall. There must have been about forty or fifty other men, all doing complicated things with trays of letters. A couple of men, but not Ted, raised their heads and glanced across at us. Even when Ted was at work he had the air of not being quite present.

He knew about us; there was something in his shoulders, the tension in his face, the fact that his hands went still. But he didn't acknowledge us.

On the way out, Mrs Geering pointed to a warehouse with closed doors. 'Girls are packing gas masks in there. The space has been requisitioned by the government. It wouldn't surprise me if I didn't find myself working here again if there's a war. It's bound to be all hands on deck, like last time.'

Afterwards, she walked with me back to the station, our shadows stretching side by side along the paving stones. 'Would you mind if I had a conversation with Mr Geering about the past?' I said.

She went deadly quiet. Finally she said in a tight voice: 'I very much doubt you'd get anywhere. He never talks about it.'

'But could I at least ask him?'

'I was saying to Maisie, he's not been himself lately.'

'I will be careful.'

'I know you will, dear. And I know you've a right to speak to him.' At the little station she let me kiss her on either cheek. She gave off a sweet, powdery smell. I wanted her to hug me but she didn't, and when I turned back she was walking away with her head down.

Christa

Travelling with Estelle was like being with a film star. She carried herself with grace and vigour, swinging along in her red hat and the camel coat nipped in at the waist. Heads turned as we raced the length of the platform at King's Cross to catch the Cambridge train. We had met at the barrier but Estelle had cut it nail-bitingly fine.

On the journey through the spring countryside, and much to the fascination of the elderly sisters who shared our compartment, she detailed the mechanical features of a tractor at work on a slope of loamy soil and commented on a herd of Friesians pressed close to a gate. Almost in the same breath, she told me that in a week's time she would be back at home writing up her dissertation, applying for jobs and lending a hand because it was one of the busiest seasons of the year. Yet when I asked questions about the actual work she'd be doing on the farm, she was rather vague. 'Maman never took to my father's rural life, so it's not really in my blood.'

'Being outside and not having to think sounds pretty appealing to me. I'm fed up with having my nose in a book.'

'Trust me, farming's fun for half an hour, then hell after that.'

On our walk from the station towards the city centre she insisted on calling in at the Fitzwilliam Museum to look at an etching by Van Dyck and a portrait by his near contemporary, Frans Hals. 'See the life in that,' said Estelle, drawing me closer. 'Can't you just imagine that man in the picture inviting you to go to bed with him?'

'Would you, if he asked?' I tried not to sound as shocked as I felt.

'Certainly not. Drunkards make hopeless lovers. He looks like one of my brother Robbe's drinking companions. Frans Hals is on the list of artists for my dissertation, by the way. His family were exiles from Antwerp, although they went north to Holland rather than crossing over to England.'

In the late spring of 1939 a word such as *exile* blew a chill breeze through even the brightest day. On newsreel we had watched German troops march through Hungary and Czechoslovakia, cheered on by crowds of civilians, while barefoot refugees, hauling suitcases or carrying an infant, headed God knew where. Arm in arm and in much more sober mood, we left the museum and did not let go of each other until we reached the ancient door of Doctor Sinclair's college where Estelle, having made enquiries of the porter, marched across a lawn signed PLEASE KEEP OFF THE GRASS. 'We might just as well be in Brussels. I can't bear all these unnecessary prohibitions.'

'If everyone did that there'd be no lawn left.'

'What's the point of grass if you can't walk on it? Show some spirit.'

When we met up again on the far side of the quad I was conscious of a distance in her manner and realised that I'd brushed up against something inflexible.

Doctor Sinclair was waiting for us at the top of a flight of narrow stairs. 'I have been watching out for you,' he told Estelle. 'When you strode off the path and onto the grass I guessed that you must be my visitor from Brussels.'

His room with its oak window seats, crammed bookshelves and blazing fire smelt of ink, pipe smoke and something tweedy and expensive. Though he offered to take Estelle's coat and arranged it carefully on a hanger, he forgot to ask for mine. He had a neat nose and quirky brows under fairish hair, which by its profusion suggested a man more concerned with matters of the mind than appearance. I judged him to be about my parents' age, in his late forties, though he seemed much more youthful. His gaze returned again and again to Estelle and at one point he shook his head, as if to clear it. When I commented on his vast array of books, he said: 'I can't resist ordering new titles and when I've read them I'm afraid I push them in anywhere they'll fit. But you could name any author and I'd find him at once.' My eyes met Estelle's – she too had registered his vanity.

A stooped man in a green apron appeared with tea and a plate of garibaldi biscuits.

'They are known as squashed fly,' I informed her as we took seats at the hearth and she grinned.

Sinclair mentioned a recent meeting with their mutual acquaintance, the Jesuit priest, Père Borland, 'My dear friend Laurence,' as he called him, pronouncing the name with an exaggerated French accent.

'You saw him last year?' said Estelle, annoyed. 'He didn't say.'

'I happened to be passing through Belgium. How is Laurence?'

'Fairly good, though like the rest of us he is worried about the prospect of war.'

'So he told me in his last letter.'

'What else did he write?'

His smile seemed almost boyish. 'That you might be interested in my current area of research, Martin Droeshout.'

Estelle looked mystified.

'The man who engraved the image of Shakespeare that is stamped on our national psyche? Droeshout was a Flemish exile, and engraving, since it could be mass-produced, enabled even mediocre artists to make a good living, provided they found the right commission.'

Throughout this discourse he had addressed only Estelle, who was seated in a very alluring pose – long legs crossed, chin in hand – though I doubted she was really listening. It was I who was forced to continue the conversation.

'Estelle showed me a portrait by the exiled painter Frans Hals in the Fitzwilliam Museum.'

'Ah yes. The Low Countries, as Mademoiselle Cornelis-Faider, being an historian, will know, have always been highly desirable, due to their excellent wool, access to the coast and the talents and education of their citizens. Anabaptists, Calvinists, Catholics, the Spanish, Dutch, Austrian and the French have all been after, at the very least, your allegiance, is that not true, Mademoiselle? And at most your land, your goods and your souls. But we

37

English have been the beneficiaries of this persecution, since so many of your best artists fled here over the years.'

'You forgot Germany in 1914,' Estelle said.

'Ah yes, Germany, the biggest thug of all.'

She changed the subject abruptly. 'How did you first meet Père Borland?'

'I spent a year in Louvain before the war studying philosophy and history. Laurence was a second-year seminarian at the time and he and I enjoyed many hours arguing about art and whether or not the profound influence of religion had been a help or a hindrance. Droeshout, for example, doubtless benefited from the post-Reformation secularisation of art in this country.'

'Did you stay in touch with Père Borland during the war?' I asked.

Sinclair bridled slightly at my interference, and his manner cooled. 'Communication between us was very difficult because Laurence was living in a country that was occupied by the Germans and I was stuck here in England. I suffer from a heart problem, so I tried to make myself useful by teaching.'

Estelle exhaled contemptuously and set aside her cup and saucer, but I persisted. 'But you and Borland did remain friends throughout?'

'Of course.'

'Doctor Sinclair, did you ever meet Estelle's mother?' This time I really had caused a stir. Estelle, who was already on her feet, paused with her hand on the chair-back. 'Fleur Cornelis-Faider,' I added helpfully, 'the Resistance heroine known as Françoise, and a close friend of Laurence Borland.'

Although he recovered in an instant, I could tell that Sinclair was weighing up his response. 'I know all about Fleur Cornelis-Faider, of course,' he flashed an appreciative smile at Estelle, 'and as a matter of fact I did once happen to be present when she came to Louvain and called on Laurence.'

'He never told me that you'd met her,' said Estelle.

'I very much doubt if he would remember an event that happened quite by chance more than a quarter of a century ago.'

'Why didn't you say anything when we came in?'

'Good Lord, it was the briefest of meetings. And I wasn't sure

38

whether you would wish to talk about her. I thought you were interested in my research.'

'What was she like?' I asked.

'In fact, her resemblance to you, Mademoiselle,' he told Estelle, 'gave me quite a turn when you first arrived.' Sinclair was now at the window seat, fumbling for a handkerchief.

'Did you like her?' I asked.

'What an odd question. Of course I—'

'It's a very good question,' interrupted Estelle. 'As I never knew my mother, I want to find out everything I can about her.'

Sinclair gave another of his whimsical laughs. 'Goodness me, I never expected the third degree. Well, I found it rather thrilling to be in the room with such a beautiful and unusual young woman' – another sideways glance at Estelle – 'but also terrifying. I was used to the polite English girls of my circle at home, all charming but unambitious. Instead, in came this tall young woman who behaved as if she owned the place and treated my rather scholarly friend Laurence almost as if he were her older brother.'

'What do you mean?' Estelle asked.

'She teased him, flirted with him, even. Given that he was a seminarian, I remember being just a little shocked.'

'*Flirted* with him?'

'Forgive me. Perhaps that's rather too strong a word. And remember this was a very long time ago. In my clumsy way I'm saying that what I'd always admired about Laurence was his single-mindedness, and whilst your mother was in the room it was hard for anyone, him included, to focus on anything but her.'

'I don't suppose you have a photograph of him?' I asked.

'Of Laurence? Of course.' He indicated a portrait, barely three inches high, of a severe-looking young man with a long chin and fierce, bespectacled eyes, wearing a dog collar. 'As a matter of fact, it was quite a revelation to glimpse Laurence as he might have been before he signed up for the priesthood. Given that I was – am – an atheist, his vocation was quite a bone of contention between us.'

A clock chimed somewhere, then another.

'I'm afraid I must dash, although we haven't even scraped the surface of Droeshout, and I had all these papers prepared for you.' He indicated a little pile on the desk.

'May I take them with me?' Estelle stuffed them into her satchel while Sinclair told her about the provenance of each. She gave his hand a cursory shake and there it was, another moment of connection: Estelle's hand, his, Fleur's. Just for a second I glimpsed Fleur through him, something in her gaze, perhaps, that Sinclair had never forgotten.

A few minutes later, Estelle was standing in the middle of the forbidden lawn gazing up at Sinclair's window. 'Did you hear what he said? He was implying that Maman and Père Borland had some kind of love affair. I don't understand it. I'd always assumed they were best friends. If she loved Laurence romantically, why did she marry Papa?'

'She could hardly have married a priest.'

'For Pete's sake, why would he become a priest if he could have Maman?' She started walking at a great pace across the quad. 'Since I've been in England, I've discovered that every single man who came across Maman seemed to fall in love with her.'

The evening was fine and quite warm and the air was smoky as we walked back to the station. On the London train we had a compartment to ourselves. For a while Estelle was preoccupied with the wide open sky and extravagant sunset, whilst I reflected upon Sinclair's rather mean decision not to have been the first to mention Fleur. She had definitely made quite an impression upon him, though not, I guessed, an entirely favourable one.

'I wish you could come to Belgium and meet my family,' Estelle said suddenly. 'Then you would understand me so much better.'

'Well I'd love to—'

'Then come. Why don't you? The minute you've finished your exams. We will need all the help we can get on the farm this summer. The harvest is hard work but fun, and then every year there's a feast because Papa's birthday is around that time too. You'd love it.'

The impulsiveness of her request, the promise of adventure and the onward speed of the train swept me up in a moment of transcendence. I could scarcely believe that Fleur's daughter should crave my company as much as I hers. The dipping sun gleamed on her face and she shielded her eyes as she smiled at me.

I crossed the compartment to link my arm through hers. 'I'll come. I'd love to.'

By the time we reached King's Cross we had made our plan. She would go home to Belgium and ask her brother Pieter to give me a few weeks' employment on the farm – I had almost no savings and would need to earn my keep. Meanwhile I would try to convince Ma that a spell in Belgium would be excellent for my French, a tonic after three years of study and a well-deserved break before I took up a teaching post in September.

Estelle

On my last visit to Harewood Road, I arrived deliberately early. Christa wasn't back from college so it was just me and Mrs Geering in the kitchen. There was meat wrapped in white paper, a cheap cut Pieter would have given to the dogs but which she was feeding through a machine called a mincer.

Frying onions, meat, sliced carrots. A cube called Oxo wrapped in foil, the size of a die. You pinched it between finger and thumb to break it up into dark brown salty crumbs for the gravy. I licked my skin clean afterwards while Mrs Geering peeled potatoes.

'I do wish you hadn't invited Christine to Belgium,' she said. 'What if war breaks out?'

'Then we'll send her home.'

'She might not be able to get out of the country.'

'Of course she will. Belgium is likely to be neutral. Nobody will stop her.'

'But think what happened to Ted . . .' She had her back to me but I knew she was fighting tears. 'I don't think I could bear it if history repeated itself . . .'

'Mr Geering managed to get home from Belgium, even during a war,' I said.

'Only just. And look how he has suffered. When he came back he was a different man.'

'You can't blame Belgium for that. It was the war.'

'It wasn't just the war. It was everything.'

'The trouble is I still don't know what really happened to him. And he hasn't said anything about Maman. I feel as if I'm going home none the wiser.'

She worked away at a potato. Her voice was strained and quiet. 'Go on then. Ask him whatever you want.'

'Are you sure?'

'I've thought it over. You deserve to know more about your mother, of course you do. I mustn't stand in your way. And underneath the surface, Ted is upset most of the time. Maybe if you draw it out of him he might feel better.' She nearly cut herself slicing the potato on the chopping board. 'You know where to find him. Tell him I need some spinach.'

It was a ten-minute walk past a walled cemetery and left at the football ground. The allotments smelled of cabbages and cinders. Half a dozen men were at work. It was a breezy day with an increasing number of clouds covering the sun. From the minute I appeared at the gate Ted Geering knew I was there, just like the visit to the factory, though he didn't raise his head. He was marking out a seedbed with string and even when I drew closer and spoke his name he didn't look up.

The sun went in and I shivered because I'd left my coat in the house. I gave him the message about spinach but he just went on tying string to sticks. He was like Oud Daan at De Eikenhoeve, inspecting the raspberry canes. That same methodical shift from one to another, total absorption. Apparently.

I sheltered in the hut while Ted fetched a knife and worked along the rows of spinach, selecting leaves. As he was wrapping them up in newspaper, I said: 'Mr Geering, I'm going home in a couple of days.'

He nodded.

'I was just wondering, before I go, would it be possible for us to have a quick conversation about my mother?'

Not a sign that he'd even heard me.

'Can you remember anything she said or did? You see, I was so young when she died. I can only use my imagination otherwise.'

The shed had to be padlocked, the key hung back round his neck on a string. Halfway through securing the lock, he paused, released the chain, opened the door again and stood just within the threshold.

'Let me look at you,' he said, turning. I stepped closer and when I was near enough he gripped my face between his hands. For an insane moment I thought he was about to kiss me. His nose was a couple of centimetres from mine and his clean breath reminded me of Pieter's. I looked him in the eye and knew he was trying to find her in me. His hands were warm and smelled of earth. Again, like Pieter's. I tried to imagine him when he was as young as my brothers. Unlined skin. Clear whites to his eyes.

'Her hair.' He picked up a lock of mine, just as he had that first afternoon in the kitchen, held it to the light and rubbed it between his fingers. 'I have never seen hair like hers since then, the way it glinted in the sun.' He released me abruptly and began sorting through his seed trays.

'We were sworn to secrecy,' he continued. 'You've got to understand that. Even our real names were kept secret. I was Grand. We were told to choose something simple that we'd easily remember for our false documents. They said: "If you're captured, the less you know the better. And when you get home, don't tell anyone how you managed it or others will suffer." So I've kept quiet.'

'There's no need any more,' I said. 'That war is over. And I won't tell a soul, I promise.'

He picked up a trowel and scraped the mud off the tines of his fork. 'She wasn't the only one. We were passed from one person to another.'

'Yes.'

'We weren't told names. We hardly saw faces. It was usually dark.'

'But you say I'm like her, so you must have seen her clearly at some point?'

'The name she used was Françoise. She was with us the longest because she escorted the two of us right to the border.'

'How long did that take? Where did you meet her? How did she hide you?'

I wished Christa was there to prevent me firing all those questions at him. He obviously found them too much because he took hold of his key, ushered me out and locked the door again. I stood in the wind, waiting while he gathered up the parcel of spinach. Stared down at a clump of rhubarb and imagined Mrs Geering cutting the stalks into chunks. 'Never cook it with water,' she told me, 'just stew it over a low heat.' She mixed it up

44

with that yellow sauce she called custard. Rhubarb fool. Sweet, pinkish brown. Fur on the teeth. I took a tin of Bird's custard home to Hanna. I bet she never used it.

Ted Geering said: 'I just walked out of the hospital tent. There were so many of us, lying on beds or stretchers or even the ground. They didn't realise I could walk so I got up from my bed and just kept on walking. I wore a blanket round my shoulders and my feet were bare. The thing is, I didn't care what happened to me. I simply told myself I should walk away from the war and not towards it. I hardly knew I was behind enemy lines.

'When I came to a village I knocked on the first door. A woman answered with a child in her arms and she hid me in a shed a bit like this one.' A smile in his voice. 'Smelt of creosote.'

I couldn't stop myself interrupting. 'Was that where you met Maman?'

'A man came for us in the night. I could hear shelling. The sky flashed. When he made me step outside I was crying and couldn't stop, but he said in English: "It's all right, you're among friends," and he made me climb into a cart full of hay.'

Ted stood with his arms folded, head down, loose strands of hair blowing in the wind. I thought I'd lost his attention. Onions were growing nearby and I caught their scent. One man was calling to another about a cure for slugs.

'Gravel,' Ted Geering murmured.

'It was because of the gas that I couldn't stand the dark, so I kept shouting out and they had to gag me and tie my hands and feet because I was fighting them all the time. I was in a terrible state. At last we came to a cottage by a canal and there was a different man in charge, very harsh, but with good English. He said if I made a single noise he would shoot me, because otherwise lots of people would die. By this time I'd been joined by another Brit who was calling himself Hébert.'

Ted Geering reached out and touched my hair again, as if he just couldn't stop himself. 'It glitters.' Then he added: 'We had to walk on and on through woods to a clearing with a hut. I fell asleep inside.'

Another pause. A strange glance at me. He was about to say something but stopped himself. Finally, after a long silence, he continued. 'When I woke, it was just me and Hébert. There was this basket of food and Hébert said we had to share it, but I think he'd eaten most of it already. We slept again for a bit and when it was getting dark Françoise came for us. The first thing I noticed about her was that she was just so *clean*.'

I laughed and he looked pleased, like a schoolboy who's cracked a good joke.

'She smelt of soap and her fingernails were pink and shining. She wore trousers and a dark-green blouse. Her teeth were lovely.'

'What sort of trousers?'

'Men's trousers with a cord to keep them up. Two of her could have fitted into that waistband. Her hair was tied up with string under a boys' cap, but at night she let it down.'

'Did she talk to you much?'

'She spoke French and I didn't. Like I said, there was this other British man with us, Hébert. He said I was slowing them down because I had to keep stopping – I was short of breath, you see, from the gas. We had to walk a long way. Françoise was sad about something. She cried quite a lot.'

'*Cried?*' In all my imaginings, Maman had never cried. 'Are you sure she was crying?'

'Oh yes. She couldn't stop herself. And when we were picked up by another man driving a load of chickens she kept shouting at him. His cart had a false bottom and we lay underneath, Hébert and me, with the chickens above us.'

I took his free hand and pressed it to my cheek. He stroked my hair with his thumb.

'After a long time we stopped. The driver opened a slat and Françoise threaded herself in beside me. There was scarcely room to breathe, and it stank of chickens. Him on my right, her on my left. We drove on a very short distance before we stopped again because a German voice was giving the driver an order. Her hip pressed against mine and suddenly she kissed me, to keep me quiet, I thought. It was a proper kiss.'

Ted Geering allowed me to draw him down to sit beside me on the little wooden dais surrounding the shed.

'The driver spoke in Flemish. Boots stamped an inch from our faces. There was a lot of squawking. I think the guards were given some chickens and then we drove on. All that time, Françoise had been holding my face and kissing me. When we were on the move we drew apart but I was a different man. I didn't know what to think. I didn't care.

'Another wood. Hébert translated for me that we were going to pass through the electrified fence at the Dutch border but we had to wait until the small hours. And first, Françoise was going to teach us how to weave through the wires, because if we got it wrong, we'd die. So we had our lesson, just inside the woods, and then Hébert seemed to be telling her we should get going. They had a bit of an argument and in the end we left him in a hiding place among some piled-up branches.

'She took me so deep into the woods that we could hardly see the sky. Then she mimed that we should bury ourselves in leaves because those woods were patrolled by dogs. We lay under a beech tree and watched the light fade. She whispered to me in French and pillowed her cheek in her hand as she looked at me. I saw a beetle in her hair and brushed it away. She started to cry again. Just a little. I kissed her cheek and her tears were cool. Everything about her was . . . lovely.

'Afterwards, I wished I had died in those woods. I've never forgotten how warm she was. How she buried her face in my neck and clung to me. She felt so pure . . .'

A long silence. I watched four magpies, one after another, land on a neighbour's plot. They pecked away amidst the furrows.

'Suddenly she pulled away from me and indicated that it was time to leave. She led me through the trees and we collected Hébert and crossed the fields, heading towards the border. I was shocked and cold and couldn't understand how she'd been able to tear herself away so easily. She walked at quite a rate and never checked to see if we were following. I couldn't bear that it was over. I remember wondering if I'd dreamt it all.'

By this point, I don't think Ted had any idea that I was still beside him. He could see only Maman. And so could I, in glimpses – a slender woman wearing a man's trousers, flitting through trees. Why had she made love to a complete stranger when time was so short?

'At one point she stopped and, from a hidden pit, she produced

47

two halves of a beer barrel,' he said. 'Then I saw the wires glinting in the moonlight. They were thin as threads, spiked, a foot or so apart, strung between rough posts. Two rows. Françoise knelt again, opened her rucksack and put on gloves. She had these rubber socks to fit over the wires. Delicate work to get the barrels in place, but she was very deft.

'Hébert was swearing. Then we heard the dogs. There was a watchtower nearby, but no sign of a sentry. Hébert muttered to me: "You fucker. What took you so long? You've killed us all. Well, I'm going first."

'I said he could, for all I cared. I wanted to stay with her but she talked to me, very low, mimed what I was to do. And when Hébert tried to push through, she spat words at him and kept him back with her hand. The dogs sounded much closer. She took hold of my jacket and spoke in halting English. "I want you go first. Yes, I'll come. But you must go now. You must go."

'She held the wire apart with the barrel like she'd shown us earlier. "Head down, arms tucked in," she'd indicated. First one set of wires, then another. It took me too long because I was shaking, but her voice was steady. "Take it easy," she said in English. "Keep your head down. Lower, lower." Then I realised that instead of following she'd gone back for Hébert. And then she was screaming at me to run. The dogs got her by the leg and she went down.'

Ted Geering went silent. I heard the sound of another man's spade cutting through soil, a vehicle somewhere. 'Mr Geering. Are you saying that you actually witnessed my mother being taken prisoner at the border?'

'They spotted Hébert in the beam of a flashlight and then I heard shots. Françoise screamed at me again and I ran and ran. Every night I'm still running. It was my fault. Hébert had kept saying to me outside the woods: "Where the fuck have you been? What was the delay, you fucker?"'

He wiped his face with his sleeve. 'Please don't tell them. Promise me you won't tell them. *Please . . .*'

When he'd calmed down, we walked side by side along the allotment path and home to Harewood Road. I felt full up, as if I'd

48

eaten too much rich food. Sated with knowledge.

Christa was home, excited about coming to Belgium. Mrs Geering had made a pink cake to celebrate my last night. She didn't ask me about the allotment at first, just put her hand on Ted's arm when he gave her the spinach. She told him to take off his boots and wash his hands. He did as he was told. We drank a glass of sherry in the front parlour. There was this false me, raising a glass, and there was the rest of me, knocked about by what he'd said.

'We'll all miss you,' Mrs Geering said.

'Not as much as I'll miss you. I wish I could stay in England forever.'

But I was lying. I kept thinking that Maman might have lived had it not been for sex with Ted Geering. I wished Christa wasn't coming to Belgium because at that moment I wanted to forget everything about her and her family. And anyway, it *was* too dangerous. Wasn't I living proof that a visitor changes everything?

In the kitchen when Mrs Geering and I were alone for a minute, she asked: 'What did he say?' She busied herself boiling milk for the Bird's custard.

I surprised myself by putting my hand on her arm and kissing her cheek. 'He told me how brave Maman was.'

She pulled away and looked at me hard.

'He told me how grateful he was she'd saved him because otherwise he couldn't have come home to you.'

But she was no fool. 'You were gone a long time. What else did he say?'

'We talked about the allotment for a while. You're right. He did get upset when I mentioned Maman. It's probably best that I'm leaving.'

'No more details about how he escaped then?'

'Only that it was a bit of a blur.'

She nodded. I could tell she was part disappointed, part relieved that I hadn't said more. I picked up the custard, she a dish of hot sponge cake on top of a layer of golden syrup. But at the kitchen door she paused. 'You will look after Christa?'

'Of course. I have to, for Maman's sake.'

49

At table in the back room we were all gentle with each other because it was my last night. Mrs Geering had a present for me, wrapped in tissue paper. Red gloves, hand-knitted, to match my hat.

Ted Geering ate very quickly, but sometimes he looked at me stealthily. When it was time for me to leave he shook my hand but wouldn't meet my eye.

Mrs Geering kissed me, just a peck on the cheek, and then again, much more heartily. 'You come back and see us any time.'

Christa walked with me halfway to the station before I sent her home to get on with her revision. She said: 'I can't wait to see you again.'

I held her at arm's length and studied her face. If only I hadn't invited her to De Eikenhoeve, I thought, I might have protected us both from this terrible complication.

I pulled away from her hug, waved her off and walked on alone. I had a new image of Maman now, and it was not the one I'd gone looking for. Caught in the flashlight behind the wire. Ted Geering's semen sticky between her thighs.

Christa

On Tuesday 6th June 1939 I left London before dawn. My examinations were over, war was approaching and in defiance of Ma's better judgement I was hurtling towards a continent already ravaged by Hitler's advance.

To my dismay, Ma insisted on accompanying me to the station. The parting had been hanging over us for weeks and I could not wait to be free of her unspoken resistance. Whilst for me the visit to Belgium was pure adventure, for her it was a matter only of dread.

She insisted on paying for a platform ticket and taking me to the carriage door, having peered through the window and found a compartment already occupied by a couple of ladies. 'Even so, be careful who you talk to. You never know, at times like this.'

'I'll be fine, Ma. And I'll write as soon as I get there.'

'But listen, there's something else.' She suddenly hauled me to one side so as not to be overheard, though the station was throbbing with noise. 'Don't forget, when we're away from home, when there's nobody around to tell us things, it can be difficult to say no.'

'No to what, Ma?'

She looked at me in agony. We both knew that I was teasing her and normally she would have blushed and laughed. 'You've read enough books. All that French stuff. You know what happens to girls. I'm just saying, I do trust you, I do, but people, men, can be very persuasive. In the heat of the moment . . .'

I held her tightly and kissed her powdery cheek. My heart bled because I thought I understood her so exactly. Though she rightly guessed that I was still a virgin, she was also probably aware that I had not been put much in the way of temptation.

She seemed diminished in her fawn coat, attempting to stem the tide not only of war but of my growing up. 'Ma, I promise I won't do anything stupid. You've met Estelle, I'll be with her family. She's not going to let me step out of line.'

She was looking over my shoulder, down the length of the platform. 'I came here to say goodbye to your Pa,' she said, 'that last time. We were just married.'

Behind me, the train was huffing cheerfully and a guard was slamming doors, and just for a moment I could feel the press of all those thousand, thousand wartime goodbyes.

'I'll come back in one piece, I promise.'

I kissed her one more time and stepped aboard, obediently found a place in the compartment she'd selected, waved frantically at her fast disappearing figure and felt the shackles of home fall away from my shoulders at last.

The landscape east of Dunkirk was a revelation. All through childhood I had been haunted by visions of Pa floundering in a cloud of poison gas and I struggled to match those images with the sunshiny fields and neat little villages flashing by. I saw myself as a needle threading its way between England and Belgium, mending the past. In two hours I would see Estelle again. Would our time together be as edgy and all-consuming as before? And what about the farm, and her family? What would they be like? Would I be welcome? Another hour. Half an hour. In ten minutes, seven, five, as we clattered through suburbs striking for their foreignness – the steeper pitch of roofs, the lack of bay windows, the prevalence of white painted shutters – I packed and repacked my handbag, left my seat far too early and stood by the door.

Estelle was waiting a little distance from the barrier, wearing a red and white dress, bare arms folded, her skin tanned. Waving frantically, I broke into a run, handed over my ticket, then threw down my suitcase in anticipation of a hug. She did put out her arms, but held me at a distance and kissed me coolly on each cheek.

'If we don't hurry, we'll miss the train,' she said. 'And that would be a real bore.'

She too carried a suitcase and told me that she had been staying in Brussels with her grandmother. In minutes she'd swept me through the crowded station and onto the little train that would carry us north to Oostervorken. We sat bolt upright on hard seats, surrounded by Flemish speakers who stared at me whenever I opened my mouth.

I told her all the news from the month or so since I'd last seen her – my graduation from college, Pa's time off work due to a sudden bout of bad headaches, the arrival of an Anderson shelter for the back garden, which Pa refused point-blank to install because he said it would ruin his rose border – but eventually her reserve silenced me. I remembered our brief spat in the quad at Doctor Sinclair's college, and it dawned on me that perhaps I didn't know Estelle as well as I thought. From time to time when our eyes met she smiled briefly, but mostly she leant her head in her hand and looked out of the window.

Having never been abroad, every detail intrigued me, from church steeples to windmills. By the time we reached Oostervorken, the carriage was almost empty, save for a couple of women with enormous shopping baskets. Estelle and I were the only passengers to alight there. Beyond a flyblown yard, there was no sign of a village or any other form of life except for a dilapidated taxicab, complete with a driver whom Estelle addressed curtly as Viktor and gave instructions to in Flemish, and whose entire business, or so she told me, consisted of waiting for the four trains which passed through daily.

Viktor's motor had no suspension and reeked of cigarettes and mould. A winding road led to a row of cottages with white shutters, a couple of shops with closed blinds and awnings and a grey stone church. When I tried to open the window it yielded an inch and then jammed. Eventually we turned into a lane so narrow that bracken and branches brushed against the car on both sides and the vehicle lurched from one rut to another until it stalled at a wide gate.

At first, after the taxi roared away, the quiet seemed uncanny, then I realised that the air was filled with birdsong.

Estelle unlatched the gate and held it open. 'Voilà.'

Unforgettable, that first glimpse of De Eikenhoeve. It seemed

53

to me, in the evening light, that the farmhouse and its surroundings were under water; no clearly defined edges, just the grey of stone, the green of leaves and the pinkish blue of the evening sky.

As my vision cleared I saw the house at the end of a curving drive. It was two storeys high – three including the attic – and had innumerable windows. The turret was straight out of a fairy tale, with a conical roof like a witch's hat. I picked up my suitcase and walked through the gate, feeling as if I were making my entrance onto a stage. The gate swung shut behind me and the heavy iron latch clunked into place.

'They will have finished dinner long ago,' said Estelle, 'but there's bound to be something to eat.'

Hens were pecking in the deep shadows of an immense oak tree and to my right, in a slight dip, was a green-painted swing. The sky was darkening and the farm, in the fading light, had taken on the texture of an oil painting. Close up, the arch, which passed right through the depth of the house, smelt of damp and animal droppings. Through it, I glimpsed the last of the evening sun slanting across a stretch of grass, a pond and a complicated bit of agricultural equipment. But Estelle left me no time to linger. Doors had been built into the sides of the arch and through one of them we entered the house along a stone passageway, past larders and sculleries, and into a kitchen furnished with a table and half a dozen chairs. Strings of onions, utensils and pans hung from the ceiling, dresser shelves were stacked with pots and clusters of labelled jars and a woman was stirring something on the stove.

'This is Hanna,' said Estelle.

Hanna embraced Estelle and gave me a nervous smile but immediately returned to her work. She had sparse hair teased into short curls, nervous, popping eyes and an air, like Ma, of having been forever on her feet.

'Our housekeeper,' Estelle added.

Hanna's longish speech in Flemish was translated by Estelle as: 'There'll be a meal ready in five minutes.'

'Will you thank her for me?'

'It's her job. I'll take you in to see Papa on the way upstairs.'

As I was marched through room after room – there seemed

to be no passageway downstairs, just interconnecting doors – I spied polished surfaces, intricate porcelain and old paintings. What on earth had Estelle been thinking when she had praised our shabby little terraced house in Harewood Road? De Eikenhoeve, by contrast, was a palace.

'They'll be in here.' She went ahead and embraced her father, leaving me at the door of a drawing room with latticed windows, an immense fireplace filled with a lavish arrangement of scented flowers, deep armchairs in a floral pattern, mirrors with elaborate gilt frames and opulent rugs covering ancient floorboards. The room's occupants, who might have seen us walking up the drive, and would certainly have heard us racing through the house, were stiffly arranged, as if they had taken up a fixed position for our meeting. Estelle's father stood on the hearthrug, bearded and ruddy-cheeked with fierce eyes, while her stepmother was perched on a delicate-legged chair, hand poised, mid-stitch, above a tapestry frame.

Tucking her needle into the canvas, she rose, smoothed the skirt of her frock and held out her hand. 'Estelle said we might expect a visitor. Christabel, is it? All the way from England. I hope your journey wasn't too arduous. If only Estelle had given me a time, I would have met you from the station.' She spoke good but heavily accented French while her husband only managed a few words in Flemish – just as well, because I was tongue-tied in the presence of the man who had once been married to Fleur Cornelis-Faider.

'He says you're most welcome,' said the stepmother. 'Please, make yourself at home. You must be famished.' She wore a highly impractical lemon-coloured dress with a white collar and everything about her was neat and restrained.

Estelle, who waited in the doorway with her arms folded, sighed audibly when her stepmother spoke. I followed her up a staircase with a banister smooth as silk to an upstairs corridor smelling of sun-baked wood. One door stood ajar. This was to be my room, overlooking the oak tree, far grander than any I had ever slept in. It boasted waxed floorboards and the unheard of luxury of a double bed covered with a spotless white quilt. From the window I saw that the drive disappeared beneath me – my room was above the arch which ran through the house – and the view was partially obscured by the dense leaves of the oak tree, which grew so close that I could almost have climbed from my window onto one of its branches. The stone windowsill was scattered with debris: leaves and twigs and a curled green caterpillar.

Estelle flung open a wardrobe door so vigorously that the coat hangers clattered together. 'There's a bathroom along the passage. And later I'll show you where I sleep.'

'Thank you. It's a beautiful room.' I couldn't help hugging her and this time there was less resistance as I caught her well-remembered scent.

At last she spoke with her old warmth: 'I am so happy that you are here. Really I am. And they'll be so shocked to find out who you are. I can't wait to see their faces.'

'You mean they don't know?'

'I told you, I haven't been home. I just wrote to say I was bringing a guest. Don't look so scared. It will be a great surprise for them.'

Places had been set for us at the end of a table in the family dining room; I had glimpsed another, vaster still and much more formal, in the centre of the house. The meal, served on chinaware decorated with oak leaves and eaten with silver cutlery similarly engraved on the handles, was succulent; the sauce richer, the raspberries plumper and the cream thicker than any I'd tasted in Watford. While we ate, Hanna stood at the door and kept up a one-sided conversation in Flemish, which Estelle only translated sporadically. 'Farm news,' she said, by way of explanation. 'And I was asking where Pieter was. Hanna says he's repairing a fence by the river.'

Hanna was surprised when I offered to help with the washing-up, but I insisted on at least clearing the table.

Estelle drummed her fingers and hissed: 'You really don't have to do that, she's paid, you know,' then swept me outside to the near darkness of the farmyard beyond the arch. There was only a sliver of moon but Estelle was as sure-footed as a night creature. A cool breeze rose from the river and the air was full of moths and perfumed with a heady blend of farm animals and wild flowers. A track sloped slightly downwards; to our right were fields grazed by horses and cows, to our left strawberry beds. Occasionally we glimpsed the glimmer of water and the flicker of a lantern.

'Pieter,' she cried.

As she ran off, all I could make out was her pale hair and the white flashes on her skirt. When I caught up I saw that she was in the arms of a tall man in shirtsleeves. A large black dog pranced excitedly at their feet, barking furiously. When Pieter glanced at me over Estelle's shoulder his eyes were amber in the lamplight. He placed his hand on the dog's head and it calmed instantly.

I thought I recognised Fleur in him when he smiled. But what I remembered most of all, lying awake later, was how his expression had changed as he watched me. Perhaps Estelle, speaking rapidly in Flemish, was explaining to him exactly who I was, because at first he looked startled, then he gripped my hand and kissed my fingertips.

Estelle

Robbe sent me a message at Grand-mère's. It was the first I'd heard from him since I'd left for London. *I'll be at the Prospero after two.* Awful timing – I was supposed to be at Bruxelles-Midi, meeting Christa at half-past three.

When I arrived he'd been drinking for hours. Thin as a rake, tartan scarf, ancient shirt and waistcoat, hair much too long. I always felt so happy when he actually bothered to turn up. He flung his arm around my shoulders and my chin brushed the fabric of his coat – the old one belonging to Pa, much too wide and in such a state it must have been to Spain and back. We sat in the window, my favourite place.

He was pale and his eyes were red. No wonder, given he smoked four or five cigarettes in the hour that I was with him. I never did get to the bottom of all that had happened in Spain to make him so jumpy. He'd witnessed a massacre, that was what he'd told Grand-mère. Crawled out from under a pile of bodies. 'It's up to him to talk if he chooses,' she said to me. 'Don't press him.' His hand trembled – too much beer and tobacco, too little food. Other women watched us through the smoke. I didn't recognise any of his friends who were lurking in the far corner. Communists, anarchists, layabouts?

'What have you been up to?' I asked. 'Nobody's been able to track you down for ages.'

'I was sick. Something I picked up. Keeps coming back and giving me the shakes.'

'Have you seen a doctor?'

'No point. We all had it. Probably the water.'

'Where are you living?'

'Oh, you know. Whoever'll put up with me for a night or two.'

'Grand-mère would have you to stay like a shot.'

'I'd die of overeating. Céleste stuffs me with pastries.' He grinned, a lamp being lit. It was a family joke, Céleste doting on Robbe, like most other women did, in fact. 'Did you finish your essay, by the way, while you were in London?'

'My *dissertation*, if you don't mind. Not yet. You know the real reason I went to England was because I wanted to meet some of the soldiers Maman saved.'

Robbe hunched over a cigarette paper, tipped out a line of tobacco and watched me with his huge, sorrowful eyes. 'Well?'

'There was one in particular who told me a lot about her. His daughter is the girl who wrote to us.'

'So he remembered Maman?'

'He did. As soon as he clapped eyes on me I could tell he'd spotted the resemblance. And when I showed him photographs he recognised her.'

I'd been wondering how much to tell Robbe about what Ted Geering had revealed, but once I was with him I knew it would be everything. Robbe's full attention was a searchlight.

'He only remembers fragments because he's never fully recovered from being gassed in the war. But he says it was Françoise – Maman – who accompanied him to the border.'

Robbe blew a perfect smoke ring, watching me. 'Did he indeed? What else?'

'There was another man with them – an English officer who called himself Hébert. He was shot.'

'At the border?'

'Yes. And Ted Geering actually witnessed Maman's arrest.'

Hand poised in the act of flicking ash. 'Are you sure?'

'Definitely. I can't get over what he told me. He'd just escaped through the fence when the dogs pulled her down. Did you know any of this?'

Robbe had made not showing his feelings into an art form, but I knew he still had them – I'd learnt to watch for a tightening at the corner of his mouth. 'Same as you. We were told she was arrested at the border near Baarle-Hertog and that an English officer was shot and killed at the same time. Not the details, nor that another man had got away. Did this Geering say anything else?'

'Once he was through the wire, he ran for it and he feels ashamed to this day. Because there's something else, Robbe. Ted Geering admitted that he and Maman had slept together. That's one of the reasons he's said nothing about it all these years – he had a new wife back home in England.'

Robbe did his thing of tipping his head backwards, sliding me a look and laughing. 'Of course they fucked each other. If you were within inches of being fried on the electrified fence wouldn't you have done the same?'

'But if they hadn't delayed, if they'd got to the border earlier ... And what about Papa and all of us? Maman knew we were all waiting for her back at De Eikenhoeve.'

It was a rare thing for Robbe to hold my hand. His was thin and hard and strong. 'War changes the rules. You don't behave as you imagine you will. Sometimes you're as calm as hell – a bullet can fall at your feet and spit grit into your eye and you walk away humming to yourself. Sometimes you can be as safe as anything, miles from the front, yet you spend the whole day shaking. Sometimes you hate the ones you're with, you're repelled by every sneeze or fart or twitch, because you think they'll get you killed and you're sick to death of them. And sometimes you would lay down your life for them, because they're all you've got and at any moment they might be dead. So if Maman and this man fucked each other just before she was captured, thank Christ, is what I say.'

'Even if they lost time because of it? Even if it made her careless?'

'That's not how it works, girl. Caution isn't always the answer.'

One of his ex-girlfriends told me that when she first met Robbe she'd been convinced he was an orphan. She said he had the eyes of a man confronted by a locked door with no key.

He ordered another drink, but I'd almost run out of time and definitely money. 'I don't have any more cash, Robbe. Have you?'

'I'll put it on the tab. By the way, I've been offered something with a magazine. I've told them I'll think about it.'

'That's great news, Robbe. Sorry, but I have to go. I'm supposed to be meeting Christa, the English girl, at the station in a quarter of an hour. She was keen to see the farm, so I invited her back.'

'What on earth for?'

'It seemed a good idea at the time. I like her company.'

'How old is this Christa?'

'A couple of years younger than me.'

'You must be crazy, letting her loose on De Eikenhoeve.' He was scrutinising me in that unnerving way of his. 'Does she know how you feel about her?'

'What do you mean?'

'Look at the state of you. All keyed up. Best frock. Come off it, Estelle.'

Damn Robbe. 'I like her. Is that a crime?'

'Shame, I was thinking you and I could have a bit of fun this summer. That's one of the reasons I wanted to meet up with you; I was going to say, why don't you stay on in Brussels? I bet my editor would give you a job.'

This was part of a pattern that upset me every time. He only dangled some prospect of us being together when he was pretty sure I wouldn't take him up on it.

'Whereas I was hoping you might come out to De Eikenhoeve sometime,' I said. 'Apparently we're all needed – it's a bumper harvest.'

'Pieter can manage without me.'

'You could meet Christa. You might like her.'

He kissed my cheek and I smelt the essence of Robbe – cigarettes and booze and something boyish in him. Tadpoles and outdoors and early morning. But I couldn't help feeling that I'd let him down and that he'd caught me out doing something I shouldn't. I protested to myself, what right had he to judge? When I stood at the barrier later and glimpsed Christa getting off the train, she was lugging a cheap suitcase and wearing too heavy a coat and for a moment I wished she hadn't come.

But as she drew closer she caught sight of me and put down the suitcase so she could wave. It was the first and only time I've seen anyone jump for joy – a double bounce on her tiptoes – and that wave of hers broke my heart because I knew, God help me, I knew I was in love with her.

Christa

I went to bed on that first night at De Eikenhoeve brimful of the fact that I was sleeping in a house once occupied by Fleur Cornelis-Faider. Everything was strange: the unaccustomed crispness of the sheets, the spacious bed, the constant slight stirring in the oak tree outside my open window, and above all the house itself, so much of it, running away from me in all directions.

Through the curtains, the midsummer night was a soft blue-grey. Fleur must have heard owls – the ancestors of those that now hooted in nearby trees – and the distant lowing of a cow. I remembered Estelle's photograph of Fleur in her loose, smock-like gown, gripping a paintbrush. Perhaps – and I sat up, wide awake now, and stared at the door – Fleur had paused sometimes in the passage outside this same bedroom, pushed open the door and perched on the low sill to peer through the branches of the oak tree to the gate and beyond. As a Resistance fighter, she must surely have been ever vigilant, waiting for signals and in fear of arrest. This deep in the countryside, it seemed to me, you could hear the least scratch of a vole's claw hundreds of yards away.

When I woke again it was because I heard rumbling underneath me and I staggered to the window, half asleep. A huge farm cart had stopped at the gate. Leaning out a little further, I heard the gate swing back against a post, then footfall, and there was Pieter Cornelis in his shirtsleeves, hatless, scanning the first-floor windows. Before I'd had a chance to draw back, he caught sight of me, grinned and waved, then turned and disappeared from view. The next moment, his cart rolled away.

I was stunned and laughing as I relived that sequence of events:

waking in a strange white bed, the sensation of subterranean movement as the heavy cart passed through the arch beneath my room, rushing to the window in my summer nightdress, Pieter's arm raised in a wave and his uplifted eyes smiling into mine.

Downstairs, Hanna was already at the kitchen stove, as if she'd been there all night. She pointed to the coffee pot, but I shook my head and said, in English, 'I'll wait for Estelle.'

Out I went, emerging from the chill of the arch to the farmyard at the back of the house and the loveliness of a June morning. Unlike an English farmyard, this was a grassy space almost large enough to be a field. Fruit trees had been trained against the old stone walls of the house, which together with its outbuildings formed three sides of a square; the fourth was made up of a shoulder-high wall, also fairly ancient, and a wide gate. A couple of white ducks dipped their heads into a reed-fringed pond.

The clear sky had that slight yellowish tinge that promises heat and the grass was dewy. To my right, a girl emerged from a low doorway and squinted in the sunlight. Having spotted me, she gaped then darted back inside. A couple of calves – orphans, I was told later – watched me from soft brown eyes and one staggered across to nudge my hip with its wet nose. The girl brought an older woman to look at me and they stood grinning and staring in their clogs and full skirts. The elder even bobbed a curtsy as I passed by, smiling shyly. I let myself out of the gate and walked self-consciously along the track Estelle and I had followed the previous evening, which plunged between hedgerows full of insects.

The sun was already warm on my neck. Fleur would have taken this same route day after day and perhaps noticed starry white flowers and a blue butterfly in the hedgerow, and a hopeful brown and white plough-horse leaning over the gate where we'd met Pieter. Further on was a low-arched bridge crossing a placid river, and to my right I could hear women's voices; a dozen or so were already at work in a field of raspberry canes. They could have been from any century, in their long-sleeved dresses, pinafores, clogs and sun hats, and though they occasionally exchanged a word or two, their fingers were never still. There must have been fifty rows of canes stretching away to the field's edge. Eventually I caught the eye of the nearest picker and gestured that I'd like to help. Somewhat reluctantly, she wagged her head towards a pile of shallow baskets and indicated that I should start on a fresh row.

The sun beat down as I worked, the fruit staining my fingers. At one point, a very elderly man with bandy legs and a black cap stood at the gate and watched us with folded arms. When I glanced up and smiled he didn't respond, and the next time I looked, he'd gone. At last, Estelle came sauntering down the lane wearing a white blouse and cotton trousers that made her look more than ever like Ingrid Bergman.

'I've been searching for you everywhere. I thought you'd want me to show you the farm this morning.'

She spent another half-hour in the field, gossiping in Flemish with the raspberry pickers, and eventually told me to leave the basket and come away.

'Don't forget I'm here to work,' I said.

'Oh for Pete's sake, they've managed fine all summer without you. They're paid by the basket. We should let them get on.'

I loved the fact that she had picked up such a very English expression from me. She took me back to the ancient, three-arched bridge over the river. The glassy water scarcely seemed to be flowing at all and the undulating landscape beyond was a patchwork of cereal crops and woodland. Rust-coloured cows were grazing in a meadow. After yesterday's journey, the anxiety of examinations and the confinement of Harewood Road, De Eikenhoeve felt like heaven.

'How long has your family farmed here?' I asked.

'Forever.'

'I can't imagine how it must feel to belong to the land.'

Perched on the low parapet, Estelle stretched out her legs and threw back her head so she could squint at the sky. 'It might seem idyllic today, but would you really want to be stuck out here in the depths of winter? With *these* people.'

'But this is your family.'

64

She gave one of her Gallic exclamations: 'Pff.'

'I suppose it could feel isolated. And I didn't realise everyone here would speak Flemish.'

'What else would you expect them to speak?'

'At least a bit of French, like you.'

'I'm the exception. Maman was French, so I made them send me to a French-speaking school in Brussels. I used to stay with my French grandparents during the week and chose a French-speaking university.'

'Didn't your mother speak Flemish too?'

'Probably not until she came here. Your face is bright red, by the way. We should get out of the sun.'

'But if your father only speaks Flemish, how did your parents manage when they first met?'

'Lord knows. Pieter thinks the village was shocked when Papa brought her home. According to him, they never really got used to the fact she was a city girl.'

Dinner was to be served at midday. 'That's if you're hungry,' said Estelle. 'Personally, I'm not bothered.'

But I was famished and keen to be introduced properly to her father and stepmother, so I rushed upstairs to wash, horrified by the sight of my sunburnt cheeks and neck.

Another detail that Estelle had omitted to mention was that her family employed a sizeable staff, not only on the farm but in the house. Aside from Hanna and a scullery maid, Lotte, who seemed to spend her entire life in the back kitchen washing and peeling fruit and vegetables, there were a couple of live-in maids called Roos and Mietje, who I later discovered had bedrooms on the floor above me.

Roos must have realised that I wasn't used to being waited on because she was subtly insolent in the way she gave my plate a little shove when she served me or stared at me contemptuously when nobody else was looking. She was by far the prettier of the two – plump-armed, clear-eyed, apple-cheeked – and she knew it. She had a way of thrusting out her hip, so that she could perch a laden tray upon it, that never failed to draw the eyes of the men.

Other women appeared on Monday mornings to strip the

beds and help with the laundry, and there were also dairymaids, a pigman, a gardener and a dozen or so labourers and their families who lived in trim little cottages on the estate. Chief among them was the steward called Oud Daan, who shared Pieter's chaotic office in an outbuilding on the far side of the arch. Despite never moving faster than a slow amble, Oud Daan was ubiquitous, and his faded blue eyes, made tiny by decades of squinting, didn't miss a trick. Often when I was at work in the fields I'd look up and see him smoking and watching me from the gate. Estelle told me that he hated change of any kind, so the presence of a foreigner was a double insult. Though he never failed to doff his cap, he wouldn't speak to me voluntarily, even after I'd learnt a few words of Flemish. My '*Goeiemorgen*' received the barest inclination of the head, and if I asked him a direct question, he simply looked blank.

His son, Jong Daan, gangly, with an abnormally small head, was famous at De Eikenhoeve for his devotion to Estelle. He would always lurk a few yards behind her, hanging his head and twirling his cap in his hands. The rest of his time was spent taking the tractor engine apart or leaning over the gate of the pigsty, mumbling away to a great sow that never seemed to budge an inch despite the onslaughts of a voracious litter. Much more competent was his friend Weber, who was said to be sweet on Mietje but dared not approach her due to his elderly mother's jealous nature, and who could be relied on to fix anything that was broken.

At midday in the smaller dining room, Mevrouw Cornelis took one look at my face and drew me to a window. Close up, she appeared younger, with clear, pale skin and, unexpected in a farmer's wife, carefully made-up lips and eyes. 'You have been in the sun too much. Come with me.'

Estelle, who had already taken a seat at table, linked her fingers behind her head and arched her back as I was escorted away. In Harewood Road, our first aid kit comprised an old tea caddy containing plasters and TCP; Mevrouw Cornelis had a polished wooden cabinet which opened to reveal numerous little drawers and cupboards with tiny labels slotted into brass holders. With her manicured fingertip, Marthe, as she now insisted I should call her, selected a jar of ointment. She then applied it to my skin as if my life depended on it.

In the meantime, we managed to agree in French that she would lend me a hat and that I must stay out of the midday sun. I told her that I should have known better because I'd recently been on a first aid course in preparation for my work as a teacher. By the time we returned to the table I felt as if the ice had been broken between us, which was just as well because Estelle and her father were silent and glowering. Hanna was hanging about in the background, waiting to serve the soup.

Marthe sat at one end of the table, Estelle's father at the other. The delayed meal began at once and we ate three delicious courses very quickly in order to keep up with Meneer Cornelis, who was clearly in a hurry. He shared my Pa's dedication, when at table, to the task at hand, and I began to wonder what on earth the exquisite Fleur had seen in him.

'I expected to be eating a sandwich in a field,' I told Estelle.

'Marthe insists on all this grandeur,' she said, pushing aside her plate.

My other attempts at general conversation, which had to be relayed through Estelle, fell on equally stony ground. 'Please thank your parents . . .'

'Marthe is not my parent,' she snapped.

'. . . for inviting me to stay.'

'*I* invited you, not them. Pieter is in charge here and he doesn't mind who I bring back.'

I was taken aback by her sharpness and didn't understand her mood at all.

'Nevertheless, I'd like you to tell them what I said,' I persisted.

She muttered a few words in Flemish and Marthe smiled at me kindly and made a lengthy reply which Estelle translated as: 'She says you're welcome.'

Having reached a dead end with Estelle, Marthe spoke to me directly in her stumbling French. 'Estelle has told us that your father was in Belgium during the war. I hope he returned home safely.'

'More or less. He was gassed, you see.'

'Gassed? What is that?'

Estelle snapped out an explanation. Meneer Cornelis nodded, shot me a look from his handsome eyes and mumbled a question in Flemish which Marthe translated: 'Your father, does he remember Fleur?'

I had anticipated shock waves whenever Fleur's name was mentioned, but nobody seemed much bothered, except Estelle. 'Pa rarely talks about the war,' I explained through Marthe, 'but he was very pleased to meet Estelle, and I'm very moved to be here – had it not been for Fleur, I'd never have been born. I'm looking forward to making myself useful on the farm, Meneer Cornelis. Would you like me to begin work this afternoon?'

Again Marthe translated and now Cornelis looked baffled. 'You may stay as long as you like as our guest,' Marthe said.

'I must earn my keep.'

Her laugh was a little strained. 'Be careful what you offer. We have always too much work.'

Estelle got to her feet and beckoned me upstairs. We dashed past three guest bedrooms, each with shutters closed but lavishly furnished.

Robbe's room was very plain, with a bizarre collection of old jam jars on the sill, some of them with bits of string tied around the rim, a pile of old comic books and a blue checked cover on the narrow bed. Estelle's mood improved as we leant out of the window overlooking the farmyard. 'I used to spend hours in here when I was little. Robbe took me fishing and we'd bring back jam jars full of river creatures and draw them, or we'd sit watching the swallows. Even though he never comes home now, Marthe keeps it ready, just in case. She adores him, but he can't stand her.'

Estelle had a corner room with a view over woods and meadows. Apart from the choice of colour – a vibrant shade of blue – the space was oddly characterless, with just a few books and no pictures. 'Most of my stuff is at Grand-mère's in Brussels,' she said. 'We should go there sometime. I'm sure she'd like to meet you. And this hallway is our gallery of family photographs. That's my other grandmother; I can just about remember her. She outlived her husband by thirty years. As you can tell, she was quite a woman.'

The De Eikenhoeve grandmother was poised in a

straight-backed chair. Her black dress was fastened high at the throat and her hair was scraped back under a plain bonnet framing a blunt nose, thin lips and cold eyes. She clasped the handle of a walking stick and appeared to be denying any connection with her husband, who stood apologetically at her side. Behind them, labourers were ranked in three tiers, clutching pitchforks or rakes and peering suspiciously at the camera. Clustered by the matriarch's knee were her three children: Estelle's Uncle Gregor, who had not survived to adulthood, her father Bernard, who had of course disappointed by marrying the flighty French-speaking Fleur, and plain little Julia, who to this day remained a spinster living on the far side of the village.

The other portraits included one of Bernard and Fleur on their wedding day, she clasping an extravagant spray of white roses and wearing an absurdly overloaded headdress, he upstanding and handsome with a crisp moustache and proud smile. I imagined Fleur's arrival here as his new bride, and the stir she must have created.

Next, Bernard's marriage to Marthe, she solemn in a plain, drop-waisted frock and deep cloche hat. At their side: Robbe, his eyebrows crinkled, as if he were pondering a tricky question; Pieter, several inches taller, fair and smiling, with his arm protectively around his little brother's shoulders; and Estelle, hair in ringlets, clutching his spare hand. And finally, a photograph of the two boys together: Robbe aged about twelve, dressed in a soft-collared white shirt, glaring beneath a mop of glossy dark hair, and open-faced Pieter, taller, broad-shouldered and muscular.

'The boys look so different from each other,' I said.

'They are different in every way. Just you wait until you meet Robbe. Aunt Julia says that by nature he is more like Maman than any of us, and I believe that is true. He's impossible to pin down.'

We were climbing a staircase to the attic floor. Estelle said: 'I expect you've been dying to see where Maman used to work on her paintings.'

A couple more steps led into a long passage. At the far end a low doorway opened into what was probably the loveliest room

69

I would ever enter in my life. It was in the turret and therefore circular, with half a dozen deep-set windows. The space might have been preserved as Fleur had left it – with a pen on the table and a soft grey cardigan thrown over the back of a chair, as if she had just a moment ago rushed out to rescue a fugitive.

Estelle collapsed onto an ancient sofa, lying on her back, hands clasped beneath her head. 'What do you think?'

'It even has a different smell to the rest of the house. The light in here must have been perfect for painting. It reminds me of the photographic studio at Sun Engraving.'

One of the windows overlooked a flower garden where Marthe, wearing a sun hat, was deadheading pink roses; another the farmyard; a third the front of the house with an oblique view of the drive and a glimpse of the swing. The walls were hung with numerous abstract impressions of trees and rivers, and over the fireplace, dominating the entire room, was an almost full-sized portrait in oils of a woman with a flood of fair hair and an upturned gaze, as if she were having a vision. The whites of her eyes were especially disturbing and her lips were heavy and sullen.

'It's by Khnopff.' Estelle had rolled onto her side so she could watch me. 'Maman studied with him for a while and he gave the picture to her as a wedding present. What do you think of it?'

'Pretty strange. And I'm not sure I'd care to meet the subject.'

'Khnopff became quite famous later on. That piece is probably worth a fortune now. But you're right, it's macabre, typically Belgian. We do have very odd personalities. Look at me, I'm half Flemish, half French, and the two sides rarely meet. In Brussels I feel entirely French, but at the farm I struggle to keep in touch with that part of myself. Most of the other paintings in here are by Maman, of course.'

I had guessed those bold oils were by Fleur. It was extraordinary to be so close to them that I could see the marks of her brush.

'Did she ever paint you?' I asked.

'By the time I came along, I doubt she had any time for art. Anyway, she didn't do portraits, and babies are notoriously tricky.'

'Do you think she brought any of her soldiers here?'

'Of course not. She'd never have put us in any kind of danger. And besides, think of the number of people who work on the farm. Who could she trust?'

With her hair spread across the cushions, Estelle looked both defiant and tragic as I knelt beside her. 'I can't thank you enough for inviting me here,' I said. 'Otherwise I'd have been working in the sales at Clements department store, and what a waste that would have been! This might be the last summer we have before a war.'

'Don't you think you'll get very bored?'

'I loved being out in the fields this morning and now Marthe has lent me a hat—'

Estelle went very still. 'As I said, I've been thinking we should go to Brussels. We could stay with my grandmother for a few days.'

'I've only been here a day. I have to earn my keep.'

'So you'd rather be at De Eikenhoeve with Marthe.'

'Not with Marthe, with you.'

She sprang up and stood with her back to the door, as if to keep me from escaping. On the wall beside her was a long mirror and I saw myself reflected there, an unexpectedly familiar image in so strange a place. 'There's something you need to understand about Marthe. She's not at all what she seems,' Estelle continued.

'Surely she's just—'

'She was employed here as a kind of untrained nursemaid when Robbe was born. Her father owns a few acres in the next village.'

'I expect your mother was glad of the help.'

'Maman had Marthe foisted upon her. My brothers say that Marthe and Papa were sleeping together long before she died.'

'How do they know?'

'They were quite old enough to have been aware of what was going on. Why do you think Maman chose to be away so much? She was driven out. One of my earliest memories is of her memorial service after the war. I was left behind while all the others went to church dressed in black. Hanna had to hold me by the waist to stop me running after them. And at the end of that day' – here she got up, opened the door and spoke much too loudly – 'as at the end of every other, Marthe climbed into Maman's bed and fucked Papa.'

Het avondmaal was the Flemish name for the evening meal, during which I struggled to keep up a conversation with Marthe whilst tackling three lavish courses for which I had no appetite at all. Once again the table had been set with an array of oak leaf-engraved silver cutlery and an even more elaborate dinner service. It felt bizarre – perhaps treacherous – to be discussing the family photographs I'd viewed and the excellence of De Eiken-hoeve's runner beans when I carried an image in my head of Marthe as a femme fatale, luring poor Bernard Cornelis between adulterous sheets. I had spent the intervening hours speculating about what had gone on. Bernard and Marthe now seemed to behave as other long-married couples of my experience: the odd understanding glance or muttered aside, the occasional touch, but nothing more sensual.

The minute the meal was over, Estelle muttered that she had work to do on her dissertation. I was struggling to keep up with her constant mood swings and felt the need to escape for a while, so I walked down to the stone bridge where the air was still heat-laden and the water beneath me like mercury. There was a faint perfume of raspberries and I could hear women's voices and the lowing of a calf. The moon, rising above the farmhouse, had waxed a little. Following my visit to Fleur's room and my conversation with Estelle, it now seemed to me that every part of that landscape was untrustworthy, too beautiful for its own good. Though I had brought with me a pen and notepad and was writing a cheerful letter to Ma, thanks to Estelle's outburst, every word felt like a lie.

After half an hour or so I heard the rumble of a cart and realised that Pieter must be home. Sure enough, within a few minutes, footsteps scrunched along the track, followed by the scuffle of a dog's paws. He loomed out of the twilight, much taller than I'd registered the previous night, a dependable figure in a soft grey shirt, face a little flushed from the warmth of the evening. That morning he'd caught me watching him from the window, and here I was again, as if posed on the bridge.

'Hanna said she'd seen you come this way.' He spoke English with a strong accent and his voice had a deep, almost guttural timbre. By the end of the conversation we had changed to a mixture of French, English and even the odd word of Flemish. 'I came to check that you weren't lost. Have you enjoyed your first day?'

'As you can imagine, there's been a great deal to learn and I'm much slower than the other women.'

The top of my head was level with his shoulder as we strolled towards the farmyard.

'It's good of you to have worked so hard,' he said, 'but there's no need.'

'There is a need. Didn't Estelle mention I'm here to work? That was the understanding. I needed a holiday job and she told me there'd be employment here.'

'You have to remember that Estelle never tells anyone anything. She seems to think that explanations are beneath her. But sure, we can find you plenty to do if that's what you want.' Pausing at a gate, he leant his arms on the post and gave me a smile that I was to revisit many times later, beginning as it did with a gleam deep in his eyes and only later touching his lips. 'The farm is remote, its own world. Since we rarely have visitors to stay, you must forgive us if we don't know how to behave. That line of trees in the far distance marks the boundary of our land, by the way.'

The expanse between the gate and the stencilled row of trees on the horizon seemed almost boundless in the fading light. I could walk all day, I thought, and never reach the end of it. 'You must be so proud to own so much land.'

'*Proud*? Of course. But I'm rather like one of my animals who doesn't question its right to be here. Essentially, all I am is the curator for future generations. I am the eldest boy and this is my inheritance.'

'Perhaps it's the same for me. My father is a printer, so I've always felt connected to books and newspapers, which is perhaps why I'm going to be an English teacher.' I stood with my hand on the gatepost, a few feet from Fleur's eldest son, framed by the luminous sky. There was no retreating now, I had to speak her name. 'When Estelle talked to you about my father, did she tell you that he was one of the English soldiers your mother saved?'

Again I expected a strong reaction, but his reply, after a beat, was casual. 'She did mention it to me briefly last night. Your father must have an astonishing story to tell.'

'He might, but he's never spoken more than a few words to me about the war. He was the victim of a gas attack.'

'Poor man. I'm old enough to remember the strain everyone was under during the war. Even in Oostervorken we saw refugees from the front line. It was a desperate time. Needless to say, my brother and I took full advantage by skipping school whenever we could – nobody minded, because we'd lost a lot of men to German labour camps and we were needed on the farm. But then our mother went missing and everything changed.'

'I believe Estelle takes after her,' I said softly. 'Pa definitely saw a likeness.'

'Did he now? My goodness. I'm quite taken aback that you should say that.' He shook his head, as if to dispel emotion. 'But you're right. Estelle does catch me unawares sometimes – when she laughs or says something she knows I won't quite like, the way her eyes go stormy in an argument.'

'I'm so sorry about your mother.'

He raised his hand and touched my face. 'As soon as I saw you, even before I knew about your father, I thought that you and I must have some kind of connection. How could we not, in the circumstances?' He whistled for the dog and we walked on – I stunned by his words and touch. 'I'm very glad that you are here,' he added, 'for whatever reason. It was such an unexpected moment this morning, seeing you at the window. Did you mind me waving?'

'Not at all. It made me laugh.'

'To me it was almost as if . . .' He held out his arm in a quaintly gallant way and we continued in profound silence, my hand lightly resting on his sleeve.

At the farmyard gate we parted because there was a fox about and Pieter needed to make sure the poultry were securely locked up. As I hurried inside, I prayed that I wouldn't meet anyone else.

I was already too full of all that had happened since the early morning, not least that unfinished sentence: *It was almost as if...*

...you had lived here for an age ...

...you had been looking out for me ...

...we had spent the night together.

Estelle

By the fourth evening I'd realised there wasn't room on that farm for me and Christa both. Ironic, given that she kept saying how vast the place was and how she was forever discovering a barn, cottage or pigsty she'd not seen before. Ironic too, that my reason for inviting her had been to make the place more tolerable. As soon as she arrived, she created gusts of feeling that enveloped me, however far apart we were.

I tried to undo what I'd set in motion – spotted the way the wind was blowing, telephoned Grand-mère in Brussels and told her to expect us. Christa thought it was because I couldn't bear to see her and Marthe so chummy together and, well, maybe that was part of it. But mostly it was Pieter.

I hadn't seen him like that with anyone else, hadn't anticipated the way he'd be so intrigued. But then, so many of us were. By the afternoon of day two, Christa was floating along the lane in Marthe's old straw hat, hand in hand with a couple of farm kids. In the evening I passed the scullery and there she was helping Lotte with the dishes on the pretext of receiving a Flemish lesson – Lotte, who never spoke to strangers, reciting: *brood, bord, vork*. Next day, Christa peeped in at the dairy and asked if she could have a go at the churn. Greta lent her a pair of clogs and she staggered about until the women were crying with laughter and had promised her a proper lesson in butter-making. Christa, demonstrating to Hanna how to draw together flour and butter with her fingertips to make English scones. Christa, hanging over the pigsty wall, obsessed by the litter of twelve piglets, trying – unsuccessfully – to make Oud Daan understand that she wanted to know how long it would be before they were sent to market. Christa, in her English frock, perched on the dairy step, one hand shading her eyes, the other holding a book, the sun picking out reddish glints in her dark hair. Sunburnt cheeks and moist upper lip; when she was reading she thrust out the lower. Eventually she realised I was there; her eyes filled with gladness and she marked the page with her finger. I sat beside her, our elbows touched and I felt absolutely in the right place with the right person.

But Pieter had also fallen under her spell. On day one I met him in the yard and he asked where she was and said he'd go and find her; said it was too dark for her to be out on her own.

'For God's sake, she's a grown woman,' I told him.

But I followed as far as the bend in the track. There she was, sitting on the bridge. He stooped to speak to her and I couldn't bear it, I turned back. The whole wretched day had been spent accommodating Christa, trying to keep her on my side, and now I had lost her again.

Jong Daan was in the yard fiddling with the hinge on the dairy door, leering at me.

The next day I saw Pieter with Oud Daan, leaning on a gate and watching Christa at work in the fields. She was wearing that same blue frock with the sailing boats and Marthe's hat.

It was that hat and how Pieter's speech slowed because he just couldn't take his eyes off her that got to me.

And then I very nearly drowned her.

Christa

Four days into my stay and my hands were stained red beneath the fingernails and in the creases on my palms and knuckles. My arms and legs were a map of scratches. I smelt of raspberries and when falling asleep at night I seemed to go on and on picking them, lifting a leaf with the back of my hand and dropping ripe fruits into the basket. Although I hadn't exactly made friends with the other pickers, we did sometimes smile at each other and had I not been a house guest we'd probably have got on even better.

On the one occasion that Estelle joined us, she moved haphazardly from cane to cane, chatting away to the other girls in Flemish until she announced that the only reason she'd come was to persuade me to go swimming with her. She'd brought me a towel but no costume. 'Why on earth would you need one? It's just the two of us.'

On our walk to the river she volunteered that it was Marthe who'd taught her to swim. 'She forced me. Gave me lessons in an indoor pool in Brussels.'

'She's not all bad then. But why did you need persuasion? I loved learning with Pa – it was one of the few things he and I did together.'

'Marthe was just performing her duty as my stepmother. The farm is full of hazards to do with water – the duck pond, ditches, the river – every child needs to know how to swim. She didn't really care,' and she swiped at the hedge with her towel.

'I still can't quite see why you're so cross with her. Of course she can never replace your mother, but aren't you glad that your father isn't facing a lonely old age?'

She stopped dead and closed her eyes as if drawing on the

dregs of her patience. 'Work it out. Who do you think had the most to gain if Maman died? You tell me.'

'Estelle, what are you suggesting?'

'Just imagine how it was in this part of Belgium during the last war. The Germans stripped the land bare, set up headquarters in the village and forced the young men into labour camps. They requisitioned every last bit of produce and sent it back to Germany. Yet De Eikenhoeve survived, as did most of its labourers. Nobody starved. Why was that, do you think?'

'I don't know. Good management?'

'What a very English response. When it comes to barbarism, good management isn't the answer. It's all about barter. What have you got that the enemy needs more than your death? Pieter says that by the end of the war there was only one pony left in the whole of north-east Belgium and it happened to belong to Marthe. Sneeuw, it was called. Marthe used to drive off in her little trap laden with stores she'd managed to tuck away in a hiding place in the cellar. Back she'd come late at night with the trap empty and De Eikenhoeve would be left alone for another week or two.'

'But isn't that a good thing, that Marthe managed to save the farm?'

'At what cost? What else did she sell? Was it Maman, do you think?'

We walked on. What Estelle was suggesting was so sinister that I felt as if the world had grown a shade darker. Half a mile or so from the bridge the path plunged into deep woodland. Eventually Estelle took a narrow fork which led through bracken to where a significant pool had formed in the river, with a sliver of wooded island in the middle. There was little movement in the water, overshadowed by ancient trees clustering the bank. On a narrow beach, Estelle turned her back for me to undo the buttons of her dress. The next moment, she had stepped out of her underwear and was picking her way across stones to the water's edge.

We kept ourselves private in Harewood Road, so I'd never seen a naked adult except in paintings. At school we used to undress for gym only down to our vests and knickers and there was

79

never time to shower before the next lesson. Of all the shocks I'd withstood since arriving here, this was the simplest and the most disturbing. Estelle glanced at me entirely without shame as the shadows passed over the long, lovely slopes of her back and thighs. In a moment of pure exhilaration, I flung off my clothes, inspired by the sheer beauty and strangeness of it all, and we joined hands and dashed into the water, yelping with cold.

We were close to the island, treading water in a patch of sunlight. Estelle threw herself backwards so that her toes pointed at the sky. I was fascinated by how her skin was stained greenish by the water and her nipples had contracted. She fanned her hands and feet back and forth to keep herself afloat.

'Did your mother swim here?'

'Of course. Pieter says she often used to bring the boys to the river for picnics. Do you remember that painting of water in her room – the one with splashes of light? Look over there. I think that's where she painted it.'

On the bank, perhaps under the willow, Fleur would have sat in her flowing gown, her sons nestling amid her skirts. For an instant I had a perfect view of her, reclining in white muslin, before I too lay on my back and stared at a translucent skin of cloud while Estelle dived under me and bobbed up close, like a mermaid.

'It was a tradition for us all to come here on Papa's feast day after the harvest was in – a kind of ritual until Papa got too old. We used to compete to see who could stay under for longest. Pieter held the record until Robbe achieved an entire circuit of the island without surfacing. I've only ever managed to get three quarters of the way round.'

'Three quarters sounds pretty good to me.'

'I'll have a go now if you like.'

As Estelle dived beneath me again, I swam slow, regular strokes until I was in much deeper water on the far side of the island. There was no sign of Estelle, so I swam on, exulting in the extraordinary freedom of being naked. In another twenty strokes or so I reached down with my foot but I was still out of my depth. After a few more strokes I tried again, but this time I seemed to tip forward, swallowed a mouthful of water and sank.

My gasp of surprise as I surfaced made me choke, so down I went again without having drawn breath. My feet were being dragged by a wholly unexpected force and my nostrils, throat and airways filled with water. For one blessed second I thought I saw a flash of sky and then the pain in my lungs blinded me, my back struck a rock and I didn't know which way the surface lay.

I'd been to lifesaving classes at school and knew that the worst response was to panic. Instead I ought to swim towards the surface or go with the current, but my legs were being pulled away so I thrashed fruitlessly and knew I was dying. There was a searing pain in my chest and head and I thought of the sunny raspberry fields and Ma in the kitchen at home making pastry.

I inhaled more water and felt as if my lungs were at bursting point. It was an hour, or a second, of descent into a monstrous suffocation – I was at the ticket barrier with Estelle and I couldn't reach her at all, and I saw Fleur again, on the riverbank, in a white gown and with her head bent over a child, and then the naked Estelle turning back to smile at me, a glint of mischief in her eye, but this time her body wasn't lithe and ripe with promise but skeletal, skin hanging off the bones, and her eyes were huge and lost. Lank hair covered her face.

Was it Fleur or Estelle? I couldn't tell. I wanted to save that woman, I reached out for her and was dimly aware that my hip grazed a rock as I put out my hands and something caught my finger, then my wrist. I was dragged upwards and heard Estelle's voice: 'For Pete's sake, stay calm.'

My head was supported and I was tugged into shallower water.

Almost the worst moment of all was that first failed attempt to breathe. Estelle pushed me face down in the mud, knelt over me and thumped my back until I heaved and spluttered and at last took in air.

'You're all right,' she gasped. 'It's OK. I forgot to tell you about that bit of the river. It gets very deep on that side of the island. You probably got caught under the overhanging rock. And there's a current.'

We lay for a moment cheek to cheek, before she sat cross-legged beside me and pulled me into her arms, holding me close and kissing my head as I wept into her neck.

81

'I thought I was going to die.'

'Of course you weren't going to die. As if I'd let you.' She cradled me so that my streaming breasts were pressed against hers and she kissed my cheek and stroked my back with her muddy hand.

I clutched her tight. 'I was taking in more and more water. I didn't know which way was up.'

'That's what happens. It's best if you just—'

'You saved my life.'

We stared at each other and shivered, gripping each other's cold, gritty bodies. I had come so far from myself, cradled in the arms of Estelle. Her mouth was close to mine and I thought she would kiss me. And I was confused, because I wanted her to, I so wanted the connection with her, with life, that I raised my head to be kissed, imagining the heat of her mouth and the fearful intimacy of her lips. I couldn't read her eyes except that they were absorbed in mine and in the movement of her hand as she brushed the hair from my face.

'You saved my life,' I said again.

'I did. But if you'd died it would have been my fault. And think of how pointless that would have been.'

She held me tight and I was still shuddering with cold and shock as she kissed my forehead, my nose, my lips. Her mouth was so soft it was like being kissed by a flower, just a momentary pressure and then a withdrawal, and her eyes were as dazed as mine must have been when we broke away. I jumped up and staggered back along the bank, oblivious to the battering I received from low-hanging branches above and sharp stones underfoot, while she hesitated, then followed behind me.

That kiss had shaken me to the core. I didn't understand myself and wouldn't have known how to look at her had she not seemed quite untroubled as we towelled ourselves vigorously and dragged our clothes over our still damp skin. This entire episode was so far from anything I knew or had imagined, yet Estelle seemed completely at ease.

'We've all fallen foul of that pool at one time or another,' she explained. 'Pieter says it's because the ground shelves so steeply into a kind of chasm under the water and the island is undercut by the river – it's easy to get out of your depth, and you can be caught out if you don't know how to manage it.'

'Thank God you were there,' I said through chattering teeth.

'I'd never let you down.' She tugged my hair, seized her own towel, dabbed at the grazes on my legs and arms then suddenly, sweetly, kissed my cheek again.

That evening, even a long-sleeved cardigan couldn't hide the cuts on my hands and wrists from sharp-eyed Marthe, who commented on them in Flemish to Estelle. This inevitably led to a low-voiced spat, and when Bernard Cornelis intervened Estelle threw down her knife and fork, shoved back her chair and left the room without even a glance at me. Marthe sat with her hands on either side of her plate, her eyes closed.

Pieter said calmly: 'I gather that Estelle took you for a swim this afternoon.'

'She did.'

'Two people have drowned in that river, even in my lifetime. Estelle ought to have been more careful.'

I put down my fork halfway through another mouthful of succulent pork and mushroom stew. 'How did they drown?'

'One was the daughter of a farmhand and was quite a strong swimmer. That was the trouble. She went down there alone and must have got too cold or something. She was fourteen years old.'

He paused while Roos darted forward to clear the plates.

'And the second?'

'The second was a stranger who'd been dead a couple of days by the time we found him. We never discovered who he was because it was during the war and the police came and took the body away. We didn't even know his nationality because his papers had turned to mush.'

Marthe said something in Flemish, clearly changing the subject. As usual, Pieter left the table before dessert, telling me that if I was interested I could accompany him on his evening round of inspection. The three of us who remained picked at a strawberry tart while I refused Marthe's offer to dress my wounds, knowing that if she saw the extent of the damage she'd be even more furious with Estelle. There was considerable tension in the air; everyone, including the servants, now knew that Pieter and I would be walking together through the dusk.

Except that I didn't want to be with Pieter that night. I wanted to be alone. The moments in the river when I had gone under for the second time and Estelle had hauled me into the air, when I had lain in her arms, looked into her frightened eyes and wondered whether her kiss would fall on my cheek or mouth were tucked away just beneath the surface and I'd had no time to work out what they meant. Because surely this wasn't how it was supposed to be between two women? I told myself that we'd acted purely out of shock and relief, but I was by no means convinced by my own argument. That wasn't how it had felt.

Outside, there was an uncanny stillness and heat to the air, and the thick, yellowish light threatened a storm. Pieter and Oud Daan were in the barn examining one of the dogs, which had been kicked by a plough horse and now lay motionless on a heap of straw.

'Poor thing,' I said.

They glanced up and I realised that Pieter's invitation, though kindly meant, had perhaps not been serious. 'He will probably have to be shot,' he said. 'We think his back is broken.'

'How did it happen?'

He shrugged. 'It's a farm. Oud Daan will deal with it.'

We left the barn, followed by the same calf who had met me that first morning. At the gate she bumped Pieter's thigh with her nose and licked his fingers until he crouched, took her head between his hands, looked her in the eyes and muttered some soothing Flemish incantation. Oud Daan, at the barn door, clicked his tongue to draw her to his side.

'This is what calves do when they lose their mother,' said Pieter. 'Attach themselves to a human being instead.'

He led me along a track that ran in the opposite direction to the one leading to the bathing pool, through a copse and into barley fields bronzed by the evening light. Here, the broad and tranquil river bore no relation at all to the wicked, primal force that had taken me to its depths.

Pieter was humming, absolutely at ease within the worn fabric of his clothes but alert to every detail or slight change in the landscape. Once or twice he paused to test a fence post or rub a head of barley between finger and thumb. At first he was silent, perhaps brooding on the sick dog, but when the path ran closer to the water he said: 'Our river is extremely slow-flowing, but we've had a very wet spring. Estelle should have warned you to stay on the near side of the island. I'm very angry with her.'

'It's my fault – I told her that I'm a good swimmer.'

'Good swimmers often get into greater difficulty because they're more confident. I hope she was properly apologetic.'

I turned away my face. 'I can't help thinking about those others who drowned. I wonder if the man you mentioned was hiding from the war?'

'More than likely. I was the one who found him. The whole thing happened soon after Maman had been taken prisoner and by that time I was pretty wild. We were all still in shock and Robbe and I truanted from school whenever we could. Well, I had my comeuppance that day – I was walking home when I saw this terrible thing in the river, a body. It seemed disrespectful just to leave it in the water but I couldn't bear to touch it, so in the end I went and fetched Oud Daan.'

'And you never found out who he was?'

'He wasn't wearing a uniform, so it was impossible to tell his nationality. Perhaps he'd got lost or tried to wade across at one of those deceptive places and was caught, like you.'

'How old were you?'

'Nine.'

He took my elbow to steer me up a path at right angles to the river, on a very slight incline. At the top, turning back, I could see De Eikenhoeve in the distance, with just one or two lights in the windows; a farm from a picture book. Very faintly, I heard a sound like a pair of hands being clapped together and Pieter winced. 'The dog,' he said.

After a pause, we walked on in a wide loop above the farm.

'You don't think the man who drowned was something to do with your mother?'

85

To my relief, he chuckled. 'Very astute, Juffrouw. Papa always insisted that our mother should keep her activities away from the farm, but I knew better.' He put a gentle hand under my elbow as we turned back towards the river. 'It was an open secret that she hid some of her fugitives here. Why wouldn't she? It's the obvious place. I even caught her at it once.'

'You *saw* her?'

'I was truanting as usual, trying to keep out of sight in the woods, and all of a sudden I came across her in a clearing, accompanied by several strangers. Do you know, I've never told anyone about that, apart from you?' He paused to pick up a stone, which he dropped into his pocket. 'Perhaps one of them was your father. Wouldn't that be something?'

'It would. Just imagine if you'd actually seen him . . .'

'He's never mentioned the woods here?'

'He doesn't talk about the war at all.'

We were entirely alone, with no sound other than the birdsong and the odd whisper from the river. 'Do you mind talking about her?' I whispered.

'Of course not. Especially to you, of all people.'

'She has always fascinated me.'

He had Estelle's way of looking right through me to something else. 'I'm bound to say she was beautiful and enchanting, of course. But you might be a little disappointed to learn that if I had to describe her in one word it would be *unreliable*. As a mother she was hopeless. I suspect that if the war had not killed her she'd have left us anyway.' He gave me a teasing glance. 'Don't look so shocked. The fact is she never took to the farm – you ask Papa or Oud Daan. My memory of her, when I was a very small boy before the war, was that she'd be either bursting with enthusiasm or bored stiff. For instance, one morning she marched Robbe and me into the yard and instructed us each to collect a newly laid egg. Hanna had to clear the table while Marthe rummaged through her sewing things so that Maman could show us how to blow the yolks into a bowl. I remember leaning on her arm and watching her prick the shell with a darning needle. And then, even better, or so I thought at the time, when Robbe's cracked he smashed it with his fist, so Marthe carried him away for his nap while Maman and I took our shells to her painting room.'

'Of course, Marthe was around when you were little boys.'

Unlike Estelle, the mention of Marthe did not seem to trouble him. 'She was indeed a fixture. So, to have our mother completely to myself was unheard of. I could hardly believe my luck when she took out her paints and showed me how to mix a colour. I remember insisting on a very dark blue. But I'd only done one or two strokes when everything changed. "Run along now to Marthe," she said. "Maman has work to do." I never did work out what I'd done to annoy her.'

Not for the first time it occurred to me that I'd had an in-finitely better experience of childhood than the Cornelis-Faider siblings. 'Perhaps she simply had something else on her mind.'

'That's true, she always did. Often I'd tiptoe to her turret room and find it empty. Then we'd be told that she'd gone into Brussels to meet with her painter friends, but that didn't explain why she never said goodbye. Every time we heard a car engine we hoped it would be Viktor's taxicab, bringing her home from the station. It wasn't until she was arrested that we understood why she'd always been so secretive.'

'I can't imagine what it must have been like to lose your mother so young.'

There was a most unnerving heat in his eyes as he smiled down at me. 'Thank you, Juffrouw Christa. Few people have paused to wonder how it must have been for me. The main difficulty, after she'd gone, was that I was responsible for Robbe and I always felt that I had to keep him from doing something really bad because nobody else could control him. Papa was completely un-approachable – absorbed in the farm and in mourning, of course. I hated it when he flew into a rage – usually something to do with Robbe. And then he married Marthe.'

'That must have been difficult for you.'

'Not really. It was inevitable.' He laughed and arched an eyebrow. 'My goodness, Juffrouw Christa, do strangers always confide their deepest secrets in you like this?'

The night was warm and breathless, busy with insects and the scent of ripe crops and nettle.

'Perhaps it's because I'm not really a stranger.'

'That's true. You're not. Anyway, Robbe and I stuck very close together until he was about sixteen. Then he wangled an allowance out of Papa and took off. I guess Papa felt sorry about not having been the perfect father. He found Robbe particularly difficult to manage and a constant distraction from the work of the farm.'

'Do you think he sympathised with what your mother was doing?'

'I doubt it. I remember a great deal of shouting. But I don't suppose for one minute that he could have stopped her.'

He took my hand as we walked on, while his dog, Swart, dashed in and out of the trees. I was transfixed by the unexpected physical contact. From time to time Pieter gave my fingers a little squeeze or his thumb worked across my palm, but we spoke as if nothing momentous was happening. 'But listen,' he added, 'it does me good to talk to you. You are a vindication of all that my mother stood for.'

'You could so easily resent me. I see that now.'

'But that would make a nonsense of her life. On the contrary, it means a great deal that you are here.'

He brought my hand to his lips and then to his cheek in a gesture that reminded me of how Ma was sometimes caressed by Pa with a swift, shy brush of the fingertips on her upper arm or back. The timing was unfortunate, though, because the gesture was witnessed by Estelle, who was perched on the farmyard gate.

'I've been looking for you everywhere,' she snapped. 'We're going to Brussels tomorrow. It's all arranged. Marthe will take us to the station. Pack a bag. We'll be gone for at least four nights.'

Estelle

The question I have asked myself many times: was there such wilfulness in me that afternoon by the river that I wanted her almost to drown so that I could save her? Why else hadn't I warned her about the deep water on the far side of the island?

Even as I dived under I had a hunch she might get into trouble. I looked up and saw her above me – graceful, small-limbed, her girlish breasts. The river was always a balm to me and I opened my eyes as it flowed past, a cool green world. When I was at my limit, I surfaced near the far tip of the island. Three quarters of a circuit, not quite as far as my record. I trod water while I got my breath back. I could see where we'd left our clothes. Christa's white towel was hanging over a branch but there was no sign of her.

I swam out to the middle of the pool and called her name. Imagined raging back to the farmhouse. *Help me. Christa's gone . . .* Holding her chill, drowned body in my arms. Writing a letter to Mrs Geering. I dived again and again, praying, praying, praying to a God I've hardly ever believed in: let me find her before it's too late.

I caught a glimmer of something pale, plunged and grabbed, first a finger, then hair, then an arm, dragging her up towards me against the current. It was a struggle and I had to fight every centimetre, but at last I got her face above water.

So it did end with her in my arms – a living girl, not a dead one. As I kissed her face and felt the weight of her, I thought: I love you and you nearly died. I should have warned you. What is the matter with me?

I could have taken her then. Gratitude shone in her eyes, she was naked and lovely and I could have stroked her breast and the inside of her thigh and she might have curled into me and it would have been so easy to make love to her, my tongue and fingers longed for her, but I did right simply to kiss her and leave her be.

Christ, I have seen corruption since then that would have made that small act of desire the merest flicker of a faulty light bulb. Two young women embracing by a river. Who would care? I would, because it was Christa and she wasn't in her right mind after I'd hauled her out of the water. She would have done anything for me in the moment of stillness afterwards.

Christa

The drive to the station in Marthe's car was brittle with good manners, hers and mine. Estelle maintained a steely silence, presumably to punish us both for last night's argument at the dinner table, and me in particular for allowing my hand to be kissed by Pieter.

On the train journey to Brussels we sat on opposite sides of the carriage, I pretending to read *Villette*, Estelle some dry-as-dust text on engraving. She hovered at the edge of my vision, head tilted down, mouth pursed, as if utterly absorbed. But I wasn't fooled. She, like me, must have been shot through with the memory of the previous afternoon, the agony and the panic, the wild relief. If I so much as turned a page she knew about it, just as I noticed when she scratched her knee with her fingertip. Occasionally, memories of the wild striving of my limbs as I reached upwards through the water, and of the kiss, her chill skin and warm mouth, surged through me. That slight, hesitant pressure of her lips had been a gateway to an altered state of being.

The kiss had been an astounding breach. Nothing in my experience had primed me for it and I refused to contemplate the possibility that Estelle had kissed me out of desire rather than affection.

The fact that she had spotted Pieter kissing my hand was yet one more complication, so all in all it was a relief to be exchanging farmland for suburbs and to be properly busy disembarking from the train and hailing a taxicab. With every passing minute, Estelle softened, until by the time we reached our destination she was teasing the taxi driver and running round to the boot to lift out our cases. Reassured, I forced all my unease to the back of my mind and determined to enjoy this new city.

'I can't wait for you to meet Grand-mère,' Estelle cried, inserting a substantial key in the lock of a once grand front door. At this house, number 7, Rue d'Orléans, Fleur had lived as *la p'tite* Mademoiselle Faider, daughter of a pâtissier, for the first eighteen years of her life and it was to this house that I had written my fateful letter. I therefore entered the high building with a sense of disbelief that I had crossed the divide between the photograph tucked away in Ma's Bible and the actual birthplace of Fleur.

In the red- and blue-flagged hall the first thing I saw, on a marble-topped table, was a framed portrait of a child.

'Maman,' said Estelle, setting down her suitcase and heading for the stairs. I lingered to pick up the photograph. As a child Fleur had been a plump little miss in buttoned boots and velvet coat, a belligerent expression in her saucer-shaped eyes. Even as a toddler she had been alluring but angry.

The stairs to the first floor were of stone, with a wrought-iron balustrade. In a dim room filled with lace doilies, table runners, curtains and cushion covers sat Madame Faider, wearing a black dress that reached almost to her neatly shod feet. Her white hair was crimped around a sweet, crinkled face. Estelle, kneeling beside her, was the only bright thing in the room. I was dimly conscious of another presence, hovering in a far corner. There was a strong smell of perfume. Madame Faider's hand in mine was rather cool and her bones felt fragile.

'Of course,' said Madame Faider with a tremulous smile. 'You are the young lady who wrote to us. We were so pleased to receive your letter, Mademoiselle.'

'I can't tell you how much it means to be here.'

Madame withdrew her hand. 'The privilege is entirely ours. Estelle will no doubt be enjoying your company. Please treat the house as your own.'

'Christa is a very well brought up young lady, unlike me,' Estelle said pertly. 'You won't even notice her.' She bobbed up to kiss her grandmother's cheek.

'Show her the shrine, Céleste,' said Madame Faider, and an ancient woman, nearly bald and stooped almost double, extended a trembling hand and drew back one of the lace curtains so

92

that a greyish light fell on a table arranged like an altar. 'I keep it for my daughter, Fleur, and my dear husband, Frédéric.'

The latter had been a bearded gentleman, rather too dapper to match my mental image of a pastry cook. Beside him was a portrait of beautiful, soft-haired Fleur, wearing a picture hat. There was also a vase of fresh flowers, a crucifix, a jade rosary, an open prayer book and a statuette of the Virgin Mary wearing white robes, a pale-blue scarf and a syrupy smile. To the right of the Virgin hung another framed photograph, this time of a bespectacled priest.

'That's Père Borland,' said Estelle.

'I remember, from our trip to Cambridge.'

'Grand-mère has a very soft spot for Père Borland.'

'I do,' agreed Grand-mère. 'He's a good man. Selfless.'

After a reverential pause we were instructed to go and enjoy ourselves.

'Don't be fooled by Grand-mère's appearance,' Estelle told me as we hauled our cases up three flights of rickety stairs. 'She's as tough as old boots.'

The house enchanted me, not only because of its association with Fleur but also with what I perceived to be its all-pervading Frenchness, and the fact that it seemed to be stuck in a time warp circa 1906, the year that Fleur had left home to marry Bernard Cornelis. The porcelain bowl and pitcher on my wash-stand, complete with glycerine soap in a white dish and a bottle of eau de cologne, the smell of vinaigrette in the dining room and the precision with which Grand-mère Faider wore her little lace collars, all seemed to me quintessentially French.

Ma would have fainted at the prospect of keeping all those rooms clean – I counted more than twenty doors. Each artefact had been complicated in some way, making it into a trap for tarnish or dust. Every surface boasted a little china tray deco-rated with garlands of leaves or flowers, on top of which were porcelain pots containing hairpins, face creams, mustard, jam, tooth powder. The keeper of all these treasures was the maid, Céleste, whose overworked ankles were so thin I felt I could have snapped them between finger and thumb.

My own home in Watford being so small, I found the forgotten spaces in that majestic house on Rue d'Orléans very enticing and insisted that Estelle show me the servants' quarters on the musty attic floor and the chambers off the kitchen passageway, where crockery was arranged in glass cupboards and there was a smell of bacon and mould. Céleste slept in a room in the basement overlooking the cobbled backyard, presumably to save her knees.

In the early days, before the pâtisserie expanded and a purpose-built bakery had been constructed a quarter of a mile from the house, all those little storerooms had been crammed with flour and sugar, and the massive kitchen table used for piping and glazing. In one room I found a mountain of metal bakeware, corroded pastry-cutters and ramekins.

Fleur's bedroom, now used by Estelle, still contained her faded patchwork quilt, hand-sewn by Céleste for her sixteenth birthday, and a doll furnished with its own tea set, wrapped in yellowing tissue paper. On the walls hung a few emphatic water-colours, street scenes that Estelle told me were her mother's early work. Most of the art in the house depicted vases of flowers, tumbledown cottages, country girls at play or queasy religious subjects such as the Sacred Heart.

No wonder Fleur's paintings, once she had reached De Eiken-hoeve, became abstract and bold. No wonder, in that disturbing portrait by Khnopff, a woman with free-flowing hair raised her eyes to the heavens. And perhaps, after all, it was no wonder that Fleur Faider had chosen to marry Bernard Cornelis who had offered a life far from these fussy rooms. Remembering how, on stepping from the taxi that first evening at De Eikenhoeve, the house and land had floated boundlessly before me, I understood that Fleur might have expected her soul to expand there too.

One evening I stood in her bedroom window, drew back the draperies and pressed my forehead to the glass so I could watch the occasional passer-by and the shuttered windows of the house opposite. The heavy fabric fell against my shoulder and the smell of dust was stifling. I could well imagine the pressure of Fleur's hands on the sill, her yearning to escape. Yet it seemed to me now, having stayed at the remote farmhouse and met her wid-owed husband, that in marrying Bernard Cornelis she had fled in altogether the wrong direction.

Estelle

Brussels was the place to be. Much better than that year-in-year-out-the-same, ghost-ridden farm. Those five days with Christa had a quality to them of cut glass or something even more precious, to do with the way I uncovered the city for her and how, because of the near drowning, we had a deeper bond, were more finely attuned to each other. In Brussels I calmed down, felt kinder, was just so happy to be with her, away from the complications of Pieter and Marthe and De Eikenhoeve.

Christa was insatiable. Wanted to see everything, go everywhere, once I had prised her out of the house, where, of course, she had worked her spell on Céleste and persuaded her to share the chores. I caught Christa clattering up and down the stairs with trays and kettles, racing through the washing-up, making her own bed and mine.

'Come on,' I kept saying. 'They manage perfectly well when we're not here.'

'But we *are* here.'

I felt useless. Stood about or pretended to work on my dissertation. I could never fathom where housework started or finished.

Christa didn't understand Brussels one bit at first. She couldn't comprehend that the buildings she admired had been paid for in blood. When I told her about the Congo she was shocked. She'd been taught to rejoice in an atlas covered with British pink splodges, so she thought it only fair that there should be a bit of Belgian orange. I had not studied at Louvain with Père Borland for nothing. Wide open, my eyes were. I told her that he gave short shrift to anyone who said what a pity it was that in the last war the Germans had burnt down our university library. 'At least they didn't destroy a civilisation,' he said, 'by rape and massacre and hacking off children's hands.' Not even the Germans had plumbed those depths. Yet.

I explained Leopold's desire to create a city as glorious as Paris or St Petersburg. And that if a man has brutal tendencies in the killing department he's likely to have shocking taste in architecture. If your army drags people from their homes at gunpoint, gives them a spade and makes them dig a mass grave, orders them to strip off their clothes and watches them shit and shudder, shoulders hunched to their ears and their knees knocking while you take your time to bark out the command, you're unlikely to look at a snug little brick cottage and say: Let's preserve that, it's pretty and means a great deal to the family who's lived there for generations. Certainly not. Let's build monolithic structures like the Palais de Justice. Show them who's boss.

I took her to the Musée des Beaux Arts because I so wanted her to love the things I loved. She asked why Belgians have such a taste for the ghoulish. Because, dear Christa, we peek into the abyss and see our own faces reflected there. Those monsters in *The Fall of the Rebel Angels* are us.

Escorted her to the Surrealists. Planted her in front of a Paul Delvaux.

It was as far as I dared go, at that stage, to remind her of the swim. Christa tipped her head to one side and went very quiet. Commented on the formal dress of the man in a suit, but not the nude woman with her splayed breasts, white skin and black triangle of curling hair. Like hers. I wanted to say: 'She isn't a patch on you. Look how her gaze turns inwards, whereas your eyes have a unique sparkle. She is insipid, compared to you.'

We avoided touching while we gazed at that picture. Desire flamed as I looked at those thin white thighs and remembered how I had so nearly slipped my hand between Christa's legs. I knew that she felt it too. There was this connection between us now, unspoken, like a silken thread.

Wanting to show her off, I left a message for Robbe at the Prospero: *I am in town with my English friend, Christa. She'd love to meet you I'm sure. Please get in touch.*

I heard nothing back.

96

I told Christa we didn't need to attend Mass on Sunday, Grand-mère would understand, but she insisted out of respect. Took the occasion very seriously, even borrowed a mantilla from Céleste and draped it over her head. I wanted to rip it off and set her hair free. All through the service I was aware of the heat of her arm, the air of reverential concentration which didn't entirely convince me.

'Ma would have been horrified to see me at Mass,' she whispered during the Communion hymn. She stayed in the pew whilst I filed up behind Céleste to receive the host. Instead of the wafer on my tongue, I thought of Christa.

After it was all over she murmured: 'Do you believe in all this? These statues and the rosary and the Sacred Heart?'

'Actually, I don't believe in anything at all.'

'I think I do. Or at least I always hope that good will triumph. I survived the river, didn't I?'

'That was down to me, not God, ungrateful girl.'

Christa

Each day, Estelle and I burst forth into the city beyond Grand-mère's house of lace and dust. She was determined to show me everything, so we walked until my feet were sore and my back ached. The times I loved best were when we'd sit in a café together. She'd order coffee or lemonade and we'd read our books and raise our heads to smile or nudge each other's foot if we'd spotted something amusing. For half an hour or so time stood still and it was just her and me in our bubble of contentment.

Whenever we took account of what was happening in the outside world, we knew that we were on the edge of a precipice. Just as in London, the newspaper headlines were full of foreboding and the prospect of war lurked in moments of strangeness on the streets. Whereas in England people had been openly buying blackout material and trying on gas masks, in neutral Belgium preparations were more discreet, though I couldn't help noticing that shopping baskets were laden with tins and shop windows announced shortages due to *unnecessary stockpiling by housewives*.

The citizens of Brussels had cause to be nervous. It had been only twenty-one years since the occupying German army had departed following its defeat in the last war. In the picture-postcard Grand Place, Estelle explained that on the 20th August 1914, the square had been crammed to the last inch with marching soldiers, and the invading German forces were so multitudinous that the troops hadn't stopped arriving for two days. Her grandparents, in their house on Rue d'Orléans, had eventually fallen asleep to the sound of marching feet and had woken the next morning to find that the pavements outside were still shaking.

As the war progressed, the population had been deliberately

starved and there had been raids on the houses of anyone suspected of assisting the enemy. Villages around Brussels were burned down, apparently at random, and if anyone protested, there were appalling reprisals. In Estelle's university town of Louvain, at the first whiff of rebellion, the invading Germans had shot 248 citizens, torched a medieval library of priceless books and banished ten thousand people from their homes.

Ma had been anxious about me travelling to Belgium and now I understood why. Hitler's evil forces were closer in space and in time. An old wall near the Manneken Pis was pitted with German bullet holes. The illusion of peace, in Brussels, was even more flimsy than it had been in Watford.

Towards the end of the first day, Estelle led me from a side street into an unremarkable little square with the statue of a woman at its centre. 'There she is. Maman. You can go and read the inscription if you like. Shall I order some lemonade?' And she flopped down at a nearby café table.

La Place Waterloo, at the convergence of five narrow streets, was cobbled and irregular in shape, its architecture a typical medley of ramshackle apartment and modern office block. Unable to find a gesture grand enough for such a moment, I glanced at Fleur's daughter, who was laughing at me from her place in the sun.

She called: 'You see what I mean about that statue of Cavell in London – just too imposing, compared to this. But they haven't got Maman right either. Her pose is far too religious, don't you think?'

'True. She looks like a saint.' Still, I gazed up at the statue, spellbound.

'You are actually behaving as if you've had a vision.' Estelle raised her arm to summon a waiter.

Despite the greenish discolouration in the folds of her gown and bird droppings on her shoulders, this bronze Fleur was heroic, with her ardent face upturned and her long hair twisted at either side of her forehead over a Grecian-style headband. Yet even I could tell that the sculpting was second-rate.

'Not exactly a Michelangelo,' Estelle said.

Bronze Fleur wore a loose belt around her narrow waist and was shod in strappy shoes with pointy toes. One hand was held to her breast, the other outstretched towards me.

FLEUR CORNELIS-FAIDER
FRANÇOISE
1888—1917
COMBATTANTE DE LA RÉSISTANCE. MARTYR. MÈRE.
MORTE POUR NOUS SAUVER

I rather admired the alliteration, and the forcefulness of *Combattante*. 'I wonder who composed the plaque,' I asked Estelle.
'Someone lacking imagination.'
'Why do you say that?'
'Can't you work it out?'
The danger signs were there. She had flung herself back in the metal chair, slender legs crossed at the calf.
'Yes. I can see why you're hurt,' I said. 'It's because they've said that she was a mother last, not first. But that's because it's a public statue.'
'Well, you've seen her now.' She drained her glass noisily through the straw. 'Next, I'm going to take you to the Galeries St Hubert and then we'll go home.'
'Don't you feel proud and thrilled when you sit here? I do, I can't get over it – that there is an actual statue of someone with whom I have a close bond.'
Estelle's eyes met mine with a cool stare. 'The bond being that you are alive and she is dead. Voilà.'

Les Galeries Royales St Hubert was an exclusive shopping arcade so hushed and expensive it was rather more religious in ambience than the cathedral. The Pâtisserie Faider retained its name even when Grand-mère had sold the business after the war, following the death of her husband. Its floor was tiled in black and white and the shelves and counters were of varnished oak. Under glass domes were heaps of pastries and gateaux, including the special cake known as La Fleur, a meringue concoction with chocolate and pistachios baked to a secret recipe. I was about to buy one as a tribute to Fleur, even though the price tag added up to an hour's fruit picking, when Estelle forestalled me by ordering the girl behind the counter to have half a dozen sent round to Rue d'Orléans, and made no attempt to pay.

'A statue and a cake,' she said. 'That's all I ever had of Maman until you wrote to us.'

That evening I was invited by Grand-mère to drink a tisane and to view the document that had announced her daughter's death. Seated in a tapestry chair with wooden arms, she showed me a worn leather writing case in which she kept a sheaf of letters. I felt a surge of pride when I saw that the latest was my own, written in March.

'I was so touched when I read it,' she told me. 'Any connection with my lost daughter comforts me. So now you are come to Belgium, like your father. Tell me, how are you finding life at De Eikenhoeve?'

'I love being out in the open, it's so beautiful. And there's so much space. Every day I discover something new and intriguing.'

'*Intriguing?*'

'On one level De Eikenhoeve is a home. On another it's like a machine or factory, with every activity in its allocated place. And on another it's an ancient farmhouse in a seemingly boundless landscape of fields and trees. Have you visited there much, Madame Faider?'

'When our daughter was betrothed we drove there in the carriage. It seemed so far away – though of course the trains bring everything much nearer these days. As you can imagine, there was some coolness between our two families. The Cornelises were as dismayed by their son's choice as we were by Fleur's.'

'How did your daughter and Meneer Cornelis meet, Madame Faider?'

'At a party they both happened to attend on one of Bernard's rare excursions to Brussels. Fleur was wearing a new green dress that she'd bought against my will – it had a sheen to it and clung to every inch of her body. Her eyes were shining when she came home and within a month she was married. What do you make of that?'

'It sounds romantic.' Apparently I'd given a very poor answer so I asked hastily: 'Did Fleur have many suitors?'

'Of course. And one in particular whom she'd known all her life.'

'Borland.'

She looked at me sharply. 'You have done your homework. Laurence Borland was the one we all thought she'd marry. In fact, the minute she was eighteen she decided that they should share a studio. The idea was that she would paint and he would work on his architecture. He was commendably reluctant to rely on family money to support him in married life, particularly as there'd been some slight difference between the two fathers in the past, but he might have known that Fleur would never put up with caution or half-heartedness.' She removed the slice of lemon from her tea with silver tongs. 'What about you? Have you a young man back in England? Estelle tells me that Pieter is very taken with you.'

'I'm sure he's just being kind.'

'It's true that Pieter is kind to everyone. He never forgets to send boxes of fruit from the farm, or a ham or butter. Sometimes he even takes the time to call in here when he's in town.'

'The farm certainly seems to be thriving.'

'Be careful with Pieter, though. Remember how young he was when he lost his mother. Men like that are always more fragile than you think.'

Tea with Grand-mère was proving to be a much less cosy affair than I'd anticipated; I felt reproved.

'I gather they're all going strong,' she continued, 'Hanna, Oud Daan, still not retired. Amazing. He must be every bit as old as me. And his son is still hankering after Estelle. Marthe comes to Brussels every month or so and keeps me up to date.'

'*Marthe?*'

'Now there's a good woman. Exquisite needlecraft. I have a sample of her work above my bed. You look shocked. I expect Estelle's told you Marthe ousted my daughter and wanted her dead. Crazy nonsense. Don't believe a word of it. Marthe is a

102

sweet woman who's worked tirelessly for De Eikenhoeve. And I'm quite sure that, unlike my daughter, she loves Bernard Cornelis very much.'

'Estelle hates Marthe.'

'Poor Marthe. The stepmother's fate, I'm afraid.'

'Were you aware at the time that your daughter was working for the Resistance, Madame Faider? Did she confide in you?'

Grand-mère replaced her teacup and drew the leather folder towards her. 'In the war, nobody confided in anyone, for obvious reasons. This is what I was going to show you; it's the letter announcing her death.'

The flimsy sheet of paper, dated 26th June 1917 and addressed to der Meneer Cornelis, was badly typed and bore the prison governor's stamp. 'My son-in-law, Bernard, forwarded us the letter, as he did anything to do with Fleur, because he couldn't bear to keep it at De Eikenhoeve.'

She spoke in a colourless voice, refusing to judge. 'My husband and I visited Freiburg three times but were never allowed to see her. Bernard might have been admitted, but he couldn't – or wouldn't – take time away from the children and the farm. And anyway, he was in a rage with Fleur for lying to him about her activities, and above all for getting caught. As you can perhaps imagine, the farm was consequently subjected to a great deal of scrutiny from the authorities.

'I don't even know if the prison staff gave her my letters. I suspect not. They all but denied her existence because they hated the bad publicity they got for holding women in prison. On the other hand they wanted to show everyone what would happen if they meddled in the Resistance. After the international backlash caused by the shooting of Edith Cavell and Gabrielle Petit, Fleur played into their hands by dying of so-called natural causes. They didn't have to go to the trouble of shooting her after all.'

'I'm so sorry, Madame Faider.'

'Imagine. My little girl. Céleste made up her bed every night with a hot-water bottle in case they suddenly allowed her home. Typhus is such a dreadful disease and wholly avoidable. Fleur would have hated the indignity of it – she was a fastidious child. My husband had nightmares and couldn't stop crying. Those months following her death were the worst of my life. We were oblivious to what was going on around us. If we'd starved to death we wouldn't have cared less. Céleste put meals on the table that we scarcely touched. Six months later my husband was dead too.'

Madame Faider recited these details like a litany. Her pale eyes never left my face and I felt shrunken in her presence, as if I were a prisoner and she my judge.

'In our family we never cease to be grateful for the choice she made,' was all I could say. 'To have given her life—'

'As I've said, my daughter did not give her life.' She gave a deep sigh. 'Her life was taken.'

'She was incredibly brave. There must have been such a high risk of capture.'

Grand-mère took a sip of her drink whilst her old eyes, almost washed of colour, fixed on me. 'Do you suppose that the Germans arrived at that particular spot on that particular night by accident? When you wrote to us, you asked if there was anything you could do to repay her courage. Well, I was wondering if you could shed any light on what happened. After all, your father must have been one of the last people to see my daughter a free woman. Perhaps he remembers something. We've never known who betrayed her to the military police. It might have been someone here in Brussels, or a nervous farm labourer close to the border, or even at De Eikenhoeve.'

Her request horrified me, especially given that Estelle had named Marthe as the possible traitor. 'I'm afraid Pa won't talk about what happened,' I said feebly.

'Such a pity. Well, there you go. It was just a thought.'

We sat a while longer in that little parlour with the loudly ticking clock and the heavily draped windows until Grand-mère seemed to doze off in her chair. I picked up the tea tray and edged my way towards the door, skirting round a number of little tables and footstools. When I glanced back, her head had dropped to one side and her hand rested upon the leather writing case and its burden of correspondence.

Estelle

Red-letter day, branded on the inside of my skull: Robbe meets Christa. How I had gloried in it, watching them from across the room and willing them to like each other. Biting my lip as they met and moved apart like a couple of cats. Disappointed that they didn't seem to hit it off. But, even so, I felt a hint of unease afterwards. I couldn't have put my finger on it at the time, but I must have sensed that pretend indifference can be a sign of noticing. Really noticing.

When Grand-père was alive, so many used to attend the Tuesday afternoon salon at Rue d'Orléans that the double doors between the drawing room and the *salle à manger* had to be flung open. Dressed up in one of Marthe's home-made frocks, muslin, with a big bow at the back, I would weave amid expensive adult knees, arms brushing against the starched aprons of three or four maids. Grand-mère's arm would restrain me while she engaged in a laborious adult conversation, me leaning into her hard bosom, bored. Or they would perch me on a pile of cushions, from which I scattered crumbs. Meringue exploding on my tongue, the crunch of pistachios, chocolate paste the consistency of toffee.

But by the summer of 1939, death or old age had decimated the audience. Monsieur and Madame Fabron still came – French to their eyeballs. She wore too strong perfume, as always, so that it gave me a headache just being in the same room. Boasted about their profits. They were exporters of Belgian glass and doing extremely well, thank you very much, due to Hitler's addiction to breaking the windows of Jewish businesses. Smug. Their daughter was married to someone *very big* in banking. A couple of ancient women from church, sisters, known collectively as

Les Desrochers, and Monsieur and Madame Vauclain, who had bought the pâtisserie and whose attitude to Grand-mère was a mixture of superior and deferential. Also a relative newcomer, Clémence Depage, the wife of Grand-mère's dentist, who had brought her youngest child, an infant, Marguerite, much to the delight of every woman present. Even I could tell she was a sweet child, with her plump cheeks and gummy smile. She had learnt the trick of clapping her hands on demand and basked in the ensuing praise.

'How lovely to be a baby,' gushed Madame Vauclain. 'Without a worry in the world.'

Clémence Depage was my favourite amongst the women, and was only about a decade older than me. We were polar opposites in other ways, she being petite and olive-skinned. I liked her attention to detail, the way she kept her children in line just by a soft word or gesture. She occasionally risked bringing her two sons to Grand-mère's genteel salon and even the naughty younger one quietened at her touch. She was his anchor. She had perfectly manicured fingernails and dead straight stocking seams. Wide eyes. And I was flattered by her attention. She had told me how much she admired me and envied my independence. When she met her husband she'd been a student of mathematics, but had given it all up to marry.

Christa behaved beautifully – she was well trained for this sort of gathering. Pretty in a frock sewn by Mrs Geering on the treadle machine in Harewood Road. Blushing when introduced as *notre invitée anglaise*. The story had to be retold, by Grand-mère, of how Christa had written to us, and how I had travelled to London and found her.

'Of course we are all so proud of our dear Fleur,' gushed La Fabron. 'We remember her so well. Such a beautiful child. Such a tragedy.'

'I was sorry never to have met her,' Clémence told Christa. 'We've only lived in the city for the past eight years. I expect Estelle has shown you her statue. I often take the children on a detour to look at her. They call her the running woman.' She received a scornful look from La Fabron, who thought everybody should have been born in Brussels.

'As you can imagine, it's hard to find the words to express my gratitude for what she did,' said Christa, in her shy French.

'How very romantic,' said Madame Vauclain, 'to have in our midst a child of the Resistance, as it were.'

'I remember how you visited the prison, Madame Faider, and weren't allowed to see your own daughter,' put in the plumper of the Desrocher sisters. 'You brought the letter announcing her death to church because you wouldn't be parted from it. The only way to comprehend it, you said, was to keep it with you at all times.'

'It was indeed a dreadful blow,' said Grand-mère after a moment's silence. 'But then most of us were suffering some kind of loss at that time. And I was proud that my daughter had been a free spirit and did what she believed to be right.'

'It's certainly true that we never knew what Fleur would get up to next,' said Madame Fabron. 'When they were children, my girls were always a little nervous about coming to play with her, if I'm honest. It usually ended with something being torn or lost.' Christa caught my eye and we nearly laughed aloud. I bet those prissy Fabron girls had bored Maman stiff.

'Of course, a war puts terrible demands upon us all,' said Madame Vauclain, whose face was indeed pinched with anxiety about the current state of affairs.

The Fabrons were convinced that Belgium must remain neutral.

'But look where that got us in the last war,' protested Monsieur Vauclain. 'Do you think that Herr Hitler will be any respecter of neutrality?'

Clémence was at the window rocking the baby. 'I am filled with dread whenever I hear that man's name,' she said.

'I think the main thing,' said Monsieur Fabron soothingly, 'is to do nothing to upset him. Which is why staying neutral is by far the best plan.'

When I made a face in the Fabrons' direction, Christa, who'd taken a bite of meringue, got the giggles, sprayed crumbs down her dress and had to leave the room.

While she was gone, Robbe showed up. What a surprise. He had his own key, so just appeared, hands in pockets, strolled over

107

to Grand-mère and gave her a smacking kiss on each cheek. She went pink with pleasure, while Céleste hobbled up, glassy-eyed, clung on to his hand and swayed in ecstasy. The other old women fluttered, looked him up and down and would no doubt later spend hours dissecting his dishevelled appearance. Their voices grew shrill at the idea of him working on a newspaper.

'How thrilling,' said Madame Fabron, hand to her throat. 'Which one? Not *Le Soir*?'

'Nothing so grand. You won't have heard of it.' He went up to Clémence and stood behind her so that he could eyeball the baby and peek at her through his fingers until she was crowing with delight.

Christa halted by the door. I saw him through her eyes: frayed collar, the smell of a disreputable bar, eyes full of laughter because of the baby. Saw her through his: cotton frock and cloud of dark hair, the exquisite angle of her elbow, the perfect line of her upper arm.

'My brother Robbe,' I said. 'A rare sighting.'

She squeezed her hands together as if to contain her joy. 'You are the last piece in my jigsaw. I'm so pleased to meet you.'

The mockery of a salute he gave her was another import from Spain. '*A piece in the jigsaw*. Is that what I am? It's a relief to have a function for a change.'

She hesitated a moment, unsure whether or not she'd offended him. Then she perched on the arm of my chair. I pressed my shoulder against her.

Grand-mère called Robbe to her side and showed off to Madame Fabron the castanets he'd bought her with the dancing couples painted on them. I could read La Fabron's mind: cheapest of the cheap.

Christa leapt forward to refill teacups. She told the Vauclains about our visit to the pâtisserie and how grand she'd found it compared to any cake shop in England. By now Céleste had recovered enough to pass round the langues de chat and Clémence rejoined the circle and fed the baby morsels of cake.

Robbe sauntered up to me and glanced across at Christa. 'How's it going?' he muttered.

'It's bearable now we're in town, but we're off back to De

Eikenhoeve on Thursday.'

'So she'll be there for the haymaking?'

'We'll see. Marthe loves her, as you can imagine. And Pieter's taken a real shine to her. He's always luring her away for twilight walks.'

'Is he indeed?' He gave her another glance as she fetched a slice of lemon for Madame Vauclain. 'What does she make of him?'

'She likes him, of course. Why wouldn't she. Don't worry, I'm keeping an eye.'

'I'm sure you are.' The look he gave me stripped me to the bone. 'I feel sorry for the poor girl. Besieged on all sides.'

'She's quite capable of taking care of herself.'

'Let's hope so. Listen, what are you doing tomorrow? Borland is in town and would like a quick word with us both. He suggested the Wiertz at three.'

Borland in town. For once in my life I was not overjoyed at the prospect of meeting him. Suddenly I wished I was back at De Eikenhoeve, only me and Christa, without the distraction of everyone else.

'And then we could go to the Prospero for dinner,' said Robbe. 'Let's show Christa the high life.' He kissed me and headed for the door. I saw him glance at Christa again before he left. She was lifting the baby from Clémence's arms and didn't notice that he'd gone – her head snapped round just as the door closed behind him.

Christa

The first time I met Robbe Cornelis was at Grand-mère's salon. I'd left the room for a few minutes and when I returned I had the impression that something foreign had blown in. There was an acrid tang to the air, like after a firework has been lit, and a fluttering among the old ladies. A dark-haired young man with unhealthily pale skin was standing by the window in a shabby leather jacket. At first I thought he must be Grand-mère's dentist come to join his wife because he was playing with the baby as if they were best friends, but of course he couldn't have been a dentist, dressed like that. When he met my eye, I felt a jolt. I saw his sister in him, and beyond her, his mother.

He glanced at me briefly, then back at the baby, who was grinning in anticipation and waving her fists, and then he looked again at my face, as if trying to remember where he'd seen it before.

My opening words when Estelle introduced us were ridiculous because I was so surprised and moved. Robbe still bore a striking resemblance to the little boy I'd seen in those photographs, glowering from beneath a mop of near-black hair with a gaze that revealed his vulnerability, although he would despise himself for showing it.

He reminded me of the lion Ma had once taken me to see, all caged up in the suburban garden of a local printer who'd bought it on a whim whilst travelling abroad. I had cried on the bus all the way home to Harewood Road because the lion was so big and the cage so small and the creature's eyes so weary of the world. But I'd felt terror too, at the danger lurking within him. After all, Robbe had recently been fighting in Spain, yet here he was in a salon filled with mostly old people and a baby.

Robbe stayed only a quarter of an hour or so and I was afraid I'd lost my one and only chance of speaking to him at any length, but as it turned out we were to meet again the next day. 'The Musée Wiertz was Maman's favourite,' said Estelle. 'She loved its madness. Although Wiertz was a second-rate artist, he persuaded the city authorities to display his paintings in perpetuity. I can't wait to see your reaction.'

There was no sign of Robbe when we arrived, punctually, at three. The gallery was actually more like a private house and, since she'd viewed its contents many times, Estelle sent me off to explore while she waited at the entrance.

A nude at a window offered a flower; another naked woman confronted a skeleton whilst pondering her own mortality; a corpse reawakened and attempted to escape its coffin; a naked woman with a book lay on her couch with her feet facing the painter, her right calf obscuring the dark place between her thighs. Wiertz's women had simpering faces, small breasts and heavy thighs, and were often posed with their buttocks thrust at the painter. His men were hairless but muscular, their genitals concealed by improbable scraps of drapery. He seemed to have had a particular obsession with breasts, backsides and severed heads.

After ten minutes or so I returned to the lobby, gleefully anticipating a conversation in which I would find out from Estelle what I was supposed to make of all this. But she was now accompanied by Robbe and another man who was dressed from head to toe in black. No one noticed me until the stranger, happening to glance my way, muttered something to Estelle and tilted his head to me in greeting. My first impression was of untidy, iron-grey hair, a quantity of beard and eyes of exceptional brightness, even behind his thick-lensed glasses.

'Christa,' said Estelle, eyes shining, 'this is Père Borland, one of my tutors at Louvain.'

'So this is the famous Mademoiselle Christabel Geering,' said Borland, taking my hand.

I felt a shiver of recognition – this after all had been Fleur's childhood sweetheart. In his black raincoat and dog collar he was very much the priest. His cheekbones were razor sharp and his expression forceful. While most people's faces were defined by curves, his was all angles.

'We met a friend of yours in Cambridge,' I told him. 'Doctor Sinclair. I recognise you from the photograph he kept on his bookcase.'

Borland's generous lips widened into a smile. 'That must have been taken decades ago. You have a very impressive memory.'

'I remember everything I'm told about Fleur Cornelis-Faider and her friends, because of what she did for my father.'

His eyes were fixed speculatively on my face. 'Ah yes. One of the men Fleur rescued.'

Behind this conversation the ground was shifting. Despite Borland's mesmeric gaze, I was aware that Robbe and Estelle were paying considerable attention to what we were saying. I murmured to Borland my old mantra about gratitude to Fleur and excitement at being in Brussels and then took a step back, allowing the three of them to resume their intense conversation. 'Louvain . . . another meeting . . . necessary fund-raising . . .'

I glanced from face to face. But wasn't it obvious? Did none of them realise that Borland's posture, the slight stoop of his shoulders, the angle at which he held his head, were strikingly similar to Robbe's?

'It has been a great pleasure to meet you,' Borland said, donning a beret, 'but, alas, I must be on my way. I have packing to do – I'm off to Rome in the morning.'

'I expect Christa's finished here,' Estelle said.

We walked together along the path in front of the museum, down the steps and onto the narrow pavement, where I recovered sufficiently to manoeuvre myself next to Borland. Brother and sister followed close behind, eager to catch every word.

'I'm so interested to learn more about Fleur,' I said.

'I'm not surprised. She was a remarkable woman.'

'I gather that you worked alongside her in the Resistance.' Borland's silence was intimidating. Nevertheless, I persevered. 'I only have tantalising little snatches of her, like when your friend Doctor Sinclair told us he'd met her in Louvain.'

'Did he? I don't remember it,' said Borland with apparent indifference.

'Doctor Sinclair said that although it was only a brief meeting, he could never forget her.'

Borland shrugged. 'As I'm sure you're aware, most people found Fleur unforgettable. Not, perhaps, an ideal trait for one whose vocation required her to be invisible.'

'And you were her childhood friend,' I persisted.

'Indeed I was.' His smile was a little more encouraging. 'Though our parents fell out when we were still quite young. My father was an architect and didn't approve of how the Faiders profited from what he called the massacre of the old city by building a new pâtisserie amidst the rubble. Fleur and I liked to believe we were Romeo and Juliet, but in fact nobody actually minded that we met up.'

We had reached the tram stop, where he took my hand and kissed it in a gesture that ought to have been disarming. However, the expression in his eye, vigilant and rather cold, didn't quite match his gallantry.

After the others had fervently embraced him we all watched as he walked away. 'Were you expecting to meet him today?' I asked.

'Sort of, but you never know with Borland.'

On the tram ride back to the city centre, Estelle and I shared a seat. She turned frequently to speak to Robbe, mostly in French, about what Borland had said – something about reviving an old publication – while I gazed out of the dirty window. Already I had begun to doubt myself. Perhaps I was completely wrong-headed, even crazily presumptuous, in suspecting that Borland and Robbe were father and son. If it were true, it would have been an almighty scandal, not least because Borland would have taken his vows by the time Robbe was born. And if it was an open secret, why hadn't Estelle or Pieter mentioned it to me?

The others were anxious to rush to the Prospero, grab an empty table, put their heads together and make plans. The idea was that they would form a group, led by Borland, to release an underground publication should war be declared. The Prospero was crowded with young people; candles were thrust into empty wine bottles; there was a cloud of smoke and nothing on the

113

menu except fish soup and bread. As I picked through the bones in my bowl I was hazily aware that another carafe of wine had been ordered.

'Where did you get this disgusting garment?' Estelle gave the sleeve of Robbe's jacket a tug.

'Spain.'

'Torn from the back of a dead *nacionalista*, I imagine.'

He grinned and lit a cigarette. Robbe Cornelis was like one of those paper fortune-tellers my school friends and I used to spend hours designing and folding during our lunch breaks. In Grand-mère's salon he had been charming and restrained, in the Musée Wiertz, with Borland, deferential and excitable. Now, in the smoky café, he pretended to be lazy-eyed and flippant. Tipping a matchbox over and over on the sticky tabletop, he scanned the room or occasionally flashed his sister a look of blazing affection.

'How's your paid work actually going?' Estelle asked.

'Pretty humdrum. Folding and stapling mostly.'

'My father also happens to be in the print trade,' I told him.

'I visited him at work,' Estelle added. 'The place is called Sun Engraving. Hugely impressive.'

'And what about you, Mademoiselle,' said Robbe. 'Will you be a printer too?'

'From September, I shall be a teacher of English and French.'

'How are you finding life at De Eikenhoeve?'

'A wonderful contrast to what I'm used to at home and it's a joy to be out in the fresh air. But it makes me all the more conscious of everything your mother gave up in order to save men such as my father.'

'Would you really want to be incarcerated in that farm forever?' he said. 'I'm sure *she* didn't.'

Estelle smiled. 'It's no use expecting Robbe to talk about Maman, by the way. He never does. Which infuriates me, because of course he must remember her a bit.'

Robbe swung forward in the chair and stared at me with dead eyes. 'What do you think of Marthe?'

'I like her. She's been very kind to me.'

'Is that so?' Without missing a beat, he dropped his voice and narrowed his eyes. 'We think she's a witch.'

'A white witch, surely.'

'He used to tell me these awful stories to frighten me,' said Estelle. 'Do you remember, Robbe? You said you'd hidden in the dairy and seen Marthe separate the milk with the blink of her eyelid. And that if she chewed her little fingernail she could disembowel a chicken, ready for the pot.'

'Quite useful skills then, for a farmer's wife,' I suggested.

Robbe took a drag on his cigarette, smiling faintly.

'There's Edouard,' cried Estelle, peering through the smoke. 'He's my best friend from college. I wondered if I might see him here. Do you mind if I go and have a word?'

After she'd left, Robbe crooked his finger and the waitress brought more wine and removed the dirty plates. He continued to flick at the matchbox with his thumbnail as he gazed across the hot and crowded room. Who was he, really? I thought it quite probable that at any moment he too might get up and leave me.

'You know Estelle saved my life the other day,' I said.

'Is that so?'

'We went swimming in the river, and like an idiot I got into trouble.'

'That's why I never go home. Much too dangerous.'

'Surely not quite as dangerous as fighting in Spain.'

His mood suddenly changed, as if he were noticing me for the first time. 'What do you really make of De Eikenhoeve?'

'It's the first farm I've ever worked on, so every day is a revelation. Full of paradoxes, don't you think? It makes me sad to see the pigs being fed and cared for one day, carted off to market the next.'

'And how is my brother Pieter dealing with his new role, now he's taken over from Papa?'

'He's been very patient with me. As I said, I know nothing about farming, but everything seems to be running smoothly. He's got Oud Daan, of course, to advise him, though it can't be easy for Pieter, with your father peering over his shoulder.'

'So Oud Daan has swapped allegiance, has he, from Papa to Pieter?'

'He seems devoted to both.'

'He's devoted to neither. It's the farm he cares about. The only way to get Oud Daan's attention is through the farm.'

'Aren't you tempted to go back sometime and see for yourself?'

'Much too busy. And it gives me the creeps, all those green spaces; having to sit through endless meals nobody really wants to eat.'

'Yes, I can see that might be a trial. Especially as they're so delicious.'

His laughter was like the crack of a pistol. 'So what have you found out about our Maman, since you've been at De Eikenhoeve?'

He was suddenly attentive and I pushed the speculation about Borland to the back of my mind. 'Estelle showed me your mother's room in the turret and Pieter told me how she'd taught him to paint eggshells. When I was a little girl, I idolised your mother, but now I can see that it's complicated being a heroine – let alone the child of one.'

Folding his arms on the tabletop, Robbe brought his face much closer to mine, so that I could see flecks of light in the irises of his dark eyes. 'I'll give you my mother if you like. I remember her very clearly, you know, despite what Estelle might think. She was always on the move. The best thing was going for walks with her. When I was really small I would hold tight to her hand, but after Estelle was born Maman was always carrying the baby and I had to twist my fingers into her skirt and tag along. Sometimes she walked so fast my feet nearly left the ground. She loved the woods, especially playing hide-and-seek. She'd leave me wandering about and then spring out from behind a tree. I can still recall the bliss of being swept up in her arms just when I thought I'd lost her forever. And when she taught me to swim I rode on her back in the river and her hair floated towards me and tickled my knees.'

'I wish I'd met her.'

'No you don't.' He took a long draught of wine then shoved aside his glass, any hint of nostalgia fading from his eyes. 'No, you don't, Mademoiselle. Because if you had, you'd miss her the way I do. I expect you think the past for me is a place full of sweet memories. The truth is, I'd rather be dragged down a cobbled street by my hair in front of a dozen weeping villagers, or lined up with my back to a wall and my face to a firing squad, than lose her again. There's nothing pretty about grief. Nothing artistic. No reason to write an ingratiating little note to an old lady in Brussels, begging for attention, like you did. Grief is filthy. There is not a day of my life, even when I'm a thousand miles from home, that I don't go looking for Maman in those woods, or race along the passage to her room and fling open the door in case she has turned up. It took months and months for them to admit to me that Maman wasn't coming back, and years longer for me to learn that she had died covered in shit and vomit and that her body had been tossed into a communal grave along with hundreds of other starved and tortured bodies.' He threw himself back in his chair and watched me. 'Is that what you were hoping to find out?'

I wanted to justify myself, to beg his forgiveness or rage at him for being unfair. I needed Estelle, who was still deep in conversation on the other side of the room. Robbe gave a long sigh, straightened his legs and lit another cigarette.

'You're right,' I murmured at last, my throat aching. 'I didn't think. I'm sorry.'

'Never mind.' He gave me a smile of sudden sweetness. 'Don't look so stricken, *ma petite anglaise*, I'm sure I'll get over it one day. Do you think she's all right, by the way?' He nodded to where Estelle was embracing people at the far table.

My voice came in breathless bursts. 'I think so. What do you mean exactly? I think she's happier in Brussels than at De Eikenhoeve.'

'You need to watch out for Estelle. She can get much too attached to people like you. Ends up being desperately hurt, every time.'

'People like me?'

He hesitated for an instant. 'The type of person who is not going to be around for long.'

'We both know it's only for a few weeks.'

'She should never have taken you to De Eikenhoeve. That place is no good for either of us.'

117

Estelle was back at our table. 'Edouard won't come over. He's almost too drunk to stand.'

'Your friend is trying to persuade me to come back for the harvest,' Robbe told her, winking at me. 'Perhaps I shall. Stir things up a little.'

'Why don't you?' she said. 'We'd love that.'

It was gone midnight. Estelle told me I looked pale and Robbe said he'd walk us back to Grand-mère's, even though it was raining and he had to cover his head with his jacket while Estelle and I huddled beneath an ancient tartan umbrella borrowed from the Prospero. At the front door, where the rain shone like needles under the lamp, he kissed Estelle on each cheek, cocked his head to one side and grinned at me. 'Au revoir, *ma petite anglaise.*'

In Grand-mère's quiet hall, Estelle shook the umbrella and left it propped crookedly on its spokes while she and I tiptoed upstairs. On the landing we held each other tightly as we said goodnight and after I'd disentangled myself I closed the door of my room, leant on it and gripped the handle as if it were a lifeline.

Estelle

After those few days in Brussels, for practically the first time since the age of around four, I was excited about going back to De Eikenhoeve. It was the most pleasurable, the easiest thing in the world, to buy a couple of tickets to Oostervorken and watch Christa select first a carriage, then a seat.

'Please close that window,' instructed an old busybody after five minutes or so. True, she had a smut on her face.

Of course, Christa, full of apology, obeyed at once, and then gazed out at the sunshiny countryside, her forehead pressed to the glass. Sometimes she glanced across at me and smiled. Her dark hair was rolled and pinned above her ears but tendrils had come adrift. We were both rather quiet, having overdone the wine at the Prospero. She was wearing the blue dress I liked best with buttons all the way down the front, and her yellow cardigan was wrapped around her shoulders. The dress was a little too tight across the breast, so that the space between the buttons strained open and I glimpsed broderie anglaise.

She said she loved looking at the wide skies and, of course, pointed out every single windmill. All English people love a windmill, she said. She'd bought a pile of postcards to send home. I envied her for having a mother who would devour every word. But come to think of it, Marthe might have done the same, had I written to her.

I was spellbound by the buttons on that frock. Imagined to myself what would happen were we ever alone together and she let me unbutton them one by one – release the strain on the fabric, press my fingertip to her breast, kiss the underside of her chin. In Brussels we'd been kept busy meeting Robbe and Grand-mère, even Père Borland. The city had held us apart.

119

Anticipating the tall hedgerows and empty rooms at De Eiken-hoeve, I felt drowsy, safe, full of anticipation.

She talked about Robbe, who I'd now seen three times in a month when usually I met him once a year, if I was lucky. Like a fool I was glad for Christa's sake that he and she seemed to have hit it off. She was worried that she might have pushed him too far by probing him about Maman. I said I doubted it – if he could face enemy snipers in Spain, he was hardly likely to mind five minutes' conversation with Christa.

'As the middle child,' she said, 'he's the one who seems to have suffered most when your mother didn't come home.'

'How do you work that out?'

'Because you were just a baby and Pieter had the farm to distract him. Robbe told me last night, while you were talking to your friend, that he's never got over your mother's death. He thinks about her all the time. Why else do you suppose he never comes back to De Eikenhoeve?'

'Because he doesn't like Marthe.'

'Yes, but all that Marthe stuff is a bit far-fetched, don't you think? Your grandmother spoke very highly of her.'

'Grand-mère likes anyone who takes the trouble to visit. Marthe knows exactly how to win her over.'

Although we spoke mostly in English, every bit of our conversation was eavesdropped upon by others. In the stuffy railway carriage my words sounded petulant. Christa crossed over so she could sit next to me, her cheek against my shoulder. 'I know it must be hard for you sometimes on the farm, but I want to make the next couple of weeks perfect, so that from now on we have only happy memories.'

We were thrown together by the lurching of the train. The old biddy with soot on her cheek smiled at us, two happy young women, bound for home.

And there was Marthe, bang on cue, waiting to meet us outside the station. I sat in the back seat and watched their two heads, Christa's young and glossy-haired, and Marthe's a smart shade of grey, set in rigid waves. I listened to their chatter and remembered other journeys with Marthe. Christa was right to ask why

120

we hated her so. There had been a time, a long way back, that I'd loved her. When I was so little that my nose was level with her thigh, I'd loved her smell. Roses – rose water. And how soft her skirts felt when I pressed my face against them. She'd made it her business to keep me close. Without her, I would have been a free-wheeling little creature, staggering along endless passageways looking for someone to notice me.

With her, it was all about small things. She had a collection of buttons, some still stitched to their card, a silk-covered sewing box for thimbles, cotton reels and needle cases, tiny notebooks filled with writing in perfect copperplate. Maman's writing had been defiant and swirly, but Marthe's was copybook even. Characterless, Robbe said.

All my treats had come in boxes. She and I made geometric shapes with matchsticks and she always let me strike one and say a prayer for my mother – in French, if I chose. If she made me a new dress she wrapped it in tissue and laid it in a box for me to unpack. She kept a box of chocolate creams bought in Les Galeries Royales St Hubert for rainy days. Her ebony dominoes exactly fitted their grey cardboard container and she had a musical box in the shape of a Swiss chalet. It played *The Blue Danube*, and when the music slowed to nothing, I closed the lid and the spring made a rasping sound.

Robbe broke that musical box. Prised up the sliver of wood that protected its mechanism and poked about until he couldn't put it back together again. We pretended it had fallen on the floor. 'Anyway,' he'd said, '*The Blue Danube* is a German tune.'

On the day Marthe married Papa, a respectable four years or so after Maman's death, I was left behind with Hanna, as usual. While they were gone, she let me scrape the cream bowl with a teaspoon. Back they all came a couple of hours later, along with half the village. The boys tore off their Sunday best and ran into the fields, but I wore a brand new lavender-coloured frock with a stiff skirt and mingled with the grown-ups.

Everyone was there. The Daans, Tante Julia, people from the farm and the village, Marthe's family – shy, determined to hold their own, I expect – and the priest. Marthe's pink hat was decorated with tiny rosebuds from the garden. The brim poked me in the eye when she kissed me and I cried until she took it off and put it on my head instead. Everybody laughed. I received lots of kisses. The neighbours drank champagne and I was allowed a sip as I wove in and out of legs and ate too much. Marthe called me her *lieveke*.

Now I came to think of it, that was the day everything changed. After that, on rainy Sunday afternoons the boys smoked in the feed store, lolled against sacks of grain, quaffed beer nicked from the cellar. Talked about Marthe.

What exactly had she got up to in the war, they wanted to know. Who had she spoken to in the village, when people asked questions about Maman? An unknown man had drowned in our river. Why?

'Basically,' said Pieter, 'Marthe has one priority. Papa. She will hang on to him at all costs, and who can blame her?'

'What costs?'

'You're too young to understand,' he said.

Until Christa, I wouldn't have dreamt of standing up for Marthe. I was on my brothers' team or I was nothing.

By the time I got out of the car to open the gate my heart was hurting. It should have been me, it should always have been me, chatting away with Marthe. Glad to be home. If I'd accepted her love all these years, how different life might have been.

Christa ran up to change. I visited the kitchen and had a chat with Hanna and Lotte. I even offered to help. Hanna laughed out loud – a rare thing for her. Told me it was good to have me back, but what had come over me? Next, I peeked into the office to find Papa or Pieter, but it was empty. It smelt of Oud Daan's cigarettes and ink and animal feed. Nothing in there had changed for years. The cane chair still stood by the window with its filthy old cushion they wouldn't let Marthe replace, and the desk was piled high with files and papers they wouldn't let her tidy.

The drawers of the filing cabinet were so crammed full they wouldn't close and the noticeboard was cluttered with charts, instructions torn off the sides of packets and ancient work rosters. All this was a legacy from Papa's reign that Pieter hadn't got around to clearing up. I sat on the captain's chair behind the desk with its studs and broken pedestal – even when I was a little girl it had only revolved halfway and then jammed. It used to irritate the hell out of Papa when I asked for a ride on that chair.

When I paid him visits he'd put up with me for a while. Let me stand alongside him while he sighed and moaned through correspondence or gave me the hole punch and a bit of scrap paper to play with. If I was lucky, he'd reach into his middle drawer and find me a cough sweet. The bottom left-hand drawer contained the farm revolver. The air rifle, for crows and squirrels and foxes, hung in the rafters above me, but the revolver for sick animals was locked away and therefore much more interesting.

Needless to say, it was Robbe who had secretly introduced it to me. He had brought me into the office one day when no one was about, sat me in the captain's chair and rummaged for the key in the cough-sweet drawer. The revolver was enclosed in a piece of grey felt. Revealing it like a conjuror, he placed it in my lap, where it felt cold and weighty through the thin cotton of my frock. I sat petrified until he took it away, raised it and squinted ahead as if he were going to fire at something through the window. I knew better than to say anything, just waited in silence until he shoved it back in the drawer and returned the key to its hiding place.

Not much sunshine ever penetrated the deep-set windows of that office. I dashed out across the yard, climbed the gate and ran down the track to the fruit fields, raising a cloud of dust as I gathered pace.

At supper Papa told us that the blackcurrants, slow to ripen, were ready now. 'All hands on deck,' he said, in jovial mood. Christa, bright-voiced and eager to please, glanced shyly at Pieter and said she'd be up at five the next morning.

'Me too,' I said.

'Well, good heavens,' said Pieter, 'put out the flags.' Everyone laughed. 'So what did you make of Brussels, Juffrouw Christa? I expect everywhere seemed rather small and scruffy compared to London.'

'Not at all. It has such special resonances for me. I especially liked visiting the pâtisserie and the statue of your mother in La

Place Waterloo. Estelle showed me everything.' She was smiling at me across the table. 'I was invited to your grandmother's salon, and I met Robbe.'

'*Robbe?*' Pieter was so surprised he glanced at me for confirmation. 'Don't tell me he turned up at Grand-mère's? Well, you *are* honoured. We haven't seen him for ages. How was he?'

'He seemed well,' I said. 'Thin and tired, perhaps.'

'What is he up to? Did you find out?'

'He mentioned some newspaper work.'

Papa was engrossed in his food. He hated any discussion of Robbe's employment prospects because they always ended in disaster. I was really hoping that Christa wouldn't mention our meeting with Borland and luckily she didn't.

'Robbe said he might come home for the haymaking, by the way,' I said.

Hope flashed across Marthe's face and Mietje, behind me, drew a sharp breath.

'Did he indeed?' said Pieter. 'What brought that on?'

'It was only a maybe. Perhaps it was thanks to Christa.'

Pieter gave her quite a look, long and smiling, until she blushed. I was so confident that she'd scarcely given him a thought all the time we were in Brussels that I no longer cared what he felt about her.

'Well, if you've persuaded Robbe to come home, you've done us all a favour. I just hope he lets us know beforehand.'

'As long as he doesn't ruin my feast,' growled Papa. 'It might be the last one if there's going to be a war.'

'You always say it's going to be the last one,' said Marthe. 'Don't you think it would be wonderful for the whole family to be together again?'

She was smiling to herself as she sliced the torte. Her dress was yellow, a colour she had always liked. And she loved cake. Usually I refused dessert but this time I accepted a small slice and she was so excited that she dropped it on the tablecloth.

Christa

On our return to De Eikenhoeve my room smelt of fresh linen and warm wood. Ignoring a letter from Ma propped on the dressing table, I flung off my travelling clothes, dressed in an old skirt and raced downstairs.

Robbe had weighed heavily on my mind all day, an ache behind the eyes that was compounded by the wine I'd drunk at the Prospero. I couldn't get out of my head the way he'd leant across the dirty tabletop and ground a cigarette end into an overflowing ashtray while he talked so bitterly about his mother.

As I hurried along the kitchen passage and out into the farmyard the perfume of drying meat and herbs, of ancient stone, of cheese and sugar, onions and smoke, felt like an assault. No wonder Robbe couldn't stand coming home, when those same smells must have greeted him every day, regardless of whether his mother was alive or dead. And what if I was right, and he wasn't even Bernard Cornelis's son? How much greater his sense of isolation?

Dinner that night was the happiest I'd known at De Eikenhoeve. There was a sort of precarious ease about the family because Estelle, the usual cause of friction, was the most affable I'd seen her. When she raised the subject of a possible visit from Robbe the atmosphere certainly changed, but there was neither a portentous silence nor a suggestion that he would be unwelcome. The subject moved on swiftly to arrangements for Bernard Cornelis's feast, which he pretended was an unwelcome ordeal, though it was obviously the highlight of his year.

Upstairs in my room, I read Ma's letter.

The news gets worse and worse. Surely Estelle's family must be worried too? This seems to be a time when we should all be in our own homes. I can't help feeling it's irresponsible of them to let you stay on. You know that the Poles are saying they're going to fight the Nazis. And bombs are exploding all over the place in London. We think it's the work of the IRA. People can get away with anything these days.

Pa misses you terribly. He's not been the same since you left. He spends most of the night sitting outside on the garden bench. I don't want to stop you having a lovely time, but we do miss you so...

I lay awake for hours thinking that I should pack my bag the following morning and return home, not just for Ma's sake, for my own. She had given me the perfect excuse to escape. Everything at De Eikenhoeve was complicated, and I found Estelle's joy nearly as intolerable as her rage. The responsibility was almost too much to bear.

As soon as it was light, I dressed and crept along the creaking upper passageways to Fleur's turret room. It was cold in there, and much of the glamour seemed to have gone. The portrait by Khnopff of the woman with a sullen mouth and languid, been-to-bed eyes dominated the one windowless wall and the rest of the furniture was shabby and tarnished. The leather surface of the desk where Fleur might have sat with Pieter painting eggshells was scratched and stained.

Her shapeless cardigan was still draped over the chair-back and this time I put it on. Soft and fine, riddled with moth holes in the ribbing at the cuffs and hem, the garment was rather too large for me. It fell well below my hips and carried the faintest possible hint, perhaps imagined, of perfume. One of the pockets contained a scrunched-up handkerchief that surely, after all these years, couldn't have been Fleur's. Choosing a window at random, I looked out across Marthe's garden to the softly undulating fields where mist clung to the land and the sky above was turning from grey to palest blue.

Fleur must have been forever awaiting a sign, a phone call or a letter. Why else would she have pushed her little boy Pieter out of the room or raced through the woods so fast that Robbe's feet scarcely touched the ground? Perhaps, from this turret, she had mapped a pathway north through woodland and fields. She might have noticed Marthe carry baby Estelle into the farmyard to look at the ducks and her young sons stride out in the wake of their father or Oud Daan. And when the coast was clear she had abandoned them all, hastening along the drive and out into the lane.

Behind me there came a rustle, as of a silk skirt. After a moment of absolute stillness I whipped round, and there indeed was a figure I barely recognised, dark-haired and wan, dressed in a pale skirt and a grey cardigan: my own reflection in the long mirror by the door, and behind me the Khnopff painting.

'I don't know you,' I whispered. This was the woman who had hastily refolded Ma's letter and thrust it into the corner of her suitcase because she could no longer pretend to herself that she was not utterly in thrall to De Eikenhoeve; the woman who knew she should but could not leave.

Estelle

Because of Christa I gave in and helped properly with the blackcurrant harvest. Dressed in the same faded shirt and blouse, day in, day out. Ate breakfast at six and walked arm in arm with her to wherever we were needed most. When it rained, I took her to the boot room and kitted her out with Maman's wellingtons, which fitted her perfectly. Pleased as punch, she pirouetted and raised her foot to examine the soles.

We splashed off down the lane, kicking up dirt until our legs were filthy and our hair hung in rat's tails. With her, I relished the smells of manure, earth, hay. She said that in the rain the river had a distinctive smell of water on water. Until then I'd never even registered that clean water had a smell. We picked blackcurrants until our hands were covered with specks of juice and stems and insects. Ate with the other women, doorstops of bread and sausage and chutney brought by Marthe. I met Marthe's eye for once and smiled.

We peed behind a hedge, Christa and me together, laughing because the grass was spiky. I was pitiable, a voyeuse, as she crouched in the grass with her legs bared, a glimpse of schoolgirl navy knickers. We staggered home at the end of the day, our skin criss-crossed with scratches, feet and hands and arms stained purple.

Time passed by much too quickly. Before Christa, days at De Eikenhoeve had dragged. With her, there were never enough seconds in a minute, minutes in an hour. Even on rainy evenings she and I passed the time so beautifully that our watch hands raced. We lay on her bed, feet in the air, turning the pages of our books until it was too dark to see. Wrapped ourselves in her quilt

128

when we got chilly or ran down to the kitchen and made hot chocolate with Hanna.

Christa said she liked the rhythm of days on a farm. I'd not noticed a rhythm before. She liked the simplicity of how one job followed another. After the rain we had a run of good weather and I explained to her that haymaking is a two-week process and that at De Eikenhoeve during the harvest we operated both in the past and the present – that the men cut the hay with a combination of scythe and horse and tractor. She and I sat on the gate watching Weber and half a dozen others wield their scythes, inching across the field, the grasses falling steadily beneath their blades. Of course she wanted to have a go and failed miserably, in fact nearly cut her leg in two. I was glad Pieter wasn't around to see her do that.

'It's biblical,' said Christa, after she'd handed the scythe back to Weber.

The tractor had broken down and all day Jong Daan's feet stuck out from beneath it while he tried to get it going again. Nobody dared speak to him. The faithful carthorses, led by Pieter, plodded the length of the far field. Oud Daan was at the hedgerow, directing operations.

Christa and I spent a couple of days picking the last of the strawberries, on our knees or bent double, the sun on our backs or the rain streaming down our necks. I had shown Christa how to balance the fruit in the palm of her hand, check its ripeness, give the stalk a little twist and place it softly in the basket so that it didn't bruise.

'Even the most perfect fruit has to be got to market fast. There are three days maximum between picking and eating,' I told her. In the scullery, Lotte hulled the misshapen strawberries and poured them into giant pans to make jam and compote to last the winter. Or the war, as it turned out.

Perhaps there are still some jars left in the cellars, gathering dust.

At the end of the day, before dinner, Christa and I took it in turns to have the first bath. We had to share the water because Pieter and Papa would be bathing too. I was so tired that I lay on the mat with my feet on a chair while Christa climbed in. Her pink shoulder, damp hair and the side of her face were visible as she soaped herself.

'I feel sorry for you, bathing after me,' she said. 'Look at all the straw I've left floating in the water. You might as well wash in soup.' Rising up, she held her hand out for the towel – her skin aglow, water dripping off her neck and thighs.

I grabbed her hot foot, bit it lightly and kissed it until she giggled. She always pretended that she wasn't embarrassed when we were naked, and she stayed with me while I bathed, perched on a chair with her knees drawn up. I found it unendurable to have her watching me like that. Asked her to soap my shoulders.

She lifted my hair and her fingertips were shy and delicate on my neck. 'Look,' she said, 'my nails will never be right again – they're all stained.' We studied our hands, side by side, hers much smaller and more slender than mine, and I kissed the fleshy part of her palm, under the thumb.

'I've got something to tell you,' I said. 'Let's go to your room.'

She tightened the towel about her shoulders and tiptoed barefoot to the door. I followed her footprints along the passage and we lay on her bed in the evening light filtered by the oak tree.

When I'd written ahead to tell Papa and Marthe I might be bringing a guest, I'd asked them to give Christa my favourite room. Marthe told me Maman used to spend time there, painting by the window. Sometimes, when I was younger, I would tiptoe upstairs and pretend to myself that I might catch her sitting with her back to me, arm raised, measuring the distance with the tip of a paintbrush.

I could almost feel the heat of Christa's body radiating towards me. Our voices were drowsy. Arms and faces seared by the sun.

Now that the threat of Pieter seemed to have floated away, there was just one thing between us. A pressure on my tongue as I finally made up my mind to tell her.

'You know what?' I said.

She rolled onto her side and propped herself up on an elbow, her damp hair falling over the pillow. Her skin was soft after the bath; there was a flush at her throat and on the curve of her breast where the towel had fallen away. By now there was a deep contrast between her tanned neck and arms and the creamy skin on the rest of her body. 'I think I know what you're going to say,' she said.

'Do you now? So you know that your father told me a secret while he and I were alone together on my last visit.'

'*Pa?*'

'Why? What did you think I was going to say?'

'Nothing. Go on.'

'Well . . .' I hesitated a moment, then forged ahead. 'He told me that he and Maman were lovers, briefly, on the night she was captured.'

'*What?* Where? How?'

'In the woods near the border.'

Christa was absolutely still as she imagined this. 'How did he put it? Did he actually say they'd made love?'

'That's certainly what he implied. They hid in the woods together for some hours.'

'No. Tell me *exactly* what he said.'

'That he had never forgotten how it felt to hold her. And the way Maman had kissed him.'

She bit her lip as if she was a little girl. Her eyebrows were messy where she'd rubbed them dry. She whispered: 'How did she kiss him?'

'Like a lover. With her tongue.' I licked my finger and smoothed her eyebrows in two long strokes. 'Maybe like this,' and I leant forward and kissed her mouth, softly, as if it might bruise, and touched just the centre of her upper lip with the tip of my tongue. 'What do you think of that?'

She blinked and moistened her lip where my tongue had been. Then she sighed. 'Do you know what, I'm not surprised. When you first visited us at Harewood Road, and we were having tea in the kitchen and Pa came in, I was sure that he and your mother had been lovers. I saw it in his eyes. I think Ma has always suspected it.' She swallowed and seemed to make a decision. 'But I'm glad, aren't you, if it made your mother happy and it was what they both wanted.'

'It doesn't really make sense to me. Only a few hours before, Maman must have been on the farm with Papa and all of us.'

'But it was the war,' she said.

'That's exactly what Robbe argued.'

'Robbe knows?'

'I told him. Yes.'

'Before you told me?'

'Honestly, Christa, does it matter?'

'Pieter?'

'I've not had a chance to tell Pieter yet.'

We stared at each other. Her eyes were clear and thoughtful and I could see myself reflected in her pupils.

'Did Pa say anything else?'

I told her everything while one tear after another spilled from the corner of her eyes onto the pillow. That an English officer calling himself Hébert (not his real name) had been shot while Maman helped Ted Geering cross the electrified wires. And that when she'd yelled at him to run, he ran.

'I had no idea about any of this,' she whispered. 'It explains so much.'

'I promised your father I wouldn't tell you, but the thing is, I've discovered that I cannot keep a secret as important as this to myself.'

'Are you saying that because of Pa ... because he and Fleur made love in the woods and then he lingered at the wire ... are you saying that might have been the reason she was captured?'

'You mustn't think that.'

'But it's possible, if they'd been half an hour earlier, they might all have got away.'

'Don't torment yourself or I'll wish I'd never said a word. It all happened such a long time ago. Who knows how it might have turned out otherwise?'

'What was Robbe's reaction?'

'The same.'

'But it still doesn't explain how the Germans knew they'd be there.'

'It might have been unlucky chance. Let's leave it at that, shall we? Anyway, now you know.' Feeling large-hearted and bountiful, I rolled off the bed, and left her to think it over.

But the next time, I was sure, it would happen.

Christa

At De Eikenhoeve we were largely cut off from the national news, but Bernard and Marthe had a radiogram in their sitting room and sometimes we'd hear the yapping voice of Herr Hitler when we passed their closed door in the evening. British and French troops had gathered in a show of military solidarity to celebrate Bastille Day and Hanna and Lotte were labelling bottled fruit and packing wooden crates with cheeses to be hidden in the further reaches of the cellars, just in case. Letters arrived almost daily from Ma, urging me to catch the first train home.

But those letters came from a distant place that had little to do with me. Much more compelling were the physical demands of each day, coupled with the knowledge that the shadows were lengthening a few minutes earlier each evening, that the leaves on the oak tree had lost their freshness and the river had become sluggish and opaque under the bridge. Summer was deepening, the hay harvest had begun and afterwards there'd be no excuse for me not to go back to England.

Despite her previous claim, it turned out that Estelle was skilful on the farm. During her early childhood, she'd learnt how to milk a cow by hand and how to tend the pigs and tickle their grateful stomachs in exactly the right spot with a long cane. She knew how to find eggs hidden amidst a heap of straw in the barn or among the reeds by the pond, and how to encourage even the most wayward hen to develop more regular laying habits. She could pick a row of strawberries before the rest of us were halfway along, and persuade a weary carthorse to make one last trip to the hayfield by clicking softly in its ear.

Working alongside her in the fields, I witnessed her transformation. It was like watching a colt stagger to its feet or a horse chestnut shake out its first green leaves. Estelle, without her anger and defensiveness, was glorious.

I was given all the credit. Even Bernard Cornelis strode up one day when I was emptying a bucket of swill into the pigpen. 'What have you done to that daughter of mine?' he asked, or something like that – my Flemish had progressed a little, but not enough to keep up with Meneer Cornelis in this rare, genial mood. I smiled, shook my head and endured a few awkward minutes of stilted conversation before at last he went away. Staring after that stolid, irascible figure, I wondered for the thousandth time what on earth had persuaded Fleur to marry him.

It was that same evening when Estelle told me that her mother and my Pa had been lovers during the hours before she was arrested. The foundations upon which my world had been built shook as I lay awake contemplating the possibility that it was not treachery that had done for Fleur Cornelis-Faider, but lust. And my father.

The sexual act, from which I had been so sheltered at home, was a constant theme at De Eikenhoeve. One night I was kept awake by the creaking of the boards above my bed, faster and faster, and when it was over I heard the heavy tread of male feet and the closing of a door. Despite my inexperience I was pretty sure what Roos was up to, and with whom, and largely thanks to Wiertz I could envisage a tangle of limbs, the spreading of her plump thighs, the panting of her sullen mouth.

And the farm, of course, was all about sex, or reproduction – the rough lick of a calf's tongue, the drowsy plunderings of a bumble bee, the hot hairy mass of an udder or the urgent sucking of a piglet at its mother's teat. In the fields, the men worked bare-chested and the women fanned themselves as they lay in the shade at mealtimes with their skirts pulled up above their knees and their blouses half undone, or they knelt at the river bank and trickled cool water between their breasts. One evening as I took the long way up to the house, by the river and along the side of the hayfield, I stumbled across lovers on the far side of a hedge. I just prevented myself in time from opening the gate to investigate the rhythmic grunts and a long female sigh.

I had been on my way back to Fleur's swing, erected by Bernard

Cornelis in a hollow behind the oak tree. This had become one of my favourite spots. The gentle motion of air on my cheeks soothed me, and I leant so far back on the ropes that my hair, at the lowest point of the arc, swept along the grass. I was hoping Estelle might come looking for me, but in the end it was Pieter who appeared on the slope above.

'Good idea,' he said, flinging himself down in the grass. He leant on his elbows and dropped his head back with exhaustion. 'Nice and cool.'

I dug my heels into the ground and the swing slowed.

'Where would we have been without you, Juffrouw Christa? I've been looking for an opportunity to thank you – not least for persuading Estelle to help us out.'

'There's no need. I'm loving it.'

He now lay full length, his arms behind his head, and closed his eyes.

'And yet you'll be leaving us soon.'

He was the image of a fallen giant, throat and forearms bare, his mouth, curved into a half-smile, very much like his mother's and Estelle's.

'Perhaps it's just as well,' he added.

'Because of the war?'

'The war, yes. And for the sake of all our poor hearts. Estelle's especially.' Shading his face with his forearm, he grinned up at me. 'Mine, you'll be glad to hear, is better guarded. But Estelle – now she has been a different woman since you came here.'

'It's the same for me,' I murmured as I got up from the swing. 'I've never had a friend like her.'

'Have you thought about what will happen to her when you go home?'

'I'm sure we'll write to each other and meet up again when we can.'

'Letters won't be enough.' He held out his hand and drew me down beside him. 'Don't look so worried, it's not your fault. Estelle seems so tough on the outside, but inside she's as soft as anything, like the rest of us.' He grinned and brushed my calf playfully with the back of his index finger. 'By the way, she tells me that you met Père Borland in Brussels. You really did have an adventurous time. I can't remember when I saw him.'

'It was quite by chance.'

He sat up and gestured to Swart, who lurched to his feet and nuzzled Pieter's hand. 'Nothing happens by chance where Borland is concerned. What did you make of him?'

'I didn't speak to him for long enough to form an opinion.'

'Oh come now, Juffrouw, you can't expect me to believe that. I've noticed how you keep your eye on us all.'

'Obviously I was very interested to meet him; I knew he'd been an important figure in your mother's life.'

'That's putting it mildly, wouldn't you say? He led Maman's memorial service, you know, in Brussels Cathedral, about five years after the war. A huge number of people came because by then Maman was recognised as a heroine of the Resistance. I remember sitting in the front row between Papa and Robbe with this great swelling of voices behind me, singing 'La Brabançonne'. According to Grand-mère, it's highly unusual for the national anthem to be sung in church and therefore the ultimate tribute to Maman. On Papa's instruction, Marthe stayed at home with Estelle, which I can't help thinking was a mistake. I'm sure both were longing to come.

'Anyway, Borland's sermon was on the subject of commitment. Having met him, you can probably imagine how powerful that was. He said Maman had been committed to the ideal of freedom; that he had been privileged to know her, and that he had never met anyone with such a potent spirit.'

'And your father was there.'

'Oh yes. He was there. He'd specifically invited Borland to give the eulogy.' A shaft of evening sunlight burnished his short hair, the same glinting gold as Estelle's.

'It must have been such a moving service, on so many counts,' I said carefully.

'Oh it was.' If he was aware of any irony, he gave nothing away, except for a slight watchfulness in his eyes, which were narrowed against the evening sun. 'For Robbe and me it was very strange to have our mother suddenly dusted off, as it were, and presented as this heroic figure. We'd got used to nobody really talking about her, and suddenly there were hundreds of people in black praising her and wanting to shake our hands. Robbe hated it, as you can imagine. He kept squirming and refused to speak to anyone. And then we all paraded to the square and Papa had to unveil her statue and we just stood there thinking: That's not our Maman. They've made her look like a saint. She wasn't a saint and she never wore her hair loose like that.'

'Oh Pieter, did you know ... has Estelle told you yet ... my father was present at her arrest?'

'What are you talking about?' He grasped my upper arm and looked at me more closely. 'Hey, what's the matter?'

'He was there. He saw it all. And he delayed her.'

The cost of telling him the full story was a flood of tears and he drew me into his arms and held me, resting his cheek in my hair and murmuring as if I were his pet calf. 'Come now. This was all so long ago. Maman would have taken full responsibility for all her decisions and perhaps, looking at it objectively, she was almost bound to get caught in the end. From what I can gather, the Resistance line she belonged to was vulnerable from start to finish. They were so unprofessional that half of Belgium could have known what was going on. She might have been betrayed by any number of people, or simply have been unlucky. Maman was far from perfect, I'm well aware of that. She was not faithful, after all.'

'What do you mean?'

'To us. She was unfaithful to Papa – we all know that – and by default she was therefore unfaithful to us. If she slept with your father I'm not really surprised because I've always suspected there must have been a few such affairs. That's war for you. But think how dangerous it was for a woman in her position to be so careless about people's trust. That's no way to win friends. So dry those tears, it's not your fault.'

He got up and pulled me to my feet, produced a large handkerchief, dabbed my face and kissed my hot forehead. 'You have brought us such joy, Juffrouw Christa. Perhaps by visiting us you have shone a light into some rather murky places, but that's OK. These things are much better out in the open.'

Like old friends, we walked to the house and I felt better, as if I'd been exonerated.

Estelle

The blow fell ten days after the hay had been cut. Oud Daan appeared at the door during dinner, cap in hand and eyes narrowed to the point of disappearing. 'I've been down to the river. Storms are coming. The hay must be brought in.'

After he'd shuffled away there remained more than a whiff of unwashed flesh.

Papa shoved his plate aside. 'Nothing ever goes right for me. That's much too early. It won't be dry. I was sure we would have a good crop this year. Typical.'

'He didn't say it would actually rain tomorrow,' Marthe said, 'just that we should begin the harvest.'

'I was relying on the barns being full this winter. With a war coming, the last thing we need is to be forced to buy in hay.'

The plates were cleared and the tart brought, but nobody ate much. All I could think about was that after the harvest there would be nothing to keep Christa at De Eikenhoeve.

I invited her to walk with me by the river. There was silence at the table when I said that, as if they all knew what was going on in my head. Everyone watched us leave. Christa said she would go upstairs to collect another layer of clothing and meet me under the arch. Our elbows touched as we stood in the hall, and it was like a jolt of electricity.

In the late evening the ducks were dawdling across the pond. 'Some of them will end up in the pot this winter,' I said. She was wearing her London raincoat. A cautious girl, Christa. The air was cool and the hedgerows full of teasels and brambles – more than a touch of autumn, though it was still high summer. Christa said she liked the thistle heads almost more than any other flower. I didn't really believe her. When she said these things they were too well-formed, as if she were trying to be a poet. I leant over the parapet of the bridge and stared down at the water.

'Please don't go home after the harvest,' I said. 'Please stay.'

'Would there be any work for me, do you think?'

'You don't have to work.'

'I do, Estelle. I've barely enough money for the journey home as it is.'

'Stay because you're my friend.'

'Ma wants me to go home. She's nervous about the war.'

'Do you always have to do what your mother says?'

She bit her lip and went rather pale. I hated myself for turning the screw.

'How can Oud Daan be so sure the rain is coming anyway?' she asked. 'This evening seems like every other.'

'He'll have looked at whether the midges are hanging low over the water, and he'll have watched how the fish are behaving, and the water voles. He can probably sniff rain in the air. He knows every inch of this farm. If we kick a pebble out of place tonight, he'll notice tomorrow morning.'

'I don't think Oud Daan's spoken more than three words to me since I've been here.'

'That's because he hates strangers. All he cares about is De Eikenhoeve, Papa and Pieter, probably in that order.'

'What about his own son?'

We laughed and set off again, the tension between us slightly lessened. I was leading her far away from everyone, along the river in the direction of Oostervorken. Above us in the hayfield the cut grass had been raked into windrows. 'Zwad, in Flemish,' I told her.

'Windrow's a much nicer word.'

The evening was fair and warm, with a pinkish light to the west. Nobody except Oud Daan could have predicted rain. Scooping up a handful of hay, I made her sniff its sweet, mellow fragrance. When she bowed her head her hair parted slightly and I wanted to kiss her there, on the nape of her neck.

Instead I said: 'I have to admit, I do love the hay harvest. It's an exact science, all this drying and raking, because if you treat the grass roughly you crush the goodness out of it. And then the animals are less healthy through the winter because they have to eat lower grade hay. There's something rather awe-inspiring about that chain of events, don't you think? Cause and effect.'

'You see, you really are a farmer's daughter.'

'Is that all I am?' I gathered up some hay and rushed at her, stuffed a handful down the neck of her dress and rubbed it into her hair. When I ran away she raced after me, shrieking with laughter, arms also full of hay. I held her at bay while she tried to reach me; she seemed to give up suddenly, then ducked under my arm and came up close. There we were, our faces inches apart, laughing.

I didn't think, I just took her face between my hands and kissed her on the mouth. This time she didn't respond at all. Her arms hung by her sides and she was utterly still. When I released her she just stared at me, then sank down in the hay as if all the strength had gone out of her. We were near the riverbank, by a grove of young birches. On the far side of the river, barley stood waist high.

'I can't survive without you,' I said. 'Do you understand?'

'Don't say that.' Her brows were drawn together and she wouldn't look at me.

'I love you, Christa.'

'I didn't know . . . I didn't think . . .'

I sat so close that our knees touched. 'You did. You did know.'

'Please don't say any more. Please don't spoil it.'

'You sound like a little girl.'

'You know damn well I'm not a little girl. You know damn well how strange this must be for me.'

'I thought you felt the same way as I do.'

She leant back on her hands and closed her eyes so that her lashes formed dark semicircles. I moved closer still, knotted my legs and arms through hers, pressed her forehead to mine. And the miracle was that she kissed me. She did. She bit her bottom lip and her eyes were stormy as she tilted her head away, but then she kissed my cheek, nose and chin with kisses soft as petals. Sighing, she touched my face and looked at me as I've never been looked at in my entire life. Her smile was tentative and wondering. Then she kissed my mouth.

140

I thought she was mine. I thought I had captured her because her mouth was so soft and daring and inquisitive. Because she let me press her down into the hay and hold her in my arms. Her hair was downy soft and her body hot through the fabric of her dress. I ached for her and was perhaps too bold and too sudden as I laid my hand on her breast and ran my tongue along her teeth. 'Christa. Christa.'

She gasped as I lay above her and edged my knee deep between her legs, and kissed the pulse in her throat. When I buried my lips in the hollow beneath her ear her hair smelt of the hayfield and I whispered words of love and longing until she seemed to melt beneath me.

But then, suddenly, I felt a pressure on my shoulder and I realised she was pushing me away.

'No. No . . .'

I kissed her lips more softly, but this time she turned aside her face. 'No. This is . . . wrong . . .'

'It's not wrong, it's right. We've known that all summer.'

'Please, Estelle. Someone will see.'

'No one will come.'

'They may come. They know we're here.'

'What do I care?'

'Please. I don't want to hurt you. This isn't what I want. I don't understand it. Please, Estelle.' She gave me another little push and this time I rolled off her.

The pain, initially, was in my belly, but with every word it spread like poison. 'How could this hurt us, if we love each other?'

'And I do love you. I do; but I'm not sure . . .'

'Then what's the matter with you? Why did you kiss me? Are you playing games with me?'

'It's not a game. I've been so happy here with you. But it's too . . . strange. Perhaps it's not real.' She was tugging at her clothes to get them straight, brushing the hay out of her hair.

'Of course it's real. Don't you know that? My God, Christa, I would die for you.'

'I don't *want* you to die for me. I just want us to be close, to love each other, like . . . Like sisters.'

141

I gripped her arms. 'I thought better of you. How do you think I feel now, to have been led on like this?'

'I didn't want to hurt you. That's the last thing I wanted.'

She tried to hold my hand but I was way beyond rescuing. I wrenched free and stood up. 'Well you have. You've broken me. I feel broken inside.'

As I ran, she called after me. 'I'm sorry, I'm so sorry.'

'Stop saying that. You're weak and despicable.'

'It's because I do love you . . .' she said, struggling to keep up. 'I can't work out what is happening.'

'Oh God, I wish you'd never written that fucking letter.'

'Estelle, please wait.'

I raced along the path, tearing my frock and stinging my legs.

Pieter and Oud Daan were on the bridge. I couldn't speak to them, just ran up the track towards the house.

Christa

Ever since our return from Brussels, or perhaps before then, in the gallery or the cathedral or when we viewed her mother's statue, I had been waiting for something to happen. Every time we touched or linked arms, I had felt an unknown craving for a different, more significant touch, further pressure on my hand, a caress somewhere a little more hidden. Every time she smiled at me, I wanted her smile to be more specific, more focused on me. When she said, after dinner, watching me: 'If it's going to rain, Christa and I should make the most of the time we have left. We'll go for a walk by the river,' I knew that this was the moment.

In my room, as I picked up my coat, I caught sight of myself in the mirror, very flushed and bright-eyed. I didn't hang about to witness Christine Geering in the act of leaving the room. I ran down to Estelle and we set off, keeping ourselves at a distance and talking about the rain. I was in an agony of yearning – for exactly what, I did not know. But if I was to return later to the house with nothing having happened between us, I thought I would disintegrate. I was as aware of her as I was of my own self, the fine blonde hairs on her forearms, the freckle on the knuckle beneath her middle finger.

But also, beyond the stillness of the evening, the voice of my conscience was still feebly chattering away: You don't really want her. Not in that way. You're mad. She's your friend. What would they say back home? Yet the further we walked from the house, the more I thought: I must touch her.

The next step was as natural as the whispering of the wind in the birch trees. I kissed her and her lips told me that she loved me. Her kiss was warmer and softer than the kisses we'd

143

exchanged after I'd nearly drowned, a kiss accompanied by the call of a drowsy bird and the rustle of some little creature nearby.

Then she kissed me again, her tongue brushing my teeth and the inside of my lip, and I wondered where her hand would fall next. She was so confident that I knew she must have done this with other women. Her knee worked its way between my thighs and I felt her fingers flutter on my stomach just beneath my navel, undoing the buttons of my dress. I opened my eyes as she touched me, and looked up at the flickering green of the birch trees and I remembered the man who had drowned in that river and been so dreadfully disfigured by the time he was discovered that even brave Pieter hadn't dared touch him. Darkness gathered in my head and I thought of Fleur flitting from tree to tree in a long pale gown and Pa stumbling after her. And far away, in Harewood Road, I knew that my parents were sitting either side of the hearth, glued to the wireless, and fearing for my future.

Estelle murmured: 'I love you, I love you, I love you, Christa,' as her hand touched my breast in an act of such astonishing intimacy that my entire body convulsed and I heard myself gasp.

'It's all right. I'll look after you. I'll be so gentle.'

'No.'

She kissed my mouth again, softly, and my legs were parting and my breasts aching. 'You are my Christa,' she whispered. 'This was meant to be.'

And then I thought of her mother, my father, like this in the woods. I saw them, even heard the crackle of dried leaves under their heads, and felt the coolness of the night air on exposed skin, the absolute need for connection. And the stealing of time, when there had been no time, the clamour of nerves, those few moments of oblivion whilst their enemy was already climbing into a van, fully armed, poised for the kill.

I felt the weight of Estelle's body, the strangeness of her touch, the salt taste of her mouth, and I knew a second before it happened that I'd detached myself from the present moment too far and that I would push her away. At once, her body hardened and her eyes went cold. I couldn't save myself, or her, as she ripped herself away from me. I was already afraid of her and her lacerating tongue; I knew myself to be guilty of everything she'd accused me of, there was nothing I could say except sorry as I stumbled back to the farmhouse.

Pieter and Oud Daan were on the bridge. 'Well,' said Pieter, 'what's the verdict? Do you think it's going to rain?'

Estelle marched away without a word.

'Of course it will rain if that's what Oud Daan says,' I muttered.

'If only it wasn't true,' said Pieter. 'But it's got very dark. Do you need a guide back to the house?'

I refused his outstretched arm. 'I'm familiar with the lane now.'

I blundered through the pitch darkness, aware of them watching me. When a cobweb brushed my face I snatched at it with both hands, clawing at thin air.

Estelle

The pain of losing Christa. Every thought crushed, sensation dulled and a throbbing knowledge that something irreversible had happened and that life would never be right again.

After she'd rejected me I went up to the loft above Maman's room in the turret. I saw Christa trail back across the farmyard, a glimpse of her yellow cardigan beneath her raincoat the only bright spot, watched her until she disappeared out of sight.

I had orchestrated this pain, worked at it with red hot pincers. That old feeling, like when the boys had disappeared and left me running along the passages looking for them until Marthe caught up with me and forced me to sit in her parlour and play dominoes. Or when the kids at school talked about their mothers. I'd wanted to slash their faces and burn the place down. Now my eyes were dry and stinging, my brain ice cold.

Why allow me to get so close and then push me away? To kiss her. Dear God, the beauty of her mouth. To feel the heat of her body, the soft curve of her breast, the ladder of her ribs. To see her mouth swollen with desire, feel her hand gentle on my shoulder, guiding me towards, not away. She had put her hands to my face so I would kiss her more deeply, allowed me to touch her. The scent of her; she was river and woods and grass and sweetness. She had quivered like a new-born lamb.

And then, 'No,' she said. 'No. No.'

I lay on my bed until dawn and relived every moment. Had she been teasing me all along, was that it? Or had I misread her completely? Perhaps she was so frightened and inexperienced that she had played along until she was in danger of getting burnt and then her tepid love had cooled. If she was such a coward, so indecisive, I wanted to have nothing to do with her.

She'd promised me everything and given me nothing. She was a wrecker, just like her father.

I considered escaping to Brussels, but that would have left her in possession of my home, my harvest. So I got up at dawn and took my breakfast to the fields. Even Hanna and Lotte were at the haymaking. It was a cloudy morning, no rain yet.

Every single person except Christa was in the fields, even the ancient ones who could barely lift a rake. I fell over a pair of infants asleep in a hay nest. Jong Daan was up in the saddle of the tractor, which was belching filthy smoke. This was the climax of his year. He was dumb with anxiety because the machine was bound to break down again at some stage. The older men and women hated the tractor and willed it to fail. In the next field the plough horses never faltered. When the tractor ground to a halt, Papa perched in the saddle, slammed the gearstick back and forth and swore at Jong Daan. Exactly the same as in other years. Weber strolled over, grinning and superior.

I claimed my usual place with a pitchfork and fed the baler. Nearly forgot myself for a while because I loved the soft piles of hay, the sweet smell of it. Innocent sounds. I took this all for granted because I believed it would always be there if I wanted it.

We heaped hay bales onto the wagon until it was on the brink of toppling. Roos perched on top and it swayed across the field, tilting perilously so she squealed and clutched at the bales. As the wagon lurched off along the lane, we all waved. There was no sign of Christa until after ten o'clock when I saw her standing at the gate, wondering what to do. I ignored her and immersed myself in working with Mietje and Roos, who probably guessed something of what was going on and were therefore enjoying themselves all the more. I knew Christa was there on the fringes, trying to catch my eye, cold-shouldered by the three of us.

I was bleeding for her.

At lunch I heard her ask Marthe if she might help with the serving. Almost weeping, she was, when she approached me with a bowl of plums.

'No thanks,' I said.

'I'll fetch you some blackcurrants if you like.'

'Don't bother.'

147

After that she worked with Marthe in the next field. Her job was to rake up loose hay and keep an eye on the children by the hedge. She was going to be a teacher after all. 'It's high time she did something useful,' I told Pieter. He looked at me reproachfully and went and chatted to her, and I felt ashamed.

The tractor recovered by the afternoon but always seemed perilously close to stalling once more, and Weber was forever fiddling about with a spanner. Pieter said it was now less likely we'd be done by tomorrow evening. Despite the strain of organising the harvest, he was the opposite of Papa – calm and endlessly patient. The women glanced at me occasionally and whispered behind their hands. They must have wondered why I was working so hard and why I kept my distance from my hitherto soulmate *de engelse vreemdeling*.

By mid-afternoon we were exhausted and kept straightening up to ease our shoulders. Suddenly I noticed a figure with a slight swagger walking slowly up from the river. Lotte dropped her rake. One of the other girls cried out: 'It's Robbe.'

And it really was him, with his shirtsleeves rolled up, a cigarette balanced on his lip, the glimmer of a smile in his eyes. The other women stopped work. One or two fell back, a bit shy, others edged closer. He shook their hands, winked at Mietje, flung his arm around my neck, kissed me and looked about him: 'Where's Christa?'

Christ. Did no one care about anyone else? I pointed to the other field and he raised an eyebrow at me. When he threw his shirt aside I saw that he had put on muscle and had a wicked-looking scar on his shoulder. Papa strode across, shook him by the hand and held him for a moment, awkward as ever. Marthe came bustling up to offer him food, but he refused. Someone must have let Pieter know, because he came striding down from the barns, ran the last few yards and hugged Robbe, then drew back and grinned. 'You've put everyone off their stride.'

'Good. I expect you've been working them into the ground.'

Christa kept her distance.

Robbe was in an excellent mood, flirting with the girls, exchanging banter with the men, asking after everyone, especially Lise, a

148

favourite of his who'd wed a distant cousin when she heard he'd gone off to Spain. We'd not seen her since, so we teased Robbe and blamed him for breaking her heart. Grass cuts in my fingers, the peppery smell of the hay, the drone of an insect, the skitter of a snake when a pitchfork jabbed a warm heap, Flemish voices. In Robbe's hands the pitchfork was an extra limb and the hay flew into the baler. He had extraordinary stamina. On form, he inspired others so that we worked faster, cracked more jokes, sang louder.

Papa strode about, egged on his men, worked alongside them until Marthe begged him to slow down for the sake of his heart. She was expert at tidying up the bales and tucking in stray ends. Pieter went back to the yard to supervise the winch and pack the hay into the barn. I caught sight of Christa sometimes and felt sick.

At teatime she sidled up and said: 'It's wonderful to be part of a ritual that has happened for centuries.'

'I'm going to Brussels on Friday morning, first thing,' I told her. 'What you do after that is up to you. Neither of us will be needed here any more.'

'Then I'll come with you to Bruxelles-Midi and take the train home.'

'Suit yourself.'

'Estelle ... please ...'

I walked away to where Robbe was examining the troublesome tractor with Weber and Jong Daan. He didn't make eye contact, just rested his arm around my waist as I stood beside him. An uncharacteristic gesture. In the circumstances, I was delighted he'd claimed me and hoped Christa had noticed. After a bit he lay down on his back so he could examine the vehicle's underbelly. Weber shoved tools into his outstretched hands, one after another. In ten minutes Robbe emerged, smutty-faced and grinning. God knows where he'd learnt mechanics. Everyone applauded and he gave an ironic bow. Christa had long since gone back to work.

By evening we'd filled another two wagonloads and were staggering with exhaustion. Robbe and I perched on top of the hay bales in Oud Daan's wagon, like we had when we were children.

I pretended not to notice what Christa was doing, but I knew that Pieter had marched up to her and was pointing out that she'd left that famous yellow cardigan on a distant fence post. We turned into the lane and lost sight of them.

Robbe lit a cigarette.

'Are you crazy?' I said. 'You'll set us on fire.'

'Of course I'm crazy. Didn't you know?'

'Why are you here, really?'

'To celebrate Papa's feast day. And it could be that I need money. And to see you, of course.'

'I'm very touched.'

There was a pause while he took a drag on his cigarette. 'So what's gone wrong between you and Christa?'

'Nothing. She's going home on Friday and I can't wait.'

'You've changed your tune.'

'I've had enough of her. I want to get back to Brussels.'

He pressed his shoulder against mine: 'Did she reject you, is that it?'

'Fuck off.'

'Or is it to do with Pieter? Has he made a play for her?'

'I've no idea.'

'Whatever happened, you're being very mean. Shouldn't you be taking care of her?'

'Don't be ridiculous. She's a grown woman.'

We reached the gate where the other labourers were clustered, waiting for Pieter to give instructions for the next day.

When the last wagon lurched into sight, Christa was up front with Pieter, tucked under his arm in fact, and he was smiling, his left hand holding the reins, his right on her shoulder just above the breast. She was smiling too, though it wasn't her normal smile. Her eyes were too bright and I knew she was hating every moment of the attention and trying to stop herself looking across at me. Everyone else stood aside and cheered them through. Not Roos, obviously. Only Robbe and Roos and I failed to cheer.

Christa

I thrashed about until dawn, reliving every catastrophic moment by the river with Estelle, then woke at eight o'clock to an eerily silent house. Downstairs, Hanna was not at the stove, the hot plates were barely warm and even Lotte was absent from her station at the scullery sink. When I knocked at Estelle's door, I found her bed empty and in the family dining room a single portion of breakfast had been left under a muslin frame.

Through the open window came the contented chook chook of the chickens and the lowing of a cow. A vast refrigerator, Hanna's pride and joy, chuntered in a distant scullery. Somewhere deep in the house a door creaked shut and I thought that Estelle might have come back for me, so I hurried from room to room, dashed back up to my bedroom, then along the first-floor passages, peering from every window in case she was under the oak tree, or by the gate, or calling to me from the drive, but there was no sign.

At the base of the turret, I happened upon a door to a staircase spiralling down into a flagged underground chamber containing a rusty wheelbarrow and other tools. If the door had slammed shut, locking me in, I'd have been lost, perhaps for days, and yet I could not resist penetrating deeper into the cellars, hoping that in the end I might emerge by the kitchen.

Electric wiring must have been laid fairly recently, and I followed a trail from one light switch to the next, from barrels of beer to piles of tarpaulins to boxes of jam jars. Each room or cell was cave-like, with low stone beams and shelves or cubbyholes, most of them empty. And gradually, as a little natural light trickled through high bottle-glass windows, I arrived in territory that felt more familiar because it was scented with preserved fruit

151

and fermentation. And there, blocking my way, was a quavering shadow, wreaking of nicotine.

I crept closer. Oud Daan was peering at me, an unlit cigarette between the finger and thumb of his right hand.

'I was lost,' I said, and when he didn't stir, I brushed past him and ran upstairs.

I tried to convince myself I didn't care what he thought, and that neither of us need ever consider the other again after Friday, but I couldn't help thinking that he'd been looking for me, perhaps with the intention of catching me out.

When at last I turned up in the hayfields, Marthe, in a full skirt and apron, like a picture-book version of a Belgian peasant, told me that she'd suggested waking me but Estelle had insisted I needed sleep. Meneer Cornelis nodded in my direction. Pieter was at work in another field and Estelle, who was toiling away with rare diligence, ignored me. Roos, whose drawstring blouse barely covered her bosom, worked like a fury on the hay wagon, rising higher and higher above the field until she had to leap down into Jong Daan's arms.

Oud Daan eventually reappeared behind me and offered me a rake with tines so worn that it was virtually useless and I spent the morning gathering up wisps of hay. No sooner had I tossed my pathetic offerings into the trailer than they blew out again.

Estelle was behaving so coldly that I was torn between an angry desire to keep my distance and a childlike longing to make up with her before it was too late. But there was no point preparing speeches or working out how we might be reconciled; she wouldn't let me near. The sky was overcast and there was little banter, only the whisper of metal through hay, the occasional muttered instruction, the grinding of the engine and bad-tempered cursing when the tractor broke down.

In the afternoon, work suddenly ceased as one labourer after another straightened up and squinted down towards the river. In my misery I followed their gaze and recognised Robbe Cornelis sauntering up the path by the hedge. There was no mistaking him, even from a distance: bare head tilted to one side, jacket hooked over one shoulder and battered satchel slung across the other.

The girls ran their fingers through their hair and brushed hay from their skirts, grinning as he greeted each one by name. Bernard Cornelis approached to embrace his prodigal son. He really did seem genuinely pleased that Robbe was home. Pieter vaulted a gate in his eagerness and the next minute the three Cornelis siblings had their arms about each other, heads pressed close. The only outsider that afternoon was me.

As I resumed my work, I was ever conscious of Estelle and Robbe in the far field. Stripped to the waist, he worked like a demon, hay flying from his pitchfork. There was about him an aura of indifference that conversely made everyone aware of him all the time, as if he were an actor in the starring role, measuring the effect of every gesture.

For some reason he pretended not to notice me. At one point he came closer to speak to Mietje but turned away at the precise moment that I glanced up. During the break he sat among the labourers and threw back his head to drink directly from one of the great demijohns of water Marthe had brought in the cart. As he lowered his eyes to wipe his mouth on his sleeve, his gaze skimmed away from mine. By the end of the afternoon he had only acknowledged my existence by looking through me.

Meanwhile, Estelle's hostility was palpable, even from a field's distance. I felt both ashamed and exposed to know that everyone must be wondering what had happened between us. Time and again I imagined flinging down my rake and walking away from them all, collecting my suitcase and heading for the station, but because the lane ran alongside the hayfield, everyone would have witnessed my departure and I couldn't bear the explanations or the ignominy of slinking away.

As the day's final load was being hitched to the plough horses, Pieter rescued me at last. 'Isn't that your cardigan on the fence post?' he said. 'Run and fetch it.'

'Thank you. I would have forgotten it.'

'I need someone to sit beside me and keep an eye on the load. Would you mind, Christa?'

We rode side by side on the wagon, the mountainous stacks of hay creaking behind us, the dog trotting ahead. This was the fifth or sixth time since the morning that the great horses had made the journey, ears flicking, their huge flanks mottled with age.

Once we were through the field gate, Pieter took the reins in one hand and hugged me close to him. 'I hope we haven't worked you too hard.'

'Not at all.'

'Estelle's such an asset when she really pulls up her sleeves, and it's all thanks to you.'

'Oh I don't think so.'

'I have a feeling you two have fallen out and I hate to see you so sad. I know what Estelle can be like.'

'I should have listened to what you said. I'm going home on Friday and these last few days are bound to be difficult for us.'

'Well, let me know if I can help. Estelle can be a tricky customer. I don't want to see you unhappy, dear Christa, and of course I don't want either of you to be hurt.'

'I'm afraid it's too late.'

He kissed the top of my head and I subsided gratefully against him so that I was tucked under his arm and my head rested on the soft fabric of his shirt. It was such a relief to be spoken to kindly and to be held close for a moment, although I was shocked to see that when we reached the open gate a crowd was waiting to cheer us through.

Roos wasn't smiling. Her eyes were full of envy, and I now saw that Estelle and Robbe were also watching, so the moment of respite became something more complicated. By the time I'd extracted myself from beneath Pieter's arm the group had split up, but I walked over to Robbe so he couldn't evade me again. 'You're back for the harvest?'

I was rewarded with a mischievous smile. 'I'm back for *you*, Mademoiselle Christa. I wanted to see what you were up to. And because talking to you at the Prospero triggered a memory. I need to show you something. But for now you'll just have to be patient.'

That night I had to endure a meal at which all the Cornelis siblings were present. We ate in the formal dining room at such a distance from the kitchen that the food was half cold by the time it arrived. There were cabinets of antique glassware and still lifes in oil of fruit and fish and dusty bottles. A massive dresser displayed an unused dinner service.

Marthe, dressed in an embroidered silk dress, took her place to her husband's right and smiled with satisfaction at the six place settings. 'Finally, we're all together again.'

Meneer Cornelis usually liked to be last at table, to make the point that he was rushed off his feet and could only just squeeze in mealtimes, but Robbe was later still. Pieter was dressed in a gleaming white shirt and his hair was damp from a bath but Robbe, when he lurched in halfway through the soup course, wore the shirt that had been crumpled up in the hay and wreaked of alcohol and tobacco.

'I had a lot of catching up to do with the lads.' Hooking his arm over the back of his chair, he waved aside Hanna's offer of soup and lit up a cigarette.

'Not at dinner,' said his father sharply. 'The rules haven't changed.'

'The smoke gets into these heavy old fabrics,' murmured Marthe. She glanced at me apologetically, aware that by this stage of my visit I understood a great deal of what was being said, and continued brightly: 'We hear you've been living in Brussels for the last few months, Robbe. How are things there?'

He gave her the sullen stare of a teenager. '*Things* are as you'd expect.'

'And you have a nice new job with a newspaper?'

'I lost it.'

'For Christ's sake,' said Bernard Cornelis.

Robbe, as he watched Mietje collect the soup plates, crumbled a roll and grinned. 'The hours were unreasonable. I couldn't stick them.'

'That's newspapers for you,' said Marthe and my heart bled for her eagerness to get something right.

Because this conversation was in Flemish I'd so far had a legitimate excuse for not joining in, but Pieter said kindly in French, 'Christa's father is in the print industry.'

'So he is. I expect he has to work shifts too,' cried Marthe, but the subject of my Pa was of course a loaded one and Estelle pushed back her chair impatiently while the men reverted to Flemish and engaged in a terse conversation about Robbe's prospects of getting another job.

'I shall probably go abroad again,' Robbe said, having taken a few mouthfuls of chicken and thrown down his knife and fork. 'But I'll need money in the meantime. That's why I'm here. I thought I could earn a few shillings helping with the harvest. I've done the equivalent of at least two days' labour already, wouldn't you say?'

'I'm sure we can—' Pieter began, but Bernard Cornelis cut in. 'I'm not paying my own son to work on his own farm.'

'It's hardly my farm,' Robbe said mildly.

'You've sponged off us enough. Stand on your own bloody two feet,' Bernard Cornelis said. 'I'd have been ashamed to ask my father—'

'Bernard . . .' Marthe placed a hand on his arm.

'What do you think, Christa,' said Estelle suddenly. 'Do you think Robbe has the right to claim money off his father?'

For a stunned moment they all glanced at me. Pieter came to my rescue. 'Let's discuss it later. You fixed the tractor, Robbe, and I definitely owe you for that. You're a genius. Where on earth did you learn about engines?'

'Any fool could have worked it out,' Robbe said with a fraternal grin.

'Well thank God the right fool arrived at the right moment. How long do you reckon on staying? You're of course welcome for as long as you want.'

'Oh yes, do stay,' said Marthe.

'I might have to, if there's no money forthcoming.'

Glancing hastily at his father's reddening face, Pieter asked: 'What's the general opinion in Brussels about whether or not our country is likely to remain neutral?'

'Of course we should remain neutral,' said Bernard Cornelis. 'What chance would we have, caught between warring nations, as usual?'

'The trouble is that no one will pay any attention to our neutrality,' said Pieter. 'The Germans have marched all over

156

Czechoslovakia, so what's to stop them marching all over us?'

'I've no doubt half the country will be delighted to toady up to Hitler,' said Robbe, looking pointedly at his father.

'What are you suggesting?'

'Given this farm's record in the last war, you're likely to do very well out of trade with the Nazis.'

'That's enough,' said Bernard and this time Robbe gave him a long, insolent smile, picked up his matches and cigarettes, and left the table.

Marthe, her eyes bright with tears, called for Hanna and the girls to clear the main course and bring in the dessert.

Estelle

On Papa's feast day, Marthe asked Christa to help in the kitchen. It was a relief that she was out of sight. I'd rather not find out how much I could make her suffer.

But while I worked in the hayfields my mind was on Christa. I knew Hanna would have set her to work, slicing onions for the beef pies and chopping parsley to garnish the hams, washing the salads and slicing the tomatoes, fetching tablecloths and heaps of plates and cutlery from the cellars, setting up the tables, decking them with flowers, hanging up the lanterns, spooning pickles from the jars, whipping the cream. The kitchen would be a hive; the women clustered round the table, munching on titbits, gossiping about who would flirt with whom at the party. That kitchen used to be my kingdom on Papa's feast day. Nose level with the tabletop, I had perched on a stool and scraped out the cream bowl.

Robbe threw himself into the work once more and even the tractor behaved when he was in the fields. By five the hay was in and it still hadn't rained. The party was due to begin at six, so I went upstairs to put on my best dress. There was no time for a bath.

I looked in the mirror – blank eyes, sulky mouth. Urged myself to forgive Christa. Told myself again: let it go, Estelle, imagine how much happier you'd feel if you and she were friends again. But I knew I wouldn't. By the time I went down, the tables were laden with food and Christa was running around trying to be useful in her best frock. The labourers had smartened themselves up and were hanging about, waiting for the party to begin, and Papa was under the arch preparing for his grand entrance. Lanterns, as yet unlit, were hanging from the barn doors and fence posts. The musicians were tuning up beside the pond and the ducks had scarpered. Beer barrels had been rolled out and tankards were at the ready. Christa avoided my eyes, and who could blame her?

I began to hate her more and more for how bad she made me feel. In the end, because of her, I ran up to Papa. 'Can we go for a swim, like in the old days?'

'Are you mad? Everything's ready.'

'Please, Papa.'

He had his eye on the beer keg and was in too mellow a mood to care.

'We'll be back within an hour. Surely the food can wait until then.'

Even I felt sorry for Marthe. She wanted everything to be perfect and the food would soon be spoiled. We were starving. Yet I grabbed a couple of bottles of wine, ran to the gate and yelled: 'Papa says, why not go for a swim?'

A pause in the chatter. Pieter stood at the head of the table, looking from face to face. Mietje and Roos and the girls from the dairy, Jong Daan, Weber, the other young people from the village. 'Shall we or shan't we?' he called. 'I tell you what, Christa's our special guest, so she must decide.' He held out his hand and she took it shyly.

Her frock skimmed her waist and flared at the hips. She had found time to brush her hair into my favourite style, in a wave above her ears, clipped into a mass at the back of her head. It hurt just to look at her.

Marthe was forcing a smile, as if to say: It's not important, it doesn't matter to me either way if you all swim while the food is kept waiting.

I waved a wine bottle. 'Let's swim.'

I ran and knew they'd follow, all the young people, two dozen or so of us hurtling down the track towards the bridge. Pieter too.

I felt wild and naughty, like a child. We raced down the lane, across the bridge and onto the path. Tiredness gone, I unbuttoned my dress as I ran, and took swigs from the bottle. In the woods, I ducked branches, yelled back at the others, dashed on.

159

I'd pulled my dress over my head well before I reached the river so I was in first, the water covering my head. I wanted to forget everything.

Robbe jumped on me. I tensed to the weight of him but was glad he still bothered to play with me. We raced round the island and came face to face with Jong Daan, poor lad. The water streamed from his hair as he bobbed beside me, tried to grab my hand and at the same time hide an erection. Roos had arrived on the bank, Mietje panting behind. They flung off their clothes and floundered into the water. Roos could hardly swim and squealed at Pieter for help. He strode up like a river god, water glinting on his chest, and floated her on his hand, her fat stomach perched on his palm.

Christa, the last to arrive – apart from poor little Lotte – stood for a minute under the trees, watching. I was absolutely sure she wouldn't dare swim because of what had happened the last time. And there was no way she'd strip in front of us all. But then she flung off her clothes and stood proudly in the cool air, with her delicate breasts and tanned arms, her dark eyes sparking defiance, slimmer and longer-limbed than most of the other girls.

A streak of white-hot desire ran through me and I ducked under and up again. Lotte, who was terrified of water and fully dressed apart from her clogs, clutched Christa's hand and squealed as they paddled. I ached to see Christa's kindness and beauty, and the stone that was my heart began to soften at last.

She glanced in my direction and away. The men were gawping. '*Zwem, Engels* Miss.' She squeezed Lotte's hand and let it go, then walked very deliberately deeper into the water, picked her way among the stones and dived under. When she bobbed up, her hair was black.

Jong Daan was chasing me and I lost sight of Christa for a while, then saw her with Pieter. 'Once round the island,' she cried in Flemish, and dived under again and, of course, we all followed. I chased her, thinking: Is she crazy? Dear God, don't let me lose her again.

My stupidity struck me at last, that I'd let these final days slip through my fingers. I remembered how I'd heaved her up through the water when she was drowning, the relief when she drew breath, cradling her in my arms, kissing her. I thought, when she comes up now, I'll hold her hand and apologise, I'll tell her we only have a few more hours together so let's make the most of them.

I bobbed up early, halfway along the far side of the island. No sign of Christa at first. And then her head appeared beside Robbe's. She was smiling at him and he was laughing and I lagged behind because it was quite obvious that she didn't need me after all.

Christa

On my last morning at De Eikenhoeve, Marthe took me aside and asked if I would mind helping out in the kitchen. 'I've had to release Mietje and Roos to the haymaking, so we really need an extra pair of hands.'

Marthe knew only too well what it was like to be cold-shouldered by Estelle so I was grateful to her, but fretful at being cooped up inside where I wasn't really needed. A couple of extra village women had already been drafted in to help prepare the mountains of food. Lotte, who rarely strung more than two or three words together, simply could not decide between a red ribbon and a yellow, and in the afternoon Marthe took me to her workroom and showed me the apricot silk bodice she'd been embroidering, proudly displayed on the dressmaker's dummy.

'Most of us like to wear traditional costume tonight,' she told me, 'though these days some of the girls prefer modern clothes, which I think is a shame. For as long as I can remember, Bernard's feast has been a rare opportunity to dress up.'

'I forget you have such a long connection with the farm.'

Her smile was somewhat less reserved than usual. 'One of my earliest memories is of leaping off a haystack here with the other children. This place always seemed heavenly to me. When Fleur offered me a job, I couldn't believe my luck.'

I had been so preoccupied with what might be happening in the harvest fields that it took me a while to realise what I was being offered. 'What was it like, working for Fleur?'

She laughed. 'I've been wondering when you would ask me that question. The answer is I loved every minute of it. I have never forgotten my first meeting with Fleur Cornelis-Faider at the welcome party they threw here when Bernard brought her

162

home from their honeymoon. We all knew that his parents weren't happy with his choice but they never missed the opportunity of putting on a show.

'We assembled in the grand dining room and Fleur came in wearing a shimmering green dress that simply bowled me over. She was sophisticated. Her hair was arranged in an elaborate style and she moved from one to another of us, shaking hands. She was much taller than we local women and she withdrew her hand too quickly from mine, but I sensed she was nervous and perhaps frightened, though some accused her of being stand-offish. Late in the afternoon she asked my name again and said that she hoped we might be friends. We were roughly the same age, you see.'

'And did you become friends?'

'Not until Pieter was born. That's when she really needed me. And we were never true friends because we weren't equals. She was my employer, first and last, although I was the one who taught her Flemish. When Robbe was born she invited me to live here as a permanent companion or nanny. Robbe was very special to me. Unlike Pieter, he was highly strung and anxious as a small child. He wouldn't fall asleep unless I was in the room, singing to him or reading a story.'

'The brothers are very different to each other,' I suggested cautiously.

'That's not unusual in families, is it? Anyway, Robbe was my excuse for staying. My parents were always nagging me to go home. They thought it was beneath me to be a servant, but once the war started I couldn't possibly leave the children when Fleur was so rarely in the house.'

'Were you aware of what she was doing?'

The question went unanswered while we listened to the clatter of dropped cutlery in the kitchen.

'I knew that it must be something of exceptional importance,' she said at last, 'to take her away from those little boys. They were so eager to please, scraping their plates clean, eyes bright, hair combed, always wanting to tell her everything. I told myself that whatever was drawing her away must really matter, if she was prepared to leave them so often. They would sit up in bed

163

for hours waiting for her to come up and kiss them goodnight, not realising that she was already gone from the house.' She spoke with so little emotion that I could not tell whether she was judging Fleur or simply stating facts.

'Marthe, do you think someone betrayed Fleur?'

'During the occupation we were all at risk of being reported for some crime or another. And people were careless.' She glanced at me a little wryly. 'I know that the children like to believe it was me.'

'But how can you bear it? Don't you want to prove them wrong?'

'It wouldn't make any difference. Robbe and Estelle will never forgive me for not being Fleur.'

She crossed to the door, then stood back to let me pass.

'Don't give up on Estelle. I was so pleased when she said she was bringing someone home. It's the first time in years. If she hasn't made it easy for you, put it down to lack of practice.'

When I went upstairs to change I saw the harvesters trailing home, bringing in the very last of the hay and actually singing. There they were, dressed in their clogs and old country clothes of muted greens and blues and yellows, carrying their tools, strung out in a long line on either side of the hay wagon driven by Oud Daan. Weber was arm in arm with Mietje, Pieter with Roos, while Robbe and Estelle lagged behind the others, deep in conversation. As they came closer I hung back, out of sight, in case anyone should glance up at my window.

An hour or so later, thirty or forty people gathered in the farmyard, including a mob of children who had their own table near the dairy adorned with balloons and parcels of sweets, wrapped by Lotte. Long trestles were so covered with food that scarcely an inch of white tablecloth was visible. Yet the minute Bernard Cornelis appeared under the arch in his best waistcoat and breeches, proud as punch, Estelle climbed onto a gate, clung on with one hand and yelled: 'Who's for a swim?'

The labourers must have been tired and hungry and it would only have taken Pieter to say: 'Let's get on with the meal,' for the moment to have passed. Instead, he looked at me. 'Well, Christa?'

164

But Estelle was already heading down the lane, leaving us no choice but to run after her. Heavy clouds had gathered and the woods were dark and gloomy, but the girls were shrieking with anticipation and dragging each other along, passing bottles of wine from hand to hand. I had a sense of hurtling headlong towards the end of my time at De Eikenhoeve, the unaccustomed wine churning my thoughts until I was beyond myself, detached from everybody else, already on my way home. Tree roots were fingers thrust deep into the earth and lichen clung like wool from the more sheltered branches.

By the time I reached the bathing pool, garments were strewn along the bank. The scene was nothing like those insipid pictures in the Musée Wiertz; these were working men and women, muscular and unselfconscious, although the men seemed more exposed than the women, their genitals vulnerable as they lunged at each other. I had a panicky sense of events veering out of control, like the evening I'd walked with Estelle to the hayfield by the birch grove on the night before the harvest. Weber was towing Mietje further downstream, where he placed his large tanned hands on her buttocks and drew her into such a deep kiss that in the end she wrapped her legs around his thighs and sank beneath the water with him.

Like an addict I sought out Estelle and there she was near the far end of the island. I felt the force of her consciousness reach out to me, though she would not relent long enough to meet my eye.

Well then, I thought, I'll go and get her. So I stripped off my clothes and grabbed Lotte's hand, but she giggled and shrieked and refused to venture more than ankle-deep.

Apparently most of the girls were reluctant to swim. They stuck to the shallows, gripping their arms round their breasts and kicking up spray to cover themselves. Some of them glanced slyly at me and then back at the men, who were using a knotted shirt as a ball, showing off, thigh-deep in the water.

Robbe, of course, was centre stage – stronger, quicker, more adept both in and out of the water, although he managed his superiority by playing the clown. His scars, a deep gouge across his right shoulder and a puckering in his abdomen, diminished the other men who had not fought and been wounded in a far-off country. Some of the braver girls waded in deeper and splashed about behind him, as if to say: Robbe, look at me, choose me. Roos bobbed up and down beside Pieter, her body round and neat as a doll's and her massive, dark-nippled breasts drawing the eyes of other men.

The water was much colder than I'd expected and after I'd released Lotte's hand I swam rapidly upstream, turned on my back and felt the weight of my hair like a cloak. Clouds were massed above the dense covering of leaves and the water was cold on my breasts. At first nobody came near me, but I knew full well that each of the Cornelis siblings must be as conscious of me as I was of them.

The next minute, Pieter broke away from Roos and was heading towards me with long slow strokes, but I didn't want to be claimed by him so I yelled: 'Shall we have a race?' and darted past.

Someone else took up the call. I didn't wait for any of them. As the water closed above me I felt a surge of joy that I had reconquered the river and shown these Belgians that in this one element at least I could hold my own. I was dimly aware of pale figures swimming beside me as we swerved round the island and took off along the far side. At first I managed to push away the memory of my last visit, then my foot hit a rock and I missed a stroke. I choked and reached upwards and someone grabbed my hand and drew me to the surface. Robbe was grinning like a water sprite as I wrenched away and headed for the shallows.

He was laughing and agile as he dived beneath me and emerged on my other side. 'Don't you want to swim a little longer?'

'I'm freezing.'

The bank was crowded and I had to search for my clothes. My thin dress was an inadequate towel and my underwear clung to my wet legs and arms.

'Drink; it will warm you.' Robbe wiped the neck of the bottle with his fist and a gulp of wine did heat me up a bit, though my hands were shaking so much I could hardly buckle my sandals.

'Do you remember I told you that I had something to show

166

you,' Robbe was dressing himself swiftly. 'Come with me now. We won't be long.'

'I'm too cold; I want to go back to the farm.'

One by one the swimmers were leaving the water, shaking themselves like dogs, the men whipping each other playfully with their rolled-up shirts, the girls tussling with the fastenings on their skirts and blouses.

'Then drink some more and put this on.' Robbe handed me his waistcoat.

Again I looked for Estelle, but she had already dressed and was scrambling up the bank and onto the path. The wine made me angrier and bolder and I was tempted to shout after her: 'Can't you behave yourself for once?' but my teeth were chattering, the wine was buzzing in my head and I no longer really cared what happened to me.

When we reached the main track, Robbe grabbed my hand and we peeled off along a path so seldom used that he had to force his way through the undergrowth. Occasionally he paused, gripped me by the waist and held the bottle to my lips. Heat had returned to my limbs and I was dizzy and excited, wanting to get back to the party but intrigued to see what he would show me. Eventually we reached an overgrown clearing, about the size of Pa's allotment, with a tumbledown hut at one side.

Robbe took my elbow. 'What do you think?'

'It's pretty.'

'See over there by the hut, or rather just in front of it. That's where your father was asleep.'

'What are you talking about? How can you possibly know that?'

His hair was drying into a mass of curls and the sparkle in his eyes seemed for once purely benevolent. 'Estelle told me that your father witnessed Maman's arrest. I've always had a vague memory of being brought here by her, and lately it's all come clear to me. She was holding Estelle in her arms and I was lagging behind because it was such a long way to the clearing. When we arrived, three men were waiting for us. I'm pretty sure one was your father.'

'How can you know that?'

167

'One was asleep and another was awake but lying in the long grass, propped up on his elbow. He didn't say much, but I did hear him murmur something in a foreign language. The third man, who was in charge but dressed very shabbily, wore his cap low on his brow and spoke very fast to Maman, in French, I think, though I didn't understand more than the odd word.'

'It's a bit of a leap to claim that one of those men was my father.'

'Well, it was the last outing that I ever had with Maman before she was arrested and I've never liked to think about it much, for obvious reasons. Also, I was sulky and disappointed at the time – she'd said she was going to show me a special place and I thought I'd have her to myself, but it turned out she was meeting all these other people. And then I got jealous of Pieter, who hadn't been forced to tag along with me and baby Estelle, but who'd followed us anyway and kept making faces at me through the trees.'

'So is this how it was, when Pa was here?' The undergrowth must have encroached in the intervening years, but even then it would have been a very secluded space. It reminded me of Hertfordshire woods and of Bank Holiday picnics with Auntie Maisie and my cousins.

'As I said, there were two foreigners. One was asleep, curled on his side with his head on his arm. One was awake, but he had no smiles for us kids. I was bored because Maman had promised me a picnic and here she was talking away to the third man in French, arguing in fact, and suddenly he made a grab for me and pressed my head to his hip so hard it hurt. Maman was angry and shouted at me to sit with the baby over by the trees. Then the argument went on until the Frenchman suddenly disappeared into the wood.

'Maman stood like a statue with her face in her hands – that was the most frightening thing. We trailed back to the house and I kept asking what was wrong but Maman wouldn't tell me. She just walked so fast through the woods that her skirt kept catching and I had to pull it free because her hands were full with Estelle, and then she got even crosser because I struggled with the gate. When we reached the bridge she sat me down and said she wished she hadn't taken me to the woods, I'd been so naughty and moody, and that if I ever told anyone what I'd seen she'd never take me on a secret outing again. She ordered me to go indoors and get washed and that was the last time I ever saw her.'

I stood at the centre of the clearing with that leaden sky above me, shivering in my summer frock, listening to the wind in the trees. 'Do the others know about this?'

'Pieter saw it all. Afterwards he told me that the Frenchman was probably a courier who'd been delivering the men to Maman so she could take over. That's how it worked.'

I wandered over to the ruins of the hut, which had all but collapsed. The grass was strewn with rotting planks and when I lifted one with my toe the ground beneath was seething with woodlice. Robbe had followed me, his shirt drying on his chest, eyes very dark and slightly unfocused. There was nothing about him that I could actually trust, not even whether he truly belonged to De Eikenhoeve, let alone if his story about my father was true, and yet the sudden blaze of his attention moved me. When he handed me the bottle I drank from it again and realised that I was faint with hunger.

'So what's going on with you and Estelle?' he asked.

'Nothing. We just had an argument.'

His head hung low and he peered from beneath his dark brows, like a wounded boy. 'You do realise that she's totally fucked up. We all are. You shouldn't have come near us. You were bound to get hurt.'

'I deserve it. Pa is at least partially to blame for your mother's arrest.'

'Maman made her choices. And I don't expect your pa was in his right mind, whatever happened. Just imagine him, lying here in this quiet and safe place. How peaceful it must have seemed to him after the battlefields. I know what it's like, you see. Your blood hammers in your veins and you want to tear your head off just to get away from the racket. You think you can't stand another minute of it, that it has to stop, but it doesn't. And as if that wasn't enough torment, then my mother came sweeping into his life.'

'But she had two children with her when they met. He *saw*

169

you. He was newly married. Didn't any of that matter to him?'

'*Matter?* What a weird word. You're racing to the border. You could be captured at any minute. It's very likely your last chance ever to touch someone. That's what war's like. Normal rules don't apply.'

I wanted to tell him that normal rules must always apply, but I couldn't find the words because the wine had thickened my lips and I was exhausted from the swim. What did I know any more about rules and how to apply them?

Robbe was standing very close, his head thrown back. 'Listen. Listen.'

All I could hear was the breeze in the leaves and birdsong. A stronger gust rippled across the clearing and I smelt rain and ancient bark. I imagined Pa here, his blood simmering with poison gas and his head full of horror. How far he must have felt from home, how sick, how broken. Then through that narrow gap in the trees, wading through the undergrowth and trailing her long skirts, Fleur Cornelis-Faider had emerged, like the Madonna, carrying a baby.

Only when Robbe put his arms around me did I realise I was crying. His mouth was harder than Estelle's and tasted of cigarettes and wine. My lips parted, but when his tongue coiled around mine I took fright and twisted my face away. 'Please don't.'

'Lie down with me,' he murmured.

I stiffened, then gave in, lay on my back and gazed up at that lowering sky. I imagined my father's utter exhaustion, the murmur of foreign voices. My body was pressed to the Belgian soil and my thoughts were blurred so that I was scarcely aware of Robbe's hand on my neck as he leant over me.

'Mademoiselle Christa, we have to do this. It's in the stars, don't you see?' He pulled me into his arms and I lay against him as he took a long swig of wine and kissed me again so that the alcohol dribbled from his mouth into mine and along the back of my throat.

'I want to go back,' I said weakly. 'To the others ...'

'No you don't.'

I looked up into his face, those dark, childishly pleading eyes,

170

the mouth that could be harsh or bitter but was now soft with desire. The sad, isolated part of me responded to his lovemaking and held on to him as his kiss became more probing and his hand on my bare, cold knee pushed up my skirt. I let him kiss me and stroke me, curious and rather touched that Robbe Cornelis, who cared for nothing, should care for me. But when his fingers got beneath my clothes I rolled onto my stomach. I didn't want my first time to be like this; not here, of all places, with a drunken stranger.

I started to crawl away, murmuring: 'Let's go back now . . .'

He grabbed my ankle and pulled me towards him again.

'Don't . . . Robbe . . .'

His weight was on me. He pulled my head round and kissed me again, and then swept his tongue across my cheek and into my ear.

'Are you really saying no?' His breath was hot in my hair. 'Can you bear to?' He propped himself up and grinned down at me. 'Don't you think you'll regret it tomorrow when you're on the train home?'

As he lowered himself once more, perhaps mistaking my hesitation for acquiescence, I looked up at the sky and thought: Don't do it again; don't let him get so near and then say you can't. Look what happened last time, with Estelle . . .

His fingers reached between my legs and found their way inside me, another shocking invasion, then he withdrew them and slid them into my mouth. 'This is how you taste. This is how much you want me. Say no, if you have to. Say no if you're sure.'

I didn't say no. I let him push me over onto my back and work his way inside me. The voice in my head said: It's right, you know, it had to happen, you've been waiting for it to happen. Because he was gentle it didn't hurt much at first, though I felt the hot power of him and thought perhaps there was poetry in this, in allowing Fleur's son to make love to me, here. But as I looked up into his blind eyes, felt the sudden violence of his thrusts and remembered again the sweetness of Estelle's touch, her gentle fingers, I felt my head go black with panic. It was Estelle I wanted, not Robbe. And whatever Robbe was seeing, as he drove himself into a frenzy, it certainly wasn't me.

171

Afterwards, I lay with a sticky wetness between my legs, panting and shivering in the cold air.

'Christ,' he said, lying on his back beside me. 'You amaze me, Christa.' His hand lay on my thigh and his fingers made their way lazily between my legs. 'Do you want me to make you come?' he whispered. 'I can show you how to do it, if you like, for future reference . . .'

I pushed his hand away. 'I want to go back to the others.'

He offered me a drag of his cigarette. For once I accepted and allowed my head to fill with smoke and faintness.

'You could come to Brussels with me, if you like. Tomorrow. Spend a few days.'

'I need . . . I need to go home.'

'Come on. Break loose. It would be fun.'

The thought of it made me desolate. I was due to travel to Brussels with Estelle, not Robbe. I imagined trailing my suitcase through the city she'd revealed to me but spending the night in some cheap room with him. He was crazy to think I would choose him when I might have been with her, in the sunshine, watching the glint of gold in her hair and attempting to second-guess her chameleon moods.

I pulled down my skirt and managed to stand up. My body felt bruised and not my own. By now I was in a desperate rush to obliterate the last hour. Robbe was in no hurry, but once we were on the main path I started to run in the feeble hope of catching up with the others.

'Christa . . .' Robbe grabbed my wrist. 'Promise me a dance. I want to dance with you later; I want to dance with the daughter of the last of the many men who fucked my mother.'

I stopped dead. 'Is that why you wanted me?'

'I could touch you forever. I could look at you forever. And each time I'd be thinking: She is the beautiful English Christa and her father was the last my mother ever saw of freedom. We all wanted you, but I'm the one who got you.'

I felt cold and sore and the loneliest I had ever been in my life.

Finally, up ahead, I could hear dance music and I knew that the feast must be well under way. As we reached the bridge, the music grew louder and then stopped abruptly. Never had the track to the farmyard seemed so long. My feet were dragging, I was sick and exhausted, then finally we were at the gate and I saw that they were all at table, that they were on their feet in the midst of toasting Bernard Cornelis, that there were just two empty places, for me and Robbe, and that Estelle was staring at me with wild eyes.

Estelle

The older ones had been drinking in our absence so everyone was mellow despite the delay. Hams oozing jelly, redcurrants, potatoes nutty and warm, stoemp because it was Papa's favourite. Peasant food, Marthe called it. Thick slices of cheese. Pickles. Those marvellous breads, desem and poppyseed.

I drank glass after glass of wine. Familiar faces in the twilight. Beloved faces, I realised at last.

When we sat down we were all mixed up; farmer, tenants, sons and daughter, friends and servants. Tante Julia patted the chair beside her and I took it reluctantly. Christa still wasn't back from the river, so Jong Daan got himself next to me on the other side and kept nudging me to offer more food.

Tante Julia was wearing her old fur coat, even on a summer evening, a twenty-year-old hat and wellington boots. 'Where's your English friend? I want to meet her.'

'She was later getting out of the water than me. I came on ahead, in case I could be useful.'

'I've been hoping you'd bring her to see me.'

'We've been too busy with the harvest.'

Tante Julia always saw straight through me. She'd said once, with that glint in her eye, that she and I were two of a kind. Why was Christa taking so long? I was beginning to feel afraid. I shouldn't have left her, even though she was with Robbe, in case she got in trouble with the river again.

'I hear that her father was one of your mother's ... fugitives ...'

'She saved him, yes.'

'How poetic, that the daughter has made a pilgrimage to De Eikenhoeve.'

174

The chat along the table was more raucous now that people weren't so hungry. And we were competing with the musicians who had got bored with hanging about and were playing much louder, wanting the dancing to start. Within half an hour the main course had been demolished. Any moment now the celebration cake would be brought out. Other people had noticed Christa's absence, and Robbe's. Pieter was peering down the table, and Marthe was looking jittery – she hated anyone to miss one of her creations.

Too late. Hanna and Mietje paraded out with the cake, which was oozing chocolate and cream. Everyone cheered and the music stopped. Still no Christa.

Pieter raised his glass to Papa and we all stood up and cheered and sang '*Lang zal hij leven*'.

'I'm just going to see if Christa's all right,' I told Tante Julia. I pushed back my chair and was already on my feet when I saw her at the gate, ashen-faced, hair still wet, eyes black and staring. She was wearing Robbe's waistcoat. Behind her, Robbe was grinning, and as I watched, he caught my eye and placed his hand on the small of her back.

'Christa,' called Pieter. '*Engels Mie . . .*' and he held her gaze along the table as he began a rendition of 'Happy Birthday' in English, which most people could only manage in fragments, with lots of noise and foot stamping. Tante Julia indicated the chair on her other side and Christa fell into it while Papa made his usual speech.

'Thanks to our forefathers for tending the land and passing it on to us in all its fertile glory, and to all those gathered round the table who are willing to spend their summer, year after year, gathering in the fruit crop and making hay.' As if they weren't his paid vassals. 'And to my son Pieter,' he cried, 'who allows me a life of ease these days, and has slipped so effortlessly into my shoes that none of you has noticed the difference.'

Laughter, as if to insist: Oh, but nobody can replace you.

'And to all the rest of the family . . .' He waved his flagon in the general direction of Tante Julia and me. 'Especially dear old Marthe, who made this wonderful cake.'

Not a word about Robbe, who had helped himself to a flagon

of beer and found a place among the lads. Papa cut slices of cake and shovelled them onto plates, but everyone groaned and said they couldn't eat another mouthful.

I was trying to work out what had happened. Where had they been, Robbe and Christa?

Tante Julia had coaxed Christa into talking to her. 'So you are the English Christa. We can speak in French, if it's easier, by the way. And your father remembers Fleur?'

'Just about. He doesn't say much.' Christa, for once, seemed tongue-tied. Her eyes were downcast and she bit her lip.

'Couldn't you manage a slice of ham, dear Juffrouw? You haven't eaten.'

The band had struck up again, for the dancing. Chairs were scraped back and partners grabbed. Boards had been laid on a square of grass and Papa led Marthe out for a polka. Pieter bowed very low to Christa and she got to her feet and took his hand but stumbled, as if she were drunk. There was no joy in her movements. He smiled down at her and steadied her and held her gently in his arms, teaching her the steps. Robbe danced with me. He was a very bad partner, full of drink and not meeting my eye at all. But still, of course, the best dancer on the floor – perfect rhythm and balance. I asked him: 'Where did you and Christa get to?' but he stared glassily past me.

The next dance was too complicated for Christa. Jong Daan invited her in amidst the stamping clogs but she soon gave up and backed away to stand in the shadows. He approached me instead. Those famished eyes of his. Greedy hands, so that I had to twitch mine free.

Hanna lit more lanterns. Robbe had managed to get hold of Christa now, dragging her back onto the dance floor, showing off with his intricate footwork, galloping her along the row. She wasn't laughing, just lurching about. He got a round of applause. The first drops of rain were falling but everybody wanted to keep going, so they kept shouting: 'It will blow over.'

Another dance struck up. Robbe hadn't let go of Christa's hand. The rain was falling faster now, huge drops that darkened fabric and the pale floor. Some of the older ones seized piles of dirty plates and tottered towards the house. This dance was

176

simple; four couples in a circle, breaking away and linking arms, rejoining the circle, breaking away again and spinning. Robbe and Christa, Pieter and Roos, Jong Daan and me, Weber and Mietje.

I pulled back from Jong Daan. I couldn't take my eyes off Christa. Robbe whirled her round faster and faster so she almost fell when they stopped. The rain was pounding down on us; our hair and shoulders were drenched. When the band played the last chords, everyone bowed and clapped, ready to rush indoors. Except for Robbe. He took Christa's face between his hands and kissed her mouth. On and on. People were yelling encouragement as the rain pounded down and the kiss didn't stop. They cheered until he released her and gave her a mock salute.

She was as limp as a puppet. Then she wiped the back of her hand across her mouth. And ran.

Christa

All night, rain lashed the window and spattered across the oak tree, and the wind swept heavy branches against the side of the house. All night, I sat upright in a corner of the room, wearing my travelling clothes, my suitcase packed by the door. At last, when I heard the rumbling of the milk wagon beneath my room, I crept to the window and peered out.

It was still raining but the sky was a lighter shade of grey and I could make out the gate where the milk wagon, driven by Oud Daan, had paused. There was quite a wait while he heaved himself out to open the gate, led the horses through, closed it and climbed back onto the driver's seat. The wagon had moved on when a dark figure emerged from the archway beneath me.

Despite the rain, Robbe was bareheaded and wore nothing to protect his clothes. He walked quite leisurely up the drive, raising his hand in what might have been a salute to whoever was watching. His jacket was slung over his shoulder and when he reached the gate he vaulted neatly over it, presumably on his way to catch up with the wagon.

Marthe was to drive Estelle and me to the station at seven. Breakfast was set out neatly in the small dining room downstairs and she was waiting for me. Pieter and Bernard had already eaten, she told me, and had gone out to survey the havoc caused by the storm. They had asked her to wish me a safe journey. She looked very drawn and spoke of the mess caused by the rain. 'But it will be the work of a minute to clear it all up,' she said when I mumbled that I was sorry I wouldn't be there to help.

Naturally, not a word was spoken about my late return from the river, or Robbe's kiss. In the kitchen, Hanna shook my hand heartily, wishing me a safe journey, and Lotte, from her habitual place in the scullery surrounded by mountains of washing-up, turned and smiled shyly. Mietje and Roos brushed past me with barely a glance. There was no sign of Estelle.

I picked up my luggage, left the house and stood under the arch, peering through a veil of rain at the oak tree, while Marthe fetched the car. After a few minutes, Pieter appeared, in cap and wellingtons. He too must have seen what had happened between Robbe and me, but his embrace was warm and brotherly. 'Dear Juffrouw Christa. I shall miss my walking companion. You have a safe journey home.'

I could barely stifle a sob of relief that he at least was prepared to forgive me. After he released me he tilted up my chin and his eyes were filled with regret. 'I hope you will remember De Eikenhoeve kindly in the months ahead, and come back and see us soon. I have a feeling that not all your memories will be happy, but I hope you understand that we mean well but are simply not used to strangers. And please send our best regards to your parents – your father especially.'

I couldn't speak, just nodded as he added: 'Things happen, you know, when people get drunk. My brother is a devil. That's all there is to it. You be safe, Juffrouw Christa.' He gave me a hasty kiss on the top of my head and stood back as the car roared up behind us.

Next moment, Estelle appeared with her suitcase, kissed Pieter and climbed into the back seat. She was as grey-faced as I and we did not speak on the drive to the station as the windscreen wipers kept up a rhythmic beat and huge droplets splashed from the trees onto the roof.

My lips formed words in response to Marthe's conversation about the journey and the weather and how much I must be looking forward to seeing England and my family again. The hedgerows were now so full-grown and overhanging that they formed a dense, dripping tunnel. When we embraced in the station yard, hastily, because of the rain, I sensed her withdrawal from my touch.

'Come back any time,' she said, turning to Estelle, who gave her a formal kiss on either cheek and stalked ahead of me into the station. On the platform, Estelle stood at a distance, glancing occasionally at her watch. Though I sat beside her in the train her body was so rigid that after a while I crossed to a place opposite and gazed out at the rain sheeting across the intricate pattern of fields, woodland and water. I wondered how it was possible to feel so much pain and not break into pieces. Estelle had taken out a book.

I could not stand the thought of parting from her, yet it was a relief to reach Bruxelles-Midi. At the barrier I put down my suitcase and tried one last time: 'Please, Estelle . . . Please forgive me.'

She turned upon me eyes devoid of expression, and quite deliberately took a step back. 'There is nothing to forgive. Goodbye, Christa. Safe journey.'

I lugged my suitcase through the station, my head full of the times when she and I had hurried through this same crowded space, shoulder to shoulder, oblivious to anyone else. With every step I was hoping she'd change her mind and come after me, but she didn't. At one point I set down my suitcase and waited while the crowd swirled past. I could not bring myself to look round, to endure one further blow, though I hoped desperately that she had followed me.

In a few minutes I reached the barrier, heaved the case along the platform and then found an empty compartment. As I climbed aboard I hesitated, but there was a woman behind me so I had no choice but to enter the train and stow my luggage. I found a seat in the corner, folded my arms and tilted my head so that my hair fell forward, hiding my face.

All the way to the Channel, I never gave up hope that Estelle would change her mind and come after me.

Estelle

Travelled with her as far as Bruxelles-Midi. Scarcely said a word. In reflective mood, to say the least.

I was thinking: What part of my life have you not stolen?

Goodness knows what was going on in her head.

At the barrier we parted. She put down her suitcase and held out her arms. I took a step back.

Registered her eyes black with pain in her white face. Saw her pick up her too heavy suitcase and turn away. Watched her merge into the crowd.

If she looks back, I told myself, I will run after her. I will. I'll kiss her. I'll tell her I will write to her, that it will all soon be better.

But she didn't look back.

I changed my mind and went after her anyway but couldn't find her. Barged through to the barrier. Saw her in the distance, stepping onto the train. One foot hesitated on the platform. Then there was nothing left of her at all.

PART TWO

August 1939—September 1942

Christa

I had fallen in love with Estelle Cornelis-Faider on the day I opened the door to her at Harewood Road and saw her red hat in a haze of spring sunshine. Now, England closed about me like a too tight glove. My home felt shrunken, dark and shabby. The air was stale with last winter's soot and a hint of damp. Ma had cooked my favourite meal but it tasted bland and the vegetables were overcooked. Inches from me at the kitchen table, Pa sniffed frequently and ploughed through his food whilst Ma told me that my cousin Paul had spent two precious days of leave erecting our Anderson shelter – rejected by Pa – in Auntie Maisie's garden, and that it was now kitted out with bunk beds and a Primus stove. And wasn't it fortunate that I was home in time for the annual trip to Teignmouth? 'Though I expect you'll find it very dull being on holiday with your old Ma and Pa after that wonderful farm.'

There was an edge to her voice and an uncharacteristic flash of jealousy in her eyes, and I knew that I couldn't possibly give her, of all people, the least hint of the seismic changes I had undergone. Although I presented my gifts from Brussels – a lace collar for Ma, chocolate for Pa – by tacit agreement nothing else was said about De Eikenhoeve until Ma and I were washing up and she could begin her interrogation. Who had I met? What had I done all day? What had I eaten? What about Estelle, her brothers, her father, her stepmother, had they been nice to me? Had they spoken about Pa? My letters had been so short, she'd assumed I'd been kept very busy. Was I glad to be home?

When I lay down at last in that small back room overlooking the privy and the washing line, I was stunned by the contrast between my present location in a two foot six inch divan, with

185

its tired mattress and worn sheets, and what had happened only a few hours previously. I flinched from the memory of how I had lain with Robbe in the clearing; the pain and a sense of disbelief and surrender followed by a deathly realisation that I had now wounded Estelle even more. And yet when Robbe had kissed me again after the dance I had not resisted him. Why hadn't that blind smile of his, those insistent hands, warned me that it wasn't finished, whatever he'd started, and that he wouldn't be happy until everyone had witnessed how he'd claimed me?

Ma, had she known what I'd done, would have expected me to pay a heavy price and I paid it. That first night I was gripped by the naked fear, white hot in its ferocity, that I might be pregnant. I imagined the complications, the mortification, the explanations that would inevitably follow. The next week, as I went through the motions of lesson preparation for the new term and of packing for our family holiday in a boarding house in Teignmouth, passed in a kind of horror that proved at least some distraction from grief.

But on the second day in Teignmouth, as I stood up to my knees in the sea, watching the waves fold over in slick grey curves and sobbing in a mire of self-pity, there it was, the familiar dragging pain in my thighs and abdomen, a leakage of blood.

After that, grief set in pure and simple. Ma accused me of being quiet and sullen, of wanting to be back among my rich Belgian friends, but I blamed my low spirits on the prospect of war. In Teignmouth, great rolls of barbed wire were stacked along the promenade and the railway station roof was being camouflaged. When pressed further, I even confided that I'd had a bit of a 'thing' with a member of the family. Of course, Ma assumed it must be one of the brothers.

'But really it was nothing,' I added hastily. 'To be honest, Estelle is the one I miss.'

There, I had spoken her name; the two syllables that sounded bell-like in my mind and acted upon me like a drug so that my blood thickened and my mind grew hazy with longing and dismay.

'Well I'm sorry we're proving so dull. I had a feeling this would happen. I remember when your Pa came back from the war that last time he never seemed to be fully in the room. But I put that down to the gas.'

I linked my arm through hers as we walked up and down the sands. Dearest Ma, who had perhaps understood all along that Pa had been bewitched by Fleur's astonishing beauty and boldness. I had succumbed to a rather more complicated version of the fate she had envisaged when Estelle invited me to De Eikenhoeve.

When I sat at breakfast in the boarding house eating toast and marmalade, I was haunted by the small dining room at De Eikenhoeve – rolls, coffee, cheeses and hams and the joyous prospect of a day in the fruit fields with Estelle. And as I stood by the sea and held the towels while my parents took a dip, all I could think of was Estelle, naked in the river, her eyes full of laughter.

Pa struck out boldly so that I had a glimpse of the man he might have been before the trenches ripped his nerves to shreds. Ma hopped and squealed and turned back to check I was keeping the corner of her towel out of the water.

As they bathed, I imagined hurling myself into the waves and swimming on and on, until I was miraculously in Belgium and walking up the lane to the farmhouse. If only I could reset the calendar. The moment I would always choose was in the birch grove with Estelle, when my courage had failed me and I had been overwhelmed by a misguided sense of what was and wasn't right.

Teignmouth symbolised all that had held me back; this mother splashing seawater onto her shoulders, this father striking out on his own, parallel to the shore, these beach huts and cafés and boarding houses, these families huddled behind windbreaks, this expectation of the way things should be conducted.

I passed the last weeks of August in a miasma of despair, writing letter after letter to Estelle, tearing up most, sending some, watching the post for replies that never came and making hardly any preparations for the start of my teaching career. And worst of all, I was faced with the ever greater certainty that I would soon be severed entirely from De Eikenhoeve, because my nation was nosediving towards a declaration of war.

Estelle

Returning to Louvain for the new term in September, I rented an attic room with a sloped ceiling and a high window overlooking other tall narrow houses a few metres away across the street. One evening, two days after my arrival, a note from Borland was pushed under my door. I had no idea that he was even back in the country.

He was seated in his green armchair by the empty hearth, pipe lit. 'And how are you, Estelle?'

My friend Jeanne had once said that Borland's voice was wasted on a priest. Too seductive. My heart was hammering. Encounters with Borland had always been disturbing, and now he was a connection to that time in the Musée Wiertz with Christa, and I so needed to speak about her to someone. 'It seems ages since I saw you in Brussels,' and I took my usual window seat where the blind grazed the top of my head.

'Ah yes, with your English friend.' He set down the pipe, held out his hand. 'Something's wrong. What is it? Come and tell me.'

I crossed the room, fell at his feet, buried my head in the crook of his elbow and sobbed like a baby. He didn't say anything, just stroked my hair. The bliss of letting go at last. I tried to calm down but kept shuddering and sniffing into his handkerchief, which was soft and old and smelt of him. At last I managed a few sentences about Christa and how I loved her – how special she'd been to me – but that Robbe had stolen her.

There was such tenderness, such humour in his eyes. 'Don't you see it was bound to happen?' he said. 'That farm is like a goldfish bowl. A beautiful woman arrives, a stranger, but with connections to your mother. And you, her children, needy for love. What did you expect?'

'Robbe can have any woman he wants. Why did he have to take her from me?'

'Did he, Estelle? Really? Was she your possession, for your exclusive use?'

I sat back on my heels in protest. 'Use? What do you mean? I love her.'

One never knew, with Borland, in which direction his morality would take him. He was a priest, after all.

'It sounds to me as if the poor girl must have had a desperate time with all you predatory Cornelises after her.'

'We're not predatory. What a terrible thing to say.'

'Are you not? Maybe take a look at it from her point of view – a naive English girl trapped in the middle of Belgium during the last summer of peacetime. I hope that Pieter behaved himself. Ah, that's better, a smile. Well thank heavens that Pieter, at least, has some boundaries. Now, I'm not the best person to advise on affairs of the heart, for obvious reasons, but I would say that you should stop feeling so sorry for yourself and think of the damage done to her. She deserves an apology.'

Typical Borland. Always an oblique point of view. 'The trouble is, I hate Robbe now,' I said.

He became a shade more remote. 'Work on that. Find a way of forgiving him.'

'I can't. It's not that easy.' I felt irritated by his response, which made me reckless. 'Have you ever forgiven Maman?'

'Forgiven her for what, exactly?'

'For marrying Papa and then sleeping with all those other men – you must have known about them. Christa's father, for instance.' He had gone very still but I was in too deep now to extricate myself. 'While I was in England, Edward Geering told me that he and Maman had been lovers. And that afterwards he witnessed Maman's arrest.'

Borland pressed tobacco into the bowl of his pipe one shred at a time as I told the story of Maman's last night, as narrated by Christa's Pa. 'So you see, they were lovers, and he's been consumed with guilt ever since because he thinks that their lovemaking caused that fatal delay.'

189

He folded the oilskin inner envelope back into the leather pouch and replaced it on the stand at his elbow.

'Does that surprise you?' I demanded.

He looked me in the eye. 'Nothing surprises me about your mother. And if it's made you unhappy, I'm sorry. I warned you not to go sniffing around in the past.'

'Do you think she'd be alive now, had it not been for Ted Geering? Is he right?'

'Actually, the subject of your mother and why she died is not entirely unrelated to why I sent you a message. I have something specific to ask. However, I need you to be very clear-headed, so perhaps this is not the best time.'

Of course I pleaded with him. Told him that seeing him again had been such a relief because there was no one else I could talk to. And yes, I would do anything for him; he could trust me. So he signalled that I should draw up the footstool and perch on that.

Borland spoke very low, as if we were in the confessional. 'I'm going to ask something of you and afterwards you'll be required to make up your mind, yes or no. If the answer is no, all I ask is that you forget this conversation and do not mention it to anyone. If yes, you must obey me without question.'

The mood had changed utterly. His eyes were fixed unflinchingly on me; his face was marble-pale and exhaustion showed in his features. From that night onwards I never saw him look anything but tired. 'Do you want me to continue or shall we leave it there?'

'Continue. Of course.'

'Unless the British and French can crush them, which seems highly unlikely, the Germans will certainly march all over us. It's only a matter of time. They've done it before and they'll do it again. We have coal, we have arable land and dairy, we have a coast. We border France and when they go for the French we will be part of what they take.'

His fingertips tapped together, tinged with bronze in that evening light. Was he aware of showing off those lovely hands? Or was he entirely unconscious, too absorbed in our discussion? I doubted it, somehow. With Borland, even when he was

190

immersed in the Eucharist during Mass, there was always a hint of the performer.

'The Germans have unfinished business following the last war. And so do I.'

Silence.

'Will you join me in resisting them?'

Sometimes, when Borland spoke, I used to imagine that the air bulged with the presence of God. That had I been a believer, I'd have heard a faint whistle as the soft wings of the Spirit descended. His eyes burned behind the lens of his glasses. We stood and he took my head between his hands so that my hair was rumpled under his palm. Perhaps he gave me a silent blessing. I even thought, when he raised my head, that he might kiss me on the lips, but instead the kiss fell on my forehead and I felt the softness of his beard.

'What about my brothers? Are you going to involve them?'

A pause. 'Would that be a problem?'

There was only one answer I could possibly give.

Back to my little attic room with its rotten window frame, to watch the reflection of the evening sky in a window opposite and plunder my heap of letters from Christa. They had arrived thick and fast since her return home. She never alluded to Robbe by name. *I wonder how everyone is . . . Please send your family my best wishes . . . My thoughts are with you all . . .* As each arrived, I had read it scornfully, with hatred and resentment, then tossed it aside, even torn one up and then had to tape it together again.

And I went back, time after time, interrogating every word, looking for vindication, for more reasons to blame her. I guessed that the versions she posted to me must have been the sixth or seventh or tenth drafts, but even then she made mistakes, crossed things out. There was strain in every phrase, like the too tight stretching of a muscle.

I'm sorry we parted on such a bad note . . .

I believe I hurt you very much and I couldn't be more sad . . .

I wish we'd had more time to talk about what happened . . .

Whining, I thought, and read on in a hurry. The middle of the letter was generally news and here her pen flowed.

Immediately she was back in England, Christa had gone on holiday with her parents. She was preparing for the start of her new life as a school teacher in a nearby town. Christa's favourite cousin Paul had joined the RAF. Christa's Ma no longer allowed her Pa to listen to the wireless in the evening because the news was so ominous.

The end was always a plea: *Do let me know how you all are . . . I long to hear from you . . . I miss you all . . . Dear Estelle, I think about you often, and do so wish we could meet up again soon. It's hard to say the right thing in a letter . . . I wish from the bottom of my heart that I could relive those last days at De Eikenhoeve. I promise you it would be different . . .*

Really, Christa?

To all these treasures I replied only once, about a fortnight after she'd left. Sat in my room at Grand-mère's and scribbled words onto the page. Like bullets, they were. My regards to Mr and Mrs Geering. Hope you are well. Shall be teaching at the university in Louvain from September, need to finish my dissertation, and so on.

Even that little note cost me. I was living a life of what ifs . . . What if I'd never brought her to Brussels and introduced her to Robbe? What if I'd been more tentative about making love to her? What if I'd been kinder to her on the last night?

Sometimes I wrote stuff like this and tore it up afterwards: *I love you, forgive me, what were you thinking of, what were we both thinking of, what does any of that matter now? Christa, be safe. Christa, have I killed your love for me stone dead? Christa, when will I see you again?*

And anyway it's him I blame.

And then Hitler invaded Poland and, snap, war was declared by Britain, France, Australia and Canada, but not Belgium.

Even more cause to hate Christa: her country had taken a definite position and done the right thing. Why did Belgium always have to be so complicated? Perched like some scruffy, near-extinct bird waiting to be potted.

Christa

My teaching career at a grammar school in St Albans began with a staff meeting in the school library where we sat in two semicircles amidst shelves of shabby cloth-bound books. Beside me was a nervy chemist called Miss Henderson, also a probationer, whose fine brown hair dangled around her spectacles and narrow nose. Following a cursory introduction of the new teachers and a review of the public examination results – encouraging but no room for complacency – the chief item on the agenda was, of course, how the school was to deal with the fact that, as of yesterday, the country was at war.

Miss Snaresbrook, our headmistress, could not impress on us enough the extra burden we would all be required to carry. She expected us to rise to the occasion for the sake of king and country, and, of course, our girls. We were likely to receive an influx of pupils and teachers evacuated from inner London, whose behaviour would doubtless be challenging compared to that of our own pupils. 'But we have been called to serve our country by nurturing our young folk and we won't let them down. I know I can rely on each one of you, as a patriot, to do her duty and work any extra hours required without complaint.'

Amidst a general murmur of assent and a few rebellious mutters, Miss Henderson whispered to me, 'I'm Elizabeth. Everyone calls me Lizzie.'

'Christine Geering.' I could barely manage a smile.

'I tried for the WRAFs because my dad bought me flying lessons and I know how to manage a plane, but they didn't want me. Miss Snaresbrook was unimpressed when she found out I'd tried to join up – she said she hoped I'd keep my mind on the job in hand. Shall we go for a cup of tea after school?'

'I can't. Sorry. I have an appointment.'

I immediately regretted my abruptness but there was no time for an apology before I was directed to join other members of the English department in a classroom where the desks had been sanded during the holidays so that all but the deepest compass marks had been erased.

The head of department, Miss Mount, handed out our timetables, class lists and the homework requirements. 'But everything may change of course. Miss Geering, you have joined the department at an awkward moment. We will all have to step up to the mark, and I'm afraid we can't allow you any slack despite your inexperience.'

Finally, I met the head of the middle school because I was to be in charge of a form of twelve- and thirteen-year-old girls. Miss Coates was a faded woman with a chignon and wearing a hand-knitted suit, who gave us a lecture about being extra vigilant for signs of nerves in the girls. She told us we were to follow the air-raid drill to the letter as it could mean the difference between life and death. In future the procedure would involve escorting the girls to the gymnasium, which was to have its roof reinforced imminently, but until that was done all middle-school girls were to be ushered down to the cloakrooms.

As soon as we were released for the day I caught the bus back to Watford and joined a queue in the Town Hall, where I was eventually interviewed by a weary young man whose shoulders were liberally sprinkled with dandruff and whose elegant entry of my name and address took up far too much of the allotted time. As he added my occupation, *School Teacher*, his pen faltered. 'We're not calling up teachers at the moment. Especially women. Didn't you read the leaflet?'

'I want to be in active service.'

'But you'll be required in the classroom.'

'I am fluent in written and spoken French and I also speak Flemish.'

'I'll put you down for Air Raid Precautions if you like. You can do that voluntarily, part-time.' He made a note and peered over my shoulder to the next woman in the queue.

'Is there anyone I can write to?' I persisted. 'Do you have an address?'

'You could try applying directly to the War Office.'

Afterwards, I sat on a park bench by the river, rested my arm on the school bag and watched a water boatman skull through the shallows. A couple of fishermen by the bridge stared intently into the fast-flowing current – I doubted they'd caught more than a stickleback all day. A family of ducks bustled in and out of the reeds and the September sunshine cast a mellow light in the willows.

If longing could transport a woman from the banks of one river to another, I should have been at De Eikenhoeve. Tucked into a zipped compartment in my bag was the pitiful correspondence I'd received from Belgium: a kind letter from Marthe in Flemish urging me to visit her again at any time, and a meticulous note from Grand-mère – in French – thanking me for mine and telling me that Estelle had now left Brussels and that the house was therefore very quiet.

There had been just one half-page note from Estelle.

I'm glad you had a safe journey home. I expect you were happy to be reunited with your parents. Please send them my kindest regards. I am looking forward to the university term starting up again, though I shall be extremely busy with a heavy teaching load and my dissertation.
Je t'embrasse,
Estelle

Nothing from Robbe, of course, but he haunted me all right, even as I sat by a sunlit river in a Watford park. Again I left Grand-mère's salon to clean myself up after I'd eaten a meringue, splashed my face under the antiquated tap and patted my skin dry with a threadbare linen towel. Again I turned the oval knob of the salon door and was confronted by a whiff of sweet cake and cologne, a flicker of attention from a number of elderly eyes and the realisation that a young stranger had appeared in the room.

Estelle, her face transfigured by pride, had led me across to him. 'My brother Robbe.'

195

Robbe in the Musée Wiertz – the shape of his head, the slant of his brows so eerily similar to the priest Borland's; Robbe hunched over the café table, chain-smoking and surly; Robbe swimming naked alongside me, shaking water from his eyes. Robbe's intense face in the clearing and the violence of his final thrusts, as if to ensure he'd left an indelible mark on me. What fun he must have had, the elusive Robbe, singling me out and bestowing upon me flashes of his lost-boy charm, luring me into the woods with his promise of a secret.

It was shame that twisted my guts and had me bent double on the park bench. Shame that I had not fought free of him, as I would have done, I needed to believe, had I not been so completely in thrall to the past. And shame that in my arrogance I had thought that De Eikenhoeve would embrace my dainty self, the prancing beneficiary of Fleur's heroism, and be enhanced by my presence.

In joining the queue at the Town Hall, I had convinced myself that active war service would at least distract me and perhaps be some reparation for the damage I had done. Instead, I had to go back to Harewood Road – shepherd's pie made from yesterday's roast, Pa's silence, Ma's excited chatter about her new colleagues, now she'd been taken on back at the print, the chore of lesson preparation – and await the first real shocks of the war.

Estelle

Half a dozen of us met regularly in Borland's office. Edouard of course, Borland's chief disciple. Francke, Jewish, knew about twelve languages and was awash with brain cells, or so Edouard said. Raymond, sickly, in a wheelchair, an engineer. Then there was Jeanne, with pale plaits and dense skin, studying medicine – a deceptively bland face. Serge, another historian, sharp as an arrow, who asked endless questions during our tutorials.

The chosen few.

Training began as fun and games. Edouard was in charge. Dogged and unimaginative but obsessively, unquestioningly, loyal to Borland. He thought everything through and expected us to be every bit as thorough.

In the early evenings we attended language classes. My already fluent French was polished to disguise a slight accent. We were taught German by a scholar who wept when he spoke of his country. He said we did not have the time to become proficient enough to speak it like a native, but at least we would soon understand those who did.

Edouard led us on excursions to Brussels, where we tested each other in cafés, railway stations and municipal offices. How would we get out of this particular building in an emergency? What would we do if we were trapped? We sought escape routes through back doors, lavatory windows, under stationary trains. We practised what to do if false papers, designed for a cursory glance, were scrutinised, say during an inspection while we were on a journey.

Lose them quickly, we decided, better without. Serge always found the best excuses, his favourite being that his papers must have been nicked by a Jew on the train. 'They'll love that,' he said.

Francke smiled obediently.

We developed new identities. 'Use your own initials,' said Edouard, 'in case you ever get in a muddle and start writing your real name by mistake.' Elisabetta Carlier was mine. Our papers were forged by a genius who worked in a print shop on Rue Ducale in Brussels. And we spent hours learning about codes from an eager mathematician who had written for the underground newspaper *La Libre Belgique* during the previous war. Delighted that his skills were to be used again, he couldn't keep his eyes off me because he'd heard of Maman but never met her.

We learnt how to pen messages in code on scraps of paper, how to commit numbers and names to memory, how to hide microfilm in our collars and the soles of shoes. We learnt that codes might be printed on pieces of silk, which could then be cut up and sewn into hems or socks or knickers.

Even flowerpots featured. 'If you're leaving a message,' Edouard said, 'agree a time and place and a signal which warns you of danger. A potted geranium normally displayed on the left of a windowsill, for instance, can be moved to the centre by way of a warning to keep away. Choose something inconspicuous that only the trained eye would notice.'

It came in most useful, that one, although we found it funny at the time that a life could depend on a flowerpot.

The dullest bit: 'When the Germans invade, you'll have to find work in Brussels. Something essential but inconspicuous – something that might be construed as a reserved occupation but will keep you close to the centre of things.'

It was all an excuse, more or less, to abandon my dissertation because I could fool myself into thinking I didn't have the time. The truth was, seventeenth-century history of art seemed more pointless to me by the minute, although Borland said history was never irrelevant; the way we should approach the teaching of history, according to him, was that the past really didn't need to have been like that.

My *heavy* teaching load consisted of ten students, who I saw twice a week. Thirty essays to read each term, though the numbers fell away gradually. Nine boys and one girl. All marking time, like me, while our feeble-minded government built laughable defences at our borders, assembled an army which it couldn't equip, peered nervously across Europe to where Poland was being carved up and millions displaced or disappeared or bundled into lorries. Our leaders seemed to have convinced themselves that those Panzer Divisions and Luftwaffe weren't going to do the same to us. Neutrality was nerve-wracking, like being under starter's orders and the gun never going off.

On Grand-mère's name day, 20th April 1940, I took my students on a train trip to Brussels. This time last year, I thought, I had just arrived in England and had only just met Christa. When the train stopped at a rural station we heard birdsong. The hedgerows were buzzing with new growth and the canals reflected pale-blue sky. Cows raised their heads from the spring grazing. Everything reminded me of Christa and I saw what she had seen. 'It's the same as England, but different,' she had said, forehead pressed to the train window.

That excursion to Brussels was the last I made in a free Belgium. It was a sunny day and the streets were crowded. Women paused to talk in shop doorways and men sat in cafés beside overflowing ashtrays. I had a craving to visit Maman's statue but there wasn't time. And, anyway, to have passed the table in the square where Christa and I had sipped lemonade might have proved my undoing.

One of the boys had a crush on me. 'If you ever want to throw away that red hat, can I have it?' He jostled close, any excuse to brush an elbow or shoulder. They were eager to tell me about their studies and ambitions – to teach, to become an academic, a civil servant. I felt such sorrow for them because they didn't seem to know what was coming.

'If there's time,' I said, 'we'll visit a cake shop where I get a discount and I'll buy you all a treat.'

We piled into the Musée des Beaux Arts and I told the students: 'You're free to wander later, but there's a painting by Bruegel I especially want to show you first.'

Winter Landscape with Skaters and Bird Trap. 'Such an innocuous little painting,' I said, and those eager young men and one woman who, if Borland turned out to be right, would be wounded or dead or transported to labour camps within a year, all peered closer. 'Some see it as a depiction of rural fun, a holiday on ice. But for me this painting is more terrible even than Bruegel's vision of hell. Look closely.'

'It's winter,' said loutish Albert and got the ripple of laughter he wanted. 'Snow, ice, bare trees. People are having fun slithering about on the ice.'

'Not that little chap,' said meticulous Dora. 'He's freezing, you can tell by his hunched shoulders.'

'And what about this contraption to the right?' I asked. 'What do you see?'

Michel: 'An old door laid horizontal but propped up at one end, with birds feeding beneath it.'

'When the maximum number of birds have ventured underneath, the trap will be sprung.' I said, 'See the most sinister detail of all: the length of rope running from the bird trap to that dark little window? Inside, someone is waiting to give it a tug, letting the door fall and, bam, a couple of dozen stunned birds will be ready for a pie.'

I told them that the painting marked a turning point in the history of European art because it was neither religious nor part of a sequence depicting the seasons. I did not tell them that it reminded me of home and that if we were to enter the painting and follow the river out of the village and into trees we would soon reach Cornelis land and De Eikenhoeve.

Of course, I swept them past the Surrealists and the Paul Delvaux – I couldn't bear Albert to make some crude jibe about that painting. When Christa and I had stood before it, side by side, there had been a throb of understanding between us. Or so I had thought.

Afterwards, I did buy them cakes at the Pâtisserie Faider. They looked at me with new respect when the staff addressed me by name. Nearly cried again when I remembered Christa with a crumb of meringue on her lower lip and her eyes brimful of laughter because of the mess she was making of her dress. At Grand-mère's salon, moments before Robbe arrived.

The students crammed the cakes into their mouths and then

I sent them off to catch the train while I attended the name-day celebrations on Rue d'Orléans.

I'd been out of touch with the rest of my family for months and had spent Christmas with Edouard's crowd in Ghent rather than go home, but an embossed invitation had arrived as usual. Silver engraving, crimped edges, written in Céleste's quavery hand. Père Borland was also invited to Grand-mère's party and had mentioned to me that he might go, he couldn't be sure. Jesuitical business had to take priority. Who knew what he was really up to? More and more, these days, he cancelled tutorials and disappeared for days on end.

My heart thudded at the possibility that Robbe might be there – it would be the first time I'd seen him since Papa's feast – but otherwise it was the same crowd as her Tuesday Salon. Céleste's knees were so bad she couldn't manage the stairs in time to answer the door, or carry a heavy teapot. Monsieur and Madame Fabron were plumper and smugger. 'The prospect of war isn't all bad news – there are opportunities, you know. I envy the Germans their strong leadership. That's what we all need.'

The Vauclains talked about the price of sugar. Sky-high since the shipping lanes had become so dangerous. 'You must remember the last war, dear Madame Faider, and how impossible it is to maintain one's standards in the pâtisserie. We've already had to cut back on the apricot glaze.'

Clémence Depage was there, minus the baby. 'I just blew in for a few minutes to wish dear Madame Faider *une bonne fête*. Marguerite is crawling now and I couldn't risk her among all this precious china, so I've left her with the maid.' She looked thinner, strained, like the rest of us.

Grand-mère wore her best lace collar and sat in state but was frailer than ever. I presented her with violet creams as usual. She held tight to my hand and said she was expecting Pieter later. 'Robbe can't come, as I expect you know, but he sent me a card.' In pride of place was an inappropriate picture of a love-bird on a garlanded branch: *Sorry not to be there. I'm travelling. Robbe.*

'I wonder where he is.' Her eyes were guileless.

Despite everything, I felt a sense of anticlimax. It turned out I'd been hoping to see him after all.

Grand-mère asked if I'd heard from Christa. 'You know, she writes to me every month,' she said with a sly glance at me. 'You can read her letters if you like.' They were in her leather writing case, Christa's impeccable script on the envelopes.

As it's now the spring term I had to cover a rounder's lesson. I'm sure the rules have changed since I was at school. Afterwards I went to the cinema with the friend – Lizzie – I told you about. She's desperate to join the WRAFs but in the meantime has hair-raising stories about what the girls get up to in chemistry.

Who was this Lizzie? I imagined the dark cinema, Lizzie shoulder to shoulder with Christa. Another woman in my place.

A neighbour's maid had been drafted in to help Céleste, but lunch went on forever as the two old women limped about. Still, the food was excellent. Terrines from the farm, quiches from the pâtisserie, bottled fruit. Tarte aux poivres. Frangipane. The gritty texture of sugar and almonds.

The conversation was stickier than the desserts, an indicator that in wartime nobody dared speak their mind. Everyone tried to avoid mentioning politics, but what else was there? One of the Fabron boys was in Germany, employed by an automobile manufacturer. 'Excellent prospects,' said Madame Fabron.

The elder Desrocher sister talked about how she looked forward to a swift conclusion ... didn't see how Britain and France could possibly hold out ... in her opinion it would be far better to join with the victors. 'Are people allowed to worship freely in Nazi Germany? Because if so, as far as I'm concerned—'

'And how about you, Madame Depage?' Madame Fabron asked sweetly. 'Is the good dentist's business thriving despite all this uncertainty?'

'He's as busy as ever, of course.'

Madame Fabron raised her eyebrows in surprise. 'You know, I used to be your husband's patient, but I've had to find someone ... closer to home. These days it seems a little profligate to call a taxicab to have one's teeth examined. One dentist is as good as another, as far as I'm concerned.'

'Doctor Depage is so sought after that I am surprised he has room for an old woman such as myself on his books,' said Grand-mère fiercely.

Clémence slipped away soon after that and I saw Madame Fabron mouth something across the table to her husband. Hateful woman.

'Keep your enemies close,' Grand-mère said when I asked why she put up with her, 'especially when they also happen to be your neighbours.'

Borland appeared a few minutes later. His dog collar and air of other-worldly austerity caused the usual flutter. Grand-mère insisted he sat beside her to say grace although the meal had already begun. He and she put their heads together and spoke sotto voce until Madame Fabron grew quite huffy. But during dessert everyone cheered up, because in came Pieter and Marthe, who seemed to have bought herself a new hat. She was bearing gifts of hand-embroidered slippers, much admired, and a couple of cheeses from the dairy. When Borland left early, Pieter escorted him to the door and they exchanged a few private words.

Afterwards, Pieter took Borland's place beside Grand-mère at the head of the table. He always looked ill at ease in a white shirt and suit and was much too tall and bulky for a salon. Marthe ate a slice of tarte; Pieter packed away the leftovers. There was an air of such desperate weariness in him that I felt sorry, briefly, that I'd not gone home and helped him out. Several young men from the estate had joined up, so he was short-handed.

When coffee was served he moved to a little armchair by the window, avoiding all those flirtatious old ladies.

The news was that he'd torn up the strawberry beds. 'If we are invaded,' he said, 'I'm not stuffing greedy German mouths with De Eikenhoeve fruit.'

Papa was permanently beside himself with anxiety and giving everyone a hard time, especially Marthe. We glanced across at her, cosied up to Grand-mère, reading out the messages from the greeting cards in her bad French accent.

Pieter said Marthe and Hanna and the maids were squirrelling things away in the cellars just as they had during the last war. Tante Julia had come to help and they'd spent days salting bacon and pickling eggs. She had repaired the henhouse. 'She's taken the place of Jong Daan,' said Pieter. 'He's disappeared, no one knows where. He didn't say a word to his father, so we have no idea if he's joined up or gone to find work in Germany. I blame you,' he gave me a sideways smile. 'Without you, there's nothing to keep him in Belgium.'

'How is Papa?'

'He doesn't say much. Just works too hard. It's almost the worst part, to see him and Oud Daan dismantling machinery and uncovering hiding places in the cellar like it's all a routine to them. But actually that's partly why I'm here – I was wondering if I could count on you this summer. I need your help, and as your big brother, I'd be happier if you were at De Eikenhoeve. Under my wing.'

I liked the thought of being under his wing. Downy, dark and warm. But he must have known I wouldn't promise any such undertaking.

'I see that Grand-mère received a card from Christa,' he added after a pause.

'What a horrible mess that was.'

'Mess?' A smile in his sleepy eyes.

'You know, the last night. Didn't you see Robbe kissing her?'

'Oh that. I certainly felt sorry for her, given Robbe's record with women.'

'I wish I'd never invited her.'

He lay back in the chair. 'I just hope he took proper precautions.'

'How do you mean, precautions?'

'There could have been any number of unpleasant after-effects ... Who knows where Robbe's been in the last few years?'

'What are you talking about? They didn't—'

'Oh come on, Estelle.'

'It was just a kiss.'

'Rather more than that, according to Roos. She saw them disappearing into the woods together.' He put his hand on mine. 'I'm sorry, I assumed you knew.'

He closed his eyes and went silent. The old people tiptoed

around him while he dosed. Marthe was helping to clear the table, so I picked up an empty dish and headed for the stairs. The basement, Céleste's world, reeked of damp. Marthe came down and started drying the dishes and she and Céleste were engaged in a stilted conversation.

I polished a few glasses but wanted to hurl them to the floor. I told Marthe that Pieter had urged me to go home to De Eikenhoeve. Marthe, her usual charming self, said: 'You know we always love to see you. However, I think you're much better off in Louvain. Don't you agree?'

It was enough to make me change my mind, just to annoy her. Of course she asked if I'd heard from Christa.

'A bit.'

'She writes to me quite often, tells me all about her work as a teacher. I love to imagine her in front of a class. Her pupils are lucky girls, don't you think? I always thought I'd like to have been a teacher.' She placed glasses one after another onto a tray. 'I trust she suffered no ill effects when she returned to England.'

'Ill effects?'

Marthe didn't answer and I blundered off down a dark passage. Standing outside in the disused yard, I wished I had some cigarettes so I could smoke.

Christa

Lizzie Henderson and I watched the invasion of Belgium on the Pathé news. Accompanied by buoyant music, the Belgian army rode its fragile tanks to the borders and shelled the oncoming Nazis. A bracing voice-over informed us that Churchill had ordered Allied troops north from France and the camera revealed soldiers waving from open-topped trucks at the pretty Belgian women who ran alongside.

At tea I told Ma and Pa there was still hope, Belgium might be saved. I didn't mention the footage of Panzer tanks ploughing through hedgerows, villages flattened, thousands of refugees fleeing in horse-drawn carts, on bicycles or on foot through those flat, defenceless fields. I didn't say that I was finding it near impossible to swallow, that every organ in my body ached, that the news of the invasion hurt far more than when we'd learnt Britain had declared war on Germany, and that I was pretty sure that Belgium was doomed.

Sure enough, eighteen days later, the Belgian army surrendered, its government fled to England, the king placed himself under house arrest and Nazi forces drove British troops relentlessly back towards the coast.

The next time I watched the newsreel I looked for Estelle amidst women picking up futile bits of debris from among the ruins of a shelled village, or gripping the reins of a little cart laden with household valuables, or sleeping under an eiderdown at the side of the road while a ragged platoon of retreating Tommies marched by. Of course she wasn't there.

A few days later during the first double lesson of the afternoon, I read a poem aloud to the Upper Fourths and wrote on the blackboard a set of tasks: *Copy Hilaire Belloc's* 'Tarantella' *into your exercise books. Answer the following questions. 1. What relevance has this poem to our world today?*

Meg Dibner shot up her hand. 'Please, Miss, why is the poem called "Tarantella"? Is it to do with a spider?' The other girls sniggered.

'Well done, Meg. The poem is inspired by the legend that when a tarantula spider bites, it injects a poison which is said to send a woman into a kind of trance that can only be cured by a most spectacular and frenzied type of dancing.'

The girls glanced at each other because they knew that the subtext of the poem must be sexual. When they had at last settled into their work I patrolled between the desks, pointed out an ink-wasting doodle on a piece of blotting paper, corrected a spelling and returned to my seat on the dais, a pile of marking before me, my temples aching in the fug of adolescent sweat.

Another girl had her hand up. 'Please, Miss, what's *tedding? The tedding and the spreading of the straw for a bedding . . .*'

'It's a word used in farming. It means to turn over the straw or dry it out.' My mouth was parched, as in the sunny hayfield. I was offering a bowl of deep-red plums to Estelle whilst Robbe, tousle-haired, walked up from the river.

The classroom overlooked a tarmac playground and neighbouring gardens; a newly dug duck pond, a poorly disguised Anderson shelter and rose bushes in early flower. On the scrap of remaining lawn a toddler was seated with his fat legs stuck out in front of him as he tore up fistfuls of grass. I couldn't shake off the notion that the fate of Belgium was somehow connected to my own behaviour at De Eikenhoeve; that the act of treacherous copulation with Robbe had been a lightning rod and through the jagged tear had flashed Hitler and his advancing armies. While Estelle paid the price, I sat snug in a Hertfordshire classroom.

A knock on the door attracted the nervous interest of everyone in the room – a sixth-form pupil had already lost a brother in the RAF – but this time it was I who was summoned to the head's office, where I found Miss Snaresbrook looking, to my initial relief, irritated rather than sympathetic. For almost a minute, whilst I stood on her Turkish rug and scanned the titles on her bookshelf, she didn't even lay down her pen.

'There's a war on,' she said. 'We can't have our teachers called out of the classroom at the least little thing, but your mother has telephoned to say that your father has been taken ill and you're needed at Shrodells Hospital. Apparently it's not life-threatening, so I'm assuming you'll wait until after the last bell.'

'My mother would not have telephoned except in an emergency.'

'As I've said, it did not sound serious.'

'Please, Miss Snaresbrook, I should like to go now. What if I were too late?'

The necklaces rattled on her bosom. We both knew she couldn't take the risk.

The hospital forecourt was bizarrely crowded with Green Line buses and I had to weave through the stench of exhaust fumes to get to the entrance. At first I couldn't work out what was happening – some kind of staff training perhaps – but then I saw that rows of stretchers were lined up, with nurses moving from one to the next, and that lying on the stretchers were naked or half-dressed men under stained blankets. What remained of their clothing was dark with blood, their faces were bruised and scarred or roughly bandaged, and there was an appalling stench. The nurses spoke in low voices and a frantic woman in civvies darted from one to the next with a pencil and notebook.

I blundered along a corridor marked ADMISSIONS, and discovered Ma perched on a long bench, clutching her handbag. Her face was ashen and her lips were trembling so much she could scarcely speak.

'One of the nurses told me that these men have just been rescued from France,' she said as an empty trolley whisked by. 'When I arrived it was calm and peaceful, and now look at it.'

Another stretcher was pushed past, bearing a man whose head was almost entirely swathed in a filthy bandage. Ma whispered that at about midday her office door had burst open and she'd been called urgently to the composing room where Pa was having some kind of nervous collapse. 'They'd carried him into Mr Smith's office and were more or less pinning him down. It took three strong men to hold him. He didn't recognise me. I've never seen him like that, not even . . .'

'Not even, Ma?'

'When we were first married. After he got back from the war, he behaved very oddly sometimes, but he was never as bad as this morning. Apparently he just got up out of his chair and swept his arm across his desk so that every bit of paper and a whole tray of letters crashed to the floor. He didn't say a word, just kept on throwing things off the desk and, when he'd destroyed his own work, he started on a neighbour's, upsetting his tray of letters and ripping up the sheets he was working on – actually *ripping* them up, hours of work, and scattering bits of paper all over the place. When they tried to get a hold of him, he rampaged across the room, hitting out at everyone. I can't tell you the havoc he caused. Oh Christine, what if they charge us for the damage?'

'Think how many years Pa has worked for them. I'm sure they won't do that.'

'A doctor came and gave him an injection and Mr Smith kindly brought us here in his car. They'll never have him back at work now.'

We waited more than an hour until a white-faced nurse wearing a stained apron appeared at our side. 'Your husband will have to stay in overnight, Mrs Geering, while the drugs wear off, but we'll want him out in the morning. You can see him for a couple of minutes.'

Beds were jammed together in the ward. There was a pungent odour of faeces, grimy flesh and something meatier, like on a hot day at the butcher's. Pa was deeply asleep, still in his work shirt, lying unnaturally straight and tidy, his inky hands resting innocently on the crisp upper sheet. His mouth was half open, so that he snored on every inhalation. Even in repose there was a withdrawn look about his face and a crust of dried tears ran from the corner of his eyes to his hairline. When we kissed him, he didn't respond at all.

It was no mystery to me why he had collapsed: news of the invasion had blared from every headline.

Belgium. Belgium. Belgium.

For days that name must have been hammering in his ears.

Even while he had stood at his desk, patiently picking out letters and words, in his head he had been stumbling through a fog of poison gas or lying in a hospital tent. He had run across exposed fields, hurled himself into a sodden ditch and come at last to what he'd believed to be a place of safety, a clearing in the midst of a quiet wood. Perhaps, in the composing room, he'd been staring at a mock-up of *Woman's Own*, a knitting pattern for a child's striped balaclava or a recipe for carrot soup, and seen instead the flare of shrapnel, a woman in pale sweeping skirts, Fleur Cornelis-Faider's bright, demanding eyes.

Estelle

While our army was still battling to resist the Nazi onslaught, Borland summoned us for the last time. We'd heard rumours of Belgian defences being mowed down, German troops parachuted into hayfields, families piled into motorcars and heading towards France or the coast, innocent civilians strafed by low-flying aircraft, our army unable to get through to defend our borders because of the thousands of refugees on the roads.

Borland's blinds were pulled down and he had lit a candle beneath his crucifix. I never had liked the brass figure nailed upon it. That emaciated Christ's gloomy face was a reproach – someone Borland loved and I couldn't.

'It's time to go our separate ways,' Borland said. 'Here at the university we'll be sitting ducks. You're of an age to be packed off to labour camps in Germany and they'll be suspicious of priests and intellectuals – especially those of us who were around in the last war – so I shall disappear for the time being. And as you well know, we all have work to do.'

He raised his arm to remove his spectacles and pinched the bone between his eye sockets. 'My last advice to you is this. Follow your gut feelings if they lead you to be more rather than less cautious. If you've agreed a code or a signal and someone makes a mistake, never trust them again. There can be no second chances. Notify Edouard if you think something's amiss. Don't investigate on your own account. And remember, it works both ways. Obey instructions to the letter, or people will be suspicious of you.

'Play to your strengths. Acknowledge your weaknesses – if you don't, someone else will find them out. Never make an exception of yourself when it comes to obeying the rules. Never ever write

211

down a name or a number. If you discover that under pressure you lack confidence, tell Edouard and he will help you fade out of the picture. Nobody will blame you.'

'What if Edouard is arrested?' asked Serge.

'Then there's me,' said Borland. 'A poor substitute, I agree. In that case I would appoint a successor to Edouard.'

'And what if you're arrested too?'

Hush.

'Arrangements will be put in place. You'll find out if the time comes.'

Borland stood at the door and said goodbye to each of us. When it was my turn, he gripped my hand and gazed at me. Those all-seeing eyes gave me nothing but love. I smelt incense as he pressed his bony cheek to mine.

I couldn't bear to let him go. In the end, he gently released my wrist and pressed my elbow to move me on.

Edouard and I travelled together on foot to Brussels, a couple of days ahead of the Nazis, camping out overnight. The entire country was on the move. Narrow lanes were completely jammed and vehicles got stuck fast in ditches. We stayed off the roads altogether, so it took an age.

Edouard was weighed down with responsibility, but, of course, didn't tell me what he and Borland had planned. Only that he had taken a job as a clerk in the Highways Department. For once I didn't even have to fend off his attempts at lovemaking. There was no time and no hiding place. Thousands had taken to the field paths. It made me nostalgic for the old days when he and I had nothing on our minds except how much he wanted me and how little I desired him.

The occupation of Brussels was relatively painless. Most German troops marched straight through the city, eyes forward, in perfect step. They were well-fed, smart and brazen.

I saw a soldier offer an apple to a little boy. The mother tugged at her son's hand. 'Say thank you to the nice man.' The soldier and the boy grinned, but the mother was white-faced.

In Rue d'Orléans we'd suddenly hear the staccato clap of

jackboots as a high-stepping platoon wheeled round the corner. School age but in Nazi uniform. Everyone disappeared off the streets as they passed by. A quarter of an hour or so later, Madame Fabron's servant came out to beat her rug and Mevrouw van der Sprenkel, newly arrived two doors down, pushed her pram to market. They avoided each other's eye.

We behaved ourselves. We had reason to. News filtered through that elsewhere refugees had been used as human shields. At Meigem, villagers were herded into a church, a grenade thrown in after them and the door slammed shut. Men were ordered to dig their own graves and then shot. I heard from Edouard that Louvain had been in the front line again and our lovely new university library torched. How could it have been otherwise, when we were caught in an historical loop?

Van der Sprenkel's eighteen-year-old son had received railway tickets through the post. This station, this train, this destination. He had gone willingly enough. There were excellent prospects in Germany, apparently. The streets were empty of teenage boys and young men. Endless instructions appeared on noticeboards and in leaflets, newspapers and via the radio. Our rations would henceforth be a third less than those of the all-conquering Germans. We must not listen to forbidden radio stations such as the BBC's Radio Belgique, since Britain was now our sworn enemy. Patriotic citizens should notify the authorities of anyone caught listening to illicit broadcasts.

Our wireless was in Grand-mère's room, where we gathered each evening at nine, Céleste stationed by the door, me in the basket chair by the fire, Grand-mère in bed, propped against lace pillows and wearing a spotless cap. One night the broadcast from Radio Belgique would be in French, the next Flemish, but the news was as grim in either language. The only comfort was that England had not yet been invaded, despite a relentless bombing campaign through the autumn. I thought of my hostel in Highgate, Christa throwing wide the door of her house in Harewood Road and me on the doorstep, fluttery with nerves.

I had never felt so close to Maman. It was a vertiginous thought – that my destiny had merged with hers. She was there in the face I saw reflected in her bedroom mirror; the shape of

213

the mouth, a gleam in the eye. Her spirit was unfurling within me, and she wanted out.

Grand-mère's dentist, Jerome Depage, whose practice was on Rue Sainte-Anne near the Palais de Justice, needed an assistant because Mademoiselle Madeleine Anselme, who'd been with him for five years, had heard that the Nazis were seeking a bilingual Belgian citizen to work at the Hotel de Ville, typing up the minutes of their nasty little meetings. A pity I hadn't got there first – that job would have come in handy.

The work as Depage's *assistante* was all about detail, good manners and, above all, routine. Things I was absolutely no good at. Clean, disinfect, polish. Scrub everything: chair, trays, sinks, shelves. Hover at Depage's elbow to hand over instruments. Answer the telephone. Write the invoices. Greet the patients. Count money. Smile. Don't flinch at a patient's bad breath, rotten tooth, yellowed tongue. Don't yawn when, for the tenth time that day, Depage runs through the patter: 'How are you today? Any pain? Any other medical problems?'

Add the tablet to make up the mouthwash, rinse the glass, wipe it dry, return it to the cupboard. Clean the bib and fold the towels. When the laundry sack is full, bundle it up and take it down to the street, where, astonishingly enough, it is still collected biweekly by Timmerman's Laundry. Fill the steriliser tray with water. Don't allow the instruments to overlap on the trays.

'For God's sake,' I wanted to shout, 'what's the point of doing everything so perfectly for one defective tooth when there's a war on, killing tens of thousands.' But after a few weeks I calmed down and came to admire Depage's meticulous approach and his expertise. Who needed toothache on top of everything else?

And then, suddenly, I came close up to a Nazi. The surgery had a street door which opened onto a flight of stairs. Usually we kept it on the latch and all our regulars knew they could simply push it open and walk straight in, but that day there was a knock, followed by a ring on the bell. Down I went, none too pleased, and found a German officer on the pavement, all by himself. Thanks to Edouard's training I recognised his rank as *oberleutnant*. He was tense, communicating in basic French that he had appalling toothache and that Depage had been recommended by one of his former employees. He had strong features, owlish glasses and his eyes were dark with pain. As I led the way up the narrow stairs I spoke loudly to give a bit of warning. The left-hand side of the staircase was hung with faded prints of birds, the right with cathedrals of Europe. I gripped the banister, took a deep breath. Our Lady of Reims. St Mark's, Venice. St Peter's, Rome.

The German said he'd been in Brussels a couple of months. He'd enjoyed the city, and was impressed by the Musée des Beaux Arts especially. Was I familiar with it?

By the way, did I by any chance speak German?

A smattering, I said.

'Ah.' He managed a laugh. 'Toothache hurts whether one is French or German.'

A deathly hush in the waiting room, where nobody even tried to behave normally – there'd been far too many sinister goings-on lately. A postman snatched off the street, bundled into a car and never seen again. A young boy hurled into prison for letting down a tyre. Teachers shopped by their pupils for refusing to begin class with the Nazi salute. Even one of our noisiest patients, a precocious ten-year-old, was silenced. Depage stood at the doorway to his surgery, pale-faced, mirror in hand. He'd been filling a tooth. His patient, a middle-aged woman, scuttled out with her hand locked round her jaw.

The officer said first in German, then French: 'Please do not let me interrupt. I can wait.'

But we insisted on showing him into the surgery right away.

The German gave me his cap, then lay back in the chair. Took off his glasses, revealing very blue eyes which roved over the wall-charts. I'd told Depage they needed an update – old-fashioned ink drawings of the anatomy of teeth: molar, canine, incisor. The essentials of oral hygiene.

Strange to have been bored one minute, the next on full alert, but my hands were steady as I fastened the bib – unlike Depage's. However, I couldn't manage a smile and I glimpsed myself, poker-faced, in the mirror opposite. The German cast me admiring glances, perhaps to win me over, and seemed to relax now there was the prospect of relief. I entered his details on a card while Depage washed his hands and prepared his instruments. *Heinrich Eichel.* He told us that he and his staff were attempting to learn Flemish but hadn't got very far yet. He asked why my German was so good. I muttered something about Flemish relatives.

He was in a great deal of pain and therefore deferential, though confident enough to have come alone, to lie back in the chair and invite a Belgian dentist to poke about with a spiked instrument and apply the drill. Depage identified a cavity behind an existing filling as the cause. 'A general anaesthetic would require a short delay, but is recommended. Or, if you prefer, the filling can be performed now.'

The *oberleutnant* didn't want Depage to knock him out. By this time something else was going on; Eichel had studied Depage's dark features and hair and recognised Sephardic descent. I wondered, had Mademoiselle Madeleine Anselme sent Eichel to Depage out of thoughtlessness or malice?

Another patient had arrived in the waiting room. Frantic whispers. Nobody left because they didn't know who might be waiting outside. The German's brow was clammy with sweat and, just once, he cried out in pain. I leant in to him with the suction tube, smelt garlic on his breath and saw that our enemy salivated and had a tongue that wagged like a pink sea creature. I could see the individual stitches on his collar and the hair follicles above his immaculately clean ears. His chest rose and fell rapidly beneath the bib and his nails were polished and cut very short. Perhaps he was vain enough to use nail powder. When the drill hit a nerve he flinched and more colour drained from his face. I wondered what he was thinking. He must have been well aware of those Belgian men and their families who'd been crammed into that church in Meigem and burned alive. Did he feel guilty and uneasy, or did he believe we were better off with his countrymen in charge?

'Suction, Mademoiselle Faider, if you please.'

Afterwards, Eichel tottered from the chair, almost weeping with gratitude. Dabbed his mouth with a handkerchief and half listened to Depage's suggestion that he take aspirin to help the pain and refrain from eating on the affected side for a day or two. He didn't offer to pay, but I could tell it was going through his mind that he should perhaps give something – he was probably obeying the rules of a Nazi handbook on how to behave like a conqueror. But he mumbled through his swollen jaw that he was very grateful and would recommend Depage to his friends.

Depage muttered: 'Please don't trouble yourself,' which I translated as: 'He would be honoured.'

A look passed between them, pleading on one side, reassuring on the other. The German knew he'd made something of a mistake, coming here. As for what else he might or might not do following this visit, we'd have to wait and see.

After he'd gone, I cleaned the instruments, Depage wrote up his notes and we dealt as usual with the other patients. By evening my employer had aged a decade. 'All day I've been turning things over in my head,' he said. 'My brother suggested I join him in the States last year, but I decided I couldn't manage it financially, with a wife and three children. I have built such a valuable practice here.'

'You are a very good dentist. That must be worth something.'

I think he was weeping. We had both recognised in Eichel the truth of our predicament. A perfectly polite, grateful German, smartly dressed; a well-educated, civilised man who, even while technically at our mercy, had been utterly unreachable. The only true connection, his ability to feel pain.

Christa

Although we heard the ear-splitting drone of planes on their way to the coast and the rattle of ack-ack guns, Watford was too far from London to be a direct target for German bombers. As a result, I was plagued by a sense of helplessness; my teaching work seemed so far removed from the actual war and my duties as an ARP warden were tedious rather than demanding. We were forever chivvying people in and out of shelters and patrolling the streets on the lookout for blackout infringements, attending drills in the church hall or first aid classes in mock-ups of a bomb site where some of us lay sprawled on the parquet floor, waiting to be bandaged.

From the slope of Oxhey Park, in the midst of a raid, we saw the night sky flare over London and heard the distant crackle of bombs falling, yet our routine continued much as ever. It was just that we were sleep-deprived and our nerves were always on edge. 'I almost want a bomb to drop somewhere close by,' Lizzie said. 'Then it would be over and done with.'

One November afternoon the journey back from school was through a sunset so dazzling that the bus driver was forced to steer with one hand shielding his eyes. The bus groaned through fields stiff with frost. By the time we reached Watford, half an hour late, it was dark and we were silhouettes on the unlit pavements. At the unheated church hall I was offered a cup of tepid tea and sent forth to knock on doors to establish if arrangements for taking shelter during an air raid, found wanting in certain households, had been improved.

By seven-thirty the streets were quiet except for the occasional dull beam of a hooded headlight or bicycle lamp and we pedestrians scurried past each other with our heads down,

218

pressed close to garden fences and hedges. Guided by the cold sheen of starlight I was able to walk briskly until, at the corner of Whippendell Road, I stopped dead in my tracks. Ahead I could see a male figure pausing to scrutinise a scrap of paper in the feeble light of a torch.

I'd have known him anywhere, despite his bulky overcoat – by the slight hunch of his broad shoulders and the way he tilted his head, by his height and leanness and by the volume of curly hair crushed beneath a wide-brimmed hat. The earth spun off its axis as I started forward: 'Robbe.'

Startled, the man turned and the weak torch-beam slid across his face.

He had a beard and steel-rimmed glasses and was far too old to be Robbe. He snapped off his torch and strode away rapidly in the direction of the town centre. I shoved my mask and gas bag into a hedge and ran after him. 'Père Borland. It *is* Père Borland, isn't it? Excuse me . . . please wait . . .'

My voice, amplified by the frosty night, was startlingly loud, but he didn't pause until, on Merton Road, he was forced to halt on the kerb as a car edged by. My hand fell on the stiff fabric of his coat. 'I'm Christabel Geering, Estelle's friend. Do you remember, we met briefly in Brussels the summer before last?'

He spoke very low and in faultless English. 'I fear you must be mistaken.'

The sleeve of his coat twitched from my grip as he stepped swiftly across the road. A cyclist swore when I tried to follow, forcing me to hesitate and check for traffic, so by the time I'd reached Market Street, my quarry had climbed into the dark interior of a waiting bus. When I reached the stop, my throat torn by the icy air, there was only empty pavement.

I ran fruitlessly after the bus for a hundred yards or so. Even when it had driven absolutely beyond reach, I still trotted on as far as the next stop before retracing my steps to retrieve my things.

Back at the church hall I handed in my clipboard and became embroiled in a long drawn-out briefing about arrangements for the weekend, when we were to receive a talk on how to treat victims of gas attacks.

I must be going mad, I thought, or was it wishful thinking? Surely Borland couldn't be in Watford when Belgium was under Nazi Occupation. And if he had been, why avoid me, the one person he was likely to know?

Ma came into the hall the moment she heard my key in the lock. 'Thank God you're home.'

'What is it? Is there a message? Has somebody called?'

'Pa's in a bit of a state. He went out to the allotment after work and stayed far too long and I cannot get him warm.'

'You've not had a visitor then, Ma?'

'Visitor? No. Were you expecting someone?'

Pa was seated by the stove, wrapped in a blanket. I took his hands in mine and attempted to rub some warmth into them. 'What is it, Pa?'

His teeth were actually chattering, although Ma had slid a hot-water bottle into his jacket and was attempting to feed him spoonfuls of soup.

'Why did you stay out so long?'

He shook his head, staring about with frightened eyes until the present was restored to him – the green and white pot-holder, the glow of the oil heater, the familiar stack of saucepans on the dresser. Finally he relaxed back in his chair, though he kept gripping its arms as if afraid that he might otherwise be blown away.

Estelle

All they wanted, our invaders told us, was that we should coop-
erate nicely. Everything would proceed exactly as before, they
said, except more efficiently. *Le Soir* featured a photograph of a
grinning German soldier raising a glass to a grinning Belgian
citizen.

But it wasn't long before it all went wrong. A few days after
Eichel's visit, a young man was pulled off the street outside the
surgery and kicked in the head and stomach by a pair of military
policemen for failing to raise his hand in a Nazi salute. Nobody
intervened. 'A friend of my niece,' murmured Madame Fabron,
'has spent three days in a prison cell for breaking the curfew after
visiting her lover. Silly girl.'

Official notices appeared like a rash across the city. CITIZENS
MUST OBSERVE ANY CURFEW IMPOSED BY . . . CERTAIN BOOKS ARE
HENCEFORTH FORBIDDEN . . . BOLSHEVIK . . . JEW . . . A photograph
of a gypsy, IF SEEN REPORT TO . . . PARK BENCHES DESIGNATED TO
NON-JEWISH BELGIAN CITIZENS ONLY . . .

In the evenings, I strolled off to the offices of a bank on Rue
de la Régence which had its own printing press in the basement,
normally used for letters and circulars. Edouard and I, left-wing
extremists, had teamed up with a bunch of right-wing financi-
ers who simply handed us a key and turned a blind eye. They
couldn't stand Hitler but wanted to have nothing to do with
the actual dirty work of resisting him, and intended to wash
their hands of us, should we get caught printing banned editions
of *La Libre Belgique*. Rue de la Régence was a favourite thor-
oughfare of the new regime. Above our heads, Nazis marched
back and forth. We printed an edition of the paper once a
fortnight – twenty thousand copies. The men did the writing

and the artwork, I collated and folded the pages once the ink was dry.

Our aim was to redress the balance of propaganda and put iron in the soul of Belgian patriots. We named Belgians shot in the last couple of months, victims of the terror that stalked our streets. *Fogelbaum, Abraham. Né le 22-6-15 à Bruxelles; Anderlecht, domicilié à Bruxelles, Avenue Clemenceau ...*

What was Fogelbaum's crime, apart from being Jewish? Letting down a tyre or two, maybe. Turning tail at the sight of a roadblock?

We printed news gleaned from the BBC, from illicit contacts abroad, from friends in high places in the Belgian administration left behind to work with the Nazi occupiers. *This regime is now telling us which part of a railway carriage we may use, is stealing the food from the mouths of our children, is capable of the massacre of men and boys. Deportation of women and children. Erasing an entire village from the face of the earth.*

On delivery day I'd pedal off with a satchel stuffed with newspapers. Dangerous and tiresome work, it was, posting through letter boxes (subscription only), deadly dull after the first couple of rounds. I was full of resentment. I'm better than this. They should at least let me do some of the writing.

One night I got caught out by a seven o'clock curfew imposed after a potshot had been taken at a German officer near the Tir National. It was rumoured that the inhabitants of half a street had been arrested and deported in revenge, even though the Nazi escaped with only a wound to the thigh. I found myself far from home, in pitch darkness. Lost.

The slow realisation of the danger I was in was like being filled from the boots up with cold water. If a Nazi patrol had swept round the corner, there'd have been a Schmeisser in my back, no argument, no excuses. My fingers were ink-stained and I still had a bundle of newspapers in my saddlebag. Christ. I jettisoned them behind a wall.

I didn't dare knock on a door to ask the way, kept on the move, pushing the bike and wincing at every rattle of the chain as I searched for clues. Did I recognise that drain cover, that tree, those half-open shutters? When I disturbed a fox slinking along the gutter, so close his tail brushed my calf, I nearly died of fright. I was too scared to ask other pedestrians the way, though I saw a couple racing from shadow to shadow. Finally I got my bearings at a road junction but had to take a roundabout route back to avoid the main thoroughfares.

I had never been so glad to be home. Céleste was still waiting up for me in the kitchen and made me a mug of hot milk, heated some brioche and gave me sliced cheese, an apple. Those were the days. She chewed on her gums to encourage me to eat but I was so shaken I could hardly raise the cup to my lips.

'She wants a word,' she said, wagging her head to indicate Grand-mère in her room above.

My heart sank.

Grand-mère was in bed, swaddled in cap and shawl and reading St Thomas Aquinas. She patted the eiderdown and I closed the door and went closer.

'I have something I wish to say.' Each word clipped.

'Look at me, I'm filthy,' I was stammering with nerves. 'Wouldn't you like me to wash first?'

'I'm surprised *Docteur* Depage lets you near his patients. His last assistant, Mademoiselle Anselme, was very neat and tidy, as I recall. Show me your hands.' She turned them over to scrutinise the nails. 'I heard you come in, three hours after the curfew. Where have you been?'

'A friend invited me for supper. We didn't notice the time.'

'Which friend?'

I nearly named Edouard but thought better of it.

'Exactly. You don't know. And what if someone asked how you're making a living these days?'

'I'm a dental nurse. I have the documents to prove it.'

'With these hands?' She wasn't smiling, far from it. 'In the top drawer you will find the gloves I wear for handling silk stockings. Use those in future when dealing with newsprint. Surgical gloves would be better still.'

How on earth did she know?

'You're not taking sufficient care,' she said. 'Remember that they will have dug out the records of your mother's activities in the last war and are almost certain to be watching you and therefore the rest of us. Why draw attention to yourself? How selfish can you be?'

'But Grand-mère—'

'I'm not interested in excuses. You're as foolish as she was.'

I'd never seen her as hard-eyed as this.

'Fleur believed it was her right to do as she wished, even under occupation, and was therefore constitutionally unfit for the work she undertook.'

'You knew what she was doing?'

'Of course I knew. Where do you suppose she lived when she was in Brussels?'

'For God's sake, Grand-mère. Why have you waited all this time to talk about her?'

'Did you need to know, until now, that she was selfish to the core of her being? I wanted you to love her memory, as I do, despite everything. I blame her father for most of her faults, because he worshipped the ground she trod. If ever I crossed her, woe betide; I had the two of them reproaching me.'

'This is your own daughter.'

'Yes, she was my daughter. And she tolerated me, perhaps even respected me sometimes. But would she listen? Laurence Borland and I were the only two who dared argue with her, so in the end she broke his heart and her own by marrying your father, more or less out of spite. The war was an opportunity to escape the trap she'd got herself into, but she left a trail of devastation at the farm, the boys running wild, poor Bernard not knowing what had hit him. Then she came to Brussels, where she plagued Laurence into teaming up with her.'

'*Plagued* him? Are you sure that's how it was?'

'If you want to worship your mother, that's fine by me. The rest of us did, after all, but now we're at war again, you need to learn the lessons of the past or you'll end up the same way she did. She believed she was invincible and that she had no enemies apart from our German occupiers.'

'Who was her enemy? Who betrayed her? Tell me.'

'The point is that it could have been anyone, right down the line, even one of the men she rescued, because her behaviour was so reckless. The reason I'm telling you this is to warn you that in

224

our line of work you need to watch your back at all times. Not to mention the fact that if you put yourself in danger, they'll come for Céleste and me too. And Depage. Is that what you want?' She again gripped my inky hand. 'When you came in, you could give me no plausible explanation. Do you understand the risk you were taking? That's all then. Lesson learnt.'

By the time I'd reached the door, she seemed to be reading again, a toy figure with cotton-wool hair snuggled under a pink silk coverlet.

In Maman's bedroom I closed the door and felt the imprint of her hand on everything, her rage and resentment against the world at large; doomed to a joyless marriage for which she had only herself to blame. Her wildly beating heart.

Christa

Neither my father nor I recovered from the night when I thought I'd encountered Borland. As time passed I became more troubled not only by the recollection of how abruptly Borland, or his double, had evaded me, but by the coincidence of my father's breakdown that same evening. Something had shaken him up so badly that in the following days we often found him standing alone in the unlit front room, watching the street, or hunched in his armchair with his hands covering his ears. If we asked him what was the matter he shook his head and either refused to answer or changed the subject. We'd lost all hope of his ever returning to work.

Most of all I was tormented by the tantalising thought that, just for an instant, I might have touched Borland's sleeve and that if he'd chosen to speak to me, he could have given me news of Estelle. In the end I decided my only prospect of unravelling the mystery was to ask the one person in England who might know the answer; Borland's friend, Doctor Sinclair, whom Estelle and I had once visited together in Cambridge.

In the midst of the Blitz, travel for civilians was a tortuous affair. We could never be sure whether trains would run, and if so, how late or if they'd be suddenly diverted to an alternative destination. Nevertheless, I set off for Cambridge on a rare free Saturday without first writing to Sinclair to ask for an appointment. He had been elusive when Estelle and I had called on him and I gambled on having a better chance of success if I took him by surprise.

Cambridge was very different to the sunlit town we had visited eighteen months previously. The station forecourt was heaped with sandbags and first-floor windows along Station

Road had been blacked out. One of the little lanes at right angles to Trumpington Street had taken a hit and, half a mile away, in the multitudinous windows of King's College Chapel, the stained glass had been replaced by tar paper. At two o'clock in the afternoon, Doctor Sinclair's college was almost deserted – only one thin student drifted into view – and when I refused to give details of the reasons for my visit, except that it was a private matter, the porter became truculent. With great reluctance he agreed to telephone through while I waited in the lobby.

Although the ensuing exchange was out of earshot, much to my relief it was obvious that Sinclair was in the building. Through the open door I saw that rows of cabbages had replaced the immaculate lawn upon which Estelle had trespassed. At last my name was registered and I was pointed in the direction of Doctor Sinclair's lodgings. A couple of very young male students glanced unashamedly at my breasts and ankles as I hurried by.

Sinclair, who could surely have timed my arrival to the second once he'd heard from the porter, nevertheless kept me waiting and made a show of surprise when he opened the door. At the writing desk in the window a pair of half-glasses and a pencil were resting on an essay. I had the distinct impression that everything had been hastily staged: the throwing down of his glasses, the rumpled hair, the harassed expression. There was no sign of the portrait of Borland. Determined to seize the initiative, I removed my coat and looked about for somewhere to put it.

Whilst most people had aged considerably since the start of the war, Sinclair had gained a little weight and looked prosperous and smart. On my previous visit with Estelle he'd mentioned the dicky heart that had prevented him from undertaking active service and I wondered how he had the nerve to appear so preoccupied when his only task was to mark essays. 'This is a most unexpected pleasure, Miss Geering. How may I help you?'

'I was wondering if you had any news from Belgium. I'm worried about my friend Estelle Cornelis-Faider.'

He made a good show of bewilderment. 'But, Miss … er … Geering, I'm as cut off from the rest of Europe as you are. Surely you might have telephoned rather than come all this way.'

'Oh, I fancied a trip out of London. Also . . . I spotted a mutual acquaintance of ours in Watford a few weeks ago.'

I'd given him a jolt.

'And who was that?'

'Père Borland. As you doubtless recall, it was he who sent you a letter of introduction to Estelle. I was assuming, if he'd been in England, that he was bound to have visited you.'

Only, perhaps, by a glance at the door leading to an inner room, did he show that he was ruffled. His voice was as well-modulated as ever. 'Goodness me. So you are here on a complete whim.'

'I'm pretty sure I saw Père Borland in Watford last month. In fact, I had a clear glimpse of his face, although he walked away quite deliberately before we had a chance to speak. But since then I've come to assume that he had been specifically avoiding me. And that he was in Watford to speak to my father.'

'Your *father*? Forgive me, but you're talking in riddles. Why would Borland visit your father?'

'I don't know. And it's no use asking Pa because he clams up if I try to raise the subject.'

Sinclair, still at his writing desk, was twitching his papers into a heap. 'Forgive me for being so slow on the uptake, but I fail to understand what you want from me.'

'When Fleur Cornelis-Faider was arrested in 1917 she had been helping two English soldiers, my father and another who used the name Hébert. Pa survived but Hébert probably didn't. From what I've gathered, your friend Laurence Borland was involved in the Resistance at that time too. So you see, there's likely to be some connection between him and my father.'

Ashes stirred and a clock ticked. 'How could Laurence possibly have been in England, given that his country is under occupation? I'm afraid you must have been mistaken.' Glancing at my face, Sinclair added more kindly: 'It seems you've had a fruitless journey, but may I at least offer you a cup of tea, Miss Geering?'

He gestured to a chair by the fire and disappeared into the next room. Apparently the outbreak of war meant that he now had to boil his own kettle because I heard him strike a match and light the gas while I automatically reached for the nearest volume – a leather-bound edition of Boswell's *Life*. None of our books in Harewood Road smelt so delicious. My hands were unsteady as I pondered whether Sinclair's offer of tea was a gesture of consolation for my rash journey or a sign that he was thinking over his response to my questions. I was as sure as I could be that my hunch had been correct, and that Borland had recently been in this room. It was to do with the missing photograph, and Sinclair's rather too slick evasion of my questions: he quite simply didn't seem sufficiently wrong-footed by the reason for my visit.

By the time he returned with almost undrinkable tea, he'd prepared a different topic of conversation. 'I wonder if your friend Estelle completed her dissertation. As I recall, she borrowed some notes of mine.'

'I've no idea. I've scarcely heard from her since I was in Belgium before the war.'

Sinclair smiled sympathetically and tapped his fingertips together. 'So you went to Belgium ...'

I set down my cup. 'Please tell me if you have any news of Estelle, and whether or not I'm right about Borland coming to England.'

'Really, Miss Geering, can't you see that all this is frankly fantastical.'

'Last time I was here you showed me a photograph of Père Borland. Would you mind if I had another look at it?'

'What a memory you have. I've packed my most precious possessions away, in the event of an air raid.'

I reached for my coat and took out a slip of paper. 'Here's my address, should you change your mind about what you're prepared to tell me. Or if you hear any news of Estelle. It would be a kindness to let me know, at least, if she is safe.'

'Don't rush off. Now you're here, I'd love to know more about your father.'

But I was desperate to leave now, as I was fighting back tears. 'If you only knew how much I miss my friend Estelle and how desperate I am for news. I've sent letter after letter via the Red Cross but have never received a reply. For all I know, she could be dead or a prisoner.'

'Believe me, if I had any news . . .'

'I don't believe anything you say. I think your friend Borland came to see you last month – he probably stayed in these very rooms. I expect he was nervous because he knew I'd spotted him in Watford. Why else would you have hidden his photograph from me?'

Even to my own ears I sounded hysterical. 'Really,' he said, 'I would not have agreed to see you if I'd known I was going to be subject to this kind of interrogation. As I've said, Miss Geering, I simply cannot help you.'

He had won, of course. Whilst I was weeping and dishevelled, he had maintained his air of bemused impassivity. With a great deal of coolness on both sides, he opened the door for me and we parted. And yet, as I walked back to the station, I did not regret my outburst. I had done something definite, if rather wild, for Estelle. And there was just a chance that I had pushed a door very slightly ajar.

Estelle

By the spring of 1941 Depage's forehead was deeply grooved and the light had gone from his clever eyes. Worn out with searching the papers and radio waves for better news, haunted by the fact that he might have got his family to the States had he not dithered, he clung on to his practice and relied on his status as a professional man. Depage was a law-abiding servant of his community, a filler-in of forms. These qualities now became dangerous.

Clémence sometimes brought the children to the surgery in the evening. She said it was too chilly in the apartment and it was good to be out and about. Sometimes she cried a little as she and I made a tisane in the kitchen. The boys, Raymonde and Davide, aged eight and six, were always equipped with satchels and exercise books, so they could work on their sums or spellings. Both had enquiring dark eyes. Raymonde was more dutiful than his younger brother, who preferred drawing cartoon figures to practising long division. Inevitably they reminded me of my own brothers, though they were small and slight and biddable by comparison. Raymonde, I sensed, was pitifully aware of his predicament and jumped if a door slammed. Marguerite, now a toddler, was a menace if left unattended. She liked to sit in my chair behind the desk and be shown the contents of the drawers.

For a while our newly formed German Military Administration didn't make a big deal of the anti-Jewish laws. We all shared the same sections of the bus and Jewish businesses ran more or less as usual. Except. The Depage dental practice had to put a notice in the window. *JOODSE, JUIVE – JEWISH-RUN.* And in spring 1941 it started. Just as the tender tips of new leaves were showing in the park, two synagogues were burned down in Antwerp, the Chief Rabbi's home was violated, Jewish assets were seized by the state, businesses liquidated or handed over to Aryan sympathisers.

Depage began to make some enquiries. In lunch breaks and after work he'd hold long conversations on the telephone. But where could he go? The borders were closed. Most of his friends were in the same boat. And then *Oberleutnant* Eichel telephoned to book a check-up; said he would come at the end of the day to save embarrassment.

He was beaming with gratitude because his tooth was better. Depage offered him a cup of coffee and was almost puppyish in his desire to please. Surely someone like Eichel wouldn't betray you or stand by and watch others mistreat you or your family? In fact, it might be a positive to have friends in high places.

We still had ground coffee in a tin imported in 1938. Depage had taught me how to make a decent pot, which I served on an oak tray. Afterwards, I sat at a discreet distance and helped out with the translation. Eichel had a smattering of French, Depage no German.

'Listen, Doctor Depage, I'm so glad we have time for a chat,' said Eichel. 'I was wondering if you could do a little bit of work for our administration and your fellow citizens. Help build a few bridges. I can offer good remuneration for you and Fräulein Estelle Cornelis-Faider, whose services we will also require. You have three children, isn't that right? I have only the two. Both girls, but there we go. The oldest in particular is very gifted. She could read before she was four years old. But you have sons, lucky man. Now, I owe you a favour, and what I am proposing will ensure that you're always held in the highest esteem by the powers that be.'

He paused for me to translate this speech into French.

'When we arrived in Brussels, I'm afraid we found that everything was pretty chaotic; proper records simply weren't kept by your former administration, whereas we Germans are ridiculed for being sticklers for bureaucracy. I recognise that our standards are abnormally high.'

Coffee, which used to be drunk on carefree mornings outside a café, was a reminder of the past and Depage had visibly relaxed. He knew that he for one was in the clear. In his own practice

– at least before my arrival – our records had been exemplary. Each patient had a buff folder which was updated after every appointment.

'We need to compile a decent register of everyone,' said Eichel. 'Their names, addresses, employment, children, cultural details, that sort of thing. Then we'll know who's who. It'll make it so much easier when it comes to ensuring everyone gets their just entitlement, you know, to education and medication, that sort of thing. Or if we have to be more draconian about ration books, should the war drag on.'

'Cultural details?' Depage's brow furrowed again.

'People in this country never seem to know their neighbours. As a German from the city of Dresden where everyone gets on with everybody else, I cannot understand how in one street in Brussels, say Rue Neuve, you can have Flemish and French families who have known each other for years but simply refuse to speak to each other. This seems like lunacy to me. How can one possibly have an effective administration in a country where two different languages are spoken within ten metres?' Depage echoed Eichel's chuckle, like a comedian's stooge. 'At the very least it would be helpful to know how people describe themselves.'

Eichel confided to me that in his previous life he had been a property lawyer. Sun streamed through the clear glass at the top of the window – the bottom was frosted, to protect patients' privacy. Eichel was tapping his fingertips together. Depage had not quite spotted the trap, whereas I was ready to punch Eichel in the balls.

'We are looking for someone respected within the Jewish community to compile a list,' he continued. 'People will be so much more compliant if it's someone of their own race asking the questions. Do you see? As I've said, there'd also be a small fee.'

Depage's smile was fixed. 'I certainly wouldn't want a fee. And I really don't understand. Tell me again why such a register would be necessary?'

'I've noticed there's quite a lot of very unpleasant anti-Semitic activity going on, even in this city, which I'd have expected to

233

be much more tolerant than the rest of Belgium. You may have heard that a kosher butcher's shop was burned down last week and a Jew was beaten up outside his synagogue yesterday. We need to be able to protect people, do you see?' Was there just a touch of shame in Eichel's eye? 'And as I've said, since even the Belgian people don't know who's who, we must find out for them. It's all perfectly straightforward. I hope you don't mind, I've recommended you at the very highest level.'

Snap went the jaws of the trap. The cup trembled in Depage's hand.

Christa

I received a letter addressed in immaculate handwriting and postmarked 4th April 1941.

Dear Miss Geering,

You will remember that you visited me in December. I do hope your journey home was uneventful. Forgive me if I was a little distracted when you called — I am so unused to receiving visitors that I was taken by surprise. You'll have to forgive a crusty old academic.

As a matter of fact, I was extremely impressed that you should have taken the trouble to visit me and I have since made a few informal enquiries on your behalf. I happen to have a colleague who used to work in the Public Records Office and I believe he might have identified the Captain 'Hébert' who you told me was with your father as he made his escape from Belgium.

I would have suggested that we meet at the Public Records Office itself, which, as I'm sure you're aware, is in Chancery Lane, but a direct hit has rendered said building inaccessible. I wondered therefore whether we might meet in an area of London that is relatively unscathed. I'm sure your free time will currently be as precious as my own, but perhaps you'd let me know, at your convenience, when would suit you.

Yours sincerely,
H. Sinclair.

Overcoming my distaste for the man, I wrote that I'd be happy to meet him during the first week of the Easter holidays, and by return of post was invited to lunch in the Rainbow Restaurant of Derry & Toms in Kensington.

To avoid complicated explanations I told Ma a half-truth and said I was off to meet a friend in town. Her sole anxiety, therefore, was that it was foolish of me to venture into central London for so frivolous a reason.

Euston Station, which had received a direct hit two months previously, had reopened and though the train was delayed at signals for twenty minutes the platform was functioning. After disembarking, passengers were funnelled between walls of sand-bags onto a wooden walkway across the former forecourt and under the monolithic entry arch.

This was my first venture into London following the Blitz. The bus edged its way past familiar buildings interspersed with mounds of rubble. Walls teetered like old teeth, scraps of wall-paper still dangling from scarred plaster, and in one spot a mirror hung from an exposed picture rail, yet people walked about as if this ludicrous cityscape was entirely normal. The immaculate mansions of Lancaster Gate, as if by divine right, were large-ly untouched, but our progress was so slow that I got off and walked south through Kensington Gardens, where the Prince Albert Memorial was firmly under wraps.

Although the more frivolous items which used to be displayed on the ground floor of the department store had been replaced by useful bags and plain hats, there was still a pleasing hint, in the neat displays and scents of new fabrics, that a more civilised world might be awaiting us beyond the current conflict. I longed to visit the roof garden but decided I didn't have time; I should have predicted that Sinclair would be late and that I would be kept waiting for nearly half an hour at the entrance to the restaurant.

He was wearing a tweed jacket and waistcoat and arrived in a hurry, smoothing his hair and checking his watch. After a sotto voce conversation with the waitress, we were escorted to a corner table, where Sinclair sat with his back to the wall, full of apology and solicitude.

I chose shepherd's pie, the cheapest and most prosaic dish on the menu, because the last thing I wanted was to be in any way indebted. I wasn't abstemious enough to turn down a glass of wine, and that moment of weakness, coupled with the fact that I'd not been honest with Ma, compromised me more than I could possibly have anticipated.

Having ordered lamb cutlets and an entire bottle, Sinclair proceeded to give me such an admiring glance that I wondered about the true motivation behind this meeting. Despite my sober coat and teaching skirt, he was effusive about my appearance. 'It does me good to see you, Miss Geering. You might have gathered that I spend my entire life with spotty youths or dusty old men. Oh, don't get me wrong – I enjoy giving lectures and tutorials, except that I am inexorably losing my best students to the war. Isn't it amazing how we feel international catastrophe on such a selfish level? But what of you, Miss Geering? How is the war treating you?'

'In my immediate family we have been fortunate so far. However, several of my pupils have been bereaved.'

Sinclair went through the motions of tasting the wine whilst wryly conveying that such rituals simply didn't matter in these grim times.

'Do you usually have much cause to be in London?' I asked.

'There are various seminars one must attend, and we academics, like everyone else, are not immune to whatever demands our country might make of us.' The flash of a self-deprecating smile was perhaps intended to suggest that he was actively engaged in some kind of important and secretive work.

The shepherd's pie was heavy on potato, low on whatever gristly meat had been ground up with the carrot and onion. Sinclair tucked into his lamb with the same efficient and distracted air with which he'd sampled the wine. He was charming to the waitress as he asked for more gravy – she was well over fifty and he chastised himself for sending her on yet another trek to the kitchens. He then asked after my father, told me a story about a near miss when he was last in the capital during a raid, and praised me for my dedication to the ARP. 'It's the kind of work I would have volunteered to do myself, were it not for this feeble heart of mine.'

To put a stop to this self-indulgence I reminded him that he had information about Hébert.

'Ah. Exactly. Now then.' He removed a typewritten sheet

237

from his inside pocket. 'As I told you, I felt so sorry that you'd trekked all the way to Cambridge for nothing that I took steps to trace this man Hébert who you mentioned. It was rather easy, I gather, because of course we knew the date and place of Fleur Cornelis-Faider's arrest and that your father had escaped. And behold, we discovered a Sergeant Raymond Hawkins of the 21st West of England Regiment, killed by the Germans whilst evading arrest near Baarle-Hertog on exactly that date. It may comfort you to know that Hawkins was in all probability a deserter, although in the circumstances the case against him was never proved. I thought that might just save your poor father a few pangs.'

I pushed my glass aside to study the document, which gave an address in Henrietta Street, Bath. 'Pa thought Hébert was a captain, not a sergeant.'

'I suspect our Hawkins was economical with the truth for the sake of self-aggrandisement, and because of course, if he really was a deserter, he'd have been keen to disguise himself.'

'May I keep this?'

'It's all yours. It was a pleasure. And of course,' a slight, inward smile, 'my help isn't entirely disinterested. I wasn't honest with you, Miss Geering, last time we met. My only excuse is that you hadn't written ahead and for the safety of all concerned my instinct was to be cautious.'

He spoke very low and I had to lean closer to catch what he was saying.

'You were quite right. Laurence Borland was in England last November, and he did visit me in Cambridge.'

I was so shaken by this abrupt confirmation that I dropped my guard. 'Is he still in England?'

'Certainly not.'

'How did he get here, in the middle of the war?'

'Now that I cannot tell you.'

'Why was he here?'

He shook his head.

'But he came to see you?'

'Because we are old friends. You'll have to accept my apology, on his behalf, for the distress he caused.'

238

'But why did he behave so strangely when he caught sight of me?'

'He wasn't supposed to be in the country, and he certainly shouldn't have taken the risk of being recognised.'

'Did he tell you he'd spoken to my father?'

He nodded. 'You see, over the years, Laurence has been tormented by the question of what really happened to Fleur, and in particular of who betrayed her. How did the military police know that she would be at the electric fence in Baarle-Hertog at that precise moment? Borland was part of the same escape line as she, and had seen her only a few days before she died. Obviously things went very wrong soon after their last meeting. He thought your father might have the answer.'

'And did he?'

'I'm afraid not. Your father was too frightened to say a word. Borland was very sorry to have upset him.'

Our foreheads were almost touching and my fingers gripped the stem of my glass. 'Perhaps you could confirm something else then,' I said in a low voice. 'When I saw Borland in Watford, I initially mistook him for Robbe Cornelis. It was the same when I met them together in Brussels: I couldn't help noticing a striking resemblance.'

Sinclair managed an appreciative smile. 'Really, Miss Geering, it's true what they say about women's intuition. You're right. I believe it happened in Louvain. As you may recall, during one of my own visits to Laurence she arrived suddenly, without notice, as was her habit. The poor man didn't stand a chance.'

'Does everybody know? Does Robbe?'

'I assume so. If you spotted the resemblance it must be fairly obvious to anyone who's paying attention. But I don't expect it's ever spoken about . . .'

He was interrupted by a third party who now hung over our table.

'Christine, I saw you from the other side of the restaurant and just had to say hello.'

I had been so engrossed that I had failed to spot the advance of Auntie Maisie, of all people, who was glaring at Sinclair, the three feathers in her hat waving furiously.

239

'Paul and I are meeting for dinner later – he's been given a new posting, so it's our last chance. Anyway, I thought I'd pop into Derry's for a bit of shopping and treat myself to a pot of tea.'

Sinclair, having risen to his feet, shook hands gravely but failed to conceal his lack of interest. Auntie Maisie was clearly unconvinced by my assertion that he was an acquaintance of Estelle's from Cambridge, and that we were here to talk about old times. Eyeing our wine glasses and the dregs in our coffee cups, which to her clearly suggested unthinkable decadence, she murmured: 'I wish Paul could have gone to university, but he was *so* keen on the RAF.'

Sinclair's aloofness deterred further questions and she backed away with an over-cheery wave. 'Oh, well, I expect I'll be seeing you very soon, Christine.'

As she crossed the room, I tackled Sinclair once more. 'You still haven't told me what Borland was doing here in England.'

'Something to do with the church. These Jesuits get about, even during a war.'

His tone was distinctly more businesslike as he gathered up his raincoat and briefcase.

'Have you still received no letters from your friends in Belgium?' he asked.

I shook my head.

'Best not to write any more, I'd say. No public channel is completely safe from enemy eyes.'

It occurred to me that during the course of this conversation Sinclair had assumed an aura of expertise and authority. From the corner of my eye I saw Auntie Maisie staring at us while she waited for the lift.

'One other thing,' he said. 'I have a colleague in the War Office who might be interested in meeting you. Did you mention you spoke French?'

'I don't believe so.'

'I must have assumed it then, from your acquaintance with Estelle.'

'I teach French, if that helps.'

'It might. The thing is, you've proved yourself to be rather resourceful. I could put in a word for you, if you liked.'

With that, he set off at speed, briefcase in one hand, hat in the other.

Unlike Auntie Maisie, he did not look back.

Estelle

A Jewish clockmaker five doors down from Jerome Depage's clinic had his windows smashed, instruments confiscated, safe raided and most of his possessions taken. One day there was a tidy display of merrily ticking old clocks, the following an ugly mass of wood and metal splinters, the next it was all boarded up. His premises had been closed down, announced a notice on the door, due to perfidious overcharging by the owner. And then the clockmaker and his family disappeared. We made discreet enquiries. They didn't seem to have been arrested; they had simply dissolved into the ether.

Meanwhile, Eichel and I were on excellent terms. He came for weekly visits, solely to check on the progress of the register, he said. Hair neatly combed, a splash of cologne behind his ears, he showed me photographs of his wife and two little girls in Dresden – blonde plaits, checked dresses. Said he was homesick. Privately, between ourselves, he admitted that he found Brussels a little grubby compared to home. Yet, I knew, if I'd stepped closer, brushed his elbow, smiled invitingly into those glinting blue eyes, his nostalgia would have found a distraction soon enough. Nor could I risk offending him by repelling his advances completely. So I strung him along. The spectre of an overbearing grandmother at death's door came in very useful and kept him at bay. Just.

Whenever he mentioned the register I brought out closely written pages laboriously compiled with the help of our patients, the rabbi, friends of friends, shopkeepers and schools. The list was going well; people trusted *Docteur* Depage. They mentioned how relieved they were not to have to deal with a German. And they took comfort from the length of the list. Better to have one's name buried amongst a hundred others than to find one-self alone on a page.

Clémence Depage and I had held a discussion about this register when I called at her apartment on Rue Van Moer, ostensibly to take her a box of almond cakes from the pâtisserie – made with the very last of the good flour, as it turned out. I chose a time on a Saturday when I knew her husband would be out. Their home consisted of five or six large rooms on two upper storeys, with long windows facing on to the street. The maid had departed some months ago, yet the apartment was impressively tidy and perfumed with the onion soup Clémence was making in the little back kitchen. Children's toys were scattered across the polished floor of the main room. The Dinky cars and a small train set presumably belonged to Davide. Marguerite lay flat on her stomach with paper and wax crayons. Her hair had been brushed meticulously into a half plait, the rest tumbled over her shoulders. The boys were at the table playing battleships.

I stood by Clémence while she stirred the soup and brewed coffee to go with the cakes. 'I've no doubt that Jerome has told you about the register . . .'

'Already I hate any mention of that register. It has become his obsession. He talks about little else. He tells me it was lucky for us that the German officer happened to turn up at his surgery, because now he has an ally. You will understand why I curse the day.'

'I can't get your husband to deviate from the task. And he doesn't see the risk. But we could, if you will allow it, use it to our advantage.'

'What good can possibly come out of something like this?'

We did not look each other in the eye – instead we watched the vigorous motion of the wooden spoon.

'What I am doing,' I said, 'is creating a second register, almost identical to the first, but with names altered and addresses changed.'

'To what purpose?'

'At worst, to cause confusion. At best, to save lives.'

Her eyes were huge, her voice low and shaky. 'Won't this put us in even more danger, when they find out what you've done?'

'I wrote the register. I will take the blame. If you'll trust me, I can save you. However, unless you feel you *have* to tell him, your husband cannot know. As you say, he believes he has made a friend in Eichel and is therefore in a good position. According to him, he's helping everyone by keeping to the rules. Personally I think the reverse is true. Eichel will wash his hands of the register the minute its true purpose is revealed. And your husband is also saying that if your family escapes you will be betraying the others we have entered on the list.' I paused long enough for her to stop stirring. 'I wanted you to know that I would do anything for you and the children.'

'What if your grandmother becomes implicated? I couldn't bear her to suffer because of us.'

'Grand-mère knows all about this. You would do the same for us, if we were in your shoes. We're all involved, Clémence.'

She licked her dry lips. 'And Jerome knows nothing about it?'

'Nothing at all.'

'Let's keep it that way,' she said.

We carried the coffee and almond cakes into the next room where the children arranged themselves in a row on the sofa, plates on bare knees, waiting for everyone to be served. Obedience, I realised, would be the death of this family.

I handed the doctored version of the register ceremoniously to Eichel when he came to collect the finished product. By way of thanks, he pressed my hand and looked warmly into my eyes as he stowed the document in his briefcase. 'If only everyone was as cooperative as you, Mademoiselle.'

We did not see Oberleutnant Eichel at the surgery after that. I took this to be a sign that the man had a modicum of shame. Or perhaps he didn't want his reputation besmirched. Or to succumb to temptation. Or perhaps, subliminally at least, he had guessed that given one iota of a chance, I would have stabbed him in the head with a periodontal probe.

Christa

By way of a pre-emptive strike, I mentioned to Ma that I'd bumped into Auntie Maisie in the tea rooms at Derry & Toms. 'Wasn't that a coincidence? She was most impressed to see me with an actual don – the one I visited in Cambridge when Estelle was here.'

However, this casual explanation obviously didn't match the account given by Auntie Maisie the next time the sisters had tea together. Usually Ma avoided confrontation and it was only when she offered to share the washing-up with me after Sunday lunch that the storm finally broke. While I scoured the pans, she rushed around behind me, wiping surfaces and sweeping the floor.

'Maisie said how surprised she'd been to bump into you in town the other day,' she began, while drying the water jug.

'It was quite a shock for us both.'

'She said she had been about to join you when she realised you were with a middle-aged man.'

'As I told you, he's a Cambridge academic.'

The jug was replaced on its hook, where it swung vigorously. 'She said you were drinking wine.'

'Is there anything wrong with that?'

'Maisie said he looked like much more than a passing acquaintance to her.'

'For heaven's sake, he's not even a friend.'

'I felt like a complete fool, not knowing who my own daughter was meeting in London.'

'Well I don't have any intention of seeing him again.'

'You see, what I can't understand is why you initially told me you were going to meet a woman friend in town.'

245

'I didn't say that, Ma. You assumed it.'

'That in itself is a kind of lie.'

There was a long pause while she scrubbed at the hob with a Brillo pad.

'So how much older than you is this Doctor Sinclair? Oh Christine, he's not married is he?'

'As a matter of fact, he's interested in Pa, not me, and his connection to the Cornelis family. Because of what happened in the war.'

But this only made things worse. 'You've not been digging up that old story again. Pa's so much more stable these days. Please don't say anything to him.'

When I showed her the typewritten sheet about Sergeant Hawkins, she was dismissive. 'How can they possibly know it was the same man? Hawkins sounds nothing like Hébert.'

Lizzie Henderson, with her science degree and flying experience, was called up in May, much to Miss Snaresbrook's chagrin. An expert puller of strings at the Home Office, our headmistress insisted that she needed all her teachers, especially the young and able, to nurture the young minds entrusted to her care. I could not help regarding my exclusion from the actual war effort as part of my banishment from De Eikenhoeve. However often I patrolled the streets at night or read Tennyson to my class as we huddled in our corner of the gym during yet another air raid, I knew that I was on the fringes of conflict, while Estelle was probably at its centre. I simply did not feel useful enough.

It transpired, however, that Sinclair really did have friends in high places. At the end of the summer term I received a letter inviting me to take an examination in written and oral French, followed by an interview at an address in Baker Street. Although I felt encouraged by my performance in the written test, the subsequent discussion with a native speaker about the state of the war, conducted at breakneck speed, was a world away from the stately pace of conversation in Grand-mère's salon in Rue d'Orléans. By the time I reached an interview room which reeked of cigarettes and Dettol, and found myself across the desk

246

from a depressed-looking officer with a list of grades in front of him, I knew I had failed.

'I was interested to meet you, Miss Geering, because you have an excellent testimonial from Doctor Sinclair and both your written and spoken French are of a high standard – not bad at all, considering you've never been in Paris.'

'I speak a little Flemish too, because I spent a summer in the countryside near Brussels.'

'However, if you were hoping to use your languages in the war effort you will be disappointed. We need native speakers, or at least those who could pass as such. As a teacher, I'm afraid your French must have become a little sullied by too much contact with your pupils. What I can do is recommend you for other essential work . . .'

He made a few more notes, and I left his office convinced that I was doomed to spend the war marking essays on 'The Lady of Shalott'. But a month later I received the news that I was to be posted with the Auxiliary Territorial Service and should present myself for basic training at Northampton on the first day of August. At last, two years into the war, I had managed to leave home, with the prospect of active service.

My fellow recruits were a mixed bag. For many of us, the ATS had been third choice and we grumbled that because we'd been working in a reserved occupation other women had signed up ahead of us and we'd lost out on the chance of a more prestigious posting. But I never really minded the khaki uniform, the hours of drill on the breezy racecourse or the interminable polishing of buttons because I was so relieved to have escaped the ever more stifling atmosphere of Harewood Road and to be doing something useful at last.

Inevitably, the scent of crushed grass, a touch of sunburn and the wide skies of Northamptonshire reminded me of De Eikenhoeve. Every salute, every swing of my arm or wheel to the right, the left, must surely bring me closer to Estelle. The prospect of being posted abroad, or at the very least trained to work in anti-aircraft, meant that I could tell her, when it was all over, that I'd made some contribution to the war effort. Towards the end of our five weeks, we sat tests in mathematics, trigonometry and languages, and former secretaries had to brush up on their typing speeds. One of the girls commented jealously that, with my superior education and background in teaching, I was bound to get a quick promotion.

But in the end I was seconded to Fanum House, a grimy office in Leicester Square, where I was to work as an Area Distribution Officer with the Board of Trade. My task was to register shortages caused by blockades, bombings, petrol rationing and the boundless demands of the armaments factories which drained resources and made mere household necessities such as scrubbing brushes or Brillo pads a rarity.

My billet was a house in Fitzroy Street, shared with six other girls. After my first day at the Board of Trade I sat on the bed in the housemaid's room on the top floor, pressed my palms to my eyes in disbelief and despair and wondered why on earth I'd exchanged the camaraderie and challenges of school for the drudgery of compiling lists at a lonely desk.

Estelle

The winter chill made the Nazis even more merciless. The latest atrocity: a German soldier was shot in the suburb of Schaerbeek and, by way of reprisal, five Belgians, selected at random, were dragged from their homes and driven away, never to be seen again.

News came from De Eikenhoeve that Papa was ill. *Short of breath*, wrote Marthe, *and taken to his bed. He's rather weak and keeps asking to see his children. Is there any chance you could come home?*

I'd never known Papa to be unwell. Filthy-tempered, hungover, wheezing, but never really ill.

I meant to go at Christmas, but we needed to put out a special edition of the newspaper. Hitler had made a mistake or two. Bombed Pearl Harbor and forced the US into the war, got his army stuck outside Moscow, freezing in their boots, and on the retreat in North Africa. For propaganda reasons, we had to take advantage of every scrap of good news. Then Grand-mère developed pneumonia and lay like a corpse, except during bouts of coughing so violent I was afraid she'd fracture her ribs.

I lugged in a couch for Céleste and we took turns keeping Grand-mère warm with our body heat. We got her through. Pushed crumbs of Vauclain brioche between her lips. They worked miracles, that bourgeois couple – pandered to the Nazi sweet tooth while eking out the flour rations, feeding the starving underbelly of Brussels. Grand-mère's chest still rattled, but she sent me back to work, where the cold in the surgery scorched my ears. The Depage children, on holiday from school, were bundled up in woolly layers, with only their wary eyes peeping out as they read ancient comics whilst their mother queued for potatoes. Depage had to warm his hands in his armpits before he could touch a patient.

The telephone in Rue d'Orléans shattered the silence of the night. 'Perhaps you will come home for the funeral, Estelle.' Marthe's voice was barely under control.

'You didn't tell me he was actually—'

'The death certificate will say heart failure. We think it was partly the foul weather. We found him on his knees in the milking parlour. It took four of us to carry him inside. When we got him into bed he closed his eyes and wouldn't wake up. The funeral is on Thursday, eleven o'clock. It would be wonderful to see you. Pieter has sent you a letter so you can show the authorities why you need to travel.'

'Is Robbe coming?' I was having trouble making sense of what Marthe was saying.

'You never know, do you? We've written to him at his last known address.'

Depage gave me the time off. Clémence would have to assist as best she could. 'I wonder if you'll ever come back,' he said, clutching my hand as if it were a lifeline. I didn't know how to answer him.

I had to pass through three barriers at the station. The last was manned by a soldier with a pustule on the point of his chin. Mean eyes. Fully armed. He'd probably been snatched from the backstreets of some small industrial town, shoved into a uniform, bullied and brutalised at a training camp, had his head filled with anti-Semitic claptrap and been marched into Belgium. All before he was eighteen.

Grand-mère had lent me an ancient black fur coat that almost reached the floor. The soldier practically licked his lips when he saw it, and couldn't help reaching out to touch the sleeve. Got me to translate Pieter's letter, word for word.

'When do you say your father died?'

'Three days ago.'

'Do you have proof of his death?' He peered myopically at Pieter's signature. 'Why do you not live at home, since you are

250

unmarried?' His gaze travelled down to my ankles, and he didn't bother to hide what he was thinking.

I'd learnt to let my mind float at such times. Reference to Grand-mère's health and my need to care for her did the trick. Sentimental, these Nazis. I imagined the poor boy staggering across the Russian Steppes, his frail shoulders burdened by half a ton of kit and his troublesome adolescent skin pounded by blizzard.

The train was late, unheated, crawled along. I snuggled into the fur, wrapped my feet in a scarf and thought of other journeys. With Marthe, when she'd collected me as a child from Grand-mère's. I'd clutch a gold-embossed cardboard box containing a plum tart from the pâtisserie, a feast of luscious textures between the teeth and on the tongue. The journey home with Christa after our few days in Brussels, the buttons straining on her cotton dress. Something in her eyes, a slight mist, which should have warned me her mind was elsewhere.

My guts tightened when I wondered what Robbe and I would say to each other.

Beyond the grimy window nothing much had changed, except there was no sign of a cow or a horse. Slaughtered, sent to Germany or tucked away in snug byres. Snowy woodland, a doddery man pulling a cart. The carriage was too quiet. Even old women returning from market had learnt not to gossip. Glanced up when someone different got on, in case it was the police.

Viktor, not Marthe, was waiting in the station yard. He'd made a few changes to the inside of his cab – a grubby sheepskin rug and a dank red velvet cushion on the back seat. Icy air whistled through splits in the roof and I had already lost the feeling in my legs. My lips were blue in the rear-view mirror.

'Have you been keeping busy, Viktor?'

'So-so.'

'I understand there's a battalion of German soldiers based just outside the village.'

No response.

'I expect that's created work for you.'

Nothing.

'Is your family well?'

'So-so.'

I had never disliked him so much. Viktor would have betrayed his own mother for a nominal fee. No wonder his son had seen the glimmer of a chance and left for Germany. 'How is Jong Viktor?' I asked. 'Have you heard from him?'

'Not a word.'

'I think I'll walk from here. I need time to think about Papa.'

I paid him too much and tumbled out onto numb feet. For several minutes taxi fumes and engine noise hung in the air; then nothing, except the descending call of a blackbird. I smelled snow and dead leaves and something metallic. Nazi steel, per-haps, creeping over the face of the earth. I'd never smelt the like, or seen such a cloak of ice. Fortnight-old snow was clamped to the hedgerows, the top of the gate, every branch. The ruts on the track were rigid with frost. For the first time in many months I felt unwatched. Truly alone.

And at last it dawned on me that Papa wouldn't be there.

See that gate to the hayfield? He'd hung it himself, adjusted it meticulously, breathing through his nose in utter concentration. Swore whenever it creaked after that. 'Worked perfectly well when I fixed it. Those bloody kids must have been swinging on it again.'

The farm gate was shut. Snow had been cleared from the drive to form a path which glinted in the moonlight.

The kitchen provided a momentary echo of the old world: Hanna at the range, the aroma of stewed meat and new-baked bread, a blaze of heat.

Don't cry, Estelle.

Hanna hugged me tight – that familiar blend of flour and cologne and ageing skin. I let Marthe hold me too, her warm cheek against my cold one. 'I'm so sorry I couldn't meet you,' she said. 'We've had to hide the car. Like last time. In case they req-uisitioned it.' They moved me into a chair, pulled off my shoes, massaged my feet, dressed me in Pieter's pullover and Marthe's sheepskin mules and gave me a cup of chocolate.

This was not right. *Chocolate*.

I staggered to my feet and made for the door.

'He's in our bedroom,' said Marthe. 'Let me take you there.'

For once I didn't pull away from her hand.

'Shall I stay, or would you like to be alone with him?'

I wanted her to stay. 'I'm all right,' I heard myself saying, so she melted away.

Papa lay in state in their frilly white bedroom, with a sheet pulled up to his chin. Grey skin translucent on yellow bone; farmer's hands crossed on his chest. I touched his cheek but jolted away from the chill of it. Even in death, his mouth was moody. He resembled his mother. My distant memory of her: knobbly temples, pinched nostrils, disapproval. Bony knees against my chest when I was brought close for a kiss on the forehead.

I expected Papa to open an eye and say: 'You've no idea how difficult it's been for me over the past year. The war has caused me no end of hardship. I'm amazed you've found the time to turn up for my funeral.'

I stared at him long and hard, wanting an answer. 'Was it you, Papa, who betrayed Maman?' Unlikely. For Papa things were pretty simple. He had loved the farm. In all probability he had been faithful to Maman and then Marthe, because he lacked the imagination to do otherwise. He could be tender – a warm hand on my arm, a wink, a fondness in his eyes. A glimpse of the man he might have been.

And then I saw that tucked around his toes was the old grey cardigan that Marthe had always left hanging over a chair in Maman's attic room, for old time's sake.

Pieter appeared in the doorway, wearing a cable pullover knitted years ago by Tante Julia, and a green scarf. I walked into his arms and held him tight. Began to cry while he kissed my hair over and over.

'Christ, I've missed you. I thought you were never coming home.'

Just three of us at supper: Pieter, Marthe, me.

Marthe looked good in black. Pale and small, her hair combed smoothly from her face. Occasionally her eyes filled and then mine did too. Hanna insisted on waiting at table, her only assistant, Lotte, who'd been promoted to maid of all work.

253

'What happened to Roos and Mietje?' I asked.

'They disappeared at the first opportunity. Rumour has it they're in Antwerp, where presumably they've found more lucrative employment,' Pieter replied.

'They've not written,' Marthe said.

'That's war for you,' Pieter said. 'People develop different allegiances.' Surely he missed Roos a little, her ever-available curves and adoring eyes.

Marthe wanted to know about my work with Depage. 'He's lucky to have an educated girl like you working for him.'

'At least I feel useful.' I hated the nervous look in her eyes when I spoke to her.

'It's a shame, because I always thought you might teach,' she said.

'Since history is my subject and the Germans are busy rewriting it, I'm glad I'm not a teacher.'

'I wonder how Christa is getting on in England,' she murmured. 'It's dreadful the way we're so cut off. I don't suppose you've heard a word.'

Pieter's fork went still for a moment and he looked at me enquiringly. I didn't reply.

The rich stew made me feel queasy and I couldn't eat dessert – said I'd prefer to take a jar of the compote back to Grand-mère. The news from the village was that a few of the boys had formed a group of the Flemish Hitler Youth League and went around bullying the old folk into giving scrap metal for the war effort – all their best pans, in fact. And a very courteous German officer had arrived at De Eikenhoeve in a smart, soft-topped car, drunk coffee in the parlour with Marthe and Pieter, apologised for the imposition and asked to inspect the barns and outbuildings in case he needed to billet his men.

'We aim for a light touch,' he had explained. 'By and large we've found the local people to be very helpful. I don't think we'll be making too many demands on you.'

'We didn't show him all the cellars,' Pieter said. A code for the food and valuables they'd squirrelled away. 'Just a couple of storerooms.' More code. So, they'd paid the German off with beer and bacon.

Marthe said: 'We wrote to Robbe at the last address we had, near Antwerp. There's been no reply. Have you heard from him, Estelle?'

'Nothing.'

A pregnant pause. We were all remembering the night of Papa's feast.

'I've had a fire lit in your mother's old room,' Marthe said. 'I thought that you and Pieter might like a glass of something there while you talk about your Papa.'

Pieter reached across the table and squeezed her hand. 'Ever thoughtful, but won't you join us?' His smile made her weep again and shake her head.

'I've a sick beast to check up on,' he told me. 'I won't be long, Estelle.'

On my way out I met my ghostly self in the hall mirror. Hair falling lank about my cheeks, collarbones exposed by the bor-rowed pullover. Upstairs, I pushed open the doors to the empty rooms. Smelt dried rose petals in one, a faint whiff of tobacco where grandfather used to sleep in another. And in Robbe's, the scent of a boy coming in from a day spent roaming the woods. Robbe had nearly always refused to take me with him. There one minute, gone the next. And an hour later, hanging upside down on the swing or rubbing down a horse.

I dared to glance into the room Christa had stayed in. Thought I caught the barest hint of her, the warm creases of her frock, her girlish flesh. I never told her that when I was young I used to imagine that Ma had escaped from the house by stepping out of the window and into the branches of the oak tree. And that I never actually slept in that room for fear of her coming back to fetch me. The rustle of fabric along the skirting, the clutch of cold, fleshless hands. A tug into the ether. '*Suis-moi, cherie, mon ange, ma bébé.*'

The bed was made up. As I stood in Christa's former bedroom, where frost had etched leaf patterns in every lattice, I felt the distance between us all unspool to infinity.

I ran up the stairs to the attic floor. High windows in the passage overlooked the farmyard, where the colours had been sucked away by cold blue moonlight. The surface of the snow had been studded by footprints, but the pond was a flat white plate. In her room, Roos had left a broken comb and an empty scent bottle. Sometimes, when I drove back from market with Pieter, I used to see her leaning out of her window. She'd catch his eye and wave. Stupid girl. Too proud to take on a village boy, too lowly for Pieter Cornelis – though her hopes must have soared whenever he fucked her in the hayloft or her own narrow bed.

The door to Maman's turret room was shut fast, but when I'd worked open the latch, the fire was lit, as promised, and Pieter was at the hearth, glass in hand, bottle by his side. He drew me in to sit at his feet, leaning against his thigh. Just him and me, in firelight, the rest in shadow. Tension oozed from me.

'I've been wanting to ask you a favour,' I murmured.

'Go on.'

I told him about the Depage family. 'We could pass them off as distant relatives. They're French-Belgian, but could learn Flemish quickly and just blend in, maybe live in a farm cottage like any other tenants. Clémence Depage would help on the farm. We've already created some papers.'

'It would be foolhardy to bring them here, Estelle. I don't trust the villagers – the dreaded Viktor, to name but one.' He lifted a strand of my hair. 'We're likely to be under surveillance, you know, because of Maman. And now Papa's gone, things will be trickier. He was a past master at keeping everyone sweet in the last war.'

'You mean he collaborated?'

'I mean he knew how and when to make compromises. He and Oud Daan were absolute geniuses at getting people to look in the wrong direction. Small irregularities with the milk yield, that sort of thing, so that De Eikenhoeve had a reputation for minor bits of subversion. The farm was fined for failing to declare the correct number of eggs and piglets and ran a nice line in black-market butter and potatoes. But in reality, Papa was providing a front for Maman. He was extremely canny, you know, beneath all that huffing and puffing. And very loyal.'

'What about Marthe? You seem to be rubbing along pretty well.'

'Since the invasion, she's been running the dairy almost single-handed. But I was wondering if you'd consider coming home, Estelle. I need your help here.'

'I can't.'

'Without Papa, it will be near impossible to keep everything going. We've heard rumours that our lads who chose to work in Germany are being treated very harshly, so I shift about the remaining few in the hope the Moffen won't count them and have them transported to labour camps. And we face penalties if we fail to maintain our quotas. They can put in a manager of their own any time they feel like it.'

Pieter was normally so cautious that it was quite disturbing to hear him use an abusive term like Moffen when alluding to the enemy.

'Isn't it in their best interests to let you get on with the job? You're the expert,' I said.

'Seventy-five per cent of what we produce is already sent across the border. Soon they'll want more. Or they could billet a hundred men on us.'

He selected another lock of my hair, twisted it round his finger, let it fall. The cold was still seeping between the floorboards, but I was huddled against his legs, my face aglow in firelight. His mouth was so close to my ear that he only needed to whisper. 'I know you're working for Borland and I applaud you for it. But you're my little sister and I want you to be safe. Come home. Think of the work we could do together on the farm, for those little Jewish children of yours, for instance.'

'You know I couldn't live at De Eikenhoeve. Please don't make it a condition of accepting the children.'

'If you were to be caught doing something illegal, they'd investigate where you worked and link you to Depage, and Grand-mère for that matter, and the trail would lead straight back here.'

'I won't get caught.'

'That's what Maman must have thought.' He got up and pulled me to my feet, cupping my face in his hands. 'When I saw you in Papa's room, just for an instant I thought you were her. The light was so dim and you had your back to me, but the way

257

your head was bent, the shape of your back, you looked just like her.' He studied me. 'For Christ's sake, Estelle, keep yourself safe. And don't forget how vulnerable we all are. Both sides will try to use us because of what the name Cornelis-Faider symbolises. I'll think about accommodating the Depage family and maybe others, if you'll think about coming home.'

The old house groaned under the sub-zero temperature as I headed for bed. Curled in the darkness, a hot-water bottle clutched to my chest, I thought that I could hear the ice shifting on the river. Imagined seeing the war out at De Eikenhoeve, retreating to this snug nest, night after night.

Four members of the Depage family in the bag. What was worth more, the lives of these Jewish children or the spasmodic delivery of an anti-Nazi rag?

The next day we processed along the lane to the village. The hay wagon had been converted into a hearse, drawn by our two remaining carthorses. Of course our best beasts had been requisitioned, or so the Germans thought. Oud Daan had hobbled these two – his favourites – prior to the inspection. Wrapped their forelegs in dirty bandages, matted their manes, dulled their coats, starved them as far as he dared. Apt that Papa's last ride should be in a home-built coffin under wreaths of holly and pine harvested from his own woods.

Oud Daan wore a coat buttoned to his throat, cap pulled down hard, scarf covering nose and mouth. His eyes, two unblinking dots, gave me the barest gleam of a greeting. Pieter drove Marthe, Hanna and a couple of other old women, using some of the last of our precious petrol. The rest of us went on foot, taking the shortcut beside the frozen river. Sometimes we heard a trickle of water, but we could have walked the entire way on ice. As we approached the village we heard the bell tolling louder with every step.

Tante Julia met us in the porch, dressed in her usual wool coat and leather boots, one of Papa's hats pulled low over her wild hair. She punched my shoulder but grief brimmed in her eyes and she and I linked arms as we walked in. In the old days, when Marthe and I came to Mass at Sint Michiels, heat used to blaze

258

from the radiators. Now the temperature inside was punishingly cold. Pressed close to Pieter and Tante Julia, I stared at Papa's coffin and felt hollowed out, wishing I'd come in time to say goodbye.

Underfoot, the blue- and white-tiled floor; overhead, the white painted arches and the wall plaques commemorating members of the Cornelis clan. Marthe, on the far side of Pieter, wore a veil. I was dressed in Grand-mère's moth-eaten fur. And behind us were the dregs of families we'd known forever. Mostly old people.

From the corner of my eye I saw Oud Daan and Hanna sitting half a metre apart, and Lotte in a far too big coat, a hand-me-down from Marthe, and beyond her, in the pew behind . . .

My guts had sensed him long before my brain. I glanced round once, twice, to convince myself that it really was him. Yes, there he was. Late, as ever. A jolt zipped up my arm and into Pieter's. I felt his shoulder twitch – he must have noticed too. And the wound was ripped open, as if it were yesterday, when I'd stood at the gate and seen Robbe gather her in his arms, her skirt crushed against his thighs, her head thrown back as the kiss deepened. I tasted her soft lips and shy tongue, felt her warm hair falling across my arm.

And then I came to myself and I was at Papa's funeral, getting on for two years into a war. The church fizzed with the drama of it. Robbe had always been a favourite in the village. I imagined the thousands of miles he must have travelled since we were last together, into dark and dangerous places. The priest had also spotted him. Gabbled through the Eucharistic prayer. We sat for the eulogy, clutching our arms to our breasts for warmth. *A pillar of the community, a tiller of the soil,* et cetera, et cetera. Pieter and Marthe went up to take Communion and some of the villagers hobbled along the aisle, mainly so they could peer into Robbe's face. I saw Marthe glance his way and blush as she came back to our pew, and Pieter acknowledge him with a raised eyebrow.

As we paraded out behind the coffin, Robbe fell in beside me. Even then I hadn't made up my mind what I would do. In the end he gave me no choice, flung his arm around my shoulders and kissed me on both cheeks. I was torn between wanting to

259

forgive him and being stuck in that moment in the farmyard, but Pieter didn't hesitate. Didn't reproach him: Where have you been all these years? Did you never once think that Papa might be missing you? Instead he held out his arms and they embraced. When they released each other a look passed between them, a fraternal flash, and I felt that old stab of exclusion, knowing they understood things that I never could. Marthe stood back, waiting to be acknowledged, and Robbe did at least touch the brim of his hat by way of recognition.

It must have taken the labourers hours to dig a grave in that iron-hard earth. We stepped forward one by one to throw soil on the coffin. I squeezed my eyes shut, and followed Papa into the grave. Imagined him fuming at being forced to lie so still. Opened my eyes and released my fistful of dirt and stones. Robbe stepped forward, stooped, then changed his mind, drew back his foot and flicked forward a clod with his toe.

A sleek automobile drew up by the churchyard gate and a German officer stepped out, dressed in an overcoat and leather gloves. The priest fell silent and we kept our eyes on the ground as Pieter strode up and shook the bastard by the hand, greeting him as Hauptmann Steiger. The German's advanced years and short sight will have been the reason he'd been posted to a backwater like Oostervorken, but that didn't stop us all thinking: Has he come for me? Had he found out that I was working for *La Libre Belgique*? Or that Marthe had hidden her little car away again and that she and Hanna were supplying food parcels to half the village? What about Pieter's treasure trove in the cellars? And Christ only knew what Robbe had been up to.

Steiger clicked his heels and saluted. Pieter inclined his head.

In German: 'I came to offer my respects, Meneer Cornelis, to you and your family.' Steiger flashed a complex smile; an I-know-I-can't-expect-you-to-love-me type of smile, but ultimately the smile of the conqueror taking the moral high ground. Nobody is forcing me to be nice to you, yet here I am.

'Your father was a good man, highly respected in the neighbourhood. It was a privilege doing business with him.'

'This is my sister, Estelle, and my brother, Robbe,' Pieter said.

'I've not had the good fortune.'

'Estelle lives in Brussels, where she is looking after our grand-mother. And Robbe, as you know, has been very ill. He came back from the mountains for Papa's sake.'

Robbe did indeed look sickly, his eyes red-rimmed, his complexion yellow.

Steiger nodded to each of us. 'I won't intrude further.' He saluted again, and headed for the car. Once his back was turned, Pieter spat into one of his bootprints. A villager gasped.

Pieter instructed Oud Daan to cram as many into the wagon as it could hold. The rest of us were to travel ahead in the van to stoke the fires in readiness for the funeral breakfast. But Robbe, behind me, muttered: 'I have a message for you, hold back,' so everything was quickly rearranged. He offered our places to a couple of old women – they would be much warmer, he told them – while he and I walked back along the river path.

I was choking on years of rage and jealousy as our boots creaked along the crust of snow. Robbe said: 'The point is, we need you, because of morale. Because you're like Maman.'

'To do what?'

'First you must promise not to say a word to anyone. Not even Pieter.'

'Why not Pieter?'

'Promise, Estelle.'

Could he really be let off so easily? This man with unwashed hair, in a coat that did not bear inspection – grubby, missing a button or two, torn at the hem – a man who had kicked dirt onto our father's grave.

'We need someone who can pass as French. Attractive if possible. Resourceful. We've lost a few people recently and we need others to take their place. In particular, we need you.'

Our breath fogged the air as we stared at each other. Robbe half-smiling, head tilted. Me breathing rapidly. Fear. Excitement.

'Why have you lost people?'

'Human error, mostly. And because too many so-called friends can be bought and sold. To tell the truth, I didn't want to involve you; it's a risky business. But Borland said it should be your decision not mine, and we do need good people.'

I had never seen him so stern.

'Unfortunately, we think they may be watching me, so I've got to keep a low profile for a while. I thought my number was up, back there in the graveyard.'

'Then why are you here? Are you mad? This is the first place they'll look.'

'Or the last. Old Steiger didn't appear to be on the alert, did he? The thing is, I wanted it to be me who had this conversation with you, not someone else. I didn't want there to be any coercion. But if Pieter ever found out, he'd kill me. He told me before the occupation, in no uncertain terms, that he wants to keep you out of trouble. A newspaper, OK. Escape lines, no.' The tip of his nose was red and he was shivering. 'So, it's up to you, but if you do decide to join us, here's the address you should go to. One o'clock, Thursday. They'll be expecting you. Or not. Your choice.'

'I'll think about it.' I was unyielding, because of his complete lack of regret for Christa.

'One more thing: if you do join us, you'll have to drop that Jewish dentist.'

'Jerome Depage?'

'You mustn't do anything to draw their attention. Jews are toxic.'

'How can you talk like that? The Depages are family friends.'

'I've told you. Drop them. There's no place for sentiment now.'

'It's not sentiment, it's loyalty.'

He was on the brink of walking away.

'Aren't you coming back to the house?' I demanded. 'You must. Everyone will be waiting for you.'

He reached into his inner pocket for cigarettes, changed his mind, suddenly looked at a loss. 'Steiger might drop in again. I really don't want any more close encounters with the likes of him.'

'But it will look strange.'

'What the fuck do I care how it looks?'

'For Papa's sake, you should come.'

'Papa.' His voice had a new timbre, low and mocking. 'Papa. Your precious Papa. I didn't give a damn about that old shit.'

Our eyes met. His stance was so familiar – the little boy provoking everyone to scold him so that he had an excuse for running away. They all hate me. Whereas, in fact, Marthe, Pieter, Papa had all forgiven him, time after time.

Under the arches of the bridge the river had frozen in circular furrows.

'Where are you going, Robbe?'

He glanced upriver, towards the woods and the bathing pond. 'Cross-country. You can keep me company some of the way, if you like.'

Such a solitary figure in his filthy coat. How many times in boyhood had he raced along that same path, to get away from us all? I yearned for the house, did not want to be out here on the borders of life, yet I followed him along the rutted path. 'Have you heard from Christa?' I asked.

'Christa?'

'Christa. The English girl.'

He laughed. 'Of course I know who you mean. And no, I haven't.'

'Do you mind?'

'Why should I?'

'Weren't you in love with her?'

'I hardly knew her. She was only here for the summer.'

He walked rapidly on and I stumbled after him. 'If you didn't care, why did you come and take her?'

'*Take* her. From whom?' He turned and walked backwards, taunting.

How I hated him then. His coat too long, shoulders crookedly held, hair matted.

'Why did you make love to her, if she meant nothing to you?'

'For Christ's sake. Because she was there. She wanted it. It had nothing to do with love. I thought it would be a laugh because of Maman and her father; a kind of symmetry. So anyway, are you coming with me any further or not?'

He glanced into my face then grunted. 'See you then, in Brussels.'

'I haven't made up my mind.'

'You will.'

He vaulted over the gate, agile as a young boy, and merged with the naked trees in the woods. Would he look back? His

263

hand went up in a casual wave, but that was all. Leaving me stricken in that frigid landscape, the sky veiled by milky cloud. So he had loved neither Christa nor Papa. But then Robbe could say one thing and mean the opposite. It was always about protecting himself from the next abandonment, or so I had come to believe.

By the time I reached the farmhouse the orange sun had dipped behind the clouds. I could hear the heavy breathing of our remaining cows in the barn and I had a vivid memory of Christa, perched on the dairy step, head raised to smile at me. I stumbled towards the phantom figure, but the print on her frock faded and her dark hair merged with the shadows.

In the crowded dining room the farmhands and villagers were drinking beer and gorging themselves on ham and cheese and pickles. 'Where's Robbe?' muttered Pieter. 'It's time for the toast.'

'He's not coming. He thought Steiger might come back and start asking questions. He's on a list, apparently.'

'I don't know why I expected anything else,' he said. I'd never seen Pieter react quite like this. His voice was as soft as ever, yet I could tell that every fibre of his being was vibrating with rage.

'He was thinking of you. He didn't want to bring trouble.'

'He has never thought of anyone except himself.'

'I thought you loved him.'

'Of course I love him. Haven't I devoted my entire life to taking care of him? Yet he could not do this one thing for me.'

'At least he came to the funeral.'

'To show his contempt, if his behaviour at the graveside was anything to go by. Why should he care about Papa? What's it to Robbe that we all spent every moment of every day trying to make it up to him that Maman wasn't coming back? Because he was the one she loved the best, and therefore the most likely to go off the rails. He owed Papa the greatest debt, yet he always treated him like shit.'

'Pieter?'

He glanced at my face, recovered rapidly and was himself again, tweaking my cheek, shaking his head. 'Never mind. It's done now. Let's get on with it, eh?'

Marthe, who'd removed her veil, had edged a little closer and was gripping a chair-back. Pieter kissed the side of her head and with his arm around her shoulder banged the table with his fist. 'Are your glasses full? Then let's have a toast. To my beloved Papa. *Proost*, Papa. *Santé*, Papa.' It was an old joke. Papa could never decide which he preferred. An excuse to have another glass. *Proost*. And another. *Santé*.

'I'm not going to make much of a speech,' Pieter said. 'However, I will say this. We all have our own memories of Papa. We know he was a contradictory soul. If he were here now, he'd be counting the cost of every loaf and at the same time chastising Hanna for not having provided enough. But he was devoted to us, his family, and to you, his people, and to the farm, to his very last breath.'

Pieter's misty eyes travelled from Marthe, who was weeping, to Tante Julia, hiding her face behind a tankard, to Hanna, who'd raised her arm to cover her eyes, Lotte, who scarcely seemed to believe she was allowed in the great dining hall, and Oud Daan, always uncomfortable inside, hanging about by the door. And all those other faces, including Viktor, who would never, ever, miss the chance of a free meal.

After the applause and another toast, Pieter built the fire higher until the ancient panelling glowed. I sat with Tante Julia, Marthe and Hanna and told them what was going on in Brussels and how Grand-mère had survived through Christmas. And I realised I wanted to be there. In that moment. With those people.

When Pieter drove me and the milk to the station the following morning, he asked: 'Why did Robbe want to talk to you alone yesterday?'

I had prepared for this. 'He wondered whether I'd heard from Christa.'

'Have you?'

'Of course not. How could I?'

'So he wasn't trying to recruit you.'

'For what?'

He glanced at me. 'And have you made up your mind?'

265

'I want to save the Depage family.'

'I meant about coming home.'

I leant my head on his upper arm and he sighed. We didn't need to say any more.

Christa

At the Board of Trade it was drummed into us that our purpose was to protect civilian morale. Now that the worst of the bombing seemed to be over, local people had to be helped to recover, so that they might return vigorously to the task of winning the war. Thus it did matter, was in fact a patriotic necessity, that a householder should be able to buy Vim and that a builder's yard should not run out of nails.

It was ironic that having wriggled out of every attempt by Ma to persuade me to work as a Saturday girl in Clements department store, I now found myself in shops day after day, interviewing owners and customers so that I might register disparities between supply and demand. Gradually I warmed to my task. For the first time, I was brought up hard against the sheer drudgery of deprivation. I would step off a bus in Tottenham and weave my way between bomb sites to the nearest Co-Op, which was half in darkness because the shattered windows had been boarded up rather than replaced, and its shelves denuded of essentials, except for jars of Camp coffee or blocks of margarine.

I would circumnavigate queues of weary women with baskets on their arms and layers of old woollens under their damp coats, hollow-eyed from spending night after night in an air-raid shelter with children mewling around their feet. The harassed manager would greet me either with cynicism or relief that here was someone who might be able to put things right. Perhaps my air of breezy efficiency reassured them that rescue was at hand, while back at my desk in Fanum House I wrote memo after memo – *Crockery: one hundred cups, seventy plates, three dozen bowls* – and held tortuous telephone conversations with suppliers, pleading and haranguing until they agreed to at least some of my requests.

At large, on the wounded streets, I felt closer to Estelle. My latest bland little letter, posted in defiance of Sinclair to Grand-mère's house on Rue d'Orléans, care of the Red Cross, had received no response, but by this time I had long since given up expecting one. Pieter I could place, striding across the farm-yard at dawn, checking the stable, barn and pigsty. Robbe and Estelle flickered in and out of view. In my imagination, Robbe zigzagged across borders, waiflike and elusive, but Estelle was surely too unforgiving and full of rage to be a safe pair of hands in any war. So what was she up to?

Since spotting Borland in Watford, the possibility of running into her had seemed tantalisingly close, even if common sense told me she was trapped in occupied Belgium. Whenever I saw a flash of red, I always pursued it round a corner or until it disappeared into the mouth of an Underground station.

I was in Sutton, in south London, one January afternoon, assessing deficiencies in the stock at the local hardware store: bolts and hinges for replacement doors, turpentine, methylated spirit, Primus stoves. Walking back to the station through an urban park, undamaged by bombs, with greenish ice covering the pond, I recalled how Estelle had taken me to the Parc de Bruxelles, where a network of wide promenades was interspersed with trees and lavish fountains. Typically, she had swerved off the main path and into a dank hollow where she insisted that Wellington had conducted a romantic assignation on the eve of Waterloo. In the face of my incredulity – 'Don't you think he'd have had other things on his mind?' – her eyes had been teasing. 'You can't bear it, a slur on your precious Iron Duke . . .'

Even when I reached a row of shops in Brighton Road, my imagination lingered in that densely planted hollow where water trickled from a muddy spring and Estelle pranced along the steep path ahead of me. I heard her call over her shoulder so clearly that I stopped dead: 'Don't take yourself so seriously, Christa.'

At that moment there was a shiver of falling masonry and a dozen roof tiles shattered at my feet. I stood on the pavement, frozen, while the pile of rubble settled and a man from across the street yelled at me to step aside. It wasn't Estelle's voice that I'd heard, it was the cracking of frozen mortar in a hastily repaired roof.

An elderly couple helped me dust myself down, fulminating about the shoddy workmanship that had been going on since the Blitz. They called it a lucky escape – that I'd stopped in my tracks just in time. 'You must have a sixth sense, dear . . .'

It was no such thing, of course. My heart was singing, as in those heady days at De Eikenhoeve, before everything was ruined. I had reached for Estelle and she had answered me with the usual contradictions – peril, rescue, remorse – her peculiar recipe for love.

Estelle

Following Robbe's instruction, I entered the stationery shop on Rue de Florence at one o'clock precisely on Thursday 29th January 1942. The smell was delicious. I soon knew the contents of every cubbyhole behind the counter. Small brown envelopes; foolscap white paper, narrow-lined; graph paper; ink, red, green, black; HB pencils; charcoal; wooden rulers; set squares; pencil sharpeners, metal or tabletop; buff folders. Even in a time of occupation, lists had to be made, accounts drawn up.

'Yes, yes, go through.' The proprietor, Monsieur Bruton, elderly with thick glasses and palsied hands, did not inspire confidence. I ducked into the chaotic back room – dirty cups on a tray, old boxes, empty bottles, a chair covered by a knitted blanket, everything dusty, as if undisturbed for years. In the far corner stood a cupboard containing a filthy old mop in a zinc bucket and a broom, beneath which lay a concealed hatch that led to the basement.

An electric light had been strung from the rafter. The whiff of chemicals took me back to Sun Engraving in Watford. There was a small hand-press here, a lamp and a magnifying glass, a collection of pens and papers and a man at work who barely raised his head as I reached the bottom of the stairs.

No sign of Borland. And no Robbe, of course. Only Edouard, who embraced me and solemnly announced that what I was embarking upon had a very considerable chance of ending with my captivity and death. 'I didn't want them to involve you,' he said. 'But Borland assured us that Fleur Cornelis-Faider's daughter would not be held back.'

He gave me all kinds of dire warning. For the next three months I would undergo intensive training, and was not to do anything that would draw attention to myself. I must stop work on *La Libre Belgique,* and soon I'd have to transfer from Depage's practice to something less volatile.

'You know things are hotting up for the Jews. We think there'll be an edict requiring them to wear the yellow star any moment now.'

'What about his children?'

'Pieter has been in touch with us about them. We suspect that Depage will have to shut up shop soon. We'll take action when we have to.'

I was to be given a new name and a Swiss passport to explain my slight accent. French papers for passing through Paris. I was to invent a nursing background and be trained in basic first aid. I would learn how to wear French clothes, style my hair in a French way. There would be a great deal of rote learning, starting with French railway timetables. The work itself would involve endless waiting. If I thought I couldn't stand the tedium, now was the time to say. And I'd be in the dark about what went on in the rest of the organisation. The less I knew, the less I could give away.

'You must think carefully about this, Estelle. People from the line have gone missing. Houses that we believed were safe have been compromised, and everyone concerned arrested. The punishment for Belgians sheltering fugitives is unspeakable. If a British airman is caught, he is usually interrogated and interned – his chances of survival are not so bad. But you would be treated as an enemy of the state as well as a source of intelligence. Beatings, starvation, mutilation of the genitals, crucifixion, electric shocks – you name it. No cruelty is considered out of bounds. And after that, you would be shot or hanged, if you're lucky; transported to a prison camp in Germany if you draw the short straw.'

'How do they find out?'

'Any number of ways. The trouble is, we have to involve dozens of people. We hammer home the need for caution, we all know the risks, but someone will be noticed in the wrong place at the wrong time, or a neighbour will get suspicious of comings and goings. Even the most loyal can be threatened or bought.'

'What will I actually be doing, Edouard?'

'You will be an escort. We need to get personnel out of Belgium and through France to Spain. Some of those you will be required to help are couriers, some spies – most, airmen who've been shot down. We have a well-established escape line, but there are . . . gaps.'

'Gaps?'

'There have been arrests. A spate of them, in fact. We're not sure why, yet. For obvious reasons, we have to be subtle in our enquiries.' Pause. 'Is this *really* what you want, Estelle?'

'Yes. Oh yes.'

'Then here's how it works. A British or Australian or Polish pilot flying over Belgium is gunned down by a Nazi plane or by ground troops. Sometimes he has an engine malfunction. Perhaps the plane catches fire and he and his crew bail out. Or a member of our own resistance becomes the target of German surveillance. The worst type of fugitive, because they tend to be unfit and poor at taking instruction, are Belgian politicians or civil servants who are required to join the government in exile. All these people need to be escorted every centimetre of the way through occupied territory to the border, across the Pyrenees and into Spain where, if we can get them to the British Consulate and on to Gibraltar, they will be relatively safe.

'That's if the British authorities believe their story and don't hand them over to the Spanish police.

'We use several different routes, but you, Estelle – Elisabetta – will be made familiar with only one of them. You will meet people along the way whose names you won't be told and whose faces you must forget. You will be entrusted with bundles of cash because people will need paying, and you will need an explanation for every step you take because at any stage you might be stopped and interrogated. Do you understand what we're asking of you?'

They took my photograph from three different angles, then released me. A cooling-off period, Edouard said. He would be in touch in due course.

Emerging into the shop, I bought a green eraser from

272

Monsieur Bruton. It was sunny that day, though painfully cold. I was walking on air. Charged with new life. My confusion gone. I had not felt so free, so sure, since before I met Christa.

I felt connected, chosen.

After all, I decided, this was my destiny.

Christa

The narrow house in Fitzrovia had been vacated by its elderly owners at the start of the Blitz. Although most of the pictures and china had been tucked away in the cellar, the house was still cluttered with dingy Victorian furniture and musty rugs. Since none of the women billeted there had either the time or the inclination to keep it neat and clean, it had the air of a hostel rather than a residence.

A month or so after my brush with mortality on a Sutton street, I was greeted by the smell of hot butter and found one of my housemates, a doctor at University College, reluctantly hosting Sinclair in the kitchen. He had brought a bottle of wine and half a dozen eggs.

'How on earth did you track me down?' I asked.

'Fanum House.' He waited for my housemate to leave the kitchen with her supper on a tray, and added: 'I have some rather sad tidings. From Belgium.'

I tried not to let him see that my heart had missed several beats.

'Laurence Borland tells me that the old farmer is dead.'

'You mean Bernard Cornelis.'

He began humming the slow movement to Mozart's Clarinet Concerto as I scrambled the remaining eggs and spooned them onto two slices of toast.

'If you wish to write something, a letter of condolence perhaps, I'm sure I could help it get through,' he said.

I had no real cause to suspect his motives, and I knew that I should be grateful to him for the research he had done on my behalf, yet I felt uneasy in his presence. He had lied to me when I visited him in Cambridge and our meeting in the Rainbow

Restaurant had caused a rift between Ma and me. I therefore made the excuse that I'd paid heed to his warning and given up writing letters to Belgium.

We sat opposite each other at the kitchen table, but I was aware that his foot occasionally brushed mine, and that as he poured himself a second glass of wine his eyes lingered disconcertingly on my face. 'I hear you're doing extremely well at Fanum House,' he said.

'Who's your connection there?'

He shook his head ruefully, as if to say he couldn't possibly divulge his source.

'And I don't suppose you're going to tell me how Père Borland managed to get in touch with you,' I added.

His smile was indulgent. 'I shouldn't really have shared the news with you. But I remembered how fierce you'd been in Cambridge, and thought you wouldn't forgive me if I withheld anything else.'

I got up abruptly and gathered the plates.

He too pushed back his chair, crossed the room and stood close enough for me to feel his body heat. 'You know, anything you want, you have only to ask,' he said softly.

'There's nothing. Thank you.'

His fingertip ran down my spine, from the strap of my brassiere to the small of my back and beyond, to the crease between my buttocks, so softly that it might almost have been a figment of my imagination. I felt his breath on my neck as he murmured: 'Or did I pick up somewhere that men don't really attract you?'

When I turned, we were practically chest to chest. 'I beg your pardon, what are you talking about?'

'I could help you so much, if you'd only let me.'

'Doctor Sinclair, if you had any further information about Estelle I hope you wouldn't keep it from me just because I refuse to offer you any favours in return.'

He half closed his eyes as if in acknowledgement of his own impeccable character as I brushed past him into the hall. Even Sinclair couldn't ignore the message of a wide-open door that allowed the dim light from the kitchen to spill onto the blacked-out street, but I didn't want to leave him in any doubt.

'Do not come to this house uninvited. I don't want you here. And if you are using whatever influence you have to manipulate what happens to me, stop. You make my flesh crawl. And I never, ever, want you to touch me again.'

His smile did not slip for a moment. He raised his hat at the threshold and disappeared.

Estelle

There was more than a hint of glamour in my new role. Aside from moments of sheer terror, I was happy, at least to begin with.

First I had to become someone different. But only gradually, so that our ever-vigilant neighbours, the Fabrons, who dined out most Saturday nights with God knows who in our arse-licking hierarchy, never quite registered what was going on. Fortunately I had a wardrobe of decent clothes bought for me by Marthe before the war. A black coat with a tightly belted waist and a jade-green hat.

For the first time I used lipstick and tried out different styles. I carried a cigarette case in a small clutch bag and drew the eyes of German soldiers in the street when I lit up, swaying my hips. On Saturdays I turned up for first aid classes at the YMCA and learnt how to apply tourniquets and to fashion a sling for a wounded arm. We were taught by a Flemish nurse, very pally with the Germans, who was forever warning us that the heartless Brits could bomb us at any time.

Dealing with Depage was the hardest thing. I told him I was looking for a new job because my work as his receptionist simply didn't pay enough.

'Of course I understand,' he said, hanging his head.

I handed in my notice at the end of March and on my last day, a fortnight later, he presented me with a copy of *Les Misérables*. I kept my chin up as I said goodbye and managed a cool look into his sorrowful eyes. I didn't allow myself to shed a tear until I was safely at Grand-mère's. She reassured me that I could put my absolute trust in Edouard and Pieter to keep their word about Clémence and the children.

The first trip I took was in late April. In order to learn the route I travelled in the slipstream of a courier smuggling micro-film out of Belgium. Sometimes we were a pair, at others we used separate carriages. I assumed the material he'd secreted in his backpack would carry a death sentence had he been caught. I'd picked up that our organisation had friends in the military HQ in Brussels. Information about troop positions, maps, railway timetables.

My escort was gloomy and taciturn on the day we set out, but I was in high spirits. US troops had arrived in England and the Nazis were about to be trounced in Russia, or so we thought. We'd not yet heard about Rommel's successes in Egypt, the fall of Crimea. Now, looking back, that journey in late spring was a kind of ecstasy. I thought I was unassailable. Deluded, therefore, on every front.

I wore my smart coat over the uniform of an obscure nursing establishment. Melted across the Belgian border with my nose in a book (short stories by Maupassant – 'Mademoiselle Fifi' is the one I remember). Papa and Marthe had taken me to Paris on my sixteenth birthday and I had returned there with Edouard in our final year as undergraduates. He had been in love with me. At first, it was all as I remembered – trees coming into leaf, flowers on a stall outside the station, shops open, hotels thriving. The Seine sparkled. Notre Dame's towers remained gloriously untouched. A girl wearing a pleated skirt was wolf-whistled as she cycled by. Then the differences began to seep into my bone marrow and dampen my spirits.

A crimson-framed swastika rippled above the porch of a posh hotel, an armoured car whisked by, a couple of Gestapo troopers glanced at me insolently from a café table. Predators. And as the day wore on, their grip became more apparent. German names on the signposts. Fat cats oozing out of limousines, impervious to the underclass shrinking in doorways, queuing for bread.

The power was cut off abruptly at six in the evening. Curfew. We slept in an empty apartment. The ashtrays were full and there were coffee grounds in a jug.

In the morning, I saw a small boy gawping as a woman was frogmarched away from a bookshop, her arm twisted up between her shoulder blades.

278

At the station I glanced coolly at the ticket inspector and handed him my ID, crafted in the basement of La Papeterie de Monsieur Bruton. I was off to nurse my poor grandmother west of Perpignan, I told him. He nodded me through.

Eastern France in May. We slowed to a halt a hundred times and saw birds flitting in and out of woodland, a man bent over his hoe, reminding me sharply of Oud Daan. The tranquil blue of the sky, an occasional glimpse of water as we reached the coast, hills in the distance, the promise of mountains. The air, when we arrived in Perpignan in the early evening, was cooler, cleaner than in Paris. The ancient streets still bustled.

My companion and I stayed with a nervy woman in a modern house on the outskirts. The two of us had hardly said half a dozen words to each other. He paid our hostess lavishly. The radio was on: French voices, music. We ate endive salad, stale cheese, fresh bread. The next morning he had a meeting to which I was not invited. I'd worked out that he must have been one of Borland's students – perhaps a few years above me at Louvain. Maybe a seminarian. Interest in women: zero.

I spent the morning sightseeing. Before the war, when Edouard and I had travelled round France as tourists, we had witnessed a society wedding here. At the end of the service the huge double doors had been flung open and the bride, on the arm of her stiff-backed groom, had floated towards us from a mystical world of stained glass, flowers and massed ranks of flickering candles. Almost worth being a believer, I teased Edouard, as the organ thundered and we gazed up at the glorious roof.

This day, under the treacherous heel of Vichy France, the cathedral doors were firmly locked. As I rattled the handle, I felt a sudden sense of unease. A lack of trust. The city basked in late spring sunshine. Women were airing their summer frocks for the first time. Awnings had been unfurled above shop windows. I passed a laden fish stall, second-hand books, cafés selling wine (though not coffee). Yet everything seemed slightly out of focus, as if someone had jogged the photographer's arm as he activated the shutter.

*

279

After Perpignan, the endless climb. First a bus, then a shepherd's path into the mountains. My shoes were inadequate. After the first slog we had gained so much altitude that I was constantly short of breath. Slept on a mildewed mattress in a climbers' hut. The next day the weather was atrocious.

Our guide through the mountains was a local boy wearing oilskins who rarely ate but occasionally swigged from a flask he kept in his hip pocket. Freezing rain peppered us like grapeshot and the wind knocked me sideways as it howled through the gullies. My shoes leaked. The guide never changed pace and I knew if I didn't keep up, nobody would wait for me.

I was supposed to be committing the route to memory but I kept my eyes on my feet, too terrified of falling to look anywhere else. Sometimes there was a sheer drop on both sides of us. We stopped for a mouthful of bread and I cracked a feeble joke. 'I'm from Belgium, remember. Bruegel is my painter of choice because my world is usually flat.' Nobody laughed.

We were now so high we saw a bird with the wingspan of a dragon. The guide grunted as we crossed the shoulder of the mountain. On the other side was Spain.

A long descent, knees howling with the strain, dipping in and out of cloud. That night we took refuge in a cottage in the foothills. A Spaniard was our host. More money changed hands. Thin soup tasting of nothing but garlic; a straw pallet and a cocoon of grey blankets. Then on down to a tinny little railway. I sat, dazed, in a toy-town carriage. Our guide bought us tickets to Barcelona and civilisation.

A bar, city buildings, a consulate. British faces. I simply could not believe the normality of it. Courtesy. Carpets. Harassed officials in rumpled suits. It didn't make sense.

We had two days to recover. Proper coffee. I slept in a small room with a white bed and terracotta tiles, surfacing from time to time as my recovering muscles ached and twitched. Sun split the shutters like a knife.

And then the journey in reverse. I was nominally in the lead now, to show I'd paid attention. At least I recognised some of the landmarks. I spotted the piercing blue of a gentian. The next time it would be just me and a guide. We were scrutinised less on the journey north.

Bruxelles-Zuid, three days later. I folded my papers into an inner pocket and was Estelle again, dental assistant, though temporarily out of work. I walked home to Rue d'Orléans as the curfew fell. Grand-mère was a skeletal presence in a chair by the front door. I'd never known her sit anywhere so draughty. Céleste was at the bottom of the stairs, a scrap of paper in her hand.

'I have a message for you,' she said.

Christa

In April 1942, I was sent to Bath after the city had been pulverised by three air raids in thirty-six hours. The railway line had survived as far as Bathampton. My first impression, as people scurried past the station beneath umbrellas or sheltered from the drenching rain, was that everything seemed fairly normal. But as I made my way along the London Road, my shoes became coated with wet plaster and I choked on the stench of burst sewer and charred timber. No end of bombed-out high streets could prepare me for a landscape so devastated that people stood about in bewilderment because they were unable to work out the topography of the place in which most of them had been born.

I saw a woman push her perambulator up to a ruined shopfront – only the facade was left, the body of the building had been flattened – and peer in the window, as if to check the price of a pair of shoes. Men clambered through the ever-shifting mountains of splintered wood, brick and glass in the hope of salvaging a few belongings. These were the old, the frail and the inadequately clothed, chewed up or simply spat out by the war, their emaciated faces rigid with shock.

The Army had been brought in to extinguish any remaining fires and clear the streets; bomb disposal experts had cordoned off entire squares, and makeshift signposts pointed to Rest Centres and a temporary mortuary. A cinema had been requisitioned by the Women's Institute for use as a relief centre and bands of robustly cheerful women were at work providing tea and sandwiches.

Conversation veered from the prosaic – 'Spam or fish paste, my lover?' – to a litany of disbelief. Nobody had been untouched;

282

everybody knew someone who'd died or been badly injured. Nobody had expected that Bath, of all places, would be treated like this. It wouldn't have been nearly so bad if a gasometer hadn't been hit, or if those wicked planes hadn't come back on three successive nights.

We then resumed the soap flakes debate. 'Any chance of getting them to send us Lux, dear? I've never got on with them cheaper brands.' The lists went on: *brooms, dustpans and brushes, crockery (all kinds), saucepans.* A woman who sat weeping for her dead mother raised her head to add: 'Bleach, that's what we'll need. I haven't been able to buy any for weeks.'

Meanwhile an endless stream of people toiled in with suitcases and bundles of possessions, most traumatised and at the end of their tether. 'I've been home for the first time since Sunday. There's nothing left except the hatstand. What *am* I going to do?'

It was twilight by the time I headed across Pulteney Bridge – en route to my billet, a school gymnasium in Lambridge – but the opportunity of visiting Hébert's widow was too good to miss. The houses in Henrietta Street were bruised and broken, yet still standing. My knock was initially greeted by silence followed by the wail of a small child, and shuffling feet. When the door opened, a woman shone the beam of a torch into my face, then spotted my uniform and said sharply: 'I've done the blackout. Not that there's much point any more.'

'It's not about the blackout.'

'The rooms are all taken. You're the fifth person who's called today. I can't possibly accommodate any more.'

'I was wondering if I could talk to you about a Captain Hawkins, who my father knew in the last war. I'm sorry if this is a bad time, it's just that—'

'Hawkins? Raymond?' She was visibly shocked. 'What about him?'

'Was Captain Hawkins your husband?'

Her expression was a mixture of suspicion and curiosity. 'Raymond weren't a captain, love. He'd just got promoted to sergeant when he disappeared.'

'I think my father and your husband were together when they

escaped from a German field hospital in 1917. I've been trying to find out exactly what happened . . .'

By now she had invited me in, closed the door and was leading me through to a gloomy back room furnished with a dining table covered by an oilcloth, an assortment of chairs, a radio and a collection of Toby jugs on the mantelpiece. A strip of canvas had been tacked across the window to cover the broken panes.

'There's nowhere else for a private chat,' she said. 'I've taken in two extra families since Monday, but I've told them I can't cook for them. They each use the stove in turn, so I've had to move all my things in here.'

She insisted on making me a cup of tea and while she was gone I lay back for a few minutes in an overstuffed armchair listening to small feet racing around overhead. I had not anticipated, when following the impulse to visit Henrietta Street, that the sorrow of the day's work would spill into the evening and exacerbate the unease I felt at taking the plunge once more into another war. Mrs Hawkins' hospitality was disarming and undeserved; I wondered how much of the circumstances of her husband's death I ought to share.

When she returned, she had removed her headscarf and apron, combed her hair into a side parting and replaced her slippers with court shoes. 'It's a pity that my daughter isn't here,' she said. 'She'd have been keen to meet you. She's off with the Wrens. I remarried, you see. Matt's with the Home Guard. I've scarcely seen him since last Friday.'

I took a sip of tea. In that stranger's room, with the clatter from the staircase and the flapping of the nearby tarpaulin, Fleur Cornelis-Faider seemed even more of a creature of fantasy than usual. Mrs Hawkins knew only that her husband had disappeared behind enemy lines and been killed at the border. Though intrigued to hear about the escape line, and how Pa had crossed the electric fence, her response was so matter-of-fact that it momentarily made me question my own obsession.

'Well you can tell your dad not to worry any more about what happened to Raymond, because I used to dread him coming home. I got this telegram saying "Missing Presumed Dead" and it were a couple of years before I knew for sure that he weren't

284

coming back. Every time someone knocked on the door, my heart sank. The night I'd married him they had to carry him home drunk, and whenever he was the worse for wear he made free with his fists or belt or whatever lay to hand. And then, finally, about a year after the war, they sent me a packet of his things and proof of his death. I'll show you if you like.'

This time she returned with a black metal tin. 'I've wondered about throwing these out. Even his mum didn't want them.'

One by one, she laid out her marriage certificate, a terse letter from Hawkins' commanding officer explaining that he'd disappeared under somewhat mysterious circumstances, another telegram, dated months later, stating that he was missing and finally the packet of possessions that had been returned by the Germans, as from a prisoner of war. A few coins, a small compass, half a box of Swan Vestas and a teaspoon.

Mrs Hawkins seemed reluctant to handle any of these items. With her permission, I examined each in turn and replaced it in the tin. The teaspoon was bent and tarnished, and had a very familiar engraving on its handle.

'What's the matter?' Mrs Hawkins had seen the expression on my face.

'I know where this came from.' I rubbed the oak leaf with my thumb and held it briefly to my chest. 'I've been there.'

'Well, help yourself to it if you like, my love. It's of no earthly use to me.'

Estelle

Robbe was in the darkest corner of the Prospero, his head sunk low. The fact that he had materialised at all was confirmation of catastrophe. And he had been weeping. I'd never seen that before.

'Borland has been arrested,' he said.

'When?' Stupid question. I couldn't take it in.

'A couple of weeks ago.'

Hunched over our beers, concealed in a cloud of smoke and a safe distance from the nearest Nazi, Robbe told me the story. Or at least a version of the story. A couple of days after I'd left Brussels, Borland was in Louvain, on his way to say Mass. Ahead of him was a woman of about thirty. Edouard had since found out that she enjoyed a bit of a reputation – was known to be making a good living while her husband languished in a German labour camp.

A pair of passing soldiers had wolf-whistled. She stuck her chin in the air. Probably had more lucrative fish to fry. The soldiers followed her, still taunting. Nobody intervened; they shut their doors tight or crossed to the other side of the street because they all knew the consequences of poking their noses into an altercation between the Moffen and the local population. The woman grew nervous and turned towards St-Jan-de-Doperkerk. Borland heard the soldiers say something along the lines of: 'Listen to me, *schatz*. You don't ignore us. Ever.'

Which is exactly what she did, because she thought she had reached sanctuary. But they grabbed her from the porch and hustled her to a spot near the wall, by trees, and shoved her down on a tombstone.

According to his own rules, Borland should have sailed on

into the church. He'd taught us that in situations such as this, we should weigh up the number of lives we might put at risk. Yet he ran to her aid. Perhaps he hoped his priesthood might save him. By the time he reached the grave, one of the soldiers had his knee on her chest and his hand on her mouth and the other was wrestling with her skirt and his fly buttons.

Borland shouted: 'Have you taken leave of your senses?'

Edouard, inside the church, heard nothing. A couple of parishioners arriving at the gate hung back. The soldiers had turned on Borland. One of them knocked him down with the butt of his revolver. When he tried to stand, they had knocked him down again. They beat him, kicked him in the guts, left him and dragged the woman away.

The bells were ringing for Mass. Borland was carried inside. Edouard patched him up and carted him home.

Three days later the Gestapo came for him, when he was still bedridden and recovering from concussion. They called him by the name Le Brun, one of his many aliases. And rather than keep him in Louvain prison with common criminals, they transported him to Brussels – first to the police station on La Rue Traversière and then to St Gilles.

Robbe was all too well-informed about what went on there because he had seduced the daughter of a handyman regularly called in to fix the plumbing. And one of the guards, not entirely loyal to the Nazi regime, sold information for the price of a couple of beers.

At first Borland seemed to think he could appeal to the law when he was charged with assaulting a German soldier in the course of his duty. 'Look at my broken nose,' he said, 'and my cracked collarbone. Now show me the soldier who is alleging I assaulted him. Where are his injuries?'

He was less confident when they asked him to name members of the escape line to Perpignan.

And: 'Who was the dark-haired Jew who visited your presbytery on Friday 23rd April? What was his business? Why did he come back the next day?'

'Where were you on the night that a train travelling between Antwerp and Ghent was derailed and a hundred passengers, all of them German troops, were injured, seven of them fatally?'

A few days later came the news – which Borland's interrogators received with manufactured outrage – that the young soldier he was alleged to have assaulted had died from his wounds. Borland was now a murderer.

Borland asked to see a lawyer. He asked to see a priest. He asked to see a photograph of the dead man and, lo and behold, was provided with one – just recognisable, with the side of his face stoved in and an arm twisted unnaturally behind him.

The interrogation was accompanied by systematic and relentless beating. According to Robbe's source, it only stopped when Borland lost consciousness, and varied between kickings, slaps to the head, lashing with belts and assaults with batons. He was given no water. They confined him to a cell in which he couldn't stand upright. They brought in Jeanne, still with her hair in plaits. Solid as a rock, hitherto. Heart of a tiger. Stripped her in front of him and vowed to rape and beat her to a pulp unless he spilled the beans. Borland and Jeanne looked each other in the eye. Neither said a word as her face was pummelled until it resembled a bleeding pumpkin and her breasts and buttocks were lacerated with the buckle of a belt.

They told him he would be shot or transported. Edouard, who'd hung about outside the prison all this time, thought he'd identified the van in which they carried him away. Followed it to Breendonk – the transit camp between Brussels and Antwerp, a mere couple of hours' drive from De Eikenhoeve. *Auffanglager*. A fortress into which people disappeared on the way to Christ knows where. And then on, by goods train probably, to some distant reach of Hitler's empire – Germany, Austria, Poland. By then we'd heard the name Ravensbrück.

'*Nacht und Nebel*,' said Robbe. 'Night and Fog, Hitler's latest punishment for resistance workers and activists. It works like this. Death isn't a sufficient deterrent. Much too tidy. Pain-free, once it's over. And where to put the bodies? The last thing he wants is to create a shrine. So instead he has people disappear. Snuffs out their very existence. It makes the relatives suffer too, never knowing whether their loved one is dead or alive. Don't say when or where they are going. Just spirit them away in cattle trucks and cargo trains. Send them somewhere they can't be found.'

'And then what?' I said.

'That's left to our imagination. Death by gassing, disease, torture, extermination, starvation or beating. The prisoner won't know when or where, only that it *will* happen. Probably when there's no work left in him. That's *Nacht und Nebel*.'

He stubbed out his latest cigarette, fixed me with dull eyes and spelt out the implications of Borland's arrest. 'We have no idea what he might have said under torture. He's the one person who knows everything. The names of at least a hundred people who are involved in our network. Safe houses, a dozen letter boxes. He knows where fugitives are hidden and who's been trained as a saboteur and codebreaker. He knows where radio operators are secretly transmitting messages to England and the names of contacts in the UK and Russia. He might have told the authorities all of this, some of it, or nothing at all.'

Robbe shoved aside the ashtray and seized my hands. I'd never seen him so deadly serious and entirely without his usual defences of cynicism or rage.

'Estelle. We want you to disappear.'

'What on earth for? It's surely far more likely that Borland has kept quiet?'

'The point is, we think it was a set-up. The whole thing: the whore, the soldiers, the arrest. How did they know where he would be saying Mass that night or that his name was Le Brun or about his connection to the Ghent train?'

'They must have been watching him.'

'It goes deeper than that. We think it could be one of our own side who betrayed him.'

'Robbe, how can you say that?'

'Face it. Not everyone loves Borland. He can be high-handed and secretive, ruthless about cutting people out of the loop. There are any number of reasons for somebody squealing – not least fear. Until we've done our investigations, you should lie low. Because of who you are, your name, your sex, you're even more vulnerable than the rest of us. All down the line you're regarded as a potential second Fleur.'

Of course, his request had the opposite effect. Or perhaps it was precisely the effect Robbe wanted.

'But we might never find out. You can't be sure it was a trap. They could have just struck lucky,' I protested.

'And you worked for a Jew. We should never have involved you, for that reason alone.'

'I'm no longer employed by Jerome Depage.'

'You're still involved with the family.'

'Not for long.'

His head went down so I couldn't see his face. Tears splashed onto his lap. 'Why do you have to be so fucking obstinate? I don't want to lose anybody else.'

It was the closest he'd ever come to telling me he loved me. I gripped his wrist and spoke softly: 'We can't let Borland down.'

'But he let *us* down. It was pure arrogance, to teach us one thing and do another. Of all people, he should have protected himself.'

'I suppose he was behaving like a priest, when he rescued that woman.'

Long pause. 'Some fucking priest. He screwed our mother.'

There it was at last, the great unsaid. I could never forget the expression on Christa's face when she first saw Borland and Robbe together in the Musée Wiertz. Confirmation of what I'd always known in my bones, the same way I knew that a hazard lurked under the smooth surface of the river at De Eikenhoeve. Papa certainly guessed it. He had an expression just for Robbe: nervousness, exasperation, anger and a kind of scorching, martyred love.

And Robbe himself? I got up and pressed his face to my belly. Felt the tension in his neck and hot tears through the fabric of my skirt. 'I won't give up unless you do,' I said.

After a few moments I released him and headed for the door. A Mof who'd been eyeing me gave me a wink. I stepped into a May evening that smelled sappy and warm.

In the house on Rue d'Orléans the old women were still in the hall, exactly as I'd left them. I told them Borland was in prison, alive as far as we knew, and helped them upstairs. Made them a meal of bread and milk and Marthe's compote. When I fell into

Maman's old bed, my hair stank of cigarettes and beer.

Face it, I told myself. Then you'll be stronger.

So I conjured up Borland's willowy, godly, egotistical self. The man who had two great passions – Maman and Christ – both of whom, I chose to think, he had loved tirelessly all his life, and in that order. I hoped that Robbe's conception had been a moment of glorious surrender; ecstasy rather than self-loathing. I thought that Borland could have been a wonderful lover, with his long clean limbs and years of pent-up desire, his lilting voice permitted at last to croon to his devilish beauty, his siren.

I didn't believe they'd broken him. I could not.

Emaciated, naked, with tousled hair full of lice and ill-fitting prison clothes. Shivering, filthy, bruised and bleeding. Forced into a cattle truck, face pressed to a gap between slats – or no, he would have given that place to another. On his knees in some quarry. I wondered if, in his imagination, he was able to grope his way to a book-filled room, a hearth, a spotless dog collar, us, his students, to the figure of that passive Christ of his, dangling from a cross.

I imagined him gasping with fever, raising a damaged hand to the bitter sky and calling upon his God.

Christa

The next time I went home to Harewood Road, the De Eikenhoeve teaspoon, wrapped in a handkerchief, was stowed away in my handbag. Along our street, nasturtiums and lobelia tumbled from hanging baskets, vivid reminders of pre-war summers.

When Ma answered the door she glowed with pleasure, then whipped off her apron as if I were a proper guest. The Derry & Toms episode when Auntie Maisie had caught me with Sinclair had not been forgiven, however, and although to have given voice to her resentment would have been unpatriotic, she was suspicious that I'd been posted to do some nebulous work in London when her friends' daughters were doing something definite such as the Ack-Ack.

We drank tea at the new version of the kitchen table, a Morrison shelter, which Pa had obediently erected but refused point-blank to use. The sad news was that my cousin Paul had been shot down somewhere over Germany. Although the dreaded telegram had arrived, 'Missing in action', Auntie Maisie still hoped that her beloved son would survive because he'd reassured her that he had undergone fail-safe training on what to do in the event of a bailout. She was clinging to the rumour that the Nazis were said to be quite kind to prisoners of war and respectful of the airmen's courage.

Meanwhile, the WI canteen was very busy. 'Pa has been keeping us in cabbages but the men always moan about the powdered eggs.'

'And your work at The Sun?'

'Still going strong. Sometimes I think I'll go blind with entering all those tiny numbers onto ledgers.'

'I'm sure you could ask for a different kind of work if you'd rather.'

'We've all got to pull our weight, though it is a shame to have come full circle.'

'And Pa?'

'Same as ever, except for this business with the shelter.' She kicked the metal cage so that it twanged. 'He refuses to budge out of bed if the siren goes, even though I've made it all snug and pleaded with him. He says he couldn't breathe if I made him lie in this thing, so we both stay upstairs. Anyway, I can't fault his patriotism.'

She produced a copy of the *Watford Observer*, which featured a photograph of Pa brandishing a prize marrow with his customary expression of stern resolution. 'Allotment keepers,' proclaimed the accompanying article, 'our urban heroes.' Whilst the mere amateurs who turned their lawns into vegetable plots managed only wormy carrots and fly-blown cabbages, Pa had grown sackfuls of potatoes, blackcurrants by the bagful, greens for his wife's canteen and so many runner beans that he had supplied maternity patients in the Peace Memorial Hospital for a month.

I took a Thermos of tea up to the allotment, where Pa received my kiss and a tin cup stoically enough, trying not to make it too obvious that he'd much rather have been left alone. When I offered to help, he handed me a hoe. A stiff wind was blowing and early fallen leaves skittered across the open land.

'I'm concerned about Ma,' I said, as Pa raised a forkful of potatoes and rubbed the soil off each one before tossing it into a sack.

A few plots along, a little girl of about two had been attached by a long rope to the tap on her grandfather's water butt and was digging the earth with a miniature trowel. A train rumbled along a distant track.

'She doesn't deserve all this worry,' I continued. 'Why won't you use the shelter you built? It's the one thing you could do for her sake.'

'I hate being shut in.'

'Can't you try to overcome that? For Ma.'

'She's all right.'

'Pa, you can't exist in a bubble. We're all in the same boat.'

'For fuck's sake,' he muttered, and I'd never heard him swear like that before, 'this is where I come to get away from you all.'

'Who is this *all*? Ma is a saint, the way she puts up with you.'

The child with the trowel sat on the damp earth with her legs thrust out, staring, whilst her grandfather dug furiously and pretended not to listen.

The conversation had begun so badly that I waited nearly half an hour before I spoke again, hoping that Pa would be regretting our spat as much as I was. 'Pa, I've got something to show you.' I produced the oak-leaf teaspoon from my bag. 'Does it mean anything to you?'

Pa, trained in the minutiae of typesetting, had always given objects far more attention than he did people. He held the spoon close to his eyes, turning it over and over. 'I don't remember.'

'Don't you? It came from the Belgian farm where you met Fleur Cornelis-Faider. While I was staying there, one of her sons showed me the clearing where they used to hide fugitive soldiers. He said he might have seen you when he was a very little boy, because his mother had brought him and baby Estelle to meet you. Do you remember?'

A lock of thick grey hair blew across his forehead and he was very still, as if listening to something beyond the wind. 'I don't remember.'

'And then last winter you had a visitor, didn't you, Pa? I know this man was in Watford because I saw him too. His name was Père Laurence Borland, though you may have known him as something different. I suspect during the war he had a beard and black curly hair. What did he say to you?'

He wiped his nose with his cuff and tears oozed so that I dreaded a collapse of the kind he'd experienced at Sun Engraving. Taking him by the elbow, I led him back to the shed and set up a rickety deckchair on the far side of it, sheltered from the wind and away from watchful eyes. At last he murmured, almost to himself: 'He was standing there by the gate. He said it was best not to mention his visit to anyone because I might do harm if I did.'

'Are you talking about Borland?'

'Le Brun. I'd have known him anywhere, because he was so harsh with us. He picked us up from the house by the canal and made us walk too fast, and he kept threatening to abandon us if we didn't do exactly as he said. When he stood over there, staring at me, I thought he was going to kill me.'

'What did he want, Pa?'

'He had such a strong French accent I could scarcely understand him. He said: "Tell me what happened after I left you with her."'

'You mean with Fleur?'

'Françoise. Like I said, Le Brun wasn't a kind person and he drove us too hard. When we got to the clearing in the woods we were so tired we dropped down and slept in the sunshine. I woke up because it had grown shady, and then I saw her coming out of the trees. Her shawl was knotted round her neck to hold a baby, and she had a basket hooked over her arm, and a little boy was clinging to her hand. She put the baby down in the shade. At first she was all smiles with Le Brun. Then they got into an argument.'

'Have you any idea what it was about?'

'They spoke in French, but I think it had something to do with the children. After a bit she went really wild and said something so fierce that it made Le Brun go quiet. He dragged the little boy close and put his finger under his chin and stared at him. That's when I got really worried, because he said something to the child that made the boy scream – I can still hear it, a wail like a wounded man abandoned in no-man's-land. Hébert said to me that someone was bound to find us now. The woman smacked the little boy and sent him away to look after the baby.

'It was a terrible row. Le Brun shouldn't have treated the child like that. Françoise was very upset. She told us to get some rest and eat, that we would be safe in the clearing, and then she went away. The food in the basket was the best we'd had in years. I offered some bread to the other child we'd spotted hiding in the woods, but he shook his head and wouldn't come any closer. Next day, Françoise returned. She looked different, her hair pulled back, and she was wearing trousers like a man. She told us that by nightfall, if we followed her and did everything she said, we would reach the border.

295

'She was so kind to me. Sometimes she would take my arm and help me along, or even hold my hand. She insisted to Hébert that it was no use rushing, we had plenty of time, and when we were waiting by the hedge for the wagon with the chickens to come and pick us up, she pressed her face to my upper arm and cried. She was just so sad, all the time. She whispered, in English, that she hoped I would be kind to her. Nobody else was, she said.'

'Is this what you told Le Brun when he came to see you?'

'Not all of it. He kept saying: "Anything else? Did you speak to anyone else? Did anyone else visit you in the clearing?"'

'You said you offered bread to a little boy who was hiding in the trees. What did he look like?'

'Just a boy; rather fair.'

'Did you tell Le Brun about this second boy?'

'I can't remember. I don't know what I said.'

'What about Estelle? Did you tell her all this, when she was here?'

'Some of it. Not about what happened in the clearing. The argument. I didn't want to upset her. Was it important? Have I done something wrong?'

'Not at all, Pa.'

We gazed out over those familiar allotments, the landscape of my childhood, while I stroked his muddy hand, leant my head against his shoulder and watched small high clouds rushing above us.

'What did he really want, do you think?' Pa said.

'He was trying to work out how the Germans knew that Fleur would be at the border that night.'

'It was because of me. I was too slow. That's what Hébert said.'

'I don't think so, Pa. I think that perhaps your Françoise was rather too careless with the people who loved her. I think that was the trouble.'

'She wasn't careless with me,' he insisted. 'She couldn't have taken better care of me.'

296

Estelle

In May 1942 it was decreed that yellow stars had to be displayed on all Jewish outer garments. The following Friday morning I visited the dental surgery for the last time, on the pretext of picking up a pair of gloves I'd left in a desk drawer. Always have a pretext, Edouard had taught us. The street door was shut, the word '*Jood*' scrawled across it in yellow paint, but it was unlocked. I climbed the stairs, past the ever-more doleful cathedral prints, and entered the waiting room.

Things had deteriorated, or rather been frozen in time. The same faded magazines were piled on the table, the cushion covers were dustier, the desk untidier. I had not been replaced, apparently. In the surgery, Depage had been preparing for the day as usual, and stood at the door, dressed in a white coat that was in need of starch.

'How did you know it was me?' I said.

'I recognised your footsteps on the stair.'

'You should keep the door locked. I could have been anyone.'

'A locked door won't stop them.'

'We need to talk. When is the first patient arriving?'

He looked almost shifty. 'It's a busy day. I'd have to check the diary.'

The diary sat unopened on the desk. 'Perhaps you could spare me a minute.'

He nodded and closed his eyes, as he used to close them when I had dropped his precious probe or banged a door.

'It's time, you know,' I said.

'I'm not shutting up the surgery.'

'You have to. Your name is on the register.'

His head was high, his mouth set. 'I need to work. I have

297

commitments here and patients to look after. Don't worry about me, I have friends.'

'Arrangements have been made for you,' I said.

'But I was responsible for the register. People gave us their names in good faith. Eichel trusted me.'

Painstakingly, as if he had a queue of patients awaiting him, he took a length of cotton cloth, daubed it with Lysol and began cleaning his trays and the arms of the chair. I was tempted, for old time's sake, to seize the cloth and take over.

'They will deport you and your family,' I said. 'Haven't you read the news? And then Christ knows what will happen to you.'

The tone of my voice made him wince. 'You and I made the register. We handed in the names. Do you think I would abandon those whose names I entered on the list?'

'Eichel gave you no choice. But now you do have a choice, to save your own skin at least. And above all, Clémence and the children. It benefits no one to make a martyr of yourself.'

'But I don't know how to live, except as a dentist. My services will always be required. You'll see.' He hesitated: 'But the children—'

'The children can be kept safe. My brothers and I will see to that.'

For the first time, his guard dropped and his eyes watered. 'Clémence and the children can pass as Belgian or French. Look at me, I can never be anything but a Jew. My name is entered on the register and, as far as I'm concerned, that is that. I will put my faith in God and *Oberleutnant* Eichel.'

For weeks I was too busy to think about Depage. A stream of messages arrived via Céleste, who was an unlikely conduit for secrets. She must have snatched at them as they blew into her dank netherworld, the basement kitchen. Later, off I'd trot to the Pâtisserie Faider for a loaf of bread. The Vauclains, stalwart souls, had dropped their standards and were padding out their stores of good flour with disgusting stuff made from ground-up beans.

When I left, a loaf tucked under my arm, I'd be followed by a pair of dishevelled labourer types. Maybe a week or so ago these two had descended on a parachute from a doomed tin-can plane.

Their eyes would be blank from exhaustion and grief because a companion had landed on the spikes of a harrow and they'd found him the next morning impaled like a sausage, or else they'd seen one of their own chased by dogs across field after field until he was torn apart or captured. Sometimes elation at still being alive made them dangerous. They were forbidden to tell me their history and I was forbidden to ask. I didn't know where they'd come from or who had hidden them. We were only given the next link in the chain.

I caught whiffs of what had happened to them, of course. Mention of being scooped up by peasant boys speaking incomprehensible Flemish, journeys on the underside of lorries or wrapped in tarpaulins on canal barges. Sometimes I took them all the way to safety but often my task was simply to hide them at Grand-mère's, where they slept in an attic nest prepared by Céleste and emerged days later, blinking like moles. They'd disappear eventually, collected by Edouard or Robbe and spirited away. We were never told their real names.

Occasionally we hid them in full sight, as family guests. They hated being in the charge of a girl and their jaws dropped even further when they met Grand-mère and Céleste, a couple of old biddies who fussed about with silver teapots and insisted on laundered napkins. Céleste, frail as a moth, sat up all night with the sewing machine, transforming their clothes into something a little more Belgian.

To a man, their language skills were atrocious. A couple – Australian – we forgave; the others, highly educated Brits, had less excuse. All were desperately ill-equipped. They were airmen, of course, geared up to navigate and drop bombs and not much else, but which idiot had trained them? IDs patently faked, clothes with British seams and labels, currency years out of date or brand-new banknotes with consecutive numbers, maps so inaccurate that the men had sometimes parachuted in error into woodland and emerged battered or with broken limbs. We worked overtime to repair the damage, heal their wounds, replace their papers, confiscate their revolvers and pummel it into their heads that they must not speak in a public place.

We never gave them a plan or told them the risks of the

onward journey, but we did crush their wilder expectations. Some thought they'd be home in a couple of days. I soon disabused them of that. 'The sea is completely out of bounds.' I listed the failed attempts to have men snatched off the beaches. 'The coastline is short, too well-patrolled and straight, with no shelter.'

Some wouldn't keep quiet. Got too high-spirited, cracked jokes and were stared at on French trains. 'They have the confidence of an English public schoolboy,' said Edouard. 'A sense of entitlement, especially to freedom.'

I closed my eyes and caught a whiff of Cambridge with Christa. The ancient stone of King's College Chapel. A stupid scrap of English lawn. Christa with her elbows clenched to her sides, hopping about in consternation because I'd broken a rule and walked on the grass.

I saw Christa in anyone English, of course. I told myself it was something to do with the size of the pores in the skin or a certain vulnerability about the eyes. I imagined that these men's English boots had walked the same pavements as hers, and I winced at the thought of their bombed cities. I tried not to dwell on that house in Harewood Road and only once gave in to temptation.

'Has Watford been bombed?'

Puzzlement. '*Watford?*'

Sometimes the men were clumsy because they were simply too tired. They had flown dozens of missions, got shot down over a Belgian field, crawled into a hedge, hidden for a week in a hayloft, been smuggled in the boot of a car to Brussels, then concealed in a Faider bread oven and Grand-mère's attic. On the trains, even sitting bolt upright in third class, they couldn't stay awake. When they yawned, they exposed teeth far too good for the labourers they were supposed to be.

Some had been to France before the war. Roared along poplar-lined roads in smart cars, got drunk on champagne under Mediterranean skies. They couldn't get used to the tension in the cities, the shadow world of horror. In Toulouse station we once halted alongside an engine pulling more than twenty closed wagons. I watched idly at first. Cattle, I thought, but as we moved away I saw something trapped in a sliding door, the fluttering end of a blue and pink scarf. Bound for Rivesaltes, probably,

Edouard told me later. He would know. His latest cover, when in France, was that of a travelling salesman supplying barbed wire to the camps. A cut-throat business, winning the contracts, he said, but highly lucrative.

I didn't point out the scarf to my protégés – best not – but they were subdued afterwards. I tried not to dwell on it myself. Borland. Scratch-marks on the roof, ankle-deep in shit, propped up in the crush by a stranger's chest or shoulder. In the morning, another half-dozen names to cross off the list; trampled, suffocated, dehydrated, driven mad. The lucky ones.

I tried to work out what might be going through the mind of the train driver. A few years ago he could have carried passengers innocently from Cologne to Berlin. Goods from Poland to Hungary. Now he'd been seconded to shuffle prison wagons across Europe, in and out of sidings; his train always low priority compared to the transport of troops or armaments. Did he remain in his cab, filling out forms during the loading and unloading? Read a newspaper or a dirty magazine? Curse because time after time he was late home for his dinner. In Toulouse station I glimpsed him leaning out, chatting to a guy in uniform; ordinary, overweight.

Even for a free woman such as myself those train journeys south were bad enough. Pressed shoulder to shoulder and, like every other passenger, in constant fear for my life. If an official stepped aboard, irritable, sleep-deprived, gnawed at by a bad diet and a worse conscience, someone was bound to suffer. There were constant checks for smugglers, refugees, Jews, resistance fighters, Maquis and foreigners. We had our bad moments: forced to escape from a railway station through a lavatory window or make a sudden dash for a departing train under the noses of the French police.

One of my men lost his papers at a meal stop – they had either fallen out of his pocket or been pinched. We made a quick search and travelled on without them. Saved by a sheer fluke. Ticket inspectors burst into our compartment, demanded that we all take out our papers, then hauled a poor man off his seat, ranted at him and shoved him away before they reached us. Lions sated with a kill.

I always relaxed a little when we reached Perpignan. There were still so many people to pay – for food, shelter, a guide through the mountains – and stories of parties such as ours tailed to some remote farmhouse by the Moffen, with entire households arrested, shot or deported. But from there on, my chief enemy was nature. Infinitely preferable, however wilful or cruel.

On the trek through the mountains, hardly a word was spoken. The air was crisp in the early morning. A climb during which I soon recognised every landmark: dense woodland, tucked-away resting places, scree slopes, deceptively shallow at first, ending in a precipice. Waking before dawn. The greyish light yellowing to the east. The peaks ancient and unforgiving. Then, touched by sunlight, shimmering, kinder, with glinting waterfalls, the distant clang of a goat's bell, a little blue flower in a crevice.

I felt very young, very small. Once, I tripped and my knee hit rock, exposing the bone. Sometimes cloud swooped down without warning and fogged the path. Winds blew strong enough to sweep us over a ridge, had we not clung together. Sometimes it was so warm in the morning that the men went bare-chested, but by evening so cold we were frozen. I didn't care. I needed nature to be a million times grander and more brutal than what was happening in the vast lowlands of central Europe.

But I always knew it was only a matter of time. The law of probability was working against me. The more often you broke the rules, the more likely you were to be caught. A weak link, a poor decision, and it would all be over. One day I'd be so frightened I could hardly get out of bed, the next gung-ho, ready for anything.

Fortnightly, on a Tuesday, the De Eikenhoeve truck arrived in Brussels laden with eggs, meat and grain to supply voracious Nazis living it up in the hotels and great houses on the Avenue Louise. Occasionally it collected essential supplies, such as tractor parts or engine oil, detergent and salt, that couldn't be bought near Oostervorken. Sometimes, in between errands, Pieter had time to drive to Rue d'Orléans and call on Grand-mère and me, if I happened to be about.

302

The minute I clapped eyes on him I felt better. He wore a checked shirt and smelt of oil and straw and warm cotton. There was reassurance in his height and breadth, though his face was lined beyond his years. His pockets were always filled with delicacies for Céleste and Grand-mère: dried peppermint and lemon balm, a couple of soft De Eikenhoeve cheeses, saucisson and raspberry cordial.

On his September visit he drove round the back of the house where rickety gates opened onto the old bakery yard. Tucked away in Grand-mère's little salon, Clémence Depage and the children were waiting. She was ashen-faced. Yesterday she had pushed Marguerite to the school gates as usual, picked up the boys and made the habitual trek across the city to the Pâtisserie Faider to queue for bread. Unlike the other customers, the Depage quartet had not re-emerged. They had brought nothing extra with them, she had left her husband no note. In the small hours they had been delivered to Rue d'Orléans in the baker's van, at the start of its rounds.

Marguerite sat like a doll on Pieter's arm as he carried her down to the truck, the boys followed in stoical silence. Clémence kissed Grand-mère again and again.

'In a world in which everything is wrong,' said Grand-mère, patting her arm, 'you can reassure yourself that you are doing the right thing.'

They had been supplied with papers proclaiming them to be Caroline Faider and her offspring, distant relations from near Saint-Omer. The father had been killed during the rout of the Allies in 1940 and since then Caroline had been dependent on the kindness of relatives. She had been offered shelter in a farm cottage at De Eikenhoeve, in return for labour in the fields.

Once they were safely installed in the lorry, Pieter returned to the house. 'And you,' he said, gripping my elbow and ushering me to a corner of the yard. 'I suppose it's no use asking you again . . .'

'Not while Grand-mère is so frail.'

'With Borland gone, we're all at risk.'

'I'm needed more than ever.'

His eyes implored me. Eyes that could penetrate a dusky copse

303

and spot a stray pup, or identify a sparrowhawk by a speck in a cloudless sky. 'You may be a liability, because of Maman.'

'Maman's name is a watchword. It's because of her that I cannot let people down.' I recognised how like Depage I sounded.

We kissed goodbye. Pieter replaced his cap and swung himself up into the lorry. Despite themselves, the light of adventure gleamed in the boys' eyes. Clémence clutched Marguerite to her skinny breast. The lorry roared and belched, reversed, gears grinding, then swung out of the yard.

I slammed the gates and bolted them fast.

PART THREE

October 1942

Christa

On the day following my interview with Fairbrother and Sinclair, I returned to Northumberland House and knocked on the door of Room 115 at eleven precisely. I shook Fairbrother's hand but barely glanced at Sinclair.

Fairbrother gestured to a seat. 'I trust you've had adequate time to reflect, Corporal Geering.'

'I've thought of nothing else.'

'And your verdict?' He picked up a pen.

'I should like to ask a couple of questions.'

He gave a small, appreciative smile. 'Fire away.'

'Who is the leader of the group known as Unit J?'

'We certainly can't disclose—' Sinclair began.

Fairbrother interrupted sharply. 'Why do you wish to know?'

'If it helps, I've worked out that his name is Laurence Borland.'

Fairbrother considered this for a moment. 'Correct.'

'What will you do with the information I give you?'

'Really,' said Sinclair, 'you cannot expect us to tell you that.'

'This is about betrayal. How can I be sure that the name won't fall into the wrong hands?'

'You'll have to trust us.' There was just a touch of his old complacency.

'I've decided that there is only one person in whom I can confide.'

Fairbrother examined his pen. He knew what was coming. 'And who might that be?'

I did not hesitate. 'Estelle Cornelis-Faider.'

'But Estelle is not here.'

'Nevertheless. She is the one.'

Estelle

I made eight trips, accompanied seventeen men, but lost one. Sixteen saved in a war that had already claimed hundreds upon hundreds of thousands.

The eighth trip was the trickiest from the start. It was autumn and I was in a low mood, with little patience for selfish English airmen. The previous night I'd received a note from Depage, who'd been ordered to report to Bruxelles-Midi with his family.

I hotfooted it round to his apartment in the early evening, before curfew. Brussels was nervy and wind-battered, all the deceptive promise of summer gone. There was a basket of children's shoes in the hallway. Depage and I sat at his dining room table, which was set with an empty plate and a glass of water. A crayon picture by Marguerite of her stick-figure family was pinned to the dresser. Half a dozen marbles, elastic bands and a couple of cigarette cards featuring Belgian royalty had accumulated in a china dish. The rest of the tableware must have been packed away.

'Don't go,' I said. 'They'll kill you when you turn up without your family.'

The zealot's light burnt in his eye. 'I told you, I have no choice.'

'You're a fool. It's suicidal.'

'It's the right thing to do.'

'Just because something's difficult, it doesn't make it right, you know. It's not too late. I can save you.'

His head was high and proud. I wanted to slap him but kissed his stubborn cheek instead and left him in the empty room.

I felt obscurely compromised, that I should abandon this person I loved, to risk everything for those I didn't.

*

And so that last journey was spent with a glowering sense of a job badly done. Haunted by the figure of Depage in his good wool coat locking his apartment door, descending the stairs with his leather suitcase banging against his knees, toiling on foot to the station because he was no longer welcome on public transport. And once there, a short-sighted peering about for the right official. I imagined him joining the back of a queue whilst smiling courageously at his fellow deportees. A dreadful surrender of identity, a needless sacrifice, so insignificant that he would not even register as a statistic.

Small wonder I had little patience with my latest duo. One boy, scarcely out of school, was called Donald – a gunner shot down on his second flight, still jabbering about the three other men who'd been in the plane. He was frightened half witless, bug-eyed. I shoved papers into his pocket, urged him to pull his cap low over his brow, told him to keep his head down and not say a word, cry if need be instead. But his companion, the pilot, was a lanky know-it-all called Phil, who had an infuriatingly buoyant manner. His heel drummed against the train floor and he cast me scathing glances each time he thought I'd made a wrong decision. Questioned my choice of routes. Was keen to show off his fluent French.

'Leave it to me,' he said when we approached the station barrier in Paris.

'Say as little as possible,' I warned him.

But he sauntered up to the policeman and smiled directly into his officious eyes. Big mistake. A volley of questions and an intense scrutiny of his papers ensued. Phil was uncrushed, even triumphant when eventually we were allowed through. 'I had a French grandmother and used to spend holidays in Provence. I've always been told that I speak like a native.'

The mountains were our ultimate test. I was told in Perpignan that as it had been raining for weeks my favourite route was all but impassable. Had it not been for Phil, I might have waited a couple of days before attempting the journey. But I wanted rid of him.

'I did a lot of trekking when I was a student,' he insisted. 'Let me know if you need any help with the navigation.'

'We'll pick up a guide tomorrow,' I said. 'Today you must simply follow me.'

The rain had stopped. Intermittent sunshine flashed over our shoulders as we toiled up through the trees. At the usual bridge a checkpoint had been installed – two soldiers with guns and dogs. Who had tipped them off?

'We'll go further upstream and wade across.' I tried to show not a hint of unease. Though the channel was narrower, the banks were steep and shelving so we couldn't easily find an entry point. The water, in full spate, churned over the rocks, but there was no time to waste if we were to reach shelter by nightfall.

'Hold my hand,' I told them. 'I'll guide you, one at a time. Brace yourselves for the force of the water. On no account allow it to shove you sideways – you must stay upright. Place your feet where I place mine; it may reach as deep as your throat, but no higher. Trust me.'

Phil hung back. 'Wait here,' he said. 'I'll find a better fording spot.'

'I know the terrain very well. Further up there's a gully where the water is dangerous. This is the only place.' But it was a struggle for power and he knew it. In truth, I had no idea how deep the river was, only that we were trapped.

I stripped off my jacket and boots, tied them round my neck and waded in. Phil headed upstream. Momentarily, I wavered at the shock of the icy, animal force of the water. But I reached across for Donald's hand, felt his vice-like grip and placed one foot after another into the unknown.

I couldn't have said for sure we'd make it – in three strides I was waist-deep and my body was whipped and aching, but there was still solid riverbed underfoot. Donald's grip loosened; I managed to grab his sleeve. Four more strides, chest-level, then waist, and we were at the other side. Alive. Exultant. Phil was still prancing about fifty metres or so upstream, searching for another entry point. I signalled for him to come back, that I would fetch him.

He hesitated on the steep bank, then lowered himself into the water. It was certainly narrower up there and the flow was broken by rocks. At first it went well – he heaved himself up onto the first stepping stone, sprang across to another. Then he missed his footing. The force of the water knocked him over. He shouted and tumbled into the churning current. We saw his arms go up and he was dashed against one rock after another before he disappeared. We waited for him to pop up like a cork, but he never did.

Christa's pale frond of an arm. Heaving her into the light, water streaming from her hair and eyes. The flicker of a pulse in her neck.

I waded in and floundered about, hoping Phil would be carried down to me. Again and again I dipped into the water because I thought I'd caught sight of his hair or clothing, staggered and was nearly swept away. This was my punishment for Christa. I had used up my river-lives on her; I had toyed with her and here was the result.

Donald lunged about on the bank, calling Phil's name, wading in and out of the water. After half an hour, when we were both nearly dead with cold and exhaustion, I grabbed him by the thin shoulders. 'We're bound to be seen if we spend any more time here. If he's alive, he'll have to find his own way. If we don't move on now, all three of us will die – either be shot in the head or get hypothermia, take your pick.'

His doggy eyes were fixed on me. In the end he followed, although I had to goad him on because he kept looking back. When we lay side by side in the mountain hut that night, even the wind, battering the window frames, could not extinguish the sound of his weeping.

Next day he was still shivering and I had to bully him into eating. 'You'll get us both killed if you're too weak to walk.'

But I was also unsettled. The episode at the river had unhinged me.

Once in Spain, Donald cheered up. On the train he sat dumbstruck, watching as we descended into agricultural territory, with farms and brooks and copses, down, down, towards civilisation. We arrived in Barcelona late in the afternoon, as the consul was about to close. I left him perched like a pigeon on a bench, shaking sporadically, and went in search of my usual contact.

From the minute I appeared in his office I knew something was wrong. His name was Keith Cheetham – or so I'd been told to call him – and his hair jutted in a thick thatch above his forehead. He was a pale, asthmatic fellow with impeccable Spanish. We went through the formalities – he thanked me for delivering the airman, listened nervously to my account, was sympathetic to the loss of Phil and regretted that he must report every detail. Finally he handed over a bundle of money for the journey home.

'And I have another message for you, of the utmost importance. A meeting has been arranged at the Café Esperanza, eleven o'clock tomorrow morning.'

I went obediently to the apartment he'd allocated me, a little green-painted room off the Via Laietana with clean white sheets, thin blankets, the noise of constant traffic. Normally I slept well in Barcelona; that night I was plagued by doubt. First Phil, next a meeting in the Esperanza. What fresh blow was about to fall?

The traffic, in my dreams, was water. The river churned in the gulley. I watched Phil take a confident step, lose his balance, give a shout of surprise. One minute he'd been an infuriating lad in borrowed clothes; the next, gone. I saw his head break like an eggshell on a jutting stone.

I stood waist-deep and my numbed hands reached for a finger, a wrist, a lock of hair. I woke with a jolt after taking one more uncertain step. My foot had found an endless drop.

I knew the Esperanza well, an old building in the Moorish style, which was accessed by a crazy courtyard with pillars and terracotta pots, and a staircase tiled in apricot and green. It had high tables with dirty white cloths and long windows. I was expecting one of my usual contacts but could see no one I recognised. There was a fair-haired Englishman behind a newspaper, but he was with a young woman. They were at a table overlooking the courtyard, she facing me directly, toying with a teaspoon.

Who was that, with the thick, dark hair falling over her shoulder, a blue hat shading one eye, a nervous expression?

My soul recognised her before my brain did.

I gripped my handbag, clamped my lips shut.

Christa.

Christa

The journey to Barcelona was scheduled to take over a week: a day's train ride to Liverpool, first class, six days on a frigate in convoy to the British naval base at Gibraltar, by rail to Madrid, where we would stay overnight, and on to Barcelona.

On board ship I shared a cabin with a couple of ATS girls bound for secretarial work in Gibraltar. I must have put a dampener on their high spirits; I blamed travel sickness for the hours I spent huddled in my bunk.

The truth was that I was entirely consumed by the prospect of seeing Estelle.

My escort was a ruddy-faced young man called Longbridge who wore tweeds and urged me to participate in a daily constitutional, as he called it, up and down the deck in the teeth of a salt-lashed wind. Apparently, he was used to dealing with refugees intent on getting out of northern Europe, or scooping up displaced politicians and airmen desperate to return to England.

Longbridge viewed resistance as a type of chess game in which the escapees had to weigh up various hazards, including the degrees of malice in the local police. Had he ever been required to organise an escape line across the Pyrenees, he would have employed the Urrugne to San Sebastián route. 'Of course some, like your friend, prefer to set off from Vichy France,' he said. 'But it's just as treacherous. The French police are merciless and even across the border in Spain there's no guarantee of safety. Far from it. Spain can hardly claim to be neutral if she's serving as a pipeline for those fleeing the Nazis.'

'What happens if someone gets caught in Spain?'

'If they're a British national they're likely to be sent to Campo de Miranda – it's a refugee camp. All kinds of flotsam and jetsam end up there, including plenty of foreigners applying to us Brits for sanctuary. We do our best, but there's a limit to the number of refugees that can be crammed into our little island, don't you think?'

On board a Spanish train I stared out at the straw-coloured plains of Andalusia, then the bleak highlands surrounding Madrid. Barcelona, bombarded by Mussolini in the closing phases of the Civil War, bore familiar scars of shrapnel and explosion.

The Hotel Monica was in the secluded Carrer de Sant Pau. My narrow room was overwhelmed by heavy mahogany furniture; double doors opened onto a balcony a foot deep that overlooked the street. In the early evening, Longbridge reappeared and took me to a neat little restaurant with red- and white-checked tablecloths. He ordered paella, which upon arrival he found disappointingly stodgy, and afterwards confided that Estelle had arrived in the city.

'The first thing you should know is that she is called Elisabetta these days. Do not address her as anything else.'

'Elisabetta.'

He beamed approvingly. 'You'll be meeting in the Café Esperanza tomorrow. Elisabetta knows it quite well and has met contacts there on a couple of previous occasions. The tables are well-spaced, so you'll have a degree of privacy. Don't worry, I'll be around to keep an eye on things.'

He watched as I dabbed at some spilt wine with a napkin. 'You should know that Elisabetta won't be expecting you. So your first challenge will be to manage her surprise.'

I pushed my plate aside.

'We should do nothing to draw attention to ourselves,' he said kindly. 'That is the key.'

From the outside, Café Esperanza was like a miniature Moorish palace. At the centre of an ornate, sunshiny courtyard was a disused fountain. Pillars supported horseshoe arches and a narrow tiled staircase led to an upper room and the reassuring chink of crockery. I had an impression of an airy, rather echoing space as we crossed to an empty table, where Longbridge unfolded a newspaper and ordered coffee.

314

And so I waited for Estelle, though with no real conviction that she would actually appear. As the hour finally approached, the terms upon which we had parted became ever more vivid. That horrific early-morning journey in her company to Bruxelles-Midi might have been yesterday. My confidence ebbed: even if she did turn up, her hostility would surely be unabated. When she saw me she would hurl abuse, ignore me, or simply walk away. Indeed, given the message I was about to deliver, this seemed the only possible reaction.

If another customer so much as dropped a teaspoon into a saucer my entire body jolted. Once or twice, Longbridge glanced round his newspaper and gave me a steadying wink or a smile. A jug of water and two tiny cups of coffee arrived. Water spilled as I lifted a glass to my lips. There was a roaring in my ears, like the sound of the sea. I longed for her to come and I wanted her to stay away.

My heart leapt each time a female paused in the doorway and looked about for a suitable table. The minute hand on my watch scarcely seemed to move at all, then rushed forwards. But as I drained the last drop of water from my glass, a woman appeared in the doorway in a dark-red hat, and with straight, blondish hair. As she scanned the room her gaze alighted briefly on Longbridge and passed on.

Haloed in the light that fell into the courtyard behind her, she was tall and slender, her complexion illuminated by some inner candle, and I was struck by the sheer temerity of having loved this woman. I think, had Longbridge not placed his large hand on mine, I would have cried out her name.

Though her gaze skimmed my face she showed no sign of recognition at first. Again she studied each table as if seeking out a friend and at last looked directly at me. This time her eyes widened and she adjusted her balance, waved as if relieved that the friend had turned up after all, then wove between the tables and smiled down at me, hand extended.

'Well, this is a nice surprise,' she said.

I somehow got to my feet and shook her hand, which was warm and strong, though her eyes were guarded. Close up, there were distinct changes; her hair, which used to be so glossy, was in poor condition and in need of a cut and she had grown so thin that her belt, although on its tightest notch, seemed not to enclose any substance. She wore a longish skirt, a somewhat crumpled blouse with a narrow blue stripe and a short jacket.

My instruction had been to treat her casually, like an old acquaintance. Recalling the frigidity with which we had parted, I had thought I might manage that, but here was the flesh-and-blood Estelle, blown across Europe and the span of three and a half years, and in some fundamental part of my being I now knew that I had never expected to see her again.

So when she grasped my hand and I registered again details that I had learnt by heart at De Eikenhoeve – how her hair swooped up from her brow and sprang into a wave, the tantalising fullness of her lower lip – I found that I was clinging to her hand as I met her gaze and made a silent plea for love and recognition. Falling against her, I pressed my face to her neck and something did break as her arms tightened around me and her cool lips fell upon my cheek. I turned my face the barest notch and whispered into her hair words I had rehearsed over and again in the solitude of my room: 'I love you. I'm staying at Hotel Monica. Carrer de Sant Pau.'

Estelle

Flashing through my mind, of course: Why are *you* here, Christa? Then sheer joy.

She had returned to me. The first words she uttered: I love you. Everything else flew away, like a heavy curtain whipped up to reveal a lit stage. Time rolled backwards. The letters I had torn into pieces reassembled themselves, I arrested her walk from the ticket barrier to the waiting train, I held her close at Papa's feast.

I had met her minder once before – Longbridge; superficially affable, ruthless underneath, and sharp.

When we hugged, Christa still fitted perfectly within my arms. I smelt that Christa warmth in her hair and felt the soft pressure of her breasts against mine. She uttered words that I had been born to hear, and I knew I was falling.

We sat and I reached for the menu whilst scanning the room for Nazi spies. My wits had disintegrated but I went through the motions; Christa was so nervous I thought that sparks might fly from her. When she bit her lower lip, two little marks appeared there and a blush came and went on her neck. I ached for her.

She had changed in subtle ways. Where there used to be softness – pliant lips, cardigans, home-made frocks – in the Esperanza, once she'd recovered from the first shock of meeting, it seemed to me that she was polished and brittle. Lipstick. Proper stockings. A lady's handbag parked beside a chair leg. That's why I hadn't recognised her at first.

She had such a job even to find simple words that I knew she could not in any way be used to this game.

'How are your parents?' I asked.

'Ma works too hard, like everyone else. Pa is a nervous wreck. My cousin Paul is missing in action. Auntie Maisie hasn't given up hope; I don't know how she'll ever recover if he doesn't come back. Paul was her pride and joy.'

'I'm sorry.' Calm down, Christa. 'And how are you enjoying teaching?'

'I no longer teach. I have a job in administration, monitoring supply and demand.'

Her top teeth again clamped down on her lower lip. She must have deviated from their script; the implication was surely that she had been transferred from a useful job to something more nebulous. Longbridge leant forward and exchanged a few words with me – asked me how I was, how long I intended to stay in Barcelona, then folded his paper so that the crossword was uppermost, and took out a pencil.

The Esperanza was a good choice, with enough space between tables and high, complicated ceilings that blurred the acoustics. Longbridge applied himself to a clue, smiling in the way of a man forced to endure the chatter of women. For all his brilliance I was pretty sure that he was oblivious to the fact that Christa had already broken the rules.

I discovered that I had picked up a knife and was pressing the blade into the stained tablecloth as I listened to that husky voice of hers, the slightly halting French. I didn't miss a detail. The buttons on her jacket were square and made of unpolished wood. And on her blouse? Tiny, mother-of-pearl, about a dozen of them.

I put off the obvious question. At first I thought she had come for a reason to do with her family, then began to realise it must be something much more disturbing. It was as if a violin string between us was vibrating at an impossibly high frequency. I decided that she had been set in motion for this one meeting. She was certainly no trained agent; her French was still heavily accented and she had next to no Spanish.

The waitress was at my elbow. 'Lemonade,' I said.

Longbridge ordered a jug and three glasses. While we waited, Christa, with a tremor in her voice, asked after the farm.

'As far as I know, they're all well, except for Papa. He died.'

The flicker of her eyelid told me that she already knew. How?

318

'Pieter and Marthe keep things going.' I leant back to study her reaction. 'You'll want to know about Robbe.'

She blinked momentarily, and I detected a very slight quickening of Longbridge's attention. 'Not especially,' she said. There was an urgent message in her eyes that I could not quite read.

'Well, he comes and goes. Same old Robbe.'

Christa smiled at the waitress who had sauntered back with a tray. After she'd gone I stirred my lemonade, which was short of both lemons and sugar. But in memory I sat at a different table, in the corner of a square, in sunshine, watching Christa, a pilgrim at a shrine as she wondered how best to behave in front of Maman's statue.

'Well,' I said, eventually. 'What other news?'

She put her lips to the glass and took a sip – she seemed not to trust herself to raise it from the table without spilling it. 'The thing is, they – we – think that too many people who work with you have been arrested. Because someone very close to you is betraying them.'

A lock of hair had fallen across one eye. She glanced nervously at Longbridge, perhaps seeking encouragement. Longbridge simply finished his lemonade and took a deeper interest in his puzzle.

'They got in touch with me because they thought I might have some idea who it was, having spent a summer at De Eikenhoeve.'

Any minute now the waitress would come swaggering across to collect our glasses.

'Go on.'

'It's your brother,' she said.

'Which brother?'

'I think you know.'

The Esperanza was spinning and blurring. She clasped my hands and our foreheads almost touched. There was no mistaking the sincerity in her eyes. I managed to say: 'Tell me his name.'

'He's betrayed you before. You know he has.'

'His name.'

'Robbe.'

I shoved my chair back from the table.

Her minder was still folding his paper as I rushed past, down the steep flight of steps, across the ornate little courtyard and into the deep shade of the street.

Christa

After she'd gone, Longbridge remained seated, perhaps in an effort to convince anybody watching that Estelle's departure had been nothing out of the ordinary. In the end, he summoned the waitress and paid the bill. I, meanwhile, must have been wearing the blind rictus grin of a woman who'd just been witnessed having a row in public.

Outside, Longbridge was far from calm. 'She didn't respond.'

'She was in shock.'

'We have no idea what she'll do next.'

'She'll do the right thing.'

There was no friendly invitation to lunch, thank goodness, just a curt order, once he had delivered me back to the hotel, that I should stay put until he returned for dinner at seven-thirty.

'Where are you going now?' I asked.

'Consular business.'

I sat at my bedroom window, reliving every second of my encounter with Estelle in the Esperanza. My hand and cheek were imprinted with her touch and her image was fresh in my mind's eye. Her long limbs and slender waist, the easy set of her shoulders, her effortless stride. It hardly mattered that for most of our conversation she had behaved like a stranger, haughty and powerful, with a dismissive curl to her lip. She was Estelle.

But as the minutes passed, my memory of her became less clear. I opened the casement from time to time and leant out over the rusted iron railing to peer into the street, though I couldn't be sure that Estelle had heard the message I'd whispered, or whether she would pay it any attention.

By the time one-thirty struck, I had seen her in every figure that passed beneath my window, and was convinced I'd never hear from her again. I caught sight of myself in the narrow, pock-marked mirror on the wardrobe door – fretful and glassy-eyed as I packed and repacked my bag, studied my map, and made a wild plan that if she didn't come soon I would run to the railway station and waylay her.

At about three I heard a brisk knock and an envelope was pushed beneath the door. An address: Apartment 14b, Carrer de l'Esparteria, and a note: *I will wait one hour. Under no circumstances allow anyone to follow you.*

I spent precious minutes identifying the address on the map and attempting to commit a route to memory. At least I had wit enough to assume that the Monica might be under surveillance, and so I walked fast, dodging occasionally down a side alley or into a shop doorway and then finding a parallel route. I had a frantic sense of time running out as I hurried through the streets, which kept slipping out of kilter. I took one wrong turn after another. Passers-by, place names, traffic, laundry drooping from balconies, graffiti, a heap of oranges in a shopfront were all obstacles designed to prevent me from reaching Estelle. I expected to feel Longbridge's hand on my shoulder at any moment.

Carrer de l'Esparteria was deeply shaded, with houses built so close on either side that there was barely space for a single vehicle to pass between. The entrance to number fourteen stood slightly open and within was a staircase leading up to a dirty landing lit by a naked bulb. I knocked on the single door and no one answered. I knocked again and it was flung open.

Estelle was now wearing a most uncharacteristic floral dress and the same narrow belt. Her hair was drawn back, exposing the fine bones of her face and her mother's swooping brows. All this I noticed in an instant, before she seized my hands, drew me inside and enclosed me in a tight embrace. My face was pressed to her neck as she kissed the top of my head and then my cheek.

Eventually we sank onto the bed. Close up, Estelle's tanned skin was sprinkled with freckles on the bridge of her nose and there was a faint flush in her cheeks. Her smile was teasing. 'Of all people, I never, ever, expected to see *you* in Barcelona. It's a miracle.'

'I didn't know what you'd think. I made them bring me.'

She cradled my face as we gazed at each other. 'I can't believe that you're here. It's a dream. Out of nowhere, out of so much shit and disaster.'

'I wish there was a better reason. That I'd had a different message.'

'So tell me. What *is* going on?'

I knew that whatever I said next would shift us far beyond the perfect moment that had begun with her opening the door and me falling into her arms. I couldn't stop time, I could only grip her hands – those competent hands with the roughened fingertips and badly cut nails – and kiss them over and over as I told her everything I knew. When I finished I whispered: 'Is it true, do you think?'

Her eyes misted with the old abstraction until I feared she would stiffen and push me away, but she nodded and flipped her head back, in surrender. 'It's true that someone is betraying us. As soon as you said it, I knew it was certain. And that it was someone close to me. But my *brother*?'

'"*Lass meine Schwester in Ruhe.*" That's what he said.' I kissed her hand and her wrist, the ivory sheen of her bones beneath her skin. 'I have tried to work out how to convince you, and where to begin.' I rocked her arm against my breast. 'I think that Laurence Borland is at the heart of everything.' I watched her face for signs of shutters flying open and light shining into dark places, but she didn't flinch. 'Borland came to England last year and tried to speak to Pa. I caught a glimpse of him and mistook him for Robbe.'

'Borland was in *England*?'

'He and Pa had met long ago, in a clearing in the woods at De Eikenhoeve. You were there too, baby Estelle.'

Perhaps the events of that afternoon were imprinted somewhere on her inner eye: a quiet green place, shadowy, innocent. A woman and her lover; a brutal rejection by a father of his son.

'That's why Robbe took me there . . . That night . . .'

When Estelle wept her eyes grew brighter. She held her chin

323

high to prevent tears from falling, but they overflowed anyway and trickled down her cheek.

'And that's where he made love to you.'

I held her closer. 'Not love ...'

'I thought he loved me,' she whispered. 'I couldn't understand why he would want to hurt me so badly.'

'On the night of your father's feast, he wasn't thinking about you or me. He was thinking about the past.'

'But you let him ...'

Her eyes were filled with sorrow and I thought she must be remembering the birch grove and how I had suddenly withdrawn from her. I knew then that I was fighting for my life and that at any moment she might become hard as glass.

'It wasn't like that. It was about ... I felt so ... powerless ...' I murmured into her hair, kissing her in between words. 'It was such a muddle. To be in the place where Pa had first set eyes on Fleur Cornelis-Faider. To have been swimming in the river where you saved me, but with the distance between us so unbridgeable that night ...'

She didn't withdraw, only ran the tip of her thumb along my lips.

'I hate to see you so nervous of me,' she said. 'I don't blame you. I was so foul to you. It's just a battle every time with me, to let things go. But now you're here. And I'm here. That has to be good enough.'

We drew the thin blanket up to our chins and curled closer. 'What do they want me to do?' she said.

'Confirm who it is. That's all, if you're able.'

'And then what?'

'Then you and I can disappear,' I said.

'What are you talking about?'

'This is our chance.'

'Disappear where?'

'We can just melt away, here, in Barcelona. Nobody knows where we are right now. And I've plenty of money.'

'You are a crazy woman. Is this what they told you to say?'

'Of course not.' I drew back so that she could see my eyes. 'They don't know that I'm in love with you.'

'In love with me . . .' It was barely a whisper.

The world, the war, fell away until they were a faint buzzing in our ears, and then nothing.

Somewhere close by, a clock struck the quarter. I put my lips to her breastbone and my hand to the top button of her dress. The birch grove shimmered in my mind's eye, and a wood by the Dutch border where my father had held Fleur Cornelis-Faider in his arms and found temporary oblivion. After a while the shadowy cloak of the past melted away entirely and there was just this living girl. I kissed the silky skin on the underside of her breast and knotted my limbs with hers so that nothing could separate us.

It was minutes before she spoke again, her voice drugged. 'You say that Pieter was there too, in the clearing?'

'He shouldn't have been, he wasn't invited. But he was watching from the trees.'

She had propped herself on her elbow and her hair swung forward and fell against my shoulder. Just before she kissed me again I saw a shadow. I would have paid it heed, should have done, had my flesh not been singing and my mouth aching for her. Her lips caressed my throat and her fingertips ran down the centre of my body.

The last words I heard as I bit on the side of her hand to prevent myself from crying out were: 'I love you, I love you.'

Estelle

After I'd bolted from the Café Esperanza, I returned to the room where I'd slept off the Via Laietana, packed my bag, dodged through the complicated network of streets and arrived at one of Edouard's boltholes. The key was concealed, as promised, behind a splinter of wood in the lintel.

Then I sent for Christa.

The tiny apartment, in the corner of the building, had two windows at right angles to each other, hung with grimy muslin curtains, a narrow bed covered by a striped cotton fabric, and a chair with a broken rush seat. There was a smell of stale bedding. The walls, at one time painted coral, had faded to a ghostly pink and the woodwork had lost all but the odd smear of varnish. When I threw back the shutters and opened the window, sunshine poured in, and a salty breeze.

A bicycle clattered by and a child screeched on the floor above.

Pressing my back to the corner of the room, I slid down between the two windows. I was stricken, like a rat in a trap. What next, Christa? I sensed her approach. Nemesis or salvation, Christa, of all people, had reached her little hand into the melting pot of Europe.

A tentative knock. I waited a moment to steady my heart before opening the door and there she was, breathless, frightened and triumphant, her hair unravelled from its combs and her cheeks flushed from running. She was the same girl who had greeted me in Harewood Road but so much more; the other half of myself.

She was almost beside herself with nerves. But she was sure of herself too; a thread of steel ran through her. After all, she had defied Longbridge and her other masters.

And me? I never could trust myself to behave well or even in my own best interest. I could only hope that I would not waste a single moment. And so, when she fell through the door, I held her close.

Perhaps that's how it had felt, being cradled to Maman's breast, when she carried me to the clearing to meet Borland, Jesuit priest, devoted, jilted, taunted lover. She had settled me in the grass, where I lay gazing up at the thousand flickering leaves, oblivious to what was happening nearby to Robbe, the poor little boy. An unwanted child. In our conversation by the frozen river after Papa's funeral, symmetry was the reason he'd given me for fucking Christa. I grieved not just for the news she'd brought, but for all that we'd made her suffer at De Eikenhoeve.

'What do they want me to do?' I asked, when I could speak.

She painted a picture for me of the life we could have together. She'd worked it all out. We'd lie low in this room for a while and then take a bus to some remote place. She had enough money saved from her teaching job to last a few months. I had fluent Spanish. We would simply disappear.

It was a glorious fantasy. After all, we fitted together perfectly. She kissed me and whispered: 'This is where we belong. Nobody else matters.'

Her lips left a fiery trail. She was sanity and softness. Her fingers were shy and her eyes liquid with love. Her hair was so soft when it brushed my skin that I gasped. I was demolished by her tenderness and her extraordinary courage. She knew me. She *knew* me. She whispered words of love into the spaces between my fingers and the hollow of my throat and the whorl of my ear. Her tongue traced the curve of my foot and the scar in my knee. I was helpless. My blood sang. She loved me. No doubt about it.

And when I knelt over her, pressed my lips to her throat and ran my hand along her hip, when I slid my tongue along her salty thigh and she arched her back and bit on my knuckle, I understood how love can break a person open. This was Christa unlatched from all she had been before. She was wide-eyed, filled with wonder, laughing. Mine.

Later, as I rested my face on her belly, I imagined my mother's skirts shushing through the bracken. My infant head was

327

pressed to the exposed skin at her throat, a small boy dragged on her hand while his brother ran unnoticed through the trees. And I remembered another woman, with another baby, who had stood by the fall of antique lace shrouding Grand-mère's window in Rue d'Orléans. Robbe crossing the cluttered salon to pull faces behind Clémence Depage's shoulder and make the baby laugh.

Pieter, a year later, in that same salon, invites me to retreat to De Eikenhoeve, safe beneath his wing. Pieter, with Marguerite perched on his arm, leads the little Depage boys to his lorry, where they sit on the high seats, frightened and proud. Their mother is trying not to cry. Pieter, at the wheel, waves me good-bye. False passports are tucked into the glove compartment. And off they go, sweeping out of the yard in a cloud of exhaust fumes.

Clémence Depage and her children nestled in a single-storey cottage on the De Eikenhoeve estate, midway between the village and the farm.

It was early evening, about six o'clock. The train left at fifteen minutes to seven. As Christa drowsed, her arms were round and smooth in the failing light.

'I have to go,' I whispered.

'Where?' She turned her face to me.

'Home.'

'You can't ...'

I stroked her hair as I kissed her. 'Tell them I'll deal with it. I need to be sure. Do you understand?'

'They'll kill you.'

Ahead of me, nearly a week away, was Brussels. In a flash I saw its thousand betrayals, its yellow felt stars and sudden acts of extreme violence. A young boy, face to the wall, arms above his head, pisses himself as a Mof puts a revolver to his ear. Watchful eyes behind lace curtains, shameful excursions to the police station, queues snaking round street corners. And here, with Christa, a bottle of wine from the south maybe, a couple of oranges, a loaf of bread for our supper. And just one more night, another day in this soft space. What difference would it make?

She didn't argue. I yearned for her to lock the door, cling to my ankles, but she simply drew the thin blanket around her naked shoulders and watched as I stuffed my spare skirt into my bag and put on my jacket.

When I sat beside her on the bed her body convulsed. We clung together. 'Tell them I will find out for sure who it is,' I said. And I wrenched myself from her arms, picked up my bag and stumbled towards the landing. 'Lock up and put the key in the gap above the lintel. Above all, don't follow me.'

She got up from the bed and leant against the door frame for support. 'I'll see you very soon,' she said, and caught a strand of my hair between finger and thumb so that I felt a slight tug as I moved away, then took the stairs two or three at a time.

At the street entrance I looked up and glimpsed her shadow before I turned and stepped out into the chill of the evening. The city was crowded, hard to navigate with traffic blocking every junction. I forced myself to take step after step, to break into a run. Would she come after me? Please, please, Christa.

Ten minutes later I had reached the station, bought a ticket and elbowed my way to the barrier. The ticket inspector, bored, glanced at my passport and asked me to confirm my name.

'Estelle,' I said.

'Elisabetta, it says here.'

'That's what I said, Elisabetta.'

It was the first of many mistakes. The banknotes I'd been given were in the bottom of my rucksack – I had forgotten to stuff them into the lining of my boots. Fortunately he didn't bother to search me. I made my feet take yet more steps along the platform and chose a crowded carriage where I'd be hemmed in by others, unable to change my mind.

In the long minutes that followed, before we drew away from the platform, I sank my head into my hands, in case she was there, somewhere, peering in. Or in case she had not followed me and the loss of her would show in my eyes.

The carriage was filled with smoke. We lurched forward, an inch at a time, then faster. I sensed relief in the passengers around me, a commitment to the journey. Every cell in my body ached for her.

Christa

The simple process of buttoning my blouse and hooking up my skirt, let alone drawing on my stockings, was almost beyond me. It took all my willpower to smooth the bed, fold the blanket and eradicate every trace of Estelle, but I worked methodically until the room was tidy and the shutters closed. About five times I stepped out onto the landing and locked the door, then went back in and checked again, in case some precious atom of her remained.

At last I crept down the dim staircase, quiet now that it was past children's bedtime, and entered the dark streets where the wind had already turned bitter and electric lights shone brazenly in that city that had no need for a blackout. I got lost many times over but somehow fumbled my way back to the Hotel Monica, where Longbridge was waiting for me in the foyer, very stern and very unlike himself.

He took one look at my face and bought me a glass of Madeira, then sat with me in the bleak, hateful bar with its wine-stained carpet that reeked of stale smoke and alcohol, within sight of the revolving doors.

'Are you going to tell me where you've been?'

'You had me watched, then.'

'Unfortunately she lost sight of you.'

'I was with Estelle.'

'Where is she now?'

'She's gone. She told me to let you know that she'll deal with the matter herself.'

He sighed and we waited a few more minutes in silence. 'You do realise that if you were followed, and if your friend is now

330

on her way back to Brussels, the odds of her being captured are staggeringly high.'

'Isn't she doing what you wanted?'

'She should have awaited further instructions.'

The bar was quiet and, of course, unheated. Each time the door revolved wind ruffled the hem of my skirt.

'She believed you then,' he said.

'Oh yes.'

'And did she confirm the name?'

'Not exactly.'

'What do you mean?'

'Simply that. I can't be sure she agrees with me.'

He was so exasperated he had to cross to the far side of the foyer and study the menu. Eventually he returned to my side. 'I have to make some urgent calls. I'll see you in the morning.'

'What will you tell them?'

His glance held just a gleam of its old humour. 'Precisely what you've said. That Estelle will deal with the matter herself.' He pushed the door briskly, was received into the revolve and delivered out onto the pavement, then peered back at me through a glass panel before settling his hat and hurrying away.

Later, a businessman who'd been eyeing me from a discreet distance approached and asked me first in Spanish then English whether I'd like an escort to dinner. One glance drove him away. For hours I sat on that red velvet banquette, starting to my feet every time the mahogany and glass door turned. I had decided that it was quite possible that Estelle would change her mind or that her train would be cancelled. She knew the name of my hotel after all.

From time to time I got up purposefully, as if to climb the stairs and go to my room. I always changed my mind and returned to the banquette. At one point I considered ordering something to eat, but could not bear to turn my back on the door. A trickle of restaurant customers came and went, despite it being clear that the Monica was not noted for its cuisine. A couple entered hand in hand, she in a fur stole and a creased skirt, he looking rather red-faced and self-satisfied as they waited for the lift.

By midnight the bar was empty and the night porter had locked the door. The lights were switched off and I was left alone under the cold security lights. In the end I had no choice but to go upstairs.

Estelle

My guide, an old boy, bow-legged, with a hacking cough, rarely said a word, simply took my money and stalked on ahead while I stumbled, time after time. At one point we lost our way and ended up back in Spain; wasted an hour retracing our steps.

The wind changed direction and lashed us with hailstones. When I missed my footing on a scree slope, I slid almost forty metres and lay with my eyes closed, my limbs heavy, sinking, too tired to get up. Only the force of a metal toecap in my hip roused me. The guide was standing over me, hands in pockets, and watched as I hauled myself to my feet.

I was so full of Christa, of leaving her behind, I could think of nothing else. All I wanted was to be back with her in the peachy light of that little room.

We crawled to a cottage high in the mountains and paid for soup, bread, a bed, blankets that failed to warm me. Our wet clothes hung from the rafters. I had to cling to the mattress to prevent myself from heading back to the train station and retracing my steps.

In another life I was still with her in that room on the Carrer de l'Esparteria. Shared wine and bread, nestled on the striped blanket, spilling crumbs. Watched her grow muzzy with alcohol and joy, lay down and held her again, forehead to forehead, blending my body with hers. Just for that, wouldn't it have been the right choice? Just to sleep with Christa cradled in my arms. The loveliness of Christa, the solace of her perfect body.

At some point in the small hours, as I lay rigid, listening to the mountain wind, the snoring of my companion and his vile cough, I thought of my brothers. The angle of Robbe's sullen head, the slight tremor in his stained fingers as he stubbed out a cigarette, the sideways glance of his dark eyes. In Grand-mère's salon he had stood close to Clémence Depage, grinning as Marguerite curled her fat hand around his finger.

I had been so sure he loved me above everyone else, Estelle, his little sister, the family glue.

What if Christa was wrong? Pieter had also been a witness to Maman's meeting in the woods. Or what if those old events were not connected to whoever was betraying us now? I couldn't be sure of anything.

Pieter had told me that Papa, in the last war was *an absolute genius at getting people to look in the wrong direction. Small irregularities with the milk yield, that sort of thing, so that De Eikenhoeve had a reputation for minor subversion.*

Harbouring the Depage family was a small irregularity, in the scheme of things.

Was it a clever decoy? Kindness? The ultimate proof that, if it was ever suspected there was a traitor in our midst, it couldn't be Pieter. Oldest son, golden boy, devoted to the farm. Who'd toiled away at languages and mathematics so he could put them to use in the family business. Patiently endured the storms brewed by Robbe's truancy and rudeness.

A typical mealtime at De Eikenhoeve when we were children: silver cutlery with the oak-leaf engraving, rainbow reflections of candles in the crystal glassware. Hanna at the sideboard, watching Papa carve.

Papa: 'Where is Robbe?'

Pieter: 'I haven't seen him since school.'

Papa: 'Well where the hell is he now?'

Pieter: 'I think his favourite cow is in calf.'

Pieter, always covering up for Robbe, never actually lied; he didn't say that they'd set off for school together but Robbe had left by lunchtime. Pieter never showed his irritation with Robbe, never complained about Papa's bad temper, never shouted at Robbe and told him to fall into line, or told tales about him.

In fact, he usually sided with Robbe. Made excuses. Kept him dancing on the edge.

I remembered Pieter and Robbe in the attic above Maman's room, talking about Marthe. 'She suggested throwing out all of Maman's art,' said Pieter. 'I told her no.' Reassurance, or a subtle goading? The sowing of seeds; Robbe's hatred for Marthe encouraged to fester.

Pieter had a working knowledge of German. At Papa's funeral he hadn't bothered to salute Steiger even though the rule was: Don't annoy the Moffen unless you have to. Unless, of course, you're making a false show of insolence because you've sold your soul to the devil and Steiger is already your friend.

A sleepwalker, twenty-four hours after leaving Perpignan, I stumbled out of Bruxelles-Midi, past officials who had always before scrutinised my papers but didn't bother that night. They must have known Elisabetta-Estelle was contaminated by treachery. Or perhaps grief had made me invisible. It was almost curfew but I walked brazenly down the middle of every street. I was courting fate, demanding to be arrested and removed from the turmoil.

Rue d'Orléans was silent and empty. I unlocked the door and stood in the hall. The house was so still I assumed they must be in bed – it was about ten o'clock. But when I reached for the lamp on the marble-topped table it wasn't there and my foot crunched on broken glass. I groped for another switch and saw, in the flood of light, that the lamp had been knocked to the floor, the glass shade smashed. I backed out into the street, ran round the corner and hid in a porch.

I knew the score. The Moffen would make an arrest, then lie in wait for friends and family to come home. After half an hour I knocked on the door of Mevrouw van der Sprenkel's house and called her name repeatedly through the letter box until the door opened a crack. 'Will you please be *quiet*?'

'What has happened to Grand-mère?'

'Where have you been all this time? They arrested her last Friday, poor soul. Ripped her out of her bed and shoved her into a car. She was only wearing her night things and was so weak they had to carry her. Didn't you know? I've heard she never reached the police station. Died on the way.'

'And Céleste?' I managed to ask.

Nothing.

335

'Céleste?' I repeated.

The door slammed in my face.

I decided, if the Nazis had really been watching the house, they'd have picked me up already, so back I went. This time I registered a foul smell in the hall. Grabbing the lamp-stand as a weapon, I crept from room to room, calling for Céleste. Every drawer had been opened in every bureau, books torn off shelves, cloths dragged from tables.

The shrine to Maman had been pulled apart, the statue of the Virgin smashed, a photograph frame stripped of its contents, the glass broken. I couldn't work out at first whose image was missing, then I realised it was Borland's. Now they could have no doubt of the connection between him and Grand-mère. And therefore me.

In Grand-mère's bedroom the sheets were in disarray, a book tossed to the floor, her glass and water bottle overturned. I could have told them that all the records she kept were in her head. In Maman's old room, everything had been ripped apart. They'd taken a few things: Christa's letters, the photograph of Maman, my dissertation. I actually smiled at the thought of the Gestapo scouring those turgid pages for clues.

They hadn't bothered with the attic floor – must have taken one look at the heaps of wormy old furniture and moth-eaten curtains and given up. Just as well. I couldn't swear we'd covered the traces of every fugitive we'd ever concealed there.

Down I went to the basement kitchen, which was surprisingly untouched, a half-peeled carrot on the table, a saucepan of water on the hob. Flies clamouring against the window led me to the little cubbyhole Céleste had converted into a bedroom.

Four shoes were arranged tidily beneath the bed – house shoes and outdoor boots. Céleste was tucked up in bed, her face turned towards me, eyes wide open. Fully dressed, in foetal position, her arms clamped to her side. We gaped at each other, she from glassy eyes which I did not think to close. I backed away, wondering: What shall I do? Where should I go? In the end I retreated to my bedroom and lay with my knees clenched to my chest, exactly like Céleste.

My stomach cramped with hunger and my head pounded.

Part of me was still in a corner of a second-class carriage rattling through France, or lying in a Spanish bedroom with Christa. I thought of Grand-mère startled by a hammering on the door, Céleste hobbling across the hall, the thunder of boots on the stairs.

Grand-mère was my constant. Cotton-wool hair and a soul as tough as old boots, tossed on the horns of history. If Christa was right, if the traitor was a brother of mine, could he have sat in her salon one minute, his too large frame spilling over the seat of a dainty armchair, devouring delicacies served by Céleste, and then delivered those same old women up to the enemy? Could he have done that?

Sleep overcame me for only a few minutes at a time and pestered me with uneasy dreams; most of the time I simply lay there, knowing that in that house I was a sitting duck and wondering why the final blow had not yet fallen.

Christa

The tortuous journey back to England was made all the lonelier by the lack of Longbridge, who'd remained in Barcelona. His replacement was an ATS sergeant with iron-grey hair set in corrugated waves, a frigid manner and a mouth clamped shut in disapproval. She didn't ask me what my mission had been in Barcelona and thankfully preferred knitting khaki socks to walks on the deck. By the time I was back in London, loss had rendered me incapable of thought, let alone work, and in desperation I ended up on the doorstep in Harewood Road, shivering and weeping.

Ma held me upright as I crossed the threshold: 'Whatever's the matter? We haven't heard from you in weeks. Where have you been?'

There was not much of the truth that I was able to tell her except that I was unwell and couldn't seem to pull myself together. Ma, with good cause to fear any hint of a damaged mind, ushered me through to the kitchen, filled the kettle, unbuttoned my coat as if I were three years old, ran upstairs to fetch my slippers, then sat beside me, patting my hands and urging me to dry my tears and cheer up; I'd soon feel better.

I was put to bed with a hot-water bottle and served a bowl of soup on a tray covered with the old blue gingham cloth embroidered with a Scottie dog that used to be my companion when I was ill as a child. I half expected Ma to bring out a jigsaw.

I lay propped on the pillows and stared out at the privy and the clothes-line, wondering how on earth I could have ended up in my Watford bedroom after I'd sent Estelle to almost certain death.

When Pa came home later, stamping his feet outside the back

338

door to shake off the mud, I heard the murmur of my parents' voices and his footsteps as he crept to the bottom of the stairs to listen for me, as he used to when I was very young and on the brink of sleep. My heart ached for all the years I had been irritated by his moroseness and silences; now I understood the effort it must have cost him to make any connection at all with his life in Harewood Road.

In the evening, news of the war blasted from the downstairs radio, the usual mix of triumph and disaster; Monty's victories in Africa offset by the sinking of British naval ships in the Atlantic. None of it touched me. The war was reduced now to one woman trapped in the Petri dish of Belgium.

When I got up to join my parents at breakfast the next day, we treated each other carefully. Pa was much more robust than he had been on my previous visit, and told me that his photograph in the *Watford Observer* had generated a pile of mail, and that he'd taken it upon himself to respond to every letter.

It being Sunday, I accompanied Ma to church, much to her joy. We stood close together, elbows touching, and sang the John Bunyan hymn about being valiant in the face of disaster. In the afternoon she knitted while I went for a walk in Cassiobury Park and peered through the dying reeds at the river. Where was Estelle now? What was she doing?

By the end of three days, I deemed myself fit enough to return to work. In the small hours of the last morning I crept downstairs. Pa was snoring heavily and it was bitterly cold. Even in the intense darkness of the blacked-out house I was sure-footed enough to find my way by torchlight to the bookshelf, where I took down the family Bible, removed the picture of Fleur Cornelis-Faider and carried her up to my room.

In bed, I curled on my side, shone the beam into her face and absorbed her image. I had tried, when younger, to penetrate those shapely eyes and that ivory skin, as if by staring long enough I might discover the essence of Fleur and even communicate with her. Now it was her daughter I sought. While the sepia Fleur had been remote and careless, Estelle was hot-blooded and passionate. For Fleur, love had meant everyone within reach immolating

339

themselves on the pyre of her martyrdom. For Estelle, it was a matter of struggling, time after time, despite everything, to do the right thing.

A board creaked on the landing; I hoped Ma would pass by my door but she opened it a crack and poked her head in. 'Are you all right, Christine? Are you sick? I heard you . . .'

She perched on the edge of the bed. A scarf protected the curlers in her hair and she wore a faded candlewick robe over a winceyette nightdress. Whereas Fleur, in the photograph, was frozen in time, her skin smooth and unblemished, Ma, who'd been no beauty even in her prime, had not aged well. Her fingers, when she took it from my hand, were swollen with arthritis.

'You used to worship this,' she said. 'And I can't say I blame you. I think Pa would have done the same if he'd known where I kept it. He's never forgotten her, you know.'

'Don't you mind, Ma?'

She scrutinised the image. 'I've become a lot more charitable recently – since meeting Estelle, actually. All I hope is that he made her happy. You know, given it was her last night.'

'Have you ever imagined what she was really like?'

'I've wasted far too much of my life doing that. The opposite of me, I expect.' She was laughing. 'But then some of us have to make soup and do the accounts and just stay alive, or what would be the point of winning a war?'

When she touched my face, her rough fingertips smelled of onions and her eyes were full of tenderness. 'Dear old love. My girl.'

Estelle

At about seven I got up, washed my face, changed my clothes and brushed my hair. I made the sign of the cross at the top of the basement stairs because I thought Céleste would have appreciated the gesture. Though actually, come to think of it, I had no idea whether she'd had a faith of her own or merely paid lip service for Grand-mère's sake.

I set out for the Prospero and, as usual, waited deep in a nearby doorway. Anticipating the fug of cigarette smoke and a few degrees of additional warmth, I longed to slip inside. The floor would be unswept from last night, the tables laden with dirty cups. My mouth watered – for some reason I anticipated pre-war bread and coffee.

But over there a man was reading a newspaper. Outdoors, on a draughty corner, despite the cold.

I was jumpy, wasn't myself, had lost Grand-mère, hadn't slept.

If I unmasked the wrong brother, how many would pay the price? The dominoes would tumble, one after another. Names would be named: the kids who ran through the fields seeking out fallen airmen, the country women who fed them, the escorts who guided them to their next hiding place, the shop owners who turned a blind eye to clandestine meetings and left messages in windows, the draftsmen who forged their passports, the officials who feigned ignorance, the landladies in Paris and Perpignan who harboured us, the mountain guides. Everyone knew someone who knew someone else.

At last, round the corner, came Robbe, wearing the usual disreputable raincoat that fell in dirty creases almost to his ankles. Hat worn low on his forehead. Perhaps he sensed me, because he looked up in the act of relighting a cigarette, and it was as if I saw his face – his beautiful, tricky face – for the first time. Borland's son, to the last cell. Not just the narrow cheekbones, those dark brows. It was the unique expression in his eyes. Both hunter and hunted, the watcher and lone wolf; the hungry boy peering through the pâtisserie window.

I saw how his hand dropped to tap ash onto the pavement. The long hard lines of his profile as he ground the butt beneath his heel. And suddenly he looked directly at me, his gaze penetrating the shadow. I thought he must have seen me before he pulled open the door and disappeared inside.

He would expect me to follow him after a few minutes if the coast was clear.

But I didn't follow.

Because now I was sure.

I stumbled, light-headed, across the city. At one point glanced over my shoulder. The man who'd been lingering outside the café had smooth brown hair, an overlarge mouth and glasses. Very thin. Was that him, ducking inside the mouth of the metro? I upped my game, dodged in and out of shops and alleys and made sure I'd lost him.

I was heading for the Pâtisserie Faider to buy a bun from Madame Vauclain, who was full of apologies: 'I can hardly bear to sell you something so paltry. In the old days, it would have been rolled in sugar but now—'

'There isn't a single raisin in the dough,' I said. 'I don't know how you get away with it.'

Her eyelid flickered. Horrified. 'If you don't like our produce, perhaps you'd like to go elsewhere.'

I flounced out.

Yes, she'd got the message and would act upon it, make sure the word got round.

I reached the stationer's shop on Rue de Florence by a devious route, darted in and bought a pencil. Grade 2B. By the time I'd crossed the street the sign was in the window in two languages: *NOUS N'AVONS PLUS D'ENCRE ROUGE . . . WE VERKOPEN NIET MEER RODE INKT . . .*

We are out of red ink.

We are betrayed. Disband. Hide. Spread the word.

I had one thought now, to reach Clémence Depage and her children, tucked away at De Eikenhoeve.

I sat on a public bench, the smoothed-out paper bag from the pâtisserie on my knee. Wrote a message to Edouard, posted it behind the usual stone in the memorial in the Place des Martyrs, then set off for the station.

I took all kinds of risks. Didn't bother with my usual trick – wait for a distraction, attach self to a woman with a screaming child, offer assistance, get waved through. Instead I flashed my papers at the barrier. All in order. So I should think; I was Estelle Cornelis-Faider and I was going home. I had probably sat in the very same carriage all through my childhood, and with Christa. Except that nobody spoke any more or smiled. We were huddled within ourselves and flinched if we saw a uniform. Anyway, I was too tired to stay upright and kept nodding off.

By the time we reached Oostervorken, the train was almost empty. Only I got out. There was an old woman in the ticket office who I didn't recognise. She gave me a mean look and insisted on scrutinising my papers. In more alert moments I would have taken the precaution of appeasing that woman or, better still, would have avoided her altogether. There was no sign of Viktor. Very odd – the first time in living memory that he hadn't been loitering there – so I had to walk.

It was late autumn, the remaining leaves were tattered and the sky skimmed with haze. Not the faintest glimmer of new life. Marthe used to say that even in the depths of winter, life simmered beneath the surface. She'd take me up close to the roses in her garden and we'd peer at their gnarled and thorny stems, searching for a hint of spring.

The afternoon sun shone milk-white as I floated along the lane. I was a phantom Estelle, with one idea in her head and the rest of her still in that upstairs room in Barcelona. The ground was wet but the surface of the lane in good repair. In a former hayfield, the winter wheat stood an inch or so tall. The oak tree was motionless and bare. Behind it, the many windows of the house were blank. I didn't even bother to wonder, as I opened the gate, who might be watching.

Instead of heading for the kitchen I went straight to the office Pieter shared with Oud Daan. The door was open but there was nobody about. Ledgers were piled on the desk, the filing cabinet had a wonky drawer that wouldn't close and bulging box files lined the shelves. I began a search, slow and systematic, for some sort of proof. At first there was nothing; no ledger with false figures that I could find. No letters from a grateful Third Reich. Nothing.

At any moment I expected the crunch of footsteps or a dog's glad bark. But I didn't appear to be in a hurry, simply sat at the desk and surveyed this kingdom where I used to come so often when I was a little girl and Papa was in charge. There were no sweets now in the middle drawer, only paper clips, a stapler and elastic bands, blotting paper, a bit of sealing wax. And, of course, the key to the other drawer, the bottom left, where Papa had kept his revolver.

Two more drawers, one labelled 'Tenants', all in order as far as I could tell. A note of the Faider family, mother and three children, installed in Cottage Number Three. 'Correspondence', all quite innocent. In the filing cabinets, receipts and records of crops and livestock. They hadn't been cleared out for years. A compartment marked 'Personal'.

And there I did find something. Amidst photographs of the labourers and indoor staff clustered round the Cornelis grandparents under the oak tree was another formal group: Maman seated, scowling Papa standing behind, his hand on her shoulder, baby Estelle on her knee, Robbe in front of Pieter, who was a head taller. Or I presumed it was Robbe. He'd been scratched out, every bit of him, with the point of a compass, in places so violently that the paper had been torn.

Proof? Of one brother's momentary dislike of the other, perhaps, a fit of rage. I searched on and found a box file amidst a row of dozens, each allocated a year in the farm's life. This one was labelled '1917/1918'.

Mostly it contained receipts and other records – prescriptions for sick livestock, a notebook with pages so ink-laden they crackled, staff records and weekly pay, an assessment of yield in Papa's painstaking handwriting, a newspaper clipping.

FARMER'S SON RETRIEVES BODY FROM RIVER

A body has been found in the Rivier Naald on De Eiken-hoeve land by young Pieter Cornelis, aged nine years. The corpse had been in the river so long that it was impossible to identify. Meneer Bernard Cornelis stated that this must be yet another young soldier, fleeing the front line. The family has paid for a modest burial out-side the churchyard in Oostervorken.

Why then, in a small brown envelope, was there a length of cord with two tags still attached, one dark green and one reddish brown? These were British tags – I had been trained to recognise and decipher them. A name, J. Symmons, engraved on both, number 2097, the letters P for rank, WG for regiment, and CE for religion.

The farmhouse was very quiet. Not a single pan rattled in the kitchen, but there was a smell of baking. I almost swooned at the sight of a tray of rolls on the table – picked one up and sniffed it, tore off a mouthful. At De Eikenhoeve there was flour in the cellars and eggs in the larder while the rest of Belgium starved.

I meandered along the passageways, climbed the stairs and reached Maman's turret room. It was full of dust, eerily silent and corpse cold. Her grey cardigan drooped over the back of the chair once more. I took off my coat, replaced it with Maman's cardigan and dropped Papa's revolver into the pocket. The picture that Christa had so disliked was still in place: a woman with upturned eyes, passive, trapped within her canvas. Is that how Maman had felt in this tower with its view of everywhere?

The land stretching away to the north had been ploughed into neat furrows and at last I spotted people at work in the former raspberry fields, digging potatoes. And there was Marthe in her rose garden beneath the tower, stooped over a near empty flower-bed.

345

Down the ancient stairs from the turret I ran and out of the side door. Marthe straightened when she saw me and put her hand to the small of her back. She wore a pale-blue overall over a black dress. Her face registered first shock then apprehension, but she managed a smile. 'Estelle. What an extraordinary surprise.'

I actually kissed her – the first spontaneous kiss since I was about four. It had a momentous effect, made her shrink away, lose all her poise.

'Oh no, don't do that. Oh my poor girl, you look done in. Where have you been? Don't tell me you walked from the station. But then you must have done, because Viktor is here, helping with the potatoes. They're going to drill for barley after Christmas. We're so short of men.'

'I'm used to walking.'

'Come into the house. You look half-starved. Where have you been all these months?'

'Did you hear about Grand-mère?'

I understood Marthe so much better that day. Her limitations. She couldn't take her eyes off Maman's cardigan – she was wondering why I'd put it on and why the right-hand pocket sagged so badly.

'I was so fond of dear Madame Faider. How could they have been so cruel to someone her age? When I think of how frail she was.' She was clutching secateurs and a skein of string.

'Any idea why she was arrested?' I asked.

'Pieter went into Brussels to find out. Estelle, I'm afraid they are looking for you. Because you were the assistant of that dentist, Depage – you know, the children we are keeping here. He was supposed to have been recording the details of all the Jews in his area, but it turns out he'd deliberately left names off the list. They made a search of his premises and then went to arrest you in Rue d'Orléans.'

'Where are his children now?'

'At school, I expect. Why do you ask? They're quite safe. Nobody here knows their real name.' We stared at each other until she dropped her gaze. 'You shouldn't have come,' she said.

'Marthe, please go and collect those children and their mother and take them to Tante Julia.'

'I can't.'

'You can. You *must*. Please.'

The secateurs slipped from her fingers. 'Forgive me.'

I held her hand to my cheek. This second-best woman. A good woman, up to a point.

'Let me give you a lift to the station first,' she said.

'I've told you, I want you to look after the children.'

'Don't let Pieter see you.'

'I must talk to Pieter. But please make sure Clémence and the children get to Tante Julia's safely. I'm relying on you.'

I left her in her garden. Willed her to summon the strength to fetch the key to the farm van, drive first to the Depage cottage, then the school and scoop up mother and children.

So this was how the equilibrium of the farm had been maintained. Everyone collusive, no questions asked. Marthe allowed to get on with her quiet life, taking food to the poor, gifts to Grand-mère, other charitable acts, as long as she saw nothing she shouldn't.

My wellingtons were lined up in the boot room. The farmyard was deep in mud; the hens rushed at me in case I happened to be carrying food, and a couple of white ducks bustled on the pond. As I passed through the gate, my shadow was long and weedy in the last of the sunshine. No need to hurry as I walked down to the former fruit fields, where Oud Daan spotted me first. He was standing over by a distant hedge, smoking a cigarette and watching proceedings, far more aged than I remembered. Hanna and one of the older labourers were at the horse's head – even at De Eikenhoeve they must be saving every drop of tractor fuel. Or perhaps, without Weber and Jong Daan, it had simply ground to a halt and nobody could repair it. Pieter wore a loose waistcoat over a checked shirt and was hauling a full sack onto the wagon.

Swart, lying by the gate, gave a pleased little moan and ambled across. Pieter's eyes widened but he soon recovered. 'My God, Estelle. What a surprise.' He walked towards me, held out his arms and drew me close. 'My dear girl. I'm so glad to see you.'

347

His jacket was rough against my cheek. 'You must be tired and hungry. Why didn't you let us know you were coming? Let me take you up to the house and find you something to eat.'

For a moment my head rested in the old, comfortable place against his shoulder. 'I've already been to the house,' I said.

'You must be exhausted. Did you come from Brussels this afternoon?'

'I did. You're right, I'm pretty tired. But I need to talk to you in private. Have you time? Might we go for a walk before it gets dark?'

'Of course. Let me just sort out a couple of things here.' He strode across to Oud Daan and muttered a few words, directed Hanna to the next row of un-dug potatoes and whistled for the dog. Crows rose up from a neighbouring field and flapped across the pale sky. I was thinking about the woman in the ticket office at Oostervorken. In the distance I heard an engine and hoped that it was Marthe in the van.

Pieter offered out his hand to me. 'My dearest Estelle, little sister. Come back to the house. Come and get warm.' My heart ached to see him against the backdrop of his vast acres, the gentle undulations of the land, the patchwork of pasture and ploughed fields.

I shook my head and so we walked down to the river and onto the path leading towards the woods and the bathing pond. The sticky earth sucked at my boots and the river was sluggish and opaque. He was talking about Grand-mère; that the Moffen had searched her house and discovered the photograph of Borland in her salon. 'It was surely a sign of her growing old that she'd not hidden it. She'd never have made such a foolish mistake in the old days. And you do know that we're all at risk because of Maman's reputation. Now there really is no choice. We'll need to lie low. You especially.'

'What do you suggest?'

'Stay here. I can keep you safe.'

Him and me. The familiar falling into step, a slight breeze, the dusk unrolling within the trees.

'I was wondering,' I said, 'if you would show me the clearing where you saw Maman on the day before she was arrested.'

348

'What are you talking about?' Even though we weren't touching, I sensed the change in him.

'You know. She was there with Laurence Borland and two English soldiers, and Robbe, and me. Remember?'

'I have no idea—'

'What did Maman say to Borland that day, Pieter? And what did you do after you'd seen all those people in the clearing? Where did you go?'

'What is the matter with you? Listen, I don't have time for games. Let's go back to the house.'

Yet he still followed me as we reached the gate into the woods.

'Stop lying to me, Pieter.' I unfurled my hand and revealed the identity discs. 'Poor man. Poor Symmons. All he wanted was somewhere to hide, I expect. Nobody had told him that De Eikenhoeve was not a safe place for fugitives any more.'

The texture of his skin had changed to clay. Life had drained from his eyes. He was not the brightest of my brothers, Pieter; the fleetest of foot, the deftest at delivering a lamb or winning the heart of the prettiest dairymaid, all these gifts were Robbe's. He was working out his options; had glanced behind my shoulder to check we were alone, and had perhaps registered what I was wearing and why it hung so strangely.

'Do you hate us all so much?' I said. 'Or is it just that you cannot bear anything to hurt your glorious farm.'

His eyes reddened. 'If you come back with me to the house I'll take care of you.'

We were deep in the woods, perhaps near the clearing where Maman had met Borland that last time. 'How have you lived with yourself all these years?' I asked. 'You must know that Maman died because you told someone about seeing her in the woods with English soldiers.'

'It was Oud Daan. He said I had to keep my eye on her, that she was a bit of a crazy woman. So I did.'

'And he told the Germans.'

'She was my mother,' he cried, like a child, and I saw him so clearly, that fair-haired little boy, left to his own devices while she took her two youngest, her favoured chicks, to the woods.

'Think about it, Estelle,' he said more calmly. 'This farm has

349

saved the lives of hundreds of Belgians. We keep them from starvation and prevent our men being sent to labour camps. It might not be heroic but it's pragmatic and it works. Maman and Borland, Robbe, what the fuck did they do? Rescue a few airmen. Publish some ridiculous newspaper or blow up the odd train. As a result they irritate our occupier no end and bring down all kinds of retribution on the heads of the innocent. If they'd only sit tight until the end of the war, we'd all be fine.'

'It's not as simple as that. We have to make clear whose side we are on.'

'I'm on your side. Our side.'

'No. No. No. You're on the side of De Eikenhoeve above all else. And Christ knows how much you have always hated Robbe.'

He didn't deny it. He didn't protest or claim that his life had not been dedicated to a systematic destruction of every single person or activity that might have made Robbe happy.

He took a step towards me. 'Come back to the house. Let's talk some more later. You need to rest.'

He hugged me. An embrace that had always been both father and brother to me. Enclosure. Strength. Reassurance. He was reaching for the weapon but I was too quick for him, had jerked free and was backing away.

'Tell me why you betrayed Maman to Oud Daan?'

'It wasn't betrayal. She was the one who let us all down.'

'And the man by the river? Was it Oud Daan who finished him off as well?'

'He was looking for Maman. We could all have been arrested if the Germans had found him on our land.'

'And Borland. And Grand-mère. Are they the price you've paid for De Eikenhoeve?'

He was paternal, sympathetic, hand outstretched, his eyes focused on the muzzle of the gun. 'I implored you not to get involved.'

'Was it that you wanted Borland to be your father too? Or that you couldn't bear the fact that Maman loved him more than anyone else?'

'Hush. Hush. I've always vowed to protect you, little sister.'

He made a lunge at me. I fired twice, at his head and heart. He fell to his knees, crushing the dead bracken as he lurched sideways. Birds crashed up through the trees.

Pieter's eyes were still fixed on me as I knelt beside him and watched him die, a faint, accommodating smile still on his lips and blood puddling beneath his head.

Mijn geliefde broer. His hair was soft and thinning slightly at the crown and his face was calm and handsome. He had been so strong. Our rock, our keeper. I kissed his still-warm cheek, closed his fingers around the handle of the gun and set off through the trees. Twigs snapped and my breathing was too loud. I aimed for the far side of the wood, planning to go across country. Not to Tante Julia, who would be receiving three children and their mother by now, but into the chequerboard of fields. It was as if, as I ran, a thread was unravelling which had been wound too tightly about my heart for my entire life.

I kept the river far to my left. Soon I would come to a lane and then more trees. It was not so cold that day; I reckoned I would be able to sleep safely in a hedgerow until morning. And tomorrow I would begin the long journey south, back to Christa.

Then I heard the distant sound of barking.

I'd been far too careless. If that woman at the ticket office had called the military police and given them my name, they must already have visited De Eikenhoeve. I was on a list because of Depage and Grand-mère and the photograph of Borland. Anyway, Oud Daan had seen me. Even on his old legs he could have limped to the office telephone and made a call.

The flat landscape had hardly any cover. Dogs had been un-leashed, a whole pack of them by the sound of it. I kept running, but only for a few moments longer. Yowling, panting, the scurry of feet and a violent animal weight had me sprawling in the mud. Another gripped my ankle in its teeth. A vice. A German voice was shouting so that the hounds drew back, watched me with pitiless eyes, their saliva dripping into my face.

A man's voice. Footfall. Grey uniform. Triumph.

'Elisabetta,' he said.

Christa

I expected retribution for my behaviour in Barcelona but received no word at all from Sinclair, Fairbrother or Longbridge when I got back to work. Desperate for news of Estelle, I dropped a note into Northumberland House requesting an appointment. I received no acknowledgement and sent a further letter.

Eventually I made my way once more through Trafalgar Square, strode purposefully across the foyer, up the stairs, and knocked on the door to Room 115. It was thrown open by a stranger in civvies who peered at me, exasperated, said he'd never heard of a Colonel Fairbrother, and escorted me back to reception.

Months after my return to England, a curt invitation appeared on my desk at the Board of Trade. On this visit, I was ushered directly into Room 115 where, to my surprise, Fairbrother and Longbridge each shook my hand as if I were a trusted colleague rather than a reprobate. I sank, bemused, into the proffered chair. Their conciliatory demeanour felt far more unnerving than the expected recriminations.

'Your trip to Barcelona did not go entirely according to plan . . .' Fairbrother said.

'I suppose not.'

Longbridge directed his gaze beyond the window.

'You will note Doctor Sinclair's absence,' Fairbrother continued. 'I have the impression that there isn't much love lost between you. Can you tell me why?'

'I scarcely know him.'

'You may speak freely.'

I hesitated, having no desire to spend another minute on the subject of Doctor Sinclair. I was desperate for news of Estelle. 'He turned up at my lodgings, quite uninvited. One could certainly say he was guilty of blurring the boundaries.'

'Would you care to expand on that?'

'Not particularly. He seemed to want to befriend me. I felt ...
manipulated.'

Fairbrother nodded. 'Alas, your misgivings appear to be
justified. As is so often the case, personal affiliations have led
to loyalties being ... compromised. Resistance needs to be a
cold-blooded affair.'

'What has happened to Estelle?'

'After meeting you in Barcelona, she returned to Brussels and
disbanded the line. Dozens of people were saved.' He attempted
a smile. 'Perhaps hundreds.'

The pause went on for so long that in the end I felt compelled
to speak. 'Thank goodness. But is *she* safe? And what about her
brothers?'

Fairbrother rested his elbows on the desktop in front of
him and steepled his fingers. 'I'm not at liberty to divulge any
information about the brothers. With regard to Estelle, I'm
afraid you must steel yourself for some very disappointing news.
Miss Cornelis-Faider was arrested within a day of her return to
Belgium.'

Unable to look me in the eye, he picked up a pencil and prodded his blotter.

'I'm very sorry. There can be little doubt about her likely fate,
I'm afraid. If she's lucky, she'll be shot. If not, she'll be deported
and sent to a prison camp in Germany or occupied Eastern
Europe. I don't expect I need to spell out what that means.' He
rose and stood behind me. 'Try to bear up, Corporal Geering.'
I sat there a moment longer. Longbridge murmured soothing
words but I said that I needed air and left the room. Somehow I
made my way downstairs and out of the building.

On the Victoria Embankment I squinted into a low sun and
watched a pair of rusty coal barges drift along the Thames. Sea-
gulls bickered on the concrete wall and a ship's horn blared down
river.

After a few minutes I heard Longbridge's soft voice. 'I'm so
sorry about your friend.' When I turned my face away he put his

hand on my arm. 'You were bound to be upset. It's far from the best outcome. However, I hope you'll take comfort from this: I wouldn't have said it at the time, but I think you did very well over there in Barcelona.'

'Can you imagine what Estelle is suffering?'

'Let's remain hopeful. If there's any news, I'll be in touch.' He patted my elbow and walked away.

I stayed put, oblivious to everything except the murky waters lapping at the Embankment wall beneath me.

PART FOUR

April 1943—Spring 1945

Estelle

My trial was quite a performance. Fresh clothes – the dress in which I'd been arrested – unironed, but clean. Booted down the corridor to the washroom to comb my hair and splash my face with freezing water. A scrap of metal revealed a foggy version of Estelle, pale and smudged with bruises. Two front teeth missing.

I was given a fistful of bread to last me the day. And then a whiff of green and outdoor air, the din of traffic. Blue sky above two lines of uniforms, rifles at the ready. A bus with blacked-out windows.

I reckoned we were heading north towards the city centre. Ordinary life proceeded only a few centimetres away. Sunshine baked the roof, which was welcome at first, but in a few minutes I started to sweat. A bicycle bell sounded very close by. We halted, at traffic lights presumably. The blackout paint on the window was scratched and I saw a jagged scribble of light. Something was thrown against the van close to my elbow. A thug, sympathiser or collaborator. I'll never know.

The guard stationed next to me was chain-smoking and stank of nicotine and garlic. When the doors were flung open I glimpsed trees in new leaf. The Boulevard du Régent. So we were near to the Parc de Bruxelles where I had teased Christa about Wellington that time, and a fifteen-minute walk at most to Grand-mère's. A tisane in the little salon. The chink of bone china and a froth of lace, a slice of crumbly white cheese from the farm, a bowl of blackcurrants.

I was prodded between another row of uniforms into a cool building with a polished marble floor. The guards' boots went clap clap clap in unison. I had hoped they might allow observers, but all I got was Luftwaffe officers in swanky uniforms, chaired by an ancient general who sat beneath the Nazi flag. That bloody eagle.

The prosecutor modelled himself on Hitler – wore the same moustache. Lots of spit from a mouth like a haemorrhoid. An interpreter stood beside me and offered the odd word in Flemish. My defence lawyer, a complete stranger, twiddled his thumbs and yawned. In the same mould as the rest. Cold eyes, regular features, iron-grey hair. He couldn't speak either French or Flemish.

The prosecutor read out the charges against me like a yapping dog. 'The prisoner has been very wicked. She has deliberately and fraudulently compiled an incomplete register of Jewish names. She has assisted in the delivery of a libellous newspaper. She has aided enemies of the state to escape the authorities. She has worked with a known spy and enemy of the people, the so-called priest, Laurence Borland, who ran an intelligence network involving dozens of gullible students – young people whom he betrayed under interrogation, to save his own skin.'

Through a high window I glimpsed treetops and drifted away, hungry and tired, but startled when I heard other names I knew only too well. Depage. Madame Faider. No mention of Edouard or my brothers, thank Christ.

Next came the first witness, my interrogator, sporting, for the first and only time, a uniform. Proudly worn and very spruce. He ran a finger along the rim of his starched collar and was red-faced in the heat. I was faint, willed myself to stay upright.

When he and I first met I had felt hopeful, idiot that I was. I thought they'd sent me to see a doctor because I was suffering from an ache in my bones and a raging temperature. He was wearing a white coat over a clean shirt and tweed jacket. Very unlike the thugs in uniform who thus far had pounded me with questions, smacked my head against the wall, kicked me in the groin. This was a clean little man with polished fingernails, far shorter than me. Breathing deeply as he ordered a female guard to unbutton my dress. I had struggled to keep my feverish wits about me because I'd begun to anticipate what was coming.

What fucking monster in this prison, I thought, gets a female guard to unbutton a woman prisoner's clothes in the name of modesty? He grew excited. There was perspiration on his upper lip though he was trying to look serious, as if he was indeed a noble physician about to perform an important operation.

'Beautiful breasts,' he said. 'What a waste.' He held a needle before my eyes – like an embroidery needle. 'What I do is insert it first into the nipple. Do you understand?'

The guards had seized my arms. I stared at the bulge in his trousers. There was a stain by the fly. He pinched my nipple between finger and thumb.

'Or perhaps you don't need further persuasion before you tell us the names of your contacts in Brussels.'

I was faced with his thinning hair and freckled scalp as he leant in very close, his wet, hot breath on my skin, peered at the nipple, found just the right spot, inserted—

'Borland,' I screamed.

'We know all about Borland. Who else?'

'I can't remember.'

Pain skewered me. It was coloured red. I fixed my mind on a striped bedcover. And my scream was a blade.

It was a nasty shock when they brought Serge into the court-room. I'd last seen him years ago in Louvain, at the time of the invasion. Wearing his own clothes and with a bruise like a squashed plum on his cheek.

They asked him: 'Is this her? Was she also there when Borland gave you orders?'

He nodded and wouldn't meet my eye.

'Is this woman, who some call Elisabetta, actually Estelle Cornelis-Faider?'

'Yes she is.'

'Is she the one who helped circulate the newspaper known as *La Libre Belgique?*'

'She is.'

'And was she later responsible for smuggling numerous enemy airmen out of the country?'

'I wouldn't say numerous.'

'Answer the question.'

'Yes.'

'Is this woman the daughter of the traitor known as Françoise who was found guilty of treason during the last legal occupation of Belgium?'

'Yes.'

'And did this woman brag about her mother and say, given the chance, she'd do exactly the same?'

'Yes.'

My defence lawyer had only a couple of surly questions.

'How did you get that bruise on your forehead?'

'I fell.'

'Did you also work for Père Borland?'

'I pretended to. To help my German friends.'

They marched him away.

Witness number three was Madame Fabron, dressed in her best navy-blue costume and hat. Hair freshly set. A dutiful expression on her calm features. Shameless woman.

Yes, she had lived next door to Madame Faider, wife of the pâtissier, Monsieur Faider, for many years, but had grown suspicious when she had witnessed comings and goings in Rue d'Orléans late at night.

Yes, she'd noticed that I'd been away on long absences.

Yes, she had met the dentist's young wife at a salon in Rue d'Orléans.

'Did you not realise, Madame Fabron, that Madame Depage was a Jew?'

'Not at the time,' she said cravenly. 'As I've explained, I felt it was my duty to look after my neighbour, Madame Faider, who was very frail. She had been rather strange and eccentric for years. I'd suggested that she employed my maid's sister, but she insisted on a woman older than herself.'

'What would you have done had you known that Madame Depage was a Jew?'

'I would have reported her to the authorities, naturally.'

'Were you aware that the prisoner had taken a job as a nurse with Clémence Depage's husband, the so-called dentist, Jerome Depage?'

'I must say I was surprised.'

'And why was that?'

360

'As far as I knew, Est— er, the prisoner, had no experience at all in medical matters. She was a student of history, I believe.'

As she left the room, Madame Fabron raised her chin but wouldn't look at me. I felt a little sorry for her. How many hours or minutes, how many conversations with daughters and husband, how many soothing tisanes would it take to realign her conscience?

My interrogator had taken to switching on a radio during our sessions together. The first time, I thought: how quaint, a wireless. It reminded me of Mozart playing on the radiogram in Marthe's sitting room at De Eikenhoeve. And in the front room at Harewood Road, another wireless, marooned on a mat with crocheted edges. Mrs Geering laughing with her hand over her mouth at some English joke.

My Mof interrogator enjoyed 'Marcha Erika'. German voices singing joyfully.

The room had white tiles, a table, an anglepoise lamp, two chairs. There was scarcely room for the two guards. On the table was a pair of pliers. He tapped my fingertips playfully, metal on flesh. Next, he took my hand as if he were Marthe and I was little Estelle and he was about to trim my nails. Instead, he tweaked my thumbnail with the pliers. See, it hurts.

'How did you come to be working for the dentist, Depage?' he asked.

'Through my grandmother. He was her dentist and she knew he required an assistant.'

'Is this your handwriting?' My dissertation. 'And this?' The register I'd made for Eichel.

'This document was supposed to name every Jew on Depage's books and in his quarter of the city. But it does not even name Depage's wife and children. Why is that? Please don't mumble.'

I attempted to take my mind elsewhere, the kitchen in Watford, Mrs Geering taking scones from the oven. A chicken clucking across the farmyard at—

'Jerome Depage is known to have reported to the mustering point in Bruxelles-Midi railway station on 20th October last year. He claimed that his wife and three children could not attend

361

because they had gone to stay in the country for the sake of the baby's health. Where is Clémence Depage?'

'I don't know.'

'I suggest you try to remember.'

'I don't know.'

The pain ripped from palm to navel to throat. He might as well have stripped the skin off my arm. Molten lava flooded up my spine, shattered my eardrums.

That's why the wireless was playing. I made too much noise.

'We had intended to call *Oberleutnant* Eichel,' explained the prosecutor apologetically. 'Unfortunately he had urgent business in Berlin. He has, however, written a statement regarding his commissioning of the register.' Said statement dwelt much on Eichel's distress that his trust in me had been so misplaced. Not a word, of course, about the moist-eyed glances he'd cast me, the pressure of his fingers and thumb on my elbow.

While the general and his pals deliberated I was sent into a little lobby above the cells. The guards avoided my eye. One of them actually brought me a glass of water, but the decision took all of five minutes.

The prosecutor yapped some more. There were no extenuating circumstances. I was found guilty of the gravest crimes. I had been part of a well-organised gang, led by the notorious Jesuit, Borland, captive of the state and condemned to death for treason. I had plotted against the Wehrmacht, including the circulation of fake newspapers containing endless lies and false allegations. I had supplied information to the enemy and helped dangerous criminals to escape the country. I had cheated the authorities and produced false documents. I was a traitor, and must be punished as such.

At the end he yelled so loudly I jumped: 'Germany will live. Death to the enemies of the Third Reich.'

The defence mumbled that I was quite young when I first came under the perfidious influence of the traitor Borland, and therefore could perhaps be shown a little leniency.

The general had a small piece of paper before him. It had been on the table all along. He found me guilty of all charges

362

and rapped out a few more words, which at last the interpreter bothered to translate in full. 'You are condemned to death.'

I was bustled into the van, went through the same journey in reverse, except that the air was cooler and dustier because the sun had gone in. It was as if I was emerging from anaesthetic and couldn't work out which bit of me had been amputated.

Christa

In October 1944, six weeks after the Allies had crossed the border into Belgium, Longbridge pulled a few strings and had me drafted to Brussels along with three other female administrators. With our troops pushing deeper into Germany, the liberated city had become a conduit for ordering and processing army supplies, and my expertise as an area distribution officer with the Board of Trade was required to help oil the wheels of the cumbersome military bureaucracy. In a handwritten note accompanying a typed memo, Longbridge suggested I might like the opportunity to make enquiries about my friends, although he warned me not to raise my hopes; there had been no news of Estelle.

Once again I travelled in a convoy, this time in an American warship. The sailors gawped at the sight of four British uniformed women, and an officer nobly surrendered his cabin to us. The tide was out when we landed near Dieppe soon after dawn, and the sun, as it rose, shone on the smooth sands, giving the illusion, just for a moment, that we would soon be treated to a French seaside resort with cafés unwinding their awnings and throwing open their doors ready for the breakfast trade. Within minutes, though, we'd glimpsed our first row of bombed-out houses, and as our jeep roared up the beach we passed the ruins of army vehicles wedged into the sand.

Although the roads and verges had been swept for mines, they were in an appalling state, and we progressed at a snail's pace, deeper into the countryside, decanting frequently as it began to rain, to help dig the jeep out of the mud. While British bombers roared overhead with ear-splitting confidence, we passed through desolate villages and ruined forests, becoming all too quickly hardened to the sight of hastily dug graves marked with crooked wooden crosses.

The roads were clogged with refugees burdened with pitifully few possessions, and it seemed to me that the entire population of Europe had been shaken loose. We begged to be allowed to offer them a lift or at least carry their baggage to the next village, and we did help a few, though we could never predict whether the ride would be greeted with embarrassing gratitude or total indifference – some people were so traumatised they had long since lost any sense of where they were going. One young mother, perhaps the most heartbreaking of all our passengers, insisted on exchanging names and addresses so she could let me know that her family had got home safely. I never did hear from her, and when I looked up her address later I discovered that hers was one of the villages that had been totally flattened as the Germans retreated.

I had to crush any idea that I deserved the thanks of these refugees; that it wasn't just a toss of the dice that had put me in a uniform, filled my belly with tea and porridge and installed me in a sturdy vehicle. The nearer we drew to Belgium, through devastated villages or cheering crowds, beneath the shell of Rouen Cathedral and on past fields scarred by artillery shells or the spattered remnants of a fighter plane, the further Estelle faded from view. The already fragile hope that she might have survived now seemed pure fantasy.

Once across the border we saw a British corporal march half a dozen ragged German POWs to a garden wall, where they slumped with exhaustion, indifferent even to the fact that their guard was leaning on his rifle whilst smoking and conducting a flirtatious conversation with the daughter of the house. His peculiar lack of vigilance was the most convincing proof yet that the war was stuttering towards its conclusion.

Brussels provided yet more shocks – not least that it seemed, at first glance, to be little changed. Most of its buildings were still in place and its citizens were out in force. In the Grande Place, the Belgian flag was flying and we uniformed Brits were mobbed by children asking for sweets and biscuits, and their parents who rushed to shake our hands. I held on to each far

365

too long and peered into their smiling eyes, wondering: can you possibly know what's happened to Estelle?

Once arrived, I didn't have a moment's free time. Our newly requisitioned offices had been so recently abandoned by the German administration that they still reeked of arrogance and fear. Nazi jackboots echoed on the parquet floor and the furniture must have borne their fingerprints. The noticeboards had been stripped and their contents crammed into wastepaper baskets; the filing cabinets gaped open and there were sacks in the yard at the back of the building stuffed with papers shredded so hastily that names and addresses were still legible. The plumbing had packed up and the lavatory bowls overflowed with Nazi waste. I returned to a little kitchen at the end of the corridor again and again to wash my hands in a bucket.

In a massive storage cupboard I found heaps of leaflets in three languages forbidding Jews entry to the Parc de Bruxelles. When I cleared out my desk drawer, I found, amidst the usual paper clips and spare nibs, a bar of German chocolate and a couple of small military buttons, each stamped with an eagle perched upon a swastika.

For some minutes I sat with those two cheap buttons before me. The threads with which they'd been sewn to a tunic were still attached. The seamstress responsible might have been slap-dash, the fact they had come adrift a sign that the Nazi regime couldn't even impose perfection on a button, but they brought me up much too close to the official who'd worn them.

Estelle

Condemned prisoners were locked up four to a cell and largely left alone. I didn't like the crowding at first. I'd rarely slept in a room with anyone else. Except Christa, of course, for a couple of hours, in Barcelona.

We went through the motions of taking care of ourselves, as if we had a future. We watched what we said. We were allowed our own clothes, though had to put shoes and outerwear in the corridors at night, Lord knows why. The window was fifteen centimetres square and barred. We cracked the odd joke. Difficult to hang yourself, we said, with three witnesses within half an arm's reach.

There were two further advantages to having been condemned to death.

Number one: No more visits to the white-tiled room with the anglepoise and the white-haired monster.

Number two: We were allowed a visitor.

In theory, at least. I waited day after day; nobody came.

Some of the women did odd bits of crochet or sewing. Since I'd refused point-blank to learn from Marthe, I was no good at either. We drew, or tried to write letters with bits of pencil on smuggled scraps of paper. Someone had a home-made pack of cards. She was kind – said that as I had no visitors of my own, if I needed something, she'd get one of hers to fetch it.

I suspected she was a plant. 'A Bruegel would be nice,' I said.

Actually, I wasn't joking. I craved a glimpse of those sturdy little people – cruel, self-absorbed, playful, frantically engaged in the moment.

When at last my name was called, my heart jolted. Inevitably, I wondered: Am I to be the one they'll choose to shoot straight

367

away, or torture again? It turned out I was to have a visitor the next day after all.

'Who?'

The guard shrugged, trained to keep her trap shut.

A knot tightened in my guts. Hope. I'd never thought to see the day when I would have given all I possessed (one pair of knickers, one vest, one worn-out dress) to see Marthe with her little basket. I remembered the days when she used to take me on the train to visit Grand-mère. There had always been a treat for the journey. An almond biscuit with my name in icing or appelflap.

Two guards escorted me into a small room with whitish walls and a concrete floor and pushed me into a seat. One, a bitch with dull eyes, reeking of sweat, plonked herself in a chair at the door. On the far side of a grille sat a large and lumpy figure. Tante Julia. Pale, depleted, sad-mouthed in the instant before she raised her head and found a smile. I smelt the outdoors, chicken shit and the smoke of her fire. I couldn't see her feet, but I would have bet she was wearing her wellington boots.

Pieter used to say that Tante Julia never actually undressed, just subtracted clothes in summer and added them in winter. She wore a dark coat I'd known all my life, sheepskin gloves, a man's scarf and a multicoloured woollen hat. Spare flesh, since I'd last seen her, hung loose under her chin. Her complexion had broken into a hundred fine lines.

She pushed items through the bars one by one. A bag of rolls from the Pâtisserie Faider. Little bursts of De Eikenhoeve: a long-sleeved woollen vest, gloves, hand-knitted socks, a pot of jam, three bars of soap, a pencil, cheese, sausage, jam, chocolate. Lovely items unearthed from the cool cellars. Even at a distance, the sausage smelt of garlic and herbs. A spoonful of jam would unleash raspberry fields, the buzzing of flies, sun on my neck.

She couldn't hide her shock at my appearance, but she settled her elbows on the ledge as if we were seated on either side of her stove.

I committed her to memory. The otherworldliness of her. The knowledge that an hour ago she'd been out on the street, in a station, on a train, at home, damping down the fire, plumping pillows, straightening a quilt. Couldn't I come back with you, *chère Tante*? I won't trouble anyone for the rest of the war. Only milk a cow, plant a row of lettuces, collect the eggs . . .

She wanted to know how they were treating me, if I had any messages, what should she bring next time? Her normally booming voice was now as frail as an old lady's.

'How are they all at the farm?' I cut in.

'German,' the guard barked. 'Or Flemish. No French.'

'Very busy,' she told me. 'Extremely short-handed. I help out there almost full-time and only go home occasionally.'

'Who's in charge?'

Evasion number one. A tightening of the lips. 'Oud Daan, I suppose. Between us we manage.'

'So Oud Daan has survived it all, despite everything.'

Evasion number two. 'Oud Daan is coming up trumps as usual. He can hardly walk, but he does actually consent to sitting up behind the tractor.' A glance at the guard. 'Which I think must be running on pond water.'

'How is Marthe?'

Tante Julia put her hand to her eyes as if shielding them from the sun. Evasion number three.

'I was hoping she might visit me,' I persisted. 'After all those years of avoiding her like the plague, I was actually looking forward to a visit from Marthe. Can you believe it?'

'I told you all along that she meant well.'

Past tense? 'But she's all right? Has she managed to keep up her flower garden?'

'The farm is doing just fine. We should have a good crop of spring wheat. The hens are laying well. I especially wanted to tell you that. You know Marthe brought some chicks over to my place, to help them survive the winter. Well, they're all flourishing.'

She was not a good actress, but I understood. The Depage children. Thank Christ.

The guard got up. Our ten minutes were gone. I couldn't help it. I asked: 'What about my friend Christa? Do you have any news of her?'

369

Tante Julia shook her head, puzzled.

'I have some laundry,' I gabbled. 'Just a petticoat, if you can bear to bring it back clean next time.'

The guard had her eye on the sausage. When I held it up she lumbered over, took the pencil and the sausage, nodded. I stuffed the fistful of filthy rayon through the bars to Tante Julia who reached for my hands. The guard made no objection when I kissed her calloused fingers. I knew then that I would not be receiving any more visitors.

Tante Julia was actually crying. 'Oh, my precious girl. Don't give up hope. Never do that. I'll see you again soon.'

The guard dragged at my arm. I swept the gifts from De Eikenhoeve into the lap of my dress. Straining back for a last glance, I saw Tante Julia grip the bars and heard her groan.

Christa

We had been allocated an apartment on Rue de l'Harmonie, near Le Jardin Botanique. Since I knew the city, I told the others that I would walk home alone because I wished to visit some old friends on the way. When I reached Rue d'Orléans, I was relieved to discover that Grand-mère's house, though very shabby, looked much as I remembered it.

Nevertheless, it took me several minutes to pluck up the courage and knock – best get it over with before the daylight faded completely and I would be forced to walk through the half-remembered streets in blackout. The door was opened by a nervous stranger who grew visibly paler when she noticed my uniform.

'Madame Faider?' I said.

She shrugged and replied in Flemish. 'I don't know anyone of that name.'

'She used to live here.' Through the half-closed door I saw the same tiles on the hall floor, the same elaborate wrought-iron banister, as well as a litter of alien possessions in the form of a battered bicycle and a perambulator, heaps of old garments and canvas bags stuffed with what looked like rubbish.

'May I come in? Is there someone here who might know where she went?'

'Nobody.' After a moment's hesitation on both sides, she closed the door.

I hung about, attempting to work out what had happened, even wondering whether I'd got the wrong address. Eventually I tried a neighbour's house, a much sprucer dwelling of the same age and design. This time I was greeted by a maid so terrified that she had to clutch the handle for support.

'May I speak to the owner of the house?' I asked in French.

The maid backed away but didn't try to keep me out – her petrified gaze was fixed on my uniform and it occurred to me that the inhabitants of Brussels must have lived in constant fear of peremptory and unexpected hammering on the door. Inside, I found myself in a different world entirely, untouched by war, the carpeted stairs freshly swept and an antique clock ticking on a marble stand. The maid, who had disappeared into a room which must have been the equivalent of Grand-mère's parlour, now re-emerged and stammered that the mistress preferred me to state my business and wait in the hall. But I was beyond good manners and walked directly past her into a snug sitting room where an elderly woman was pretending to read a newspaper beside a blazing fire.

'What is this?' she demanded. 'You've frightened my maid half to death.'

'I'm sorry to call so late. I don't have much time. My name is Christabel Geering. I was in Brussels before the war, and I stayed with your neighbour, Madame Faider, for a couple of nights. I am a close friend of her granddaughter, Estelle.'

By the time I'd finished this speech, I remembered that this woman had been one of the guests at Grand-mère's salon. Heaving herself to her feet, she flapped at me with the newspaper as if I were a fly. 'What are you doing here? How dare you come in without an invitation?'

'I simply wanted to know what has happened to Madame Faider. As I recall, you were a friend of hers. I met you—'

'She died. She was very old. What did you expect? Now, if you don't mind—'

'I'm sorry to hear that. Do you know anything about her granddaughter, Estelle?'

'That girl? Nothing at all. No. You'll have to leave. I simply don't know. There's been a war. We all had to make sacrifices. I kept a low profile.'

'What about her grandsons?'

The sheer rage of the woman was driving me from the room. She was gesturing to the maid to open the door. 'This is quite outrageous, if you come back I shall be forced to call

372

the police. What is the name of your regiment?'

The door slammed behind me and I found myself walking in no particular direction, simply to get away from her inexplicable forcefulness. In the end I got my bearings and set off for my lodgings, passing through the silent Place des Martyrs and stumbling from one street corner to another in this looking-glass world, where everything was outwardly more or less the same but also irretrievably changed.

Estelle

A rush of activity in the small hours. Pack your things. What a joke. Half a dozen items at most in a small cloth sack. A bit of lavender soap left from Tante Julia's visit. I had shared the rest out double quick, before a guard took them. The clothes on my back. Tante Julia's gloves.

Might there be the smallest glimmer of an opportunity to escape in the transition from prison to transport? St Gilles Prison, near the centre of Brussels, was so close to the people and places we loved. Perhaps Edouard was loitering nearby, ready to snatch me away. We stepped along the hated corridor for the last time, past rusty metal doors, into the grey light of day and a wall of uniforms and glinting weaponry.

Far too many of us piled into the van. At first I thought, this will be OK, there's plenty of space in this compartment, but then seven prisoners were crammed onto a bench designed for two. No air. The driver pulled out, gears grinding, the screech of brakes, someone shouting, lurching over potholes I probably used to bump over whilst riding my bicycle, saddlebag laden with forbidden newspapers.

I wasn't alone in praying for a volley of gunshots, the throwing open of doors. Death or liberation.

At first we didn't understand what was happening to us. We kept waiting for someone to explain. Miles and miles of road, no food, no water. Aix-la-Chapelle. Düsseldorf. Each time bundled into a dirty cell, herded together like sheep. Then on. At last, on the way to Cologne, stomach cramping after a dribble of bad soup, I worked it out. *Nacht und Nebel*. We were disappearing, had dropped into the abyss. Already nobody knew where we were.

We hardly knew ourselves. I even looked forward to roll call, to prove that my number was still on a list. I pinched my arm. I am here. I am Estelle.

We spent two days stuffed into the cattle truck of a train. Knot holes in the wooden slats were our only chance of discovering our location. We had acquired other prisoners, Flemish, Dutch, French, and we behaved according to our individual temperaments: weeping, defiant, sick, sleepy, cold, angry, violent. Or kind. I tried to be kind. I hung on to the thread of a smile that used to be me.

On the train, there was a benefit to being tall. Another woman's hair in my mouth and the hot trickle of her urine on my calf, but my head was up above the rest, gasping. It was so tempting to fight for the best place, near the door or in a corner. Bread and water were flung at us when the great doors were slid open a few inches before being slammed shut again.

At times, we were turfed out beside the track to relieve ourselves at gunpoint, but each time I crouched in the gravel my insides seized up. I had contemplated crawling under the wagon – too low – or just running. I thought: a few seconds, a blast of gunfire and it will all be over. Pain, then blessed, blessed oblivion.

We were loaded into lorries somewhere near Cologne and driven to the prison. We longed to lie down, but no, instead we were herded into a vast shower room.

'Take off your clothes. *Sich beeilen.* Put in basket. Stand still.'

We had heard rumours of what happened to prisoners in showers. A dreadful silence fell. Christ. The nozzles above us were dry. In front of me a woman shat herself, filth oozing down her inner leg. I placed my hand on her shoulder.

Could these be my feet on the bare concrete, the rather long feet of Estelle Cornelis-Faider? Feet that used to kick and squirm when Marthe perched me on her knee and fastened my shoes? Feet that had carried me to England and back, luxuriated in a bath while Christa sat beside me, excited and nervous and ready to bolt?

We waited a minute, or an hour, shuddering, muttering, praying, weeping, before half a dozen guards came in with buckets and tossed the contents over us without warning. Disinfectant, scarcely diluted. One woman howled and put her hand to her eye. Then there was a hissing above us and cold water let rip from the shower heads. Water. We shrieked and hopped from foot to foot and clutched our arms around our bodies as we waited for them to deliver our clothes. Most of us were crying. It turned out we hadn't wanted to be dead after all.

St Gilles now seemed the cosy option. At least I could place it on a map. In Cologne I had no idea where the prison was in relation to anywhere else. The lorry's tyres had crunched and lurched on the broken roads because the city had been flattened by the Allies. We took some comfort in that.

Half a dozen of us were pushed into a cell designed for two at most. For Christ's sake, I thought, why go to the trouble of keeping us here? Send us home. We promise to sit out the war quietly. Anything but this endless shouting, the thud of baton on bone when we stumble, a bucket in the corner of the cell, six women shitting from the fear and filthy food, wiping ourselves with our skirts.

Except I wouldn't have stayed quiet, of course. I would have risen from the ashes of myself.

Christa

For days I was confined to the office, typing orders and drawing up invoices. I did make the occasional surreptitious call to the Red Cross during a tea break or when I was supposed to be calling a depot in Saint-Omer, but I never succeeded in getting through. In the evenings I volunteered at the YMCA where a rest centre had been set up for Allied soldiers who'd been given a couple of days' leave from fighting on the front line.

The men were sent back from Germany in their hundreds, stinking of mud and sweat, their eyes blank with exhaustion. They had stories of friends shot, tanks blown up, battalions of half-starved German infantry huddled behind hedges, waiting to take potshots at the advancing army. We made them tea and poured them weak beer, sat beside them to help them compose letters home or watched them sleep through the concerts given in their honour.

Eventually, after putting in endless requests, I was allowed an afternoon off and joined a queue of largely silent Belgian citizens seeking news of loved ones who'd disappeared during the occupation. When I finally reached the information desk I was left to wait while the official entered Estelle's name in a register, then shuffled off to check whether there was a file on her. I could see him through the frosted glass, a middle-aged man with tremulous hands and an academic's unwavering thoroughness, opening and shutting drawers and leafing through vast piles of paperwork. At last he returned, sympathetic but weary, and said he would have to conduct further searches but could I return the following week? My case number was 3,082.

There was just time, that same afternoon, to visit the Pâtisserie Faider, which was still in business, although its gilded paintwork had been neglected and its displays of luscious cakes replaced by a doleful tray of rolls. Behind the counter was Madame Vauclain, skinnier and more sharp-featured than I remembered. Once I'd reminded her of my name and nationality she gazed upon me with dawning recognition, then bustled round the counter and kissed me vigorously.

'How smart you look, *chère Mademoiselle* Geering. But what are you doing in Brussels?'

I told her about my job, then the reception I'd received in Rue d'Orléans, and she clapped her hand to her mouth. 'Don't tell me you haven't heard the dreadful news about Madame Faider and Estelle?'

She insisted on taking me through to a neat back office, where she shooed away an assistant and poured me a cup of extraordinarily good coffee. 'Poor Madame Faider was arrested in the autumn of 1942. Unfortunately – or perhaps fortunately for her – she breathed her last on the way to prison. Imagine the cruelty of a regime that arrests an aged woman at the dead of night. What did they expect? A few days later the body of her maid was discovered in the basement.

'And then they must have lain in wait for Estelle. We don't know the details of her arrest, only that she was taken to St Gilles. We tried to visit her there, of course, but they wouldn't let us in. Only close relatives of the prisoner, they said, so we sent for her aunt from Oostervorken.

'Julia Cornelis can't have set foot in Brussels for years. She came here first to see if we had any cakes that she might take to Estelle. She was behaving like a sleepwalker, completely lost in the city, so I went with her and waited outside. At least she was admitted, if only for a few minutes. And she saw Estelle. Afterwards, as I walked her to the station, she could barely speak. All I could get out of her was: "She'll be all right. Of course she will. She's Estelle."'

'And then?' I whispered.

'We don't know. We think she was in a convoy that left for Breendonk in April last year. After that, it's anybody's guess. Oh, my dear girl, there are so many like her, simply disappeared. Everybody is looking for someone.'

'What about the rest of the family?'

'I've not heard from the farm, if that's what you're wondering.' For the first time she looked evasive, and her sharp brown eyes shifted above my head to the clock over the mantel.

'So you don't know—?'

'No idea. But then why would I? Apart from Madame Faider, only Estelle was a regular visitor here. She never failed to call in if she was in town. Even then, she was always in a hurry or I was too busy to talk.'

Our eyes met briefly, and I glimpsed another world in hers; one from which I was completely excluded. Madame Vauclain's survival, I realised, must have been due at least in part to her not sharing information with every passing acquaintance.

Though it was now dark, I made a pilgrimage to the obscure little square where Estelle had once shown me the bronze of her mother. Fearing that a sledgehammer might have been taken to the plinth and the flattened metal carted off to a munitions factory, I peered through the gloom – but there was Fleur Cornelis-Faider, poised in mid-flight. 'Heil Hitler' had been scrawled across the plaque, pigeon droppings adorned her shoulders and litter had accumulated at her feet, but perhaps in order to draw attention to Fleur's failure to survive the last war, the Nazis had left her in place.

I walked around her several times. That day in the square, as I had fumbled for the right words, I had turned to see Estelle laughing at me, and not altogether kindly. She had raised her hand to summon the waiter, unconsciously displaying the ineffable superiority of her mother's legacy.

I stepped forward and pressed my head against the statue's unyielding skirt.

I'll find you, I will. I've done it before. I'll do it again.

Estelle

At Waldheim, we so-called educated types from the Low Countries were crammed in with child murderers and thieves. The guards taunted us: Look where it's got you.

I wished I'd learnt to sew, because the ones who could had by far the easiest time. Instead, I had to sort rags into different colours and textures. And when I was too slow at that, I had to strip the stalks from feathers until my fingers bled. A few weeks later it was nets. For what? The nylon ropes cut us to the bone. My hands were wrecked in any case; missing most of my nails, I couldn't get a grip.

One day we queued for hours in a corridor, wondering what was next. We soon found out. A big-breasted woman with hands like slabs of clay took a pair of scissors, slash, slash, never mind the ears. Then a razor. Weeks later, the cuts in my scalp were still festering. 'It's a matter of hygiene,' she'd snapped. I caught a glimpse of myself in the metal panel of a door. Bonehead.

My possessions now reduced to one cup, one plate, one canvas bag in which to put my ration of bread, I held tight to what I could remember, for fear of disappearing altogether. De Eikenhoeve came to me in fits and starts, although I was forced to make some of it up. The beds were an obsession. That white bed in the room above the arch which had been Christa's. The smell of laundered sheets. My own bed with its bright quilt.

And food of course. I tried to avoid thinking about the kitchen at De Eikenhoeve, though my thoughts often swerved in that direction. A fat round loaf resting on a baking tray. A bowl of mushroom soup. Raspberries sprinkled with brown sugar. I was all stomach; even my toenails were starving.

No. Pull on your wellingtons, Estelle. Slosh across the farmyard.

Lift the latch. The gate is sodden with rain. The hedgerows are crushed with it. The cow parsley reeks of summer.

We heard rumours all the time, passed from lip to ear in the latrines or dinner queue. The Allies are in France, in Belgium, on German soil. That's why we're being shifted again. The good news was that the Nazis were in retreat. The very bad news, that any moment they were likely to slaughter the lot of us. We were too much trouble, could bear witness to too many atrocities, and anyway why should we be allowed to survive when the name of every game was punishment? Would it be decapitation, cheaper than a bullet, quicker than a hanging? My choice would be back to a wall, hands pressed to stone, eyes on the sky.

We were piled into yet another lorry. As we rumbled on and on, my sluggish brain reached once more for home.

Christa

On my first free Saturday, I boarded a train from Bruxelles-Midi to Oostervorken. Like everything else in Belgium, three months post-liberation, the railway was showing signs of severe neglect, the trains running an hour and a half late, with torn seats, broken luggage racks and unheated carriages. I even heard someone mutter that things had operated far more efficiently under the Nazis.

The countryside was stark and rain-soaked, with the first shoots of winter wheat pricking the soil and the hedgerows naked. We regularly juddered to a halt, often alongside the burnt-out remains of military vehicles and houses with their windows boarded up. My fellow passengers cast the odd timorous glance when a newcomer entered, but otherwise refused to meet anyone's eye.

By the time I reached Oostervorken I was almost alone, save for a small woman in a black headscarf whose nervous eyes darted towards the exit then back to me, no doubt planning her escape route should I turn on her.

The familiar platform was veiled by steadily falling rain and the same driver, Viktor, was in attendance outside the station. When I asked if he would take me to De Eikenhoeve he heaved himself reluctantly out of his seat and cranked the engine. Both he and his cab had acquired five years of additional grime and the roof leaked so that the back seat was now damp as well as being infused with cigarettes, mildew and the odour of unwashed male. One windscreen wiper stuttered and the other didn't work at all.

At first I took comfort from the fact that at least this one local institution had survived, but as we left the village it occurred to me that the fact that Viktor was still mobile suggested that his first priority during the occupation had been to stay in business. At whatever cost.

Viktor gave no sign that he recognised me and I was certainly in no mood for conversation. When I did say, in my rusty Flemish: 'I expect things are very much altered at De Eikenhoeve,' he made no attempt to respond.

I managed to stay composed until we turned into the lane leading to the farm. 'Here will do.'

Again, he didn't seem to hear me.

'I said drop me here.'

'It's another couple of kilometres.'

'It doesn't matter.'

He ground to a halt but left the engine running and didn't open the door for me. Umbrella in one hand, handbag in the other, I retreated into the verge while he made angry manoeuvres in the mushy entrance to a field.

Beyond the hedgerow, the hayfield now lay fallow and was occupied by weeds. I struggled to keep my footing as I slithered along the lane, nerves clamouring beneath the dripping trees. There, at the turn in the lane, was the shut gate, and beyond it the tree that gave De Eikenhoeve its name.

I made no attempt to lift the bar at first. Five years had made no mark upon that sodden wood and the past rushed through me. The visible section of the farmhouse behind the naked oak was lower than I remembered, the windows deeper set into the wall, the gables in the steep roof smaller.

The quiet was unnerving; no mutter of distant machinery, not a single cow lowing, no hens clucking, only the steady patter of rain.

With every second, more changes became apparent; dandelions clustered between paving stones, walls in need of repair where the rendering had fallen away. I knew precisely how it would smell beneath that archway, of mortar and chicken droppings, cattle and old leather harnesses. There was no knocker on the door, so I would have to throw it open and shout to get someone's attention.

In the event, my voice failed, and anyway it was immediately clear that no one would come. In Lotte's scullery a few dirty plates had been left in the sink and a filthy tea towel was draped over the drying rack. The state of the kitchen was even more unsettling – as if a flood had swept everything aside and left only a trail of silt. Windowpanes were smashed, pans were missing from the racks, crockery was randomly stacked and the floor was filthy.

The dressmaker's dummy lay on its side in Marthe's little parlour, which looked as if it had been clumsily searched – drawers thrown open, a tangle of fabric and thread, her beautiful medicine chest torn apart and its contents strewn across the floor.

'Marthe,' I called, and then, with even less confidence: 'Hanna . . .'

The yard outside the window was also empty, though the mud had been recently trampled, and there, by the farmyard gate, with eyes like slits fixed upon me, was a frail old man wearing a cloth cap and smoking a cigarette.

Or perhaps he was a figment of my imagination. Swathed in a long brown trench coat, head sunk deep within his collar, he merged with the dismal tones of sky and earth; I had to look twice to make sure he was there. The window was jammed, so I knocked on the pane. He didn't move a muscle. In the end I ran back the way I had come and by the time I reached the farmyard there was no sign of Oud Daan or anyone else.

At Bernard Cornelis's feast, the band had gathered up its instruments as the tablecloths grew dark with rain and everyone headed indoors, except for Robbe and me. Now I trudged to the gate, picking my way between the puddles and the worst of the mud until I reached the spot where Oud Daan had stood.

The track down to the river, which I remembered as a deep channel between high hedgerows, was starkly fringed by dead thorns and the spiky remains of bracken. I reached for the latch—

'Can I help you?'

I'd heard no footfall. The voice was Flemish, male, somewhat harsh, but not forgotten.

I gasped and whipped around. 'I have come to see . . .'

We gazed at each other.

It was certainly Robbe Cornelis, with those conker-dark eyes and the features of a Leonardo angel, and though it took him a while to recognise me, a woman in a British Army cap and raincoat, I saw the colour ebb from his cheeks.

'Christa.'

I didn't take his outstretched hand, just stood there with the rain splashing down.

'However did you get here?' he said.

'I was looking for Estelle.'

He stared at me as if I were mad. '*Estelle?* Don't you know what happened?'

I tried to take him in, this thin man wearing corduroy trousers and a jacket that was far too large for him, probably his brother's. Robbe Cornelis, who I had named as a traitor. 'I know she was arrested,' I said.

'She was sent on one of the transports to Germany. Edouard is looking for her. He's been gone for months.'

'Is it possible she's alive?'

He shrugged. 'Christ knows. From what I've heard, I hope not.'

'Is there anyone else here, apart from you?'

'Just a couple of old men.' He gestured towards the house. 'Do you want to come inside?'

When I shook my head he removed cigarettes from his pocket, flicked open the pack with his thumbnail, made a slight gesture to offer me one, then lit up under the shelter of my umbrella so that his gaunt face came very close to mine.

'Then let's go down to the river,' he said, unlatching the gate.

I followed him along the familiar track which used to be crowded with thigh-high nettles, flickering butterflies and small pink flowers.

It was several minutes before he spoke again. 'It seems we owe you a favour, Juffrouw Christa. Apparently, you saved us all.'

'But not Estelle.'

'Based on your evidence, my sister came back to Brussels and spread the word that we'd been betrayed. Our unit was disbanded.'

'Did you see her?'

'Only briefly, outside a café. I thought she would follow me inside so I waited for an hour but she never came. She'd left a note for Edouard, but by the time he found it she'd already left the city.'

Compared to his brother, he was not an easy walking companion. His hair caught in a spoke of my umbrella and he lacked the countryman's rolling stride.

'She came here,' he added. 'To deal with Pieter. And then she was arrested.'

'*Deal* with him.'

'Shot him.'

Rain drifted across the river in a mist. Robbe, though drenched, seemed oblivious to the discomfort as he gestured downstream with his cigarette. 'Do you want me to show you?'

Without waiting for an answer, he took the path he and I had walked that night, behind the other bathers. At times, the mud oozed over the top of my shoes and I had to drag my foot free.

'After I'd spotted Estelle in Brussels, and Edouard read her note, we got hold of a vehicle and drove through the night. Fortunately, we decided to walk the last half-mile or so, because we saw a German truck pulled up outside the house.

'We waited until dawn and got hold of Lotte when she came creeping out into the yard – not that she was of any use to us, she could hardly speak for fright. Nobody's seen her since. In the end we worked out that Estelle had come home and walked with Pieter into the woods, and that Marthe had driven off in a great hurry and none of them had come back. Later that evening the Germans had arrived to search the house. They'd already arrested Estelle.'

'How did they know she was here?'

'Any number of ways. They were on the lookout for her. She was crazy to come to De Eikenhoeve. She was probably followed from Brussels, or an official spotted her at the station.

'So Edouard and I went looking for Pieter. I knew exactly where he'd be. Swart and Oud Daan were there beside the body. We buried him where he'd fallen. The *Abwehr* never found out. Nobody did, except me and Edouard and Oud Daan.'

We walked on without speaking, along the track which led to the bathing pond, and then up the almost invisible path to the clearing. The skirt of my coat was spattered with mud and my stockings were torn. Pieter's grave was unmarked, close to the fallen-down hut, and almost invisible after nearly two years – just a very slight bulge in the long grass.

'Did you understand why she killed him?' I said.

'I'm not sure that's the right question, Juffrouw Christa. The question is surely: How did *you* feel, Robbe, when you came into this clearing and saw your dead brother? The answer is I felt very sorry that she'd shot him in the head and chest. I wished she'd shot him in both feet and both hands and left him writhing in agony until Oud Daan got here.'

His vehemence diminished me. It seemed that everything I had felt thus far had been on too small a scale.

'I thought it was you,' I said. 'I told her it was you.'

He gave a bark of laughter. 'Of course you did.'

'How did she know? How did she work it out?'

'Because we're her brothers. She knew what we were capable of, and who we loved.'

'Who *do* you love, Robbe?'

'I loved my father.'

At once I realised that this was the inescapable truth. I should have known it when I saw Borland and Robbe together in the Musée Wiertz – not just by the similarities in their posture, but by the way that Robbe had stood a little apart, shy, proud, a touch overawed. And how Borland had inspired him, lit him from within.

Robbe was taut with grief, coiled within himself. 'Pieter could never forgive me for being Borland's son.'

'Did you not realise?'

'I couldn't see past his sympathy. He never ceased to remind me that I was a bastard and I didn't belong, simply by promising that it made no difference to him at all. Then he got my father arrested.' He had acquired a new gesture – rubbing the palm of his hand across his hair. 'And probably my mother too, if he told Oud Daan he'd seen her here in the clearing with three men.'

Peering through the wintry trees, the dripping branches, the bracken stalks and brambles, I saw Pieter, the fair-haired boy, crouched in the undergrowth, watching his mother's world unravel, and felt another rush of sadness that in the end this place had been his burial ground, and he had not deserved anywhere so lovely or so peaceful.

'It was Oud Daan who betrayed your mother, then.'

'Oud Daan would betray himself if he thought it would save De Eikenhoeve.'

'Why is he still here? How can you bear to look at him?'

'He's all I've got. Him and the farm. It's a kind of rough justice to see him grinding on and on, attempting to keep it all going.'

'You hate the farm.'

He actually laughed. 'Ironic. I always felt unwanted here, like a cuckoo. And now I'm the farm's best hope. What do you make of that?'

'You'll stay then?'

'Who knows?' He shook his head and shrugged. 'We should leave,' he added. 'It will be dark soon.'

He was right, of course, but I was so close to Estelle that I could have stayed forever. At the last minute I turned back but the clearing was empty, not a flicker of a woman's hair or dress among the trees.

At one point on the way back, uninvited, Robbe linked his arm through mine and joined me beneath the umbrella. 'We found Marthe's body upstream. There was a Jewish family staying in one of the cottages – she took them to Tante Julia's for safety's sake, left the farm van by the church, went in to pray and that was the last anyone saw of her. She'd stuffed her pockets with stones. You stirred up a fucking hornets' nest, Juffrouw Christa.'

When we reached the farmyard, he said: 'I could drive you to the station if you like. I still have a vehicle.'

I shook my head. We parted by the oak tree, where he simply hunched his shoulders, then returned to the house.

But I could not bring myself to leave De Eikenhoeve just yet, or even to open the gate.

After a few moments, I heard running footsteps. 'Christa.' Robbe seemed more vigorous, as if he'd made up his mind to do something. 'Christa. I'm sorry for what I did. To you and Estelle.'

388

I nodded. The rain had stopped at last and as he lifted the latch for me I furled my umbrella. We pressed each other's hand gravely, then the gate swung shut behind me with a decisive thud, and I walked away.

Estelle

This place is called Mauthausen. Somewhere in Austria? I'm not entirely sure.

So I am lost, along with hundreds of thousands of others. We are ants. We are weeds. From a distance, we bags of bones, we staggering corpses, all look the same.

I regret to say I have rather lost hope.

Some women pray for death, but I'm not so stupid. I warn myself, if death was anything good, we would yearn for it, as we yearn for sleep, not fight it every inch of the way. If it were kind, it would come and carry us gently away, to some dark and warm place. We'd surely have an inkling that it was better than this, and wish to go there.

Or perhaps this is already death – somewhere along the line I fell over onto the other side and it's turned out to be more of the same. Perhaps death is an endless shuffling from one chamber of hell to the next.

Christa gave me a choice. She said: Stay with me in Barcelona. I thought I'd made the right choice, but this is not what I chose. I didn't see this coming.

We have come to the end of the world. Pain is too short a word, suffering too soft, agony too dramatic. No smiles, no warmth, no food, no drink, no cleanliness, no rest, no peace, no sleep, no friendship, kindness or love. No hope.

We are debased. We are the opposite of yes. We are the living dead.

I've worked out that the first twenty-four hours in a new place are crucial. Definitely the most likely time for everything to fall apart. For a start, it's when most people get called out of the line. This way to the huts, that way to the shower blocks. We watch them go and our feeble prayers, or whatever you may call them, barely reach halfway across the yard. We can afford to be generous, and feel a bit sorry for them, because today it isn't us. We spend most of our mental energy trying not to imagine how it feels to be in one of those queues.

So. First assess the tent or cell or hut to which we've been assigned, how many women to a board at night, where to hide shoes – best to sleep in them. The state of the latrines – graded from unspeakable to squalid. Find a routine. Manage the routine. Then leave and visit another place.

I resurrect Grand-père Faider demonstrating how to pipe an éclair, his clean hands, smeared spectacles, the innocent task of easing cream through a nozzle, the smell of flour and melted butter. I perch in the window seat in Père Borland's tutorial room, watching the embers glow in his hearth. I was always on edge there, under the eye of the dying Christ, because there was always far too much left unsaid. Too many secrets. Or I walk along an English canal with Christa and note how the sun finds a glimmer of red in her dark hair.

Last week, the guards played a game with a couple of prisoners who claimed they were too weak to work. We were forced to watch. First, the women were driven into the yard, then they were told to strip. We stood in a wind that could sever a neck, blown in from Czechoslovakia, stinking of death, latrines, rotten meat, burning. The women worked too slowly, fumbling with buttons and laces. Whimpered. Stepped out of their thin dresses. Our greedy eyes examined the soles of their shoes, assessing if they were better than ours, while they doubled up in the cold, bones as sharp as coat hangers.

Once they were women who bothered about what they wore, dressed their hair in front of a mirror. Sat in a chair by a window, reading to a child, wrote a letter, perhaps a love letter. They had stupid arguments with their husbands about lateness or untidiness or because they'd spent too much on a hat or a pair of gloves. They sat on a beach and toasted their knees in the sun. Ran laughing through rain. Brushed their teeth at night and first thing in the morning. Blushed when a piece of bare flesh was

391

exposed, say at the doctor's surgery. Exchanged views on books and politics over coffee or lunch. Boiled water in a kettle and poured it over tea leaves. Ran to catch a bus. Stood at a kitchen table, baking a cake.

Hoses were unfurled. A couple of other prisoners, the strongest, were ordered to step forward and hold the nozzles. Jets of icy water hit naked flesh. They shrieked and screamed. The guards laughed and lit cigarettes. We averted our eyes but were shouted at to watch – 'It will be you next' – as the women were knocked over by the force of the water. The guards shouted for it to be switched off. Kicked the women until they raised themselves on all fours, kicked them upright. Had the water turned back on.

I looked at the sky. Pale blue behind white clouds. In a month or so, it would be spring, calving time at De Eikenhoeve.

There's a boy in the trees.

Pieter, oldest son, responsible Pieter, loving Pieter, steady Pieter. I can never forget the look in his eyes when I stood at the gate of the old raspberry field that last time. Before he smiled at me.

One woman had fallen again but this time she didn't get up. She didn't even twitch when the guard approached, stood over her in the puddle of water and booted her in the groin. The other woman was on her knees. Bored, he shot them both in the head. The kneeling woman fell like a puppet released from its strings.

Christa

Estelle's Tante Julia wrote to me care of the Pâtisserie Faider, inviting me to visit her in Oostervorken. I took a train a few days before Christmas, by which time most of Brussels was without heating fuel and there were rumours that the Germans were threatening to break through the American lines, march back to the city and inflict dreadful reprisals on its population. We were all so war-weary that we would have believed any rumour, yet been too exhausted to act upon it. I had received the inevitable letter from Ma wishing me a happy Christmas, telling me how much she missed me and hoping I would soon be home.

I had only met Tante Julia once, at Bernard Cornelis's birthday feast, and that night I had been so full of Robbe and Estelle that I'd been unable to pay her much attention. Her cottage was about a mile from Oostervorken, very isolated, and a far cry from the grandeur of De Eikenhoeve. A young boy was attempting to shoo a dozen or so chickens into their hutch in the yard. His eyes, when he caught sight of me, were curious but unafraid.

Julia Cornelis had a well-worn, kindly face, with none of the petulance of her older brother. When she came to the door she was wearing wellington boots and her wild white hair was tied up in a scarf. She stared when she saw me, as if she couldn't work out who I was, and I saw a glimmer of Estelle in her cheekbones and the way her hair lifted from her temples. She was holding a little girl by the hand, who wore a miniature version of her own headgear.

They led me into a snug kitchen, a room perhaps deliberately preserved in the past, with a blue- and coral-tiled floor and an unvarnished table where another lad was hunched, tongue caught between his teeth, writing in an exercise book. The slight woman who was working at the stove greeted me shyly. She introduced herself as Clémence Depage, and reminded me that we'd met briefly, at Grand-mère's salon, before the war.

'I remember,' was all I managed to say as I took a seat and tried to calm myself. The room was both orderly and cluttered, every surface covered with something purposeful: hanks of twine, scissors, a penknife, rough glazed vases and pots, a basket of dried lavender and a can of engine oil.

'Robbe told me you'd been asking about Estelle,' Tante Julia said.

Clémence removed the pan from the stove and wiped her hands on her apron. 'Come,' she said, taking a protesting Marguerite by the hand and nodding towards the boy so that he followed obediently. While Julia talked, I could hear their low voices in the next room.

'I was the last to see Estelle,' Julia continued, 'when I visited St Gilles. We'd received word that she was on the list for deportation and Edouard realised that I was the one person they might allow in. They tend to be sentimental about elderly relatives.'

'How was she?'

'Like herself. Thin. Tired. As you'd expect.' She bit her lip and wouldn't look me in the eye.

'Do you think she will have survived?'

'I can't say.' I could tell that her instinct was to disclose as little as possible; she'd braced herself for a difficult conversation. 'She's a very tough girl, as you know. Even so, the chances are slim.'

The coals spat in the stove. Its heat was so unaccustomed that I could feel it sapping my energy. A cat, curled on a cushion, gave a mighty yawn.

'I am in love with her, you know,' I said.

She looked at me sternly, went to a cupboard and produced a small brown paper package. 'She gave me this, in the prison.'

My hands shook as I fumbled with the knot, so that in the end she found a knife and cut it open for me. Inside was a crumpled garment, a plain cream-coloured petticoat, stained and torn.

'I was about to wash it, as she'd asked, except I thought, but

394

this isn't anything Estelle would wear. So I looked more closely and discovered this scrap of paper rolled in the hem . . .'

It was the merest fragment of cheap paper, grown soggy with time and inscribed with a blunt pencil.

Christa.

Estelle

And yet love is always there when you least expect it, a seed. Yesterday, between them, two women propped me up on the march home from the potato fields and yelled at me when I threatened to fall down and sleep. Today I couldn't get up from the mattress, my bones were too heavy. They covered me and brought me water, squeezed my hand and stroked my head.

They said: 'Do you know what? We've heard that the Allies really are coming. The Red Cross will arrive soon in white vans with bread and tea and clean blankets. They will help us to return home.'

But they haven't come yet. Instead, more prisoners arrive, even though there's not a single scrap of room for them. I am shoved to the wall, knees clenched to my stomach. The woman beside me digs her elbow into my back and I smell her fear. She stinks of it. If she allows it to take over, and she screams and thrashes, we're both done for, so I reach out and find the bone which is her wrist, then her hand, which I hold tight. She pulls away but I don't let go and gradually she calms down and puts her forehead to the back of my neck.

There are hundreds of us, packed like carcasses, too weak to speak, but I hold this one woman's hand against my breast.

I visit England. The view of Kent from the train window is full of overlapping curves.

An English street of small brick houses, each one attached to the next. A trim front door, number 13. Mrs Geering is home and leads me down the little hall, where a pattern of flowers is pressed into the wallpaper painted dark green. She's sifting cocoa into a mixing bowl and I'm tempted to run my fingertip along the rim.

I sit on a wooden stool at the table and rest my elbows on the checked cloth. There's a faint smell of gas and the brown linoleum doesn't quite meet the edge of the stove. Mrs Geering's shoulders are weary and her fawn skirt has gone baggy, but I think she's beautiful. Anxious, yes, but filled with grace, on a mission to do the right thing.

Christa isn't there. Her raincoat hangs on a hook by the front door and the cup with the yellow flowers that she uses is upside down on a wooden rack by the sink.

'She'll be back any minute,' says her mother.

And just when I can't bear it any longer, when I've convinced myself that I'm not going to see her this time, the door flies open. She's wearing a blue dress with sailing boats printed on it. She hesitates for a moment and then she smiles, a heavenly smile. Her dark eyes brim with wonder.

My heart cracks apart. It does every time I think of her.

Christa.

Christa

At the beginning of 1945, while the Allied and Russian armies were battling towards Berlin, we began to see more young men on the streets of Brussels, liberated from the labour camps for which they'd volunteered or been sent to at the start of the occupation. The Vauclains made it their mission to feed them up and usually one or two strangers were lurking behind the pâtisserie counter, eating sandwiches stuffed with black-market beef sausage retrieved from a hiding place under the kitchens.

The latest arrival, a Jewish boy called Martin, had ended up in a camp named Auschwitz and was in a far worse state than any I'd seen. His eyes were dead and when I perched on a stool beside him he flinched. Only when Madame Vauclain had introduced me as a friend of Estelle Cornelis-Faider, also known as Elisabetta, did he manage a smile, and I saw a flicker of life in him, like the stuttering wick of a candle. After the camp had been liberated, he and a couple of compatriots had been put on a train, but only he had survived the journey home. One died of a fever he'd developed in the camp, the other had simply eaten too much of a meal provided by his well-meaning liberator and hadn't been able to stop vomiting.

Eventually, Madame Vauclain gave Martin a job as keeper of the yard and kitchens. His home was in Antwerp, but he couldn't bring himself to face whatever news awaited him there. When he, together with his entire family, two sisters and both parents, had been rounded up and processed at Breendonk Camp in 1941, he'd lost sight of them all.

After this conversation I stayed away from the pâtisserie for several days, but by the Saturday had recovered sufficiently to take a bus to St Gilles Prison. Its name was notorious, even in

England, because Edith Cavell had been interned there prior to facing the firing squad. I hoped Estelle, whilst an inmate, had appreciated the irony.

Even on a Saturday the prison was busy with new arrivals, and while I watched, several vans drew up and were kept waiting while the huge iron doors swung open. It was a vast edifice, more like a castle than a modern prison, adorned with crenellations and turrets. The latest intake of criminals, according to Madame Vauclain, were the opposite of resisters. Men and women who'd collaborated with the Nazis were being arrested in their thousands.

Madame Vauclain did not mince her words. 'They've got what's coming to them. The ones who were afraid or intimidated, I can just about forgive. The ones who went willingly to the enemy and told on their neighbours I regard as irredeemable.'

I stood under a tree opposite the main entrance for nearly an hour, reliving the afternoon I had spent with Estelle in Barcelona. Perhaps from the very first moment that I had stepped into that little bedroom, both of us had known that she wouldn't be running away with me. But if I could have predicted her fate, I would have locked the door and tied her up. I would have called on Longbridge and all the weight of the British secret service. I would have risked a lifetime's furious reproaches rather than let her leave.

But Estelle would have broken free, whatever tricks I'd tried. Of course she would. She was, after all, her mother's daughter.

As the spring advanced and more and more refugees and prisoners returned home, Madame Vauclain and I volunteered to join the reception committee set up to welcome travellers at Bruxelles-Midi. The authorities had been alerted to the fact that many returning exiles, having endured years of imprisonment and an interminable journey, were arriving at the station but that nobody was expecting them.

That terminus soon became my obsession. It was the only place I wanted to be. The trains rumbled in more or less at random, often hours later than scheduled; proper passenger trains with ten or more carriages, belching smoke as if exhausted by the long

399

haul across Europe. There was always a hiatus before the doors were flung open, either from within or by the porters who raced the length of the platform.

Gradually the passengers would disembark, some leaping out boldly, some so frail that they had to turn round and step off backwards, clutching the handrail. We soon knew how to pick out the ex-prisoners discharged from concentration camps. Usually travelling alone, they avoided eye contact, especially with officials, clung to their pathetic bits of luggage and wore a strange collection of laundered but ill-fitting clothes. When they reached the barrier they hung back, fumbling for their papers. Their fingers shook as they handed them over, and they watched the documents fiercely until they were returned.

Sometimes their eyes burned with expectation, but mostly they seemed without hope.

I could always tell if someone had managed to get word through to their families and arranged to be met. A little group would be clustered at the barrier, hugging each other as the locomotive pulled in. Occasionally there was a yelp of recognition as they were reunited with a mother, an uncle, a brother. I saw relatives who'd been waiting quietly give a cry, burst through the barrier and hurl themselves along the platform, only to halt in front of some fragile figure, afraid that they might break.

Once I saw a lame old man approach a young woman with whom I'd been talking for a few minutes before the train arrived. 'My husband is coming home,' she'd said to me with pride. 'He telephoned me last night. He was arrested because he carried a pregnant woman, a Jew, in his taxicab. Can you imagine? I haven't seen him for eighteen months, so I've scrounged rations from the neighbours and cooked a feast.'

Now, as the old man came closer, I saw her stiffen and her expression change from disbelief to horror. This balding, grey-skinned stranger, upon whose outstretched hand the skin hung raggedly, was her Lazarus, raised from beyond the tomb, and she simply hadn't recognised him.

Other travellers had the blind look of those determined to conceal any emotion or reveal how much their tortured feet were hurting. These I approached with my clipboard and gentle questions. After a few minutes they followed me obediently to the trestle tables set up by the ladies of the Red Cross. I spoke softly, offered to carry their bags and smiled into their eyes. It was the best I could do. Nobody left without having been given an address where they could stay. Most refused point-blank to avail themselves of the waiting transport.

I hope none of them guessed that each time I greeted them I was hiding disappointment. That much as I rejoiced in their homecoming, I could not help wishing with all my heart that they had been Estelle.

I return to the station day after day, whenever a train is scheduled to arrive from Austria, Germany or Switzerland. Each time I wait until all the passengers have disembarked and the last stragglers have trailed along the platform. I have been known to run the length of the train, in case she might be too frail to alight by herself. If a train is late, I never mind. In fact, I tell myself that the wait will surely improve the chances of her being on board.

Sometimes I indulge in the fantasy that she won't come by train at all; that I will bump into her one day in the Pâtisserie Faider or that I will glimpse her in the Parc de Bruxelles. If I see a woman in a red hat or camel coat my blood quickens and I always run a few steps towards her, just in case.

We have heard that Mauthausen, where quite a few Belgian women ended up, was one of the last camps to be liberated. In the final dragging months of the war, when the avenging Allied armies were storming across the borders, the Nazis emptied the concentration camps and drove the surviving prisoners into gas chambers or onto trucks or trains or on foot into the deeper reaches of Europe. Of the prisoners who survived those forced marches, who did not die of starvation or exhaustion, many ended up in Mauthausen.

And because Mauthausen was liberated only a short while ago, and because it could take many weeks for the former inmates to recover enough to absorb adequate nourishment and be issued with clothes and travel passes, it could take some of them a very long time to find their way home.

So I won't give up. I will never give up. Until the last prisoner is back, until there is no work left for me to do and my money runs out, and even beyond, I shall return to the station every day. Because when she comes home, I need to be at the barrier. In fact, I don't belong anywhere else. And she mustn't be one of those lonely souls who climbs down from the train and gazes along the platform, sick and weary but with just a glimmer of remaining hope, only to find that the world has moved on so far and so fast that nobody who loves her is waiting.

Acknowledgements

With thanks to my travelling companion, Charonne Boulton and to Joan Scanlon and Charlotte Beckett for reading an early draft. To Kirsty Dunseath for her meticulous and revelatory editing and, as ever, to my agent Mark Lucas, for his inspirational encouragement, creativity and support.

I am particularly indebted to the following:
Musée Nationale de la Resistance, Brussels
The St Bride Library (of the print)
Sun Printers archive http://www.sunprintershistory.com/history.html
Steve Cook, David Swinburne and the Royal Literary Fund.

A selection of books:
The Defence of the Realm, Christopher Andrew (Allen Lane, 2009)
Brussels for Pleasure, Derek Blyth (Pallas Athene 2003)
The Sorrow of Belgium, Hugo Claus (Random House, 1990)
A Quiet Woman's War, William Etherington (Mousehold Press, 2002)
M19 Escape and Evasion, 1939–1945, M.R.D Foot & J.M. Langley (The Bodley Head, 1979)
Resistance, M.R.D Foot (Eyre Methuen, 1976)
Wartime: Britain 1939–1945, Juliet Gardiner (Headline Book Publishing, 2004)
'Mission Paradise': A World War Two Memoir, Marjory Rae Lewis. (New Generation Publishing, 2015)
Between Silk and Cyanide, Leo Marks (Harper Colllins, 1999)
Gaston's War, Allan Mayer (Presidio Press 1988)

Public Servant, Private Woman, Dame Alix Meynell (Victor Gollancz, 1988)

Little Cyclone, Airey Neave (Biteback Publishing 2013)

Why the Allies Won, Richard Overy (Jonathan Cape, 1995)

Charlotte Brontë's Promised Land, Eric Ruijssenaars (The Brontë Society, 2000)

Edith Cavell, Diana Souhami (Quercus, 2010)

I'll Walk Beside You, Mary Trevelyan (Longman's 1946)

The German Occupation of Belgium 1940–1944, Werner Warmbrunn (Peter Lang Publishing 1993).

MI6, Nigel West (Weidenfeld & Nicolson, 1983)

blog and newsletter

For literary discussion, author insight,
book news, exclusive content,
recipes and giveaways, visit the
Weidenfeld & Nicolson blog and
sign up for the newsletter at:

www.wnblog.co.uk

For breaking news, reviews and exclusive competitions
Follow us 🐦 @wnbooks
Find us 📘 facebook.com/WeidenfeldandNicolson